KEYS TO THE KINGDOM

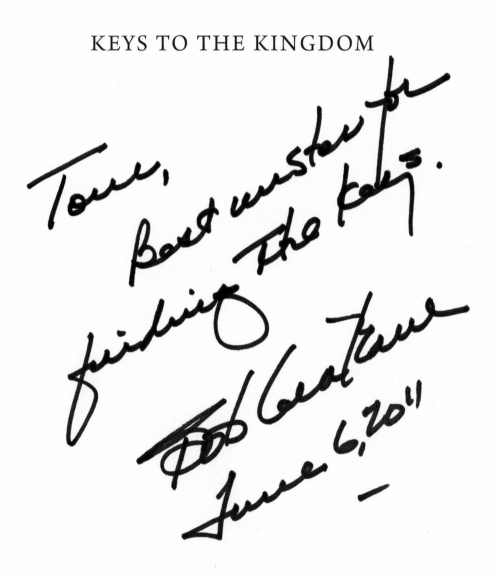

Tom,

Best wishes for finding the keys.

Bob Graham

June 6, 2011

KEYS *to the* KINGDOM

SENATOR BOB GRAHAM

★ ★ ★ ★ ★

Vanguard Press
A Member of the Perseus Books Group

Published by Vanguard Press
A Member of the Perseus Books Group

Set in 12 point Arno Pro

Library of Congress Cataloging-in-Publication Data
Graham, Bob, 1936-
  Keys to the kingdom : a novel of suspense / Senator Bob Graham.
   p. cm.
  ISBN 978-1-59315-660-2 (alk. paper)
  1. Political fiction. I. Title.
  PS3607.R3364K49 2011
  813'.6—dc22
                        2011000934

E-book ISBN 978-1-59315-669-5

Vanguard Press books are available at special discounts for bulk purchases in
the U.S. by corporations, institutions, and other organizations. For more
information, please contact the Special Markets Department at the Perseus
Books Group, 2300 Chestnut Street, Suite 200, Philadelphia, PA 19103, or call
(800) 810-4145, ext. 5000, or e-mail special.markets@perseusbooks.com.

10 9 8 7 6 5 4 3 2 1

In wartime, truth is so precious that she should always be attended by a bodyguard of lies.

—WINSTON CHURCHILL

PROLOGUE

September 19
Mumbai, India

On General Post Office Road, across from the Chhatrapai Shivaji Terminus, a cluster of middle school girls in their blue-and-white uniform skirts and blouses from Anjuman Islam School, chattered about weekend plans as their teacher tried to hurry them along toward the train station. But Mamata Bakht, a head taller than the others and standing out from the crowd, had other things on her mind.

Lost in her own world, staring up at the beautiful, cloudless blue sky, she thought back to the school day. In algebra class, Ms. Patel had scolded her for not paying attention.

"Mamata, you are very bright, but you must apply yourself and not let your mind wander."

"I am sorry," Mamata had responded in a quivering voice.

"I'll judge that by the results of your weekend homework assignment. I don't want to have to speak about this to your grandparents."

That would make things even worse. Bappa and Umma were very good to her and she was deeply devoted to them. And if they knew the reason she couldn't concentrate on her studies was that she missed her mother so much, they would feel very hurt. They had explained to her that it would not be a good thing for a girl of her age and bright future to be living under the same conditions as her mother at this important time in her life. But no one seemed to be able to explain to her why Mamma couldn't be here in Mumbai with her.

"Come along now, girls! The trains will not wait for you," Ms. Patel admonished.

As the final strains of the call to Friday prayer from Jama Masjid, Mumbai's oldest and largest mosque, faded away, they were suddenly replaced by the penetrating long and short bleats of an emergency vehicle. Their attention suddenly riveted, the girls and their teacher leaned into the street to follow the yellow ambulance with green-checkered markings as it weaved through the automobiles and trucks moving to clear a path.

"Ms. Patel, what is happening?" Mamata asked with alarm. So many things—even an unexpected noise—frightened her these days.

"There must have been an accident or possibly someone is having a heart attack," the teacher responded. "The ambulance is speeding to help before it is too late. The authorities and our people understand the urgency of providing treatment. Girls, you are fortunate to live in such a modern city."

Directly in front of them the ambulance, with topside lights ablaze, swerved left toward the cavernous Victorian building. They crossed the street with a thousand or more of the concerned or curious.

Mamata was shocked to see the ambulance slam through the line of nineteenth-century streetlights that separated the red-tiled open-air entrance from the station's main terminal and jolt to a halt against a structural column, scattering two score of passengers lounging on green railway benches.

Treading carefully to avoid the shards of glass, she moved closer, near enough to see the backs of the two occupants splayed forward in the space between the seat and dashboard as a plume of white smoke billowed from beneath the vehicle, obscuring it in an opaque veil.

Then, a white strobe of light penetrated the haze and the earth seemed to explode. Mamata was instantly blinded. She heard the collapsing ceiling and cupola fifty feet above and the screams from her classmates. She crumpled under the fragments of steel, concrete, brick, and glass.

And then nothing.

ELEVEN WEEKS
EARLIER . . .

★ ★ ★ ★ ★

JULY 6

New York Times
"Over the Horizon"
BY JOHN BILLINGTON

While America's attention has been focused on the president's decision to return combat troops to Iraq and the pending decision on whether to increase troop levels in Afghanistan, more ominous threats have gone largely unnoticed and unattended.

In the last decade and a half, a nuclear arms race has accelerated in South Asia. China, India, and especially Pakistan have substantially increased their arsenals of nuclear weapons of mass destruction; in the case of Pakistan, from less than 20 in 2000 to an estimated 40 to 60 today.

During the same period, the accumulation of biological and chemical weapons of mass destruction has escalated in Central Asian and Middle Eastern countries such as Iran and Syria. Through superior intelligence and the assistance of a regional ally, the United States seized tons of materials in the Red Sea intended for additional WMDs. This shipment was interdicted, but many others have made it through porous borders.

Surrogates of nation-states and even surrogates of other terrorist organizations are becoming more restive, unwilling to supinely comply with dictates of their former masters. Hezbollah, the Lebanese-based paramilitary organization which has now become a political party and vacillates between being part of the governing coalition in Lebanon and being its primary opposition, is the premier example of this greater independence.

The potential danger of this independence is captured in the reality that no nation-state would be so irrational as to deliver a weapon of mass destruction bearing its home address, real or virtual. The United States has a policy of nuclear annihilation should a nuclear weapon be detonated here or against an ally or U.S. interest abroad. While it may be an oxymoron, a "rational state" that decides to use a weapon of mass destruction would try to keep its hands clean by leaving the dirty work of delivery to a surrogate. Thus WMDs will likely be transferred to groups such as Hezbollah that in turn will exercise a significant, if not singular, role in the decisions of when and against whom to use them.

Add to these what I consider to be the most dangerous risk that can still be contained—the emergence of Saudi Arabia as a nuclear state.

The congressional inquiry into the 9/11 attacks left several secrets unanswered. The top three are Saudi Arabia's full role in the preparation for and the execution of the plot; the kingdom's willingness and capacity to collaborate in future terrorist actions against the United States; and why this and the prior administration conducted a cover-up that thus far has frustrated finding the answers to the first two questions.

Now, there is an even more ominous unknown. Does Saudi Arabia have the bomb? One of America's leading journalists on intelligence has estimated that Israel has up to two hundred nuclear devices. Iran continues to reject international efforts to halt its nuclear weapons program. Given Saudi Arabia's hostile relations with both nations and its economic stake in protecting oil production, it is hard to imagine that the kingdom has not directed a portion of its newly acquired, vastly enlarged petrowealth to becoming a nuclear state. A recent publication has suggested the Saudi nuclear aspirations might have been facilitated by renegade Pakistani nuclear scientist, Dr. A. Q. Khan.

When that is achieved it will be impossible to frustrate the nuclear ambitions of other Middle Eastern states such as Egypt and Turkey, an escalation of nuclear capability that will destabilize an already volatile region.

In 1914 the fuse for World War I was ignited at Sarajevo with the assassination of Austro-Hungarian Archduke Franz Ferdinand. The set pieces for World War III are now in place in Central Asia and the Middle East. Avoiding another such calamity—this time with nuclear, biological, or chemical weapons—should be the highest priority of American foreign policy. The United States should take prompt action to prevent this potential conflict from becoming a reality.

John Billington, a retired U.S. senator (D-Florida), was chair of the Senate Select Committee on Intelligence.

JULY 15

Washington, D.C.

All right, Tony thought, *let's end this thing.*

As he had tens of thousands of times since he took up the game at the age of eight, Tony bounced the ball three times with his right hand, paused to assess his prey, tossed the ball directly over the center line of his body, grunted, rotated, and snapped. The ball rocketed toward the ad court, clipped the net, and ricocheted wide.

"Let," Mark Block cried.

It couldn't have been any later than 7:20, but already the wet heat of Washington pressed down. Tony wiped his face on his T-shirt sleeve and repeated his ritual. This time the ball caught the corner, and, lunging, Mark got a racquet on it. Tony set up, coiled, and whipped a topspin forehand down the line that Mark could only wave at.

Game, set, and yet another match.

"Congratulations," Mark said with no hint of sincerity, "that's only twelve straight points. In case you haven't noticed, I'm gaining on you."

Tony laughed. "Which is why I've had such trouble sleeping. Good game."

They shook hands across the net.

Mark Block played a fair game. Reports—mostly of his own—had him doing well in the tennis tournaments at the Potomac Racquet Club. But he was doing more for his post–congressional staff reputation as a partner in a tony K Street law firm defending the affluent from charges of white-collar crime. Of course he was nowhere near Tony's league in tennis, but few were. Once a week they met at a public court on Capitol Hill and, for a little exercise and the pleasure of his company, Tony ran him around a bit. Today had been somewhat different: three or four times Tony had cursed himself for lapses in concentration and general sloppiness.

Courtside, they toweled off and guzzled their water bottles.

"Amigo, what's happened to you?" Mark asked. "Where's that McEnroe fierceness they used to write about? Today you were like an absent-minded professor. Play like that next time, and you're going down."

"Play like that next time and I'll deserve to." Tony clapped him on the back. "And think what a nice boost to your confidence that would be." Tony was a few years past the days when he used to smash racquets on the court and launch into tirades at the umpires, but this morning he was distracted. Maybe it was the testimony he was writing for his boss, Ambassador William Talbott. Maybe it was his increasing obsession with the alluring Carol Watson. Whatever, he wasn't doing a good job of keeping it together.

"Oh, and one more thing," Mark added. "Billington wants to talk to you; says it's urgent."

"If it's urgent, why didn't you tell me before the match?"

"Because knowing how you feel about Billington, you would have abandoned me and my vain hopes of beating you and rushed to call him."

Tony nodded his agreement, then asked, "What's a former senator, safely retired back to Florida, got to say that's urgent?"

"Beats me," Mark replied.

Tony recalled the first time he'd heard Mark's voice, authoritative, with a hint of Brooklyn. Tony had been at his desk deep in the State Department when a call came through from a Mark Block, a staffer for Florida Democratic senator and former governor John Billington.

Billington he knew. In fact on Tony's fifth birthday, the then-governor had given him what turned out to be the greatest gift of his life. On that day—June 4, 1980—he and his family and nearly three thousand other anxious Marielitos had been crammed for three days in a brutally hot hanger at Trumbo Naval Air Station in Key West awaiting their fate. Nerves frayed. Tempers flared.

Then a gray-haired man in a blue suit arrived and climbed up on a chair. "Mi nombre es Gobernador John Billington," he'd announced in a clear, steady voice, and not an hour later Tony and his family were on a school bus bound for their new lives as Americans.

"We're putting together a team to investigate the intelligence community's handling of 9/11," Block had said, explaining the reason for his call, "both before and after. The senator wants the INR's perspective, and your name keeps coming up."

"We screwed up too?" Tony asked.

"Not that I know of," Mark responded with a chuckle. "In fact, INR is one of the few organizations the senator is impressed with. The agency and the bureau are doing their usual cover-your-ass act. He likes what he's heard about your energy and smarts. He's also looking for imagination and a willingness to take some chances."

Tony smiled and recalled why he had chosen to go with the State Department's Bureau of Intelligence and Research. With his top ranking in Georgetown's Foreign Service program and near-proficiency in Arabic and Pashto, he'd had offers from all the big intelligence and defense agencies after he completed his Army ROTC commitment. What he liked about INR was that with just three hundred professionals, it was leaner, more adroit, and more cerebral. And it tended to get it right on the big issues like the collapse of the Soviet Union and Iraq's nonexistent weapons of mass destruction. They were academics, but no Tom Clancy caricatures.

"And," Mark continued, "it didn't hurt that you grew up in Hialeah."

Tony appreciated the comment. Hialeah was a dark-blue, blue-collar town. Some yahoos looked down their noses, more so since Hialeah was four-out-of-five Cuban. If you grew up there, you had to be tough.

"Which leads me to ask," Mark said, "how you got from Hialeah to the INR."

With an intensity undiminished by time, Tony traced his sojourn from Guanabacoa to Miami. The Ramos family had waited for years to escape the oppressive tyranny of Cuba. Finally, the spring 1980 opening of the port of Mariel and the willingness of cousins exiled in Miami to pick them up on a chartered boat gave them their chance. It was a daily struggle for his father, a former shortstop, now a home siding salesman; his mother, a housewife turned sewing machine operator; and Tony and his younger sister to keep the family together, make the transition to America, and keep its hopes alive. "After I was okay in English," Tony continued, "I got pretty good at school. A Jesuit priest urged me to apply to Georgetown, where I got an Army ROTC, not a tennis, scholarship. That's how I got from Hialeah to Washington."

"That's the kind of story Billington respects." Mark paused, and Tony could sense him skimming his CV. "I see you graduated near the top of your class in Middle Eastern area studies. With your Arabic and special operations experience, those are the skill sets we're looking for. And bringing home the NCAA tennis singles title shows a lot of discipline. I'd like to set up an interview for Friday, okay?"

Trying to disguise his excitement, Tony replied, "Okay."

At 10:15 Friday morning Tony arrived at the senator's hideaway in the Capitol, one of seventy offices secreted throughout the Senate wing. Ranging from cubbyholes to ornate suites, they were assigned depending on that truest acknowledgment of status in the upper chamber, seniority. As seventeenth in years of Senate service, Billington had a room that overlooked the east lawn, decorated with furniture from the Senate storeroom and landscape art of his state.

"Mr. Ramos, have a seat," the senator greeted Tony.

"Thank you." He sat on the end of the sofa closest to Billington's desk.

The approving smile and tilt of the head indicated the senator was intrigued with Tony's athletic grace and presence. "Mr. Ramos, before we go to the subject of our meeting, may I ask if you had a relative with your name who played infield for the Havana Sugar Kings? As I recall, you look a great deal like him."

Impressed but not flustered, Tony replied, "Yes sir. That was my grandfather in the old Florida International League. I'm surprised you would remember that."

Billington placed his hands behind his head and stretched out in the desk chair. "My father loved baseball. When I was growing up, we had season tickets to the Miami Sun Sox, and he and I drove in from the farm to almost every home game. The Sugar Kings were the dominant team in the league. Dad especially liked your grandfather's grit and hustle."

"I wish I'd been able to see him play."

"You would have been proud. I remember when Dad told the sports editor of the *Post* about Tony Ramos and several of the other Cuban ballplayers. He said the Washington Senators should pick them up; the only thing they could do would be to improve the weakest team in the American League. But that was a couple of years before Jackie Robinson broke the color line, and the Senators were not about to do that in a southern-culture town like this one."

"That was my grandfather's dream, to play in the major leagues, and I know he would want me to thank your father."

Billington paused to pour two glasses of water. After offering one to Tony he sipped and continued, "That was yesterday and today is now. I'd like to ask a question."

"Yes sir."

"Mark Block is not an easy grader, and he has given you very high marks. I'm satisfied you have several of the aptitudes we will need for the inquiry, so I'm more interested in motivation. Why do you want to break your INR career path to take this on?"

Tony leaned forward. "I think the president has fundamentally mischaracterized 9/11 as the beginning of a war on terrorism. It is not a war unless we make it one. This is not a war. It is an intelligence and paramilitary operation against a relatively small and enormously outgunned enemy."

"What do you mean by 'relatively small'?" the senator asked.

"A week after 9/11, my current boss asked the head of the INR how many terrorists were there in the world?"

"And what did he estimate?"

"He said if you define a terrorist as a person who has been through training camps like al-Qaeda's in Afghanistan, or Hezbollah's in Syria or Lebanon, and who belongs to an organization prepared to use those acquired skills, he estimated 100,000. I don't disparage that figure, but it's hardly the Viet Cong, or Saddam Hussein in the Persian Gulf."

"So, that's why you want to join our inquiry staff?"

"Yes sir. To understand the nature, objectives, and capabilities of our enemy. And also to understand why we have exaggerated its threat. Those are some of the questions I think your inquiry can answer."

"Tony, that is a very thoughtful statement of our mission. I want you on the team."

JULY 15
Washington, D.C.

Bag slung over his left shoulder, Tony waved goodbye to Mark as he walked to his 2005 black Mustang and began the short ride to the State Department gym. While he was growing up in Hialeah, the Mustang had been a symbol of all he yearned for. Black was an affirmation of his ethnic pride. The twenty-minute drive was Tony's chance to focus on his agenda for the day.

He showered and dressed in a patterned black Zegna suit. He was not one of the fitness-obsessed regulars in the gym, but he spent enough time on the treadmill and free weights to stay in competitive tennis shape. After his special ops training, it almost seemed like spa treatment. As Tony examined the reflection of his six-foot frame in the mirror, adjusting his Ann Hand red American eagle print tie, he took satisfaction that he weighed five pounds less in his mid-thirties than at his Georgetown graduation, and the same as when he left the military.

Heads turned as he stepped into the elevator. He wasn't called the "Will Smith" of State for nothing.

On Monday, he'd been notified of an 8:45 meeting in the office of his boss, Ambassador William Talbott, assistant secretary of state for Central and South Asia. When he arrived, Tony was surprised to see his next-door-office mate and occasional nemesis, Benjamin Willis Brewster, leaning over Talbott's desk.

"Mr. Ambassador, the Saudis are dumfounded with the rush to leave Iraq again," Brewster intoned in his aristocratic New England accent. "Less than eighteen months after we pulled our combat troops out of Iraq, the country was tearing itself apart in a civil war, and the president has sent them back in again. Now there is serious consideration of transferring a division of those soldiers to Afghanistan. In my judgment the kingdom is legitimately concerned with our vacillation, and if we reduce our new troop commitment precipitously, Iraq will implode into even more violent conflict and an eventual Yugoslavian-style partition."

Shit, thought Tony as he entered the office. *The jerk's given in to two of the longest-running diseases at State: Arabism—an excessive affection for the Muslim world—and going native—allowing that affection to distort your loyalties.*

Talbott stood as he saw Tony and pointed to an empty chair.

Brewster glanced condescendingly over his left shoulder at Tony and then continued. "And at a practical level this administration has reached the same conclusion. Its rationale is not what might happen in the future but how to keep Iraq from unraveling while it is still in charge. As long as this administration is in power, Iraq will be the priority, so why waste our credibility at the White House and on the Hill by taking a contrary position?"

Tony could say there were few people he didn't like or who didn't like him. Benjamin W. Brewster was a notable exception. A couple of years behind Tony in age and service, he had the same portfolio for Saudi Arabia that Tony held for Afghanistan. Raised amongst old money and hereditary privilege, Brewster had a cultivated aversion to those he considered his inferiors. Tony, a street-smart Miami Cuban, was near the top of his most-disdained list. This was not the first time they had been in open conflict for Talbott's attention and support.

Talbott turned to Tony. "Mr. Brewster is making the case that Thursday's testimony to the Foreign Relations Committee should give equal weight to maintaining our position in Iraq as to expanding our troop strength in Afghanistan. Has he convinced you?"

"In a word, no," Tony responded.

Brewster turned to face him. "Ramos, you're locked into the notion that the war in Iraq was, and always will be, a mistake. You've lost whatever capacity you had to be pragmatic and strategic."

Tony started to rise from his seat toward Brewster, but a disapproving glance from Talbott sat him back down again. He contented himself to fantasize about punching Brewster in his soft, bulbous stomach.

"Mr. Brewster," Tony declared, "I know you don't like to compare today's war in Iraq with Vietnam in the 1960s and President Johnson's determination to avoid a military defeat on his watch. But that is just the trap we have slipped into, whether you call it surge or reset or some other macho word. The objective of your Iraq strategy is to save this president that embarrassment, and paying for it with more body bags. How many more Americans do we have to sacrifice to allow the president to declare 'I didn't lose a war'?"

"They're all volunteers," said Brewster. "They knew what they were signing up for."

So typical, thought Tony. *It's so easy to fight a war from behind a desk thousands of miles away.* He wished for a moment that there was still a draft and that he could be the one to kick Brewster's fat ass around in boot camp.

Tony simply replied, "And since you brought up Yugoslavia, let me remind you Iraq was also a made-up country, created at the end of World War I, putting people who despised each other under the same flag. The idea that you can take disparate tribes and make them live together only works under a despotic strongman, like Tito or Saddam. And what have we accomplished? Just making Iraq an easy take for Iran instead of maintaining a balance of power in the region."

"And what is your grand strategy, Mr. Kennan?"

Tony inwardly cringed at Brewster's reference to the architect of the Cold War containment strategy against the Soviets. It was historical name–dropping, just to impress the boss. Fortunately, Talbott's unchanging expression betrayed no such effect.

"To cut our losses from your war and get back in the game where it counts."

They glared at each other until Talbott warned, "Gentlemen, this is a serious policy issue and what we decide here might actually make a difference."

"Ambassador, it surely will," Tony responded. "Afghanistan is central. If we fail there, Kabul will go to the Taliban, and Pakistan, already shaky as hell, to al-Qaeda. There will be a firestorm in India. The nations with the sixth- and seventh-largest stashes of nuclear weapons will be eyeball to eyeball and no one will back down."

Brewster interrupted imperiously. "Mr. Ramos, the president and the Congress have agreed—and you know that doesn't happen often in this partisan city—that Iraq is the priority. What are your credentials to go before the Senate Foreign Relations committee and challenge them?"

"Common sense and a responsibility to use it for the American people. If we had not been distracted into Iraq, al-Qaeda would have long since been dispatched. Instead, it has been strengthened. Next to al-Qaeda, the primary beneficiary of our Iraq misadventures has been Iran. We have converted Iraq from being Iran's primary regional rival into Iran's Shia surrogate."

Tony recalled an incident Senator Billington had described during the early days of the 2002 inquiry. The senator had just returned from Central Command in Tampa. The purpose was a briefing on the state of the Afghanistan war. The briefing was military-crisp and the outcome upbeat. The United States and its foreign and indigenous allies were rolling the Taliban. Billington was reassured until he was asked to join Central Command's commander in his private office. Behind closed doors he was told the truth.

"Senator, we are no longer engaged in a war in Afghanistan," the general said.

Clearly surprised, Billington asked the general to explain.

"To prepare for a war in Iraq, military and intelligence personnel are being withdrawn. The predators, which have been a key part of our air superiority, are being relocated. The special ops units which have been working with the Northern Alliance since before the Russians were kicked out are being moved west and replaced with units from Colombia. Those units performed in an exemplary manner in the South American jungles, but there aren't many jungles or Spanish speakers in Afghanistan. Senator, we could eliminate al-Qaeda, Osama bin Laden, and the rest of them here and now, but not if we don't have the soldiers and equipment to do it."

Billington said that was the first time he fully realized that the decision to go to war with Iraq had already been made and that the consequences of that decision were playing out in real time in Afghanistan.

The general continued. "After we finish the job there, my next priority would be Somalia. It has no effective government to control the growing number of terrorist cells. Next would be Yemen. Its president is willing to help in the war on its home-grown terrorists, but he has no capabilities.

"Iraq, that's another story. Our intelligence there is very unsatisfactory. Some Europeans know more about Iraq's weapons of mass destruction than we do, but we don't want to listen."

Tony thought what a different world it would be if we had listened to the general.

Up to a point, Talbott appreciated what he called healthy debate. He had reached that point and passed it. "Sit down," he commanded, "both of you. Mr. Ramos, I want you to continue working on my testimony as we discussed yesterday. I want to see it no later than three o'clock. Mr. Brewster, I have another assignment for you. Report back here at five."

Brewster followed Tony through the office door. When they were out of Talbott's range, Tony turned. "The Saudi portfolio must be pretty fucking dull if all you've got to do is suck up to the ambassador. Or is it just part of your overall career path?"

Brewster smiled condescendingly. "You know, Ramos, if I'd been brought up the way you were, I suppose I would be just as jealous and resentful."

Tony entered his office and slammed the door.

His windowless cubbyhole was on the second floor of the Marshall wing of the Truman Building, the official name of the Department of State headquarters. Tony had also been attracted to the INR by the diversity of challenges its mission offered. He experienced this range of topics—the continuing conflict in Kashmir, the economic surge of Singapore—in his first years of INR service. In May of his second year, after the latest military suppression of Buddhist monks in Myanmar, he was tapped to pull together and analyze all the open-source and clandestine intelligence. He produced an options paper for the secretary of state that she used in a speech to the Asia Society. But Myanmar was beyond the White House's attention span. After her words there was no action.

Tony's gray metal desk was covered with eighteen memos from the CIA and National Security Agency, the two agencies INR depended on for most of its raw clandestine intelligence; five cables from Kabul; and a short stack of pink telephone slips, arranged in order of priority.

Before turning to all of these competing demands, Tony retrieved Senator Billington's recent op-ed from the *New York Times* website and reread it carefully from the beginning. One line popped out at him:

The congressional inquiry into the 9/11 attacks left several secrets unanswered . . .

For everyone else, this seemed to be old news. Yet John Billington was one of the few individuals Tony had met in public life who seemed to be able to take in the big picture—past, present, and future—in one view. He was one of the few who truly understood the Shakespearean quotation carved onto the entablature of the National Archives building on Constitution Avenue: "What's past is prologue." And by the end of the op-ed, he had certainly made his case.

> The United States should take prompt action to prevent this potential conflict from becoming a reality.

Billington had a reputation for not mincing words, and Tony was impressed that in supposed retirement, he was still so engaged. Resurfacing the suggestions that the Saudis could have been involved with the al-Qaeda attacks was pretty damn provocative. No wonder there'd been a firestorm of protest over the piece. But Saudi Arabia was another analyst's territory. Tony had his hands full with Afghanistan.

And his interest in Afghanistan was very personal. At graduation he was commissioned into the army as a second lieutenant. With his athletic ability and facility for language, he was a natural for special operations. With basic and advanced training completed, Tony was assigned to a mixed unit of army and intelligence officers preparing to be inserted with the Northern Alliance in Afghanistan.

Since the Taliban had taken control of the country after the forced eviction of the Soviets, this tribe of tribes operating downhill from the Himalayas had emerged as the primary resistance force.

One memory had never left him—as vivid and searing as the day it happened.

On a cold April morning, Tony was on his horse bareback, hidden in the niche of a hill overlooking a grassland valley. On the near side of the opening was a wooden-fenced enclosure that in other times had confined sheep and goats. A scattering of men dressed in the rough pants and parkas of these highlands sat on the top railings. From the south entrance to the enclosure a horse convoy of a dozen men and three fully clothed women entered. They stopped in front of recently cut stakes driven into the muddy ground at the center of the enclosure.

With their robes wrapped around their waists and hands strapped tightly together, the women were pulled from their wooden seats and dragged to the poles.

On the hill, Tony turned to his partner Amal. In colloquial Pashto, he asked, "What in the hell is going on?"

Shifting on his steed, eyes focused on the scene below, Amal responded in kind, "I don't know but it looks like Sharia law being fulfilled."

"What are they doing?" Tony asked urgently.

"In past times this would have been within the families. Now, they are also an offense against Allah and society."

"And what does that mean?"

Amal waited to respond until the women had each been roped against a stake. Four men encircled each of them and unsheathed their swords. They cut loose the women's cotton chadaris, leaving them exposed to the eyes of the males and the swirls of icy, gusty wind.

"They have violated the rules of cohabitation, found with a nonfamily male in a compromising circumstance," answered Amal. "The sanction is humiliation and flogging. It may be death when their bodies are returned to the family. This is the Taliban way."

From bags hung over the rumps of each horse, the men uncoiled leather whips. From his shoulder holster, Tony removed an M4 and nudged his horse toward the narrow path leading to the valley. Amal, surprised and confused, haltingly followed.

"Be careful, my friend," Amal called out, inadvertently alerting the men below that they were not alone. Now using elemental English, he added, "They are doing what they have been told to do."

"I don't give a fuck," Tony replied.

He fired the first burst a meter above the captor's heads, rattling the trees that encircled the flogging field. The dozen returned fire. One shot tore through the neck of Tony's horse, which collapsed and threw

Tony to the rough ground. Using the dead animal as cover, he pulled off another round. Two men keeled over. The remaining ten ran for the woods, with Tony kicking up sods of earth at their heels.

Still mounted, Amal passed Tony and cut the women free. He sliced up his night sack to give them a minimum of warmth and concealment. As Tony closed the distance on foot, Amal shouted out, "Only in our country a month, already a savior."

Returning his mind to the present, Tony faced his current challenge: the fact that Afghanistan was again slipping back to the Taliban. *Our commander on the ground tells us he needs at least 30,000 more troops, and he's pretty damn sure they're not going to come from the Belgians. Still, the administration is focused on avoiding a total fiasco in Iraq by sending the troops back, which they hope will save the November elections.* Tony was among those who had always considered Iraq an optional war that had trumped the United States' legitimate strategic interests in Afghanistan and Pakistan. And the reality was that Afghanistan and Iraq were, and always had been, irreconcilable competitors for our attention and resources.

The president had stated that Iran could be the fuse of World War III. But all evidence suggested it would much more likely be along the Indian-Pak border or in the triangle of Israel, Palestine, and Syria. If the intelligence community would try as hard as Billington to get the administration's attention on a possible Saudi nuclear bomb and its consequences, we'd all be a lot better off.

The BlackBerry rang. "Tony, this is John Billington."

"Senator." Tony was always pleased to hear his voice.

"What are you up to, young man?"

"Not feeling very young, that's for sure. Believe it or not, I was just reading your op-ed in the *Times*. You seem to be the one voice of enlightenment these days. Other than that, it's pretty grim."

"Still trying to explain Afghanistan to the Philistines?"

"You must be tapping my phone. But you didn't call about my problems."

"True. I've got a favor to ask. A big one and I need to discuss it face-to-face."

"Senator, honestly, I'm under water here, but if there's something I could do—"

Billington plowed ahead, oblivious to Tony's protests. "There have been some inexplicable developments here. For the first time, Tony, for the first time in my life, I'm feeling vulnerable. I'm scared."

This was not standard operating procedure for John Billington. "What's happened?" Tony asked.

"I don't feel comfortable telling you on the phone."

"Senator, I'm buried in this testimony, but as soon as I can break free—"

"I need your help and time is not on my side." Tony was starting to get alarmed. This really wasn't like Billington.

"Can you give me a couple of days, Senator, to put out some fires and clean things up here a little?"

"I think I can wait that long," Billington replied. "But I need you down here as soon as possible."

"I'll be there," Tony assured him.

Tony used the interoffice line to call Florence Wilkens, Ambassador Talbott's assistant.

"Ms. Wilkens, I need a favor: personal leave on Friday and Monday. Could you clear it for me?"

"Mr. Ramos, I think that is doable."

JULY 15
Washington, D.C.

With less than two hours before it was due, Tony tried to refocus on Ambassador Talbott's Afghanistan testimony. He struggled to clarify the current American options: bad and worse. He pulled his BlackBerry from its holster and started to call Billington. "There's no way I can go to Miami this weekend," he said to an empty room. Then he remembered why he admired the man so much.

In October of 2002 the president's war scream on Iraq was at full throat. He had enumerated a series of horrors necessitating armed intervention: an Iraq spy was collaborating with al-Qaeda in Prague, proving Saddam Hussein and bin Laden were in cahoots; Iraq was a training ground and source of supply for terrorists; the British had confirmed Iraq had weapons of mass destruction and the means to deploy them on forty-five minutes' notice.

Billington had a different take. Certain close advisers of the current president had served in an earlier administration and considered it had shut down the Persian Gulf War juggernaut before it finished the job of toppling Saddam. They saw 9/11 as a pretext for settling old scores, and an inexperienced and persuadable chief executive as the means of doing so. Billington had also concluded that the information on Saddam's weapons of mass destruction was suspect and the Taliban and al-Qaeda posed far greater threats of killing Americans than did Saddam. Discarding his staff-prepared text, Billington took to the Senate floor and let it rip. "Turning our back on Afghanistan to fight a war of choice against Iraq will be the single greatest national security blunder since Pearl Harbor. Those of you who would grant this power to the president, you, too, will have blood on your hands."

This passion from the usually mild-mannered Billington caused some stir on the floor and the press gallery, but not enough to keep seventy-seven Senate votes from authorizing war in Iraq.

Tony's cell rang. He glanced at the caller ID. *Carol!*

In the charmingly earthy lilt of the Upper South, Carol Watson asked, "Is this a good time to talk?"

"Does the question imply that you're talking to me again?" Tony asked.

"I called, didn't I?"

"You did. I'm just surprised."

"In a good way, I hope."

"In a very good way." After the way Carol had severed diplomatic relations between them two months before, when she declared he'd blown her off for work for the last time, Tony had doubts he'd ever see her again. He'd become fascinated with her and the subtle ways she wasn't like other women with whom he'd been involved, and the breakup hit him hard, harder than he'd even suspected it would. Up till now, she hadn't answered his calls, texts, emails, tweets, not even a few letters. Had she, all the while, been missing him just as intensely?

Carol coughed. "Sorry. I woke up with a little chest cold. I thought about calling in sick, but I've got too much to do, so I came into work." She went on as if they had just spoken the day before.

"Carol, all you serious distance runners are always complaining about something: a cramp, a strained knee, a twisted ankle. A little sneeze isn't going to keep you down."

"That's what I love about you, Tony, always so sympathetic and understanding."

"Carol, I've really missed you," Tony confessed.

She worked for the Treasury Department's Office of Terrorism and Financial Intelligence, the United States' elite forensic accounting agency. They had met just before running in the last Marine Corps half marathon. Her blond hair was short, framing sparkling blue eyes and smooth white skin. Her tight Adidas outfit had accentuated her conditioned body as she lifted her leg to stretch against the concrete wall that separated the Iwo Jima monument from the traffic flow on Arlington Boulevard. Tony was intrigued and immediately set about to get to know her better. What he'd found so far was not the typical young Washington go-getter, willing to do just about anything or do in anyone to rise up the ladder. So he'd been playing it fairly cool with her, yearning to experience her on a deeper level, when she'd thrown him over. And now, inexplicably, she was back.

Uncharacteristically, Tony didn't know what to say next, so he settled for, "Uh, what is it you, uh, want to talk about, Carol?"

"I just got handed a case from Justice," she explained. "There seems to have been a kickback deal going between the Saudis and a British defense contractor. A lot of the action is in your part of the world. Could you fit me into your schedule, say, at three?"

"I don't know anything about a Saudi-Brits deal," Tony replied. "There's no reason I should have been briefed in. Maybe you should be talking with Benjamin Brewster; he's paid to stay up to speed on the Saudis."

"If I wanted to talk to Benjamin Brewster, I would have called him. I want to talk to you."

"I can't argue with your taste. But I don't understand why Justice is investigating a corruption case when we don't have a dog in the fight?"

"I don't either. That's what we need to figure out."

He liked the word "we" but hoped her renewed interest was not limited to his knowledge of the Arabian Peninsula.

"So what about this afternoon?" Carol persisted.

Florence Wilkens, Ambassador Talbott's executive assistant, stuck her head into Tony's office. "Mr. Ramos, Congressional Liaison is on me for the final draft of the secretary's testimony. If we don't get it to the committee by four, somebody will have some explaining to do, and that would be you. When can the secretary expect it?"

Tony was torn. He wanted to burnish his already good relationship with Ambassador Talbott, and he knew how important this testimony was. But if he put Carol off now, that would definitely be the absolute end between them. He couldn't get her deep-blue eyes out of his mind. He could hear her gentle breathing on the phone.

"I'll meet you at three," he told her. "How about the steps of the Lincoln Memorial."

"You got it," Carol replied.

Tony wondered just what "it" was. Punching off his BlackBerry, he turned to Ms. Wilkens. "Ma'am, it will be on your desk before three."

At twenty minutes before three, Tony removed his tie and left his suit coat draped over his chair back. He took the elevator to Secretary Talbott's office and laid the eighteen pages on Wilkens's desk. She looked up, acknowledged Tony with a nod, grabbed the file, and disappeared into the secretary's adjoining office. "So much for collegiality," Tony muttered.

The Lincoln Memorial is just down the 23rd Street hill from State. Although Washington is a thousand miles north of Hialeah, Tony thought the summers were more oppressive. He attributed it to the lack of ocean breeze and to traffic congestion. And the overabundance of hot air.

Carol sat about halfway up the memorial's steps, on the side so that the marble temple shaded her from the sun while she waited for Tony. From her vantage point, she could see the buses unloading tour groups at the Vietnam Veterans Memorial and families who had come to honor a relative. There were always several visitors with sheets of paper, rubbing a name from one of the granite panels. She remembered attending the funeral service of a Tennessee National Guard sergeant, the husband of a close friend from high school, who was killed in Iraq. He had left two young children, traumatized by their loss and fear of the future without a father. How many more granite walls would America erect?

As he crossed Memorial Circle, Tony observed Carol for a few moments before she spotted him. In her short black skirt and long-sleeve linen blouse he found her just as provocative as in her Adidas. As she leaned down to secure a file from her brindle folder, he recalled the small image of a rose tattooed on the outer slope of her left breast. If he were slightly closer, he could probably spot it now. It was one of the many riddles about Carol. Why would a woman as seemingly traditional and reticent about sex as Carol have a rose provocatively adorning her breast? Tony had thought he was close to being ready to ask her about it when she threw him over.

Tony had had only two serious relationships with women. When he was on the tour, he had traveled and lived with a Swedish pro. They made quite a contrasting pair in mixed doubles: he left-handed, she right; she composed, he always a threat to explode over a missed line call; he a dark African-Hispanic-Cuban mix, she golden blonde and snowflake white. Their lovemaking was as competitive as their tennis. The relationship ended with Tony's professional tennis career.

Three years ago there had been a Hill staffer who lived next to him on Seventh Street. Tony thought this might be the one, but he lost out to her boss and she was now the first lady of an Indiana congressional district.

He didn't know what to make of Carol. She was cute and smart and resourceful, but very insecure and wary in social settings. Tony rather liked the lack of predictability; every occasion with Carol had been a new discovery, as with the rose.

She smiled when she saw him. That was a good sign. "Hi," he said.

"Hi, yourself," she replied.

"Let's find a bench."

They walked back toward Constitution Avenue, by a row of elm trees that shielded them from the noise of the constant traffic. Carol sat on one of the railway station–style wooden benches scattered throughout the Mall. Tony took his place next to her, stretching out his arm behind her back. He pulled in close till he could feel the cup of her bra pressing against his chest wall.

Carol arched, separating herself from him. Surprised and visibly stung, he betrayed a look that she picked up on. She removed Kleenex from her purse and dabbed her nose. "I don't want you to catch my cold."

Was that the real message?

"Carol, if you don't want to do this . . . " He hoped she got the double meaning of his message.

"No, it's just, I've got a flight to Zurich tonight. And in case you've got anything, too, I don't want to pick it up and complicate my own condition. You know, you can get a bacterial super infection on top of a virus, and then you could have real problems."

Tony had to admit, this sounded just like the Carol he had come to know and love. "Zurich? Why there?"

She seemed to soften and moved a little closer. She fanned through the first twenty or so pages of her file. Strangely, Tony felt increasingly comfortable. After the months of no contact, this seemed something like a return to normalcy. At least, it had that potential.

"Here's what I've learned so far: In the mid-eighties, the Saudis were sweating the war between Iraq and Iran. The royal family was convinced the kingdom needed to beef up its air force. They decided they were too reliant on our birds. So they negotiated tough with the Germans and French, but finally ended up with the Brits' BAE Tornados."

"How much did the Brits stick them for?"

"Thirty-six billion pounds for seventy-one fighter jets and replacement parts."

"Wow. The king must have really felt Saddam Hussein breathing down his neck. I don't know the exchange rate then, but that's got to come to around a billion dollars per?"

"A little less, but more than twice what the Saudis would have paid for our F-15."

"OK. So where does Switzerland fit in?"

"The big deal leaked out five or so years ago. The British Serious Fraud Office was mucking around with some BAE files and realized the company had been making under-the-table payments to several of the princes in the Saudi royal family. It started with toys—a gold Rolls Royce here, a Mayfair apartment there. Then it turned to cash, and that's where the Swiss come in. Zurich-Alliance was the bank where the pounds changed hands under the protection of the Swiss bank secrecy laws. The Serious Fraud folks had verified that BAE Systems had forked over about two billion pounds when they had the rug pulled out from under them."

Tony stiffened, "Two billion pounds? Hell, that's better than a five percent payoff. And you say they might have found even more if what?"

"If Prime Minister Tony Blair hadn't stepped in and shut them down. He slammed the door on any more snooping around, saying it was a threat to one of Britain's most important strategic relationships."

"Sounds like he learned his national security politics from *The West Wing.*"

"I know. The *Guardian* newspaper broke the story. It was a hell of a stink. It was one of the things that eventually forced Blair into early retirement."

"I'm getting the feeling this wasn't the end of the story."

"Not quite. The guys who came in after Blair managed to deepen the cover-up, even convincing the House of Lords to keep a blanket over the scandal. But the action went on; only, the stage shifted here. This past February, Justice announced it was starting its own investigation.

At first, they were looking to the FBI to do the full job, but gave up on its forensics accounting capabilities and called in our office."

Tony leaned back on the bench and recalled a late-night session during the 9/11 inquiry. In the Capitol's fourth-floor secure room, committee members were questioning an FBI agent. Where did the money come from to support the hijackers? Billington pressed for more details on bank records. The besieged agent spluttered for a while, then finally said that the FBI was restricted in its access to the accounts. The senator blew up, stormed out of the room, got the attorney general on the phone, and demanded he get somebody competent on the case. The AG wasn't happy, but the following week the Treasury's Office of Terrorism and Financial Intelligence, the TFI, was brought in. Almost overnight they had a team on the case and were smelling smoke. But by this time it was November 2002; the final report had to be voted on in early December, and the clock ran out.

"So, how can I help?" Tony asked.

"Well, for starters, is there a history of foreign contractors bribing members of the Saudi royal family?"

"A long one. It even has a name—facilitation payments. Considered standard operating procedure. The Brits must have really wanted that contract. Do we know who got the money?"

"No, but I intend to find out."

"What's your plan?"

"Since I got the file last week I've been reviewing the intelligence traffic from '90 to '92. One of my colleagues has done a FinCEN search."

"What in the hell is that?"

"It's a network of national financial crimes enforcement agencies. This has given us a map of the relationships among the relevant parties, like the Saudi defense minister in the late eighties and the princes who were on the take."

Tony perked up. "You're into my bailiwick now. What's your confidence level in FinCEN?"

"Very high. And for the raw data we rely on SWIFT."

"You could lose your mind keeping track of the Washington acronyms. And SWIFT would be? . . ."

"When I first learned about it, it was 'Need to Know' and I couldn't have told you. But then the *New York Times* broke the story on SWIFT, so it's public knowledge. Don't ask me what the letters mean, but it's a massive computer system that tracks all the wire transfers throughout the world. It's really impressive."

Tony shook his head. "It still doesn't add up. Justice didn't give a shit about the Saudis' role in 9/11. What's with the sudden awakening?"

She reached for another Kleenex and shrugged. "Isn't that odd?"

"OK, next question: The Swiss protect secret bank accounts like Coca-Cola protects its secret formula. What makes you think your trip to Zurich will get you more than a nice fondue?"

"You're right. It used to be near-impossible to get Bern's cooperation. But since the scandal over Swiss banks setting up schemes for U.S. gazillionaires to avoid our taxes, not to mention the revelations about aiding the Nazis in stealing Jewish property, they want to play nice. So they've given us the green light to look at BAE's records at Zurich-Alliance."

Tony grinned. "If you really loved me, you'd invite me to come along."

She matched him with a playful grin of her own. "I expect you to be waiting with dutiful devotion for my return."

As she pecked Tony on the cheek, he caught another fleeting glimpse of the tiny rose.

———————

Tony took twice the usual time to walk back to the Marshall wing, trying to sort things out with Carol. Had she purposely flashed the rose? Was she coming on to him at the end there, or just trying to make him suffer? Were they really back on again, or did she simply want his help on this project? Should he have forced the issue more, or be patient and wait for things to happen? She was hard to figure.

JULY 16
The Lakes, Florida

John Billington's morning walk was his only daily exercise, and his first stop was always the same: three blocks from his townhouse in The Lakes. That was where his fourth daughter, Kendall, lived with her husband and two children in a one-story ranch home backing up to one of the artificial lakes that gave the town its name. Billington's family had built The Lakes on its former dairy farm. It was one of the projects that had made the Billingtons among the prosperous in the Sunshine State and had laid the groundwork for John's political career. As he rounded the corner, his granddaughter Eloise ran from her porch to greet him.

"Doodle," she called, "come see our new puppy!"

From behind her, a bichon frise leapt out, its head up and tail wagging furiously. John reached down to take it in his arms as Eloise hugged his knees. "Eloise," he said, "you are almost as cute as this puppy. What's her name?"

"Milly," the child announced. The puppy had been named after John's wife, Eloise's grandmother. "I have a storybook. Read it to me till the bus comes? Please?"

At eight, Eloise was the youngest of Billington's granddaughters and the only one living in The Lakes. Her large black eyes and lush eyelashes gave her an exotic presence beyond her years.

When Kendall was Eloise's age, John was running for governor. A lingering regret was his absence from many of the family's special occasions in those tumultuous years. He pledged to be more a part of his grandchildren's lives than he had of any of their mothers'.

Sitting on a bench in the front yard, with Eloise close beside and Milly in her arms, John opened *On the Farm*. He read about the cows and chickens and the family that cared for them. He couldn't resist adding some of his own boyhood cow stories from his years on the dairy farm. Eloise giggled and flirted with her grandfather, running her fingers through his white hair.

The lumbering yellow school bus approached. Hand in hand, they walked to meet it, Milly bounding ahead.

"I love you, Doodle," she said, as she climbed the steps. "Can we finish the story tonight?"

"And I love you very much. I'll come over after supper." John gave her a kiss.

Rolling her eyes in embarrassment, Eloise said, "Can we read two books?"

John was proud of The Lakes. From fifty years of vision and hard work, a new town had grown. The morning walk through the curving tree-lined streets was a chance to feel that gratification and monitor what was going on. "The palms are looking ragged. Check with the park super," he noted in the small spiral notebook he always carried.

The turning point of his walk was a neighborhood shopping center. At the Food Spot, he greeted the regular customers and the female Bangladeshi clerk. Although he had been retired for three years, most of his neighbors continued to ask for his advice and help with their problems.

Dressed for his job as a roofer, Jose Rico was standing in line for his daily lottery ticket. "Senator," he said, "my brother in Nicaragua, he is trying to get a student visa to study computers at Miami Dade College. At the embassy they told him no; could you help?"

John wrote the information in his notebook and promised to look into it.

With the *New York Times* and *Miami Herald* under his arm, he headed home. He could not deny he liked the attention. In retirement and out of the spotlight, requests for assistance gave him a reason to call the friends and agencies he had depended on over those years. It kept him in the game. The walk gave him time to think.

A typical south Florida midsummer shower interrupted. He turned off the sidewalk toward a portico-covered park bench to sit it out.

He reflected on the reaction to his op-ed piece. In the days after it ran in the *Times*, he had received a number of hostile emails and calls from a political officer at the Saudi embassy. Inferring that Billington had access to classified information, the man challenged him to disclose the source of his assertion that the kingdom was developing nuclear capability. Billington told him his access to that sort of information had ended long ago; his opinion piece had simply put two and two together. The Saudi seemed unconvinced.

As the rain intensified, Billington's Samsung cell phone rang. He recognized Tony Ramos's State Department number. "Everything okay?" Billington asked without any preliminaries.

"I've gotten clearance for the weekend," Tony reported. Billington felt a wave of reassurance come over him.

"Would four o'clock on Friday, in your office, be okay?"

"Excellent, my friend."

"Any material I should bring?"

"No. I'll have a memo with some of my thoughts. That should be sufficient."

"I'll see you on Friday, Senator."

Before he met with Tony, Billington wanted to have everything in order. He had already prepared a memo outlining his analysis of Saudi objectives, likely actions, and steps that needed to be taken. Each time he remembered something else, he jotted it in his notebook. As a backup, he had given a copy of the material to Mildred and asked her to deliver it to Tony if . . . Well, it was just that a man of his age had to have plans made.

During and after the inquiry he had led on the performance of the American intelligence community relative to the 9/11 tragedy, John had developed a fatherly attachment to this young intelligence officer detailed to the inquiry by the Bureau of Intelligence and Research. He identified with Tony and admired the intelligence and determination that had brought him from an immigrant youth in Hialeah to his present position in politics and national security. Both men cultivated social graces and an interest in people. Both prized their private time as their most productive. Above all, John Billington felt a bond of shared values and commitment with Tony.

Toward the end of the 9/11 inquiry, a review of FBI files suggested that information on two hijackers living in San Diego was inconsistent between the files at the central office in Washington and those at the field office in San Diego. The bureau protested to Billington when he announced that five staff members were going to San Diego to look into it. It was a gutsy move, with the White House threatening his job at State, but Tony requested to be put on the San Diego team. His digging unearthed the support that Hamza al-Dossari, the cultural officer at the Saudi consulate in L.A., and Omar al-Harbi, whom the FBI had labeled a Saudi agent based in San Diego, had given two of the 9/11 hijackers. Tony was the kind of man you wanted by your side when conditions were toughest.

As the rain slackened, Billington crossed the dampened street and turned left. A five-foot concrete wall separated him from a row of townhomes. Halfway down the block, he became aware of a vehicle that seemed to be following him. He quickened his pace, looking over his shoulder. A rapidly accelerating black Ford F-150 pickup swerved from the far side of the street, throwing up trails of rainwater. It turned sharply and jumped the curb.

Billington ran, leaping as high as his seventy-one-year-old legs would lift him. The grill and headlight smashed into his thigh and abdomen, twisting and throwing him against the wall. His head snapped forward against the concrete. He slid to the sidewalk, blood hemorrhaging from his gashed forehead. The pickup scraped the wall, U-turned with a screech, and sped from the scene.

Ed Feathers and Jack Wells, friends and commuters who had become accustomed to seeing Billington on his strolls, happened to be passing by and rushed to his aid. Ed called 911 on his cell phone. Billington was slumped on the sidewalk, his shoulder supported by the now scarlet wall. His dark-blue golf shirt was wet with blood and rain.

"Mildred," he moaned, "Mildred." Ed gently grasped Billington's head and shoulders to lay him on the concrete.

Ed Feathers for many years had been the comptroller of the Billington family companies. He called Mildred.

In less than five minutes Mildred Billington was kneeling by her husband.

"John. What happened?"

No response.

"I love you so much; I'll take care of you." She leaned forward.

"I think I'm badly hurt."

"The ambulance will be here soon; rest."

"My back." He dropped into unconsciousness.

The lime-green emergency van arrived with its red, white, and blue lights cycling and its siren screaming. Doors flew open as two emergency medical technicians launched themselves toward the victim. One reached into his red plastic case for a pressure bandage. The other looked down Billington's throat. "Airway open."

Tilting his head close to the senator's mouth, he observed the quivering, irregular, shallow and rapid wisps. "He's breathing." He took his wrist. "There's circulation, but it's going south, weak and thready; pulse is 115. He's in shock."

Protecting the spinal column, the two attached a neck brace and gently secured Billington's immobilized body to a backboard and taped small sandbags alongside his head. Though still unconscious, he winced.

Two minutes had passed by the time three paramedics arrived in an ambulance and took control. While one attached a cardiac monitor and oxygen mask, a second inserted IV lines into Billington's arms and attached them to saline bags. The third paramedic opened a collapsible stretcher, then held the undulating bags above John's head as the first two lifted him onto the stretcher and loaded him into the rear of the ambulance.

The vehicle rushed northward toward the Columbus Clinic Emergency Room. Mildred followed with Ed.

JULY 16

Above the Pacific ★ *Los Angeles, California*

The Singapore Airlines A340 executed a three-degree deviation to the south as it passed over Amchitka Island, eleven hours into a sixteen-hour flight from Singapore to Los Angeles. In the first-class cabin, Laura Billington interrupted her review of photo images and peered down at this spit of land and tundra that intruded on an otherwise undisturbed North Pacific.

With her bare feet curled under her and an iPad on her lap, Laura reviewed the first images of the shoot two days earlier in Bangkok. Eighty-year-old King Bhumibol Adulyadej, Rama IX of Thailand, surrounded by his family of three generations—thirteen men, women, and children—displayed the toothy smile of the genial grandfather rather than the imperial bearing of the longest-serving monarch in the world. She had been contracted to portray him for *Vanity Fair*. The palace had agreed. It was in the second hour in the stateroom of the royal palace that the king revealed the gravitas of the monarchy and the royal functions he had performed most of his adult life. Laura found the assignment surprisingly interesting and the king not only an accessible subject but also an avid amateur photographer.

"Ms. Billington," the young Chinese flight attendant said, "we will be serving a meal in twenty minutes. Would you care for a drink before the lunch?"

As Laura turned in her seat, exposing an inch of skin between her Joe's Jeans and a sweatshirt embossed with a golden Thai pagoda, her eyes fixed on the young woman with a mixture of incredulity and revulsion. Laura had perfected the ability, not uncommon among the more egocentric movie stars, of projecting the message with a single look that the onlooker was violating her precious and altogether entitled privacy merely by being in her presence.

"Thank you," she said with a brittle smile and an air of great and magnanimously granted tolerance, "I'll let you know."

As the shaken young woman backed away, bowing at the waist, Laura refocused on the images. After forty-five minutes she had selected ten with the most promise to find their way into the November edition of *Vanity Fair*. On the memo pad from Raffles Hotel she jotted the names, titles, logistics, and individual idiosyncrasies that might support the captions accompanying the royal family in print.

Her thoughts turned to the next assignment. Every few months she would review her offers, select those that intrigued her, organize her acceptances into geographically convenient segments, and notify the clients. Laura realized her practice was becoming excessively political and royal, not producing the income necessary to sustain her lifestyle. So a year earlier, she had accepted an assignment from *GQ* to photograph the chief executive officer of the private equity firm Peninsular Partners, in his office in Long Beach.

From her travel bag Laura selected a briefing book prepared by her research assistant on Peninsular and its leader. She reread the sections that interested her:

> Peninsular was established in 1990 by former members of the administration then in office. The firm focuses on investments in the high-tech and oil and gas sectors. Peninsular is a top-tier private equity firm with a successful track record. Its most recent fund has just over $10 billion in capital commitments to pursue investments globally.
>
> Since leaving his high position with the Department of Energy in January of 1993, Roland Jeralewski has served as the firm's managing partner. That same year the headquarters of the firm moved from New York to Long Beach, California. In November of 2003 *Fortune* magazine recognized Jeralewski as one of America's 100 most successful business executives. Known for his capacity to charm foreign leaders and his demanding leadership style, he was ranked two years ago as the 15th-highest compensated American executive.

Laura looked at the photograph attached to the memo: Jeralewski surrounded by men in white gowns and red-and-white turbans. Dressed in khaki pants and short-sleeve shirt, with his finger pointed at the apparent leader of the group, he was frozen by the photograph as a dominating figure amidst a group of supplicants. Laura repositioned her feet. She liked strong men. Her father had been her first experience with a dominant male. Although their relationship had deteriorated in her late adolescence, he still had her respect, if not her love. The first of a series, her break with her father had come when he tried to throw his rope around her rebellious neck. Laura applied for admission to Kenworth College in Colorado. He had objected to her selection, describing Kenworth as a ski resort posing as an educational institution for overindulged, snooty, and snotty kids. She enrolled in spite of his objection, and he consented to pay the $25,000 annual tuition. Her father's forebodings were confirmed when as a sophomore Laura told him she had moved in with her "very understanding" boyfriend and that together they had volunteered in the reelection campaign of Senator Horace Volker of Colorado, whom her father considered the most ideological and intemperate of the right-wing neo-cons.

The final straw came when Laura revealed she was dropping out after three undistinguished semesters "to follow her heart" to the London School of Photography. That was when Billington unleashed the colorful vocabulary of profanity he had learned on the cattle farm of his youth. He said she could follow her heart to hell, "but not with my money." For the last ten years father and daughter had hardly spoken.

As photography became a career, Laura had serial romantic relations. Many of the men had the characteristics she saw in the photograph of Jeralewski.

She reached for the pad of buttons above her and rang for the flight attendant. In moments she arrived over Laura's right shoulder. With her eyes never turning to engage the young woman, Laura ordered, "I am now ready for my meal. First I would like a Maker's Mark on the rocks, then the shrimp and scallop salad."

Finally she looked up. The brittle smile returned as she said, "I trust this will not be as uninteresting as the dinner you served last evening."

The attendant nodded and backed away.

Laura's advance man had emailed a description of Peninsular Tower locations. The warmest would be the Japanese garden in the rear; the most austere, Jeralewski's penthouse office. *GQ* had requested shots that captured Jeralewski's authoritarian demeanor. Laura selected the penthouse. Starting with location photos at sunrise, followed by interiors, she calculated the session should not last more than six hours.

The flight attendant arrived with the drink. Laura looked at it with the most abject disappointment and said, "I was so hoping for more youthful ice cubes; if the airline has any, that is." Again, the attendant retreated.

———

The giant airliner touched down at Los Angeles International at 1:10 in the afternoon. Laura gathered her materials, purse, and shoulder bag and inserted her well-pedicured feet into Versace slippers. She exited through the first-class cabin door and awaited her staff of four at the end of the skyway as they emerged from the tourist section. The three men and one woman showed the consequences of a transpacific flight in tight quarters. Their faded jeans and T-shirts were rumpled and stained, and their faces were those of the sleep deprived. In silence, Laura led them down the terminal to the baggage claim carousel, where she was met by her limousine driver, her crew by a driver with a white Dodge van.

At curbside Laura said, "We'll meet tomorrow morning at 5:30 at the Ocean Boulevard entrance to Peninsular Towers. Jaime, check that arrangements have been made for the office to be open. If there are changes, call me. Any questions?"

None coming from her bedraggled crew, she wrapped up: "It's been a demanding three weeks, with one more"—Laura let a stutter slip out, a childhood characteristic she strove to contain—"day to go. We'll celebrate when we get back to London."

With the staff baggage and twenty metallic cases of equipment loaded, the Dodge pulled into the airport traffic and headed to the Long Beach Marriott.

Laura settled back in the Lincoln Town Car for the thirty-five-minute drive to the Beverly Hills Hotel. She opened her iPhone and scanned the eighteen voicemails that had accumulated during the flight. She deleted all but one: her sister Kendall had left an urgent message.

"Kendall, it's Laura. I just got to L.A."

In a strained and whispering voice, Kendall said, "Laura, I'm so glad you called. Daddy was badly injured in a hit-and-run accident this morning. He's still in surgery. The doctors aren't optimistic. Mom has completely broken down. Please get here as soon as possible."

Laura stiffened, as she seemed to every time her father was mentioned. "I am so sorry. Please let Mother know I'm thinking of her." Laura could visualize her father wandering to the edge of the street, unaware of the traffic until it was too late.

"I'll get there as soon as I can. But—"

"Please hurry. Laura, there isn't much time."

"I understand, Kendall, but I've just gotten in from an international flight, and I've got a whole bunch of things lined up here in L.A. and—"

"I'm sure you're very busy, as always, Laura, but this is one situation that can't be put on hold for you. If you want to see your father alive—"

"You've made your point, Kendall, I'm going to do my best to come as soon as—"

"Or maybe you don't," her sister interrupted, continuing her own thought. "But I'd think you'd feel you owed it to your mother, at least, to be by her side at a time like this."

It had been almost ten years since she last saw him. Her father had lived a long life and had more than his share of achievements and recognition. If this was his time, so be it. But that was not language Kendall, or the other girls, for that matter, could possibly understand.

"I'll be there soon," Laura said.

As soon as she hung up, she realized she was crying.

JULY 16–17
Los Angeles ★ Long Beach, California

The Beverly Hills was one of Laura's favorite hotels. Its South of France ambience amidst the palm trees of Southern California appealed to her. And there were few places as ideal for connecting and being seen as its venerable Polo Lounge. There she had met Warren Beatty, her professional breakout, with a spread in *Rolling Stone* magazine.

But this afternoon she was tired, with demanding and emotional days ahead. After checking into her suite, she called Kendall.

"How's Mother?"

"Resting in the visitors' lounge. Daddy's in Intensive Care. We're still waiting for some definitive word. Laura, it is very depressing here; we're pretty much down to prayers."

"I'll be there as soon as I finish here. Tell Mother I love her."

"Laura, Mother needs you. All of your sisters are here to take control of the situation now," Kendall emitted a pained gasp, "and what might happen. You would be a great emotional boost to her and a help to the rest of us."

"Kendall, I'm not here on a vacation. I made this professional commitment months ago. There are many people depending on me. I can't just up and leave."

"Laura," Kendall screamed, "your father may not live another twenty-four hours. I don't care what you thought of him or what your personal history might have been. He—we—deserve your being here before he is gone. And no one is going to forget it if you are not here for the end."

The connection cut off. Laura stared at the phone incredulously for a moment. "Point made, as usual, Kendall," she said.

———

Laura spent the next two hours in the spa, took a light room-service dinner, and was asleep by 8:30.

She arrived at Peninsular Tower promptly at 5:30. "John," she glowered at the lighting technician, "when the sun is fully up, the reflection will overwhelm Jeralewski. Move the lights and umbrellas to the rear of the yard, under the palm fronds."

With the lighting as she had directed, Laura snapped test images of John, examined them, and waved the gear further into the shadows until satisfied. "Okay, we'll go with that."

At 8:15 the equipment was broken down and moved to the penthouse offices. At twenty-seven floors of glass curtain wall, the Peninsular Tower dominated the Long Beach waterfront. The reception area for the penthouse offices was decorated in modern Spartan. Except for the occasional Warhol or Hiler, the tone was eggshell white. The surroundings softly echoed serious, prosperous business.

Forty minutes of setup and light-checking in the managing partner's office passed before Jeralewski arrived. Laura rose, responding to his nod. He was deeply tanned, with prominent cheekbones and chiseled features. In a throaty voice that suggested roots somewhere in Central Europe, he said, "Ms. Billington, welcome to Peninsular."

He was shorter than Laura had anticipated, no more than five feet, eight. His suit was suavely Global Executive, British pearl-grey wool with an indigo pattern in an Italian cut. The flapless coat accentuated Jeralewski's trim, muscular buttocks. Cuff links bearing the seal of the president of the United States of America adorned his French blue shirt. The only noticeable concession to the West Coast was his tasseled oxblood loafers.

None of the modernism of the lobby invaded his office. More like those on Capitol Hill, Jeralewski's walls were covered with photographs of the occupant with prominent figures. The most important officials from the Reagan and first Bush administrations were represented, with no fewer than thirteen depictions of the two presidents. The wall-to-wall carpeting provided an innocuous stage for a Heriz Persian rug. Through her mother Laura knew about these rugs and calculated she stood on more than $300,000 of ancient wool. The furniture seemed lifted from a London men's club. The chief executive's mahogany desk anchored the near side of the room, facing a plush semicircle of silk-upholstered chairs. Light streamed in through a floor-to-ceiling glass pane facing the ports of Long Beach and Los Angeles and on to the Pacific horizon.

"Please, Ms. Billington, take a seat."

Laura eased into the centermost of the chairs, and before she could offer the standard formalities, Jeralewski interjected, "I have heard and read a great deal about you. Your work is compelling, particularly your recent portrait of President Putin, and I am pleased the magazine accepted our suggestion and selected you to take the photographs."

Accepted their suggestion? They had asked *GQ* for her? That wasn't how it was done. She waited for more. After a long pause he said, "I wonder if I might have a few private words with you after our session?"

Laura felt a slight moistening of her underarms. She had had sufficient experience with the flattery of high-profile subjects not to be surprised by his words. Yet she did feel oddly anxious and uncomfortable in his company.

She said stiffly, "Of course. Now, shall we begin?"

Jeralewski rose, brushed a spot of imperfection from his coat. His Naval Academy ring caught the glint of the morning sunshine. "Where?"

"If you please, here. I prefer to do the portrait at the beginning and then the informals."

With the subject before the camera, Laura was dissatisfied with the intensity of the light. "John," she implored, "drop a double scrim over the key light." Satisfied at last, she began.

An hour and twenty minutes into the shoot, as Laura captured Jeralewski "reviewing" office papers, the credenza phone rang. "Ms. George, I'm occupied," he announced sternly. "Please handle my calls until Ms. Billington is finished."

He was quiet for several seconds, then, "I'll take the call."

With the phone tucked under his chin, Jeralewski scribbled on a note pad. "Mr. Chairman," he said, "I have no reason to suspect our understandings have been altered without permission." For two minutes he listened, frowning. "This is not the time for this conversation. Could you come to my office after three?" Laura snapped the shutter.

Another hour of candids: Jeralewski conversing with colleagues and bystanders in the garden and at the formal entrance of the Peninsular building. Laura was winding up. She was confident *GQ* would be pleased.

As her staff was dismantling the photographic gear, Laura's iPhone hummed.

"Laura, Kendall . . . " A pause conveyed the message. "Daddy died twenty minutes ago. He never recovered consciousness. The doctors said he was in no pain." Another longer pause. "The rest of us are all here. Mother's in no condition to make plans. We hope you can be here tonight."

Now that he was dead, a strange mixture of—what?—relief, shame, sorrow, and anger swept over her. Were things still that complicated between her and her dad? *Well, I can't think about that now.* Laura looked at her watch. "I'll get the next flight I can," she said.

As Laura came back into the executive suite, Ms. George was sitting at her desk near the entrance to Jeralewski's office.

"I'm terribly sorry," Laura said, "but there's been a family emergency. I will have to postpone my meeting with Mr. Jeralewski."

JULY 17

Washington, D.C.

As was Ben Brewster's norm, at five o'clock he was preparing to call it a day. He could not resist poking his head, centered by quarter-inch-thick bifocals and topped by a scalp so hairless it reflected light, into Tony's office.

Tony looked up. His hope that this was the beginning of peace negotiations was short-lived.

"Have you heard the Cuban national anthem?"

"Brewster, I really don't need any of your paranoid xenophobic shit," Tony replied.

Undaunted, Brewster continued. "Last February, I was at Foxy's bar on Jost Van Dyke in the British Virgin Islands—"

"And I'll bet they could spot a fellow virgin when they saw one."

"No, listen: I was walking up to the bar from our catamaran. Foxy himself, an old, skinny black guy with a big smile, was sitting under a coconut tree by the front door strumming a ukulele. He asked me, 'You ever heard the Cuban national anthem?' Without waiting for an answer he sang, 'Row, row, row, your boat gently down the stream—'"

Tony picked up a yellow government-issue pencil and mentally calculated the minimum number of moves to maneuver the point into Brewster's anal region, when he recalled his Tuesday promise to Carol. "Before I drive this up your ass, would you like to act like a professional for a change?"

Brewster lowered his flabby and bulging buttocks onto Tony's guest chair. It emitted a squeak of protest.

"What've you got?" Brewster asked.

"I've been told that DOJ has opened an investigation of a corruption case involving BAE and the Saudis. It struck me as strange that we would be prying into a case involving our best ally and a crowd we'd gone out of our way to protect after 9/11. You're supposed to be our expert on all things Saudi—what's up?"

Brewster looked taken by surprise. "Where'd you get this from?"

"Let's just say I heard it around." Tony knew that if the situation were reversed, Brewster would never divulge a source to someone on his own level. In Washington, information was the real currency of power.

Brewster squirmed in the chair. "Maybe one of our defense firms is still pissed off over losing those F-15 sales."

"Got to be more to it than that."

"I dunno. You know how much weight those Beltway bandits swing at 1600 Pennsylvania."

Tony was about to respond when Brewster rose abruptly. "Sorry I couldn't be of more help. See you tomorrow; maybe we can sing the National Anthem together."

Tony brandished the pencil threateningly as Brewster stuck out his mighty ass in provocation. "I'm not worried," he said. "I'm told your aim has fallen off since you left the tennis circuit." He gave a foppish sort of wave as he exited the office, closing Tony's door behind him.

As soon as he was back in his own office, Brewster closed that door, too, and moved across to the window. He punched ten digits into his Droid, waited several seconds, and then punched in four more.

Another pause and then he said, "I need to speak with Mr. Jeralewski."

JULY 17

Washington, D.C. ★ Zurich, Switzerland

About six in the evening, while he was immersed in the latest cable from Kabul, Tony's Blackberry rang. It was his Uncle Luis from Hialeah.

"Tony," he said in Spanish with a solemn voice, "your friend Senator Billington has been killed in a car wreck. The radio says he was at Columbus Hospital and he never regained his senses."

"What!" Tony said, stunned. He felt his body go suddenly slack. "Is there any more?"

"Not that I know, but I'll keep listening."

"Thank you, are you doing okay?"

"Yes, thank the Lord."

Tony leaned back. He realized his hands were shaking. He had talked with the senator the day before and made reservations for a trip to Miami to see him and consider his requests for help.

He called Mrs. Billington, leaving his message of condolence with the third daughter, Suzanne. She relayed the funeral arrangements. He booked a turnaround flight to Tallahassee on Wednesday that would get him to the state capital in time for the funeral.

Since Georgetown, Tony had drifted from his Catholic upbringing but retained a belief in a Supreme Being. He offered up a silent prayer for his friend.

Promptly at three o'clock, Carol presented her papers to Franz Schmidt, manager of the personal accounts section of the Zurich-Alliance Bank. A warm shower and two hours of sleep had washed away the initial jet lag of her night flight from Dulles.

Rising to inspect the papers, Schmidt offered Carol the facing chair. "Welcome, Ms. Watson. We have been anticipating your arrival. I trust your arrangements have been satisfactory."

"Quite." Carol responded. "This is a beautiful city, and I hope to get to know it better while I am here on my government's business."

Schmidt moved a manila folder to the center of his desk. He did so with the assurance and élan of one who had spent a career overseeing the financial needs of some of the world's wealthiest and most celebrated clients. "I am pleased you will have that opportunity, although I must say, your assignment is challenging and for us rather novel."

"Novel?"

"Yes. As you know, we Swiss have prided ourselves on a tradition of confidentiality in our private banking relationships. This would be particularly true of our official and special clients."

"My government appreciates your discretion. However," Carol paused as she sought the words to describe what to her was an opaque assignment, "in this instance we have concerns about a corrupt relationship that might compromise decisions affecting our national security. My government is gratified by the offer of cooperation extended by yours, and Zurich-Alliance."

Schmidt lifted his brown-rimmed glasses. "It is my understanding you are specifically interested in the records reflecting transfers from the British corporation BAE Systems to certain Saudi clients of this bank during the period April to June 1991. Correct?"

"At least that appears to be the point of origination of my government's interest."

"Ms. Watson, I am certain you are aware of the sensitivity of these records and the degree of departure from standard practice for the bank to voluntarily agree to provide you with access?"

It seemed to Carol as if she were fighting a duel, only instead of foils, the politest and most carefully chosen of words were the weapons.

"Mr. Schmidt, as you might have been informed, I was one of the Treasury officials involved in the investigation of UBS."

Whether Mr. Schmidt was aware of her involvement or not, he was intimately familiar with the UBS case. After years of protracted and often

contentious negotiations, UBS had agreed to reveal to
the names of 4,450 wealthy American clients holdin
billion in offshore accounts and suspected of evading

"And as you also might know," she continued, "ur
treaty with your government, the U.S. is pursuing no   , ... fraud
but also similar financial crimes such as money laundering and corruption. It is under this authority and with the insights our Treasury Department has gained in pursuing UBS and other financial institutions
that I am investigating the designated accounts. I am confident of my
ability to fulfill my assignment, and your assistance in doing so will be
very much appreciated." Looking directly at Schmidt, over the green-
shaded bank office desk light, she added, "In exchange, you can be assured of my professionalism and discretion."

"Thank you for those assurances. I have made arrangements for a
private office here in our section to be at your disposal." Rising again,
he indicated the door and led Carol from his office.

With the door secure and the manila file before her, Carol turned
from the cover sheet marked "Account 67-H39-4" and dated for the
Swiss fiscal year, the calendar year 1991, to the following pages of entries. The first nineteen pages reflected in chronological order a series
of credits to the account, primarily from European and North American sources, in amounts denominated in British pounds, Euros, and
U.S. and Canadian dollars, most in excess of seven figures.

On page 20 was an April 11, 1991, entry for 100 million British
pounds from BAE Systems Inc. Carol noted similar entries in May,
June, and July. Even with the closest inspection, she failed to detect further BAE entries until October, when, on the first Wednesday, 250 million British pounds had been credited from BAE, with the same
amount on the same day in November and December.

Carol looked up on hearing a light knock on the wooden door. Mr.
Schmidt opened it and indicated it was the normal five o'clock closing
of the bank, but magnanimously assured Carol she was welcome to stay
as long as she might wish. Otherwise, he extended an invitation for dinner at his home. With the second stage of travel weariness descending,
Carol accepted, returning her files to him for safekeeping.

Even in July, there was a crispness in the early evening air. Carol was glad she'd thought of bringing a light coat. She slipped it on as she stepped from the bank entrance into the street. This casual distraction contributed to her failure to note a man with paunchy jowls in a heavier trench coat falling into step behind her.

JULY 18

Miami International Airport

"OK, what you got?" Miami-Dade Police sergeant George Whitten snapped into the phone.

"One mucho pissed-off hombre," Mario Cartaya replied. "Says he just got back from a business trip to Vegas and can't find his truck in the Flamingo Garage. Says he's looked all over—no truck."

"Can you put him on the phone?"

"Yeah, he's standin' right beside me."

"Hello, this is Ramon Diaz."

Sergeant Whitten lifted a form from his desk's left-hand drawer and cradled the phone between his right ear and shoulder. "Mr. Diego, can you tell me what happened?"

"My name is Diaz," the man replied with annoyance. "What happened was, I went to the Nurserymen's meeting in Vegas. I go every summer. Left last Saturday and parked my truck here around four o'clock. Third level, section P; I made a note. I came back a couple hours ago and started lookin' for it, and it ain't there. So I went down to the exit box to tell somebody, and now I'm talking to you."

Whitten filled in the blanks on the form as Diaz provided the information. "Ramon Juan Diaz. I live at the Tropical Nursery at 18645 Southwest 262nd Street in Redland, Florida, zip 33031."

"What kinda truck were you driving and do you know the tag number?"

"It's a Ford F-150, 2004 model. Painted black. I'll have to get back to you with the license plate."

"Do you want a copy of this form for an insurance claim?"

"Hell no. I just want my truck back. What are you going to do about it?"

"Well," Whitten sighed, "we have over a dozen cars called in missing from this place every year. Each is reported to the state vehicle data center and to the Miami-Dade detective bureau to follow up."

"And how many of those have you found?"

"Some, but most of them are taken right over there to the Miami River," Whitten waved in the general direction of northeast, "put on a boat for someplace in the Caribbean, and that's the last they'll see of the U.S.A."

There was no reply from Diaz.

"The detective will check the video from the cameras we have in the garage. You say it was Flamingo 3-P from 4:00 p.m. on the 12th till today?"

"That's right."

"Mr. Diaz, if you would come over to my office—Mr. Cartaya can give you directions—and sign this missing vehicle form. I'll call you if the detectives come up with anything."

Diaz handed the phone back to Cartaya. "God damn, just more paperwork shit."

While the distraught nurseryman called his brother in Sweetwater to give him a ride home, Cartaya wrote out the directions to the airport police office.

JULY 18–21

Zurich ✶ Washington, D.C.

It was Carol's fifth day in Zurich. The initial cordiality was beginning to wear thin. It had begun on Day Two.

Carol worked through the 1992 version of the credits she had reviewed on Thursday. She saw a continued pattern: on the first Wednesday of each month, payments into the account from BAE Systems Inc. of 250 million British pounds per month—through October of 1992—for a total over the thirteen months of 3.25 billion pounds. What she had not seen were any disbursements.

"Mr. Schmidt," Carol asked when she was back in his office, "I have completed both fiscal years' review of credit transactions. I now need the disbursement information."

"Ms. Watson, I am not sure you are authorized to inspect those transactions."

"Mr. Schmidt," Carol reacted with uncharacteristic sharpness, "I am authorized to conduct a complete audit of the account. What I have seen thus far is consistent with findings of the British Serious Fraud Office. What I have not seen is what it was denied—records of disbursements out of the account. I thank you for your hospitality and assistance, but I must be able to examine all transactions."

"I will review it with my superiors."

It was almost four o'clock when Schmidt reported that the general counsel of Zurich-Alliance had opined that the authorization to inspect that Carol proffered was limited to credits. Stunned and angered, Carol called the U.S. Department of the Treasury and spoke to Assistant Secretary for Finance and Intelligence Samuel Shorstein. She transmitted the information that 3.65 billion pounds had been credited to a numbered account stated to be under the control of members of the Saudi royal family, but her authorization did not extend to a review of where the money had gone.

"Ms. Watson, the Department of Justice cleared the authorization with the Swiss banking officials. I am stunned you are being blocked. It's ten in the morning here; I'll be back with you before noon."

It was 5:30 in Zurich when Carol next heard Shorstein's voice on her cell. "This is inexplicable, but apparently the guys at Justice and State screwed up. I have our legals on it, and I think we can get it resolved over the weekend. At any rate, you're in luck. July is a good month to be in the mountains."

And it was. Carol would have an unexpected chance to fulfill her desire to get to know Zurich and visit a few of the surrounding alpine villages. On Saturday night she dined alone at the hotel restaurant. She became aware of a man wearing a heavy coat, sitting awkwardly in a darkened corner, who seemed to be unusually attentive. Strange for July, that coat.

On Sunday, the same man, again overdressed for the train to Zermatt, was behind her in the economy-class car. At the Museum of Mountain Art, he was observing the landscapes from about twenty feet behind her back. He maneuvered forward, through the small cluster of art patrons, until he was standing behind Carol's left shoulder. He bored in like a giant grizzly appraising its next morsel. The perverse intensity of his black eyes sent a quiver down Carol's spine.

She had to get out of here. Whatever she did, she just had to get out.

She hurried through the crowd and made her way across the lobby and down the alcove into the ladies room. She went over to the row of sinks and placed her palms firmly on the counter to steady herself. She looked at herself in the mirror. Watching herself tremble made her tremble even more.

Take deep breaths. This is probably nothing. Even if he's following, it's probably just to hit on you. Still, she wasn't going to take the chance. She quickly decided to dismiss the rest of the exhibit and abandon her plan to tour other villages.

Tentatively, she opened the ladies room door and peered outside to see if he was hanging around. The coast looked clear.

Not running, but striding too fast for comfort, she dashed out onto the street, carefully looking all around at each juncture.

She spotted an available taxi across the street, got in, and locked the door. The driver turned around in surprise. She told him she wanted to go to the train station. She arrived barely in time to catch the 3:26 to Zurich.

––––––––––

Midday Monday, the assistant secretary called back.

"Mr. Shorstein," Carol said, "I have this suspicion I am being followed," and she recounted the instances in which the same man had been in her vicinity.

"Carol, I'll ask our counsel general in Zurich to contact the Swiss authorities. If you feel in any way endangered, here is her name and local number." He repeated the information. "Now, the good news. We have clearance for you to complete the review. The papers have been approved in Bern and the approvals transmitted to the bank officer. Maybe you'll be able to wrap this up and leave your unwanted companion."

Promptly at 12:30, Carol was again in Franz Schmidt's office. Chagrined, he apologized for the interruption on Friday and gave her two additional manila folders and access to the same office she had used three days earlier.

From April to July of fiscal year 1991, there were no unexpected disbursements. Each month transfers had been made to yet other numbered accounts at banks in Saudi Arabia. Carol assumed they represented individual members of the extended royal family. The amounts varied month to month, but rarely were these remittances for amounts less than the equivalent of 15 million U.S. dollars.

Her search became more interesting and consistent after October 1991. For the last three months of that year, a single wire transfer disbursement of the full 250 million pounds was made, on the day of receipt, to the Anglo-Cayman Bank in George Town, Grand Cayman. This practice continued into 1992 until it stopped suddenly in October.

Carol took the next hour to verify her accounts and records and review the notes she had made. She pushed the envelope with Mr. Schmidt when she asked permission to copy the pages of the statements on which credits and disbursements of relevance to her inquiry were entered. Possibly intimidated by her ability to reverse his earlier refusals, he acceded to her request.

Satisfied, at 2:00 she confirmed her 5:15 flight back to Dulles.

"Ms. Watson, I am so regretful at our misunderstanding and the inconvenience it caused you," Schmidt conveyed as she was leaving. "We are unaccustomed to the inspection of our accounts and are rather clumsy at it, as your tax inspectors have also experienced. I hope you will accept Zurich-Alliance's, and our government's, apologies."

"Thank you, Mr. Schmidt. I know you were carrying out your responsibilities as you were instructed. The information you have made available will be very valuable to my superiors and our government."

As her two pieces of luggage were placed in the trunk of the airport taxi, the jowly man stood secluded behind the transfer stand. As it had been with several of his recent assignments, he was not informed of the purpose of his surveillance, only given specific tasks. Here, they had been to monitor and report on the young woman's activities and movements. In contrast to other recent duties, it had been clean and non-confrontational. He would submit his encrypted report and return to his temporary residence.

———————

From the Zurich Airport lounge, Carol called Tony.

"Well, I got as far as I'm going to get here. I'll be at Dulles at 7:30 tonight. Could you arrange your very loaded social schedule to pick me up?"

"I'll think about it," Tony teased.

"You'd better think about it hard, my boy."

Yes!

JULY 21

Washington, D.C.

At 7:30 Monday evening, Tony was waiting for Carol at the International Arrivals area at Dulles. Every time the automatic doors opened, the crowd perked up, waiting to see if the emerging traveler was their loved one.

Carol stepped through the automatic doors, pushing a Smart Cart. The casual blouse she wore fell loosely over tight Calvin Klein jeans. She turned and her face brightened. Tony approached and hugged her around her bared midriff. She gave him a kiss full on the lips, followed by a light one on his neck.

As they left Dulles in the black Mustang, Carol sat as close to Tony as the center console and gearshift would allow. He recounted the news of Senator Billington's tragic and unexpected death. Then, after a pause he said, "Carol, I've really missed you, not just since you've been gone but . . . since you've been gone . . . from me."

"Tony," Carol said softly as she turned to him, "I missed you and needed you."

He felt an electric jolt, right around the middle of his chest. "Needed? How?"

"Well, in lots of ways. But I do need to get your advice on a piece of business."

"Okay." His mind was on other things as he steered the Mustang onto the Dulles Access Road.

"After a speed bump that seems to have been constructed here—not Zurich—the bank officers were gracious and helpful. They must be taking the IRS investigations seriously and want to repair their reputation with us. Anyhow, listen to this: From April to July of '91, 400 million pounds were transferred by BAE to a numbered Saudi account. Then from October '91 to October '92 there were monthly transfers of 250 million pounds each from London to the same account at Zurich-Alliance."

"Wow."

"Tony Blair was especially protective of that account."

"The plot thickens."

"But the October-to-October BAE transfers didn't stay in the numbered account long. It was all sent back west to the Anglo-Cayman Bank in Grand Cayman on the day of receipt. All three billion, two hundred fifty million pounds."

"What do you think was going on?"

"My bank liaison said there was a connection between BAE and an American defense firm. He said that what I saw in the '91 and '92 accounts was not the whole of the relationship. He speculated it involved a military operation the Brits and U.S. wanted to keep undercover from the Israelis."

"That could explain DOJ's interest. If you didn't know it, you're a damn smart girl."

"And that's where I need your help, smart boy. Intelligence on a national security matter like that wouldn't be in TFI database, but it could be in INR's."

"I can take a look," Tony offered. "Is there anything else?"

He noticed a ripple run through Carol's shoulders. "Yes," she said. "There was a man who seemed to be following me. He was at the hotel restaurant where I had dinner, on the train to Zermatt, and stood next to me at an art gallery. He didn't say or do anything, but he gave me a fish-eyed look and was so close he was practically breathing down my neck. I finally had to run away from him and stayed in my hotel room once I got back to Zurich."

"Did you tell anybody?"

"My boss, Mr. Shorstein. He alerted our counsel general in Zurich, but I don't know if she did anything. It probably doesn't amount to a hill of beans but he creeped me out, made me feel as if I were under surveillance."

"Do you think it could have been the bank was pissed off that you had pressed them further than they wanted to go, or maybe the Saudis? It was their accounts you were nosing into."

"I honestly don't know."

"I'll look into it tomorrow."

Carol leaned over the console and rubbed her perfumed cheek on Tony's neck. "You are so sweet."

———————

Carol's apartment was on the fourth floor of The Greenwich, in the row of residential buildings stretching north along Connecticut Avenue across the street from the National Zoo. Tony carried Carol's two bags to the elevator.

The apartment perfectly fit the profile of other young, single, first-rung-on-the-salary-scale professional women's apartments in Washington. The small living-dining room and adjoining kitchen were bare except for a few necessities and a clutch of family photographs with Carol, what appeared to be her parents, and a young child. Since he had noticed it the first time he was in her apartment, Tony had wondered who the little girl was, but had never found the right moment to ask. The place was obviously for sleeping and preparing for work and little else.

Tony placed the luggage in the equally small bedroom.

"I'm really grungy," Carol said. "I've been in this outfit since Zurich. I need to jump in the shower. Make yourself comfortable. I won't be long."

Tony welcomed her idea. *How comfortable?* he wondered.

As she turned, he clasped her wrist to keep her from leaving. "Carol, I've had a long time to think about it while we weren't seeing each other, and I really don't want to let you out of my life again."

"Well, that's up to you, I guess," she replied.

"We're both ready to take this to the next level. I want our relation-ship to be . . . deeper."

"Deeper, huh?" Carol had a mischievous glint in her eye.

"I've never waited this long to . . . you know."

"Your forbearance is admirable."

"Carol, I love you, and I want to *love* you."

"We'll have to see about that." Despite her words, her eyes still be-trayed that sparkle.

"I'd like to see about it . . . tonight."

"If you don't let me get into the shower, you're not going to want to get anywhere near me."

As he sat on the IKEA couch watching the Washington Nationals' pathetic effort to look like a major-league baseball team, Tony replayed the just-completed conversation in his mind. Maybe it was her southern upbringing; maybe it was her wariness of former professional athletes; maybe it was his skin color; maybe it was that she didn't think Tony was in this for the long haul. Maybe it was this, maybe it was that, but every time Tony had gotten close to intimacy with Carol, she had emo-tionally backed away. At least, that was the vibe she gave off. But now, it was as if she were communicating a different message. If it was ever going to happen, now was the time.

While Tony overanalyzed in the living room, Carol peeled off her clothes in the bathroom and turned on the shower. She washed her hair with the Gucci shampoo from the Zurich duty-free shop. The Molton Brown soap was from her hotel room. She was smoothing the lather up and down her long legs when she suddenly heard the roar of the Na-tionals fans.

The shower curtain flung open behind her. She gasped as Tony, naked, stretched his muscular right leg into the tub. Carol jerked the curtain shut, leaving only the leg protruding into her space.

"'But you're lovely, with your smile so warm and your cheeks so soft,'" Tony crooned through the plastic barrier. "All of your cheeks so soft. And getting softer by the minute, I presume."

With the showerhead pouring water on her head and shoulders, Carol pulled back the curtain, "You presume correctly."

Tony almost leaped into the tub. Stomach to stomach, they swayed as he sang on, "'There is nothing for me but to love you, and the way you look tonight.'" Carol reached down for the bar of soap on the tub floor. Tony cupped her breasts, bowed to nuzzle and gently kiss her erect nipples. Carol soaped him with rotating strokes, beginning with his chest, stroking down to his groin.

From behind, he held her loosely around her waist. She eased back on his forearms, completely relaxed in his grasp.

Together they stepped out on the tile floor. They each toweled the other, but couldn't wait until they were completely dry, as if all the time they had waited had built up in a pressure cooker. With their moisture dampening the bedsheets, they lay there together, absorbing the pleasure of their first intimacy.

Tony pulled back. "I have a condom."

"No need," Carol said. "I'm taken care of."

That was a surprise.

"And I want you 'just the way you are tonight.'" Feeling her insides throbbing, she whispered, "Tony, it's been a long time since I felt for a man the way I do for you."

He rolled over, his upper body supported with his left elbow. He held his position, gazing at her naked and glistening body. She was all his now. He kissed her, encircling her parted, moistened lips.

He climbed on top and entered her. Carol wrapped her legs around his thighs and pulled them up to his buttocks. The two of them were in complete harmony, moving in unison. After a passionate eternity of rhythmic plunging, they climaxed together. Then, still entangled, they rested.

They were sheltered in each other's arms. The tension of a long day, tinged with sadness and travel weariness, had dissolved in each other's embrace. Intertwined, they slept.

An hour later, Carol rose to use the bathroom. When she returned Tony was lying on his back awake. He reached out, pulled her toward him.

Their physical connections gradually became tenser, erotic. Their pace quickened. With Tony still on his back, Carol rolled on top, as if needing to assert her equality. Her breasts swayed before him, the rose further enflaming Tony's desire as she guided him into her again. They made love until their mutual climax left them drained and exhausted.

This time, it was Tony who woke first. As he gazed at her sleeping form, he couldn't stop thinking about that rose tattoo and yearned to know the story behind it.

JULY 22–23

Washington, D.C. ✶ The Lakes ✶ Tallahassee, Florida

As promised, Tony's first call was to Samuel Shorstein. Informed that the assistant secretary was en route to an international conference on terrorist financing in Amman, Tony spoke with Shorstein's deputy, John Oxtoby.

"I am generally familiar with Ms. Watson's situation in Zurich. I've followed up on a directive from Secretary Shorstein Monday to the FBI legate in Bern."

"What was his take?" Tony asked.

"Frankly, he thinks Ms. Watson might have overreacted and read more into the situation than was warranted. I understand this was one of her first assignments, maybe even one of her first foreign travels of any type. In a different culture innocent acts can be seen as threatening."

"Mr. Oxtoby, Carol—I mean, Ms. Watson—may be a relative novice to foreign travel, but she is very levelheaded. Secretary Shorstein would not have given her this assignment otherwise."

"Excuse my intrusion, Mr. Ramos, but do you have any form of relationship with Ms. Watson—a relationship that could affect your objectivity?"

Tony squirmed, his thoughts flashing back to last evening. "We are friends and have consulted on professional matters of mutual interest."

"I'll note your evaluation and ask the station in Bern to keep her file active. If anything pops up, Ms. Watson will be notified. Thank you for your interest."

John Billington's only instructions for his funeral had been to include "America the Beautiful" and end with a bagpiper, dressed in a blue and green tartan kilt, playing "Amazing Grace."

The last notes of Billington's first request hung in the humid afternoon air as Reverend Jeffrey Frantz, the family minister at The Lakes Congregational Church, led the overflow gathering of friends, political associates, and admirers in prayer. The Bangladeshi clerk at the store where the senator had bought his last two newspapers sat in a side pew, weeping while consoling her adolescent daughter.

By the time Laura arrived and squirmed uncomfortably into the end of the family pew, Reverend Frantz was beginning his eulogy. "You know, my friends, you can discern a lot about an individual from the stories others tell about him. So yesterday afternoon, when I met with Mildred Billington and four of her and John's five daughters, I asked the girls—they're certainly not girls anymore, though I've known them all since they were—I asked each of the daughters what story their mother told most often about their father. And you know what? They all agreed. It was about when the parents had first met."

Laura glanced down the pew at her sisters, all of whom seemed engrossed in the story, their eyes forward to the lectern and not on her.

"Mildred Moore met John Billington as a freshman at the University of Florida. Struggling with a required course in the physical sciences, she had come on a warm October morning to the administration building in hopes of securing a tutor. By chance, John was leaving as she was walking up the stairs.

"He paused and introduced himself with a sincere, but unlikely-to-be-successful pickup line, 'My name is John Billington. Usually students only come here when they're in trouble; what's your problem?'

"'Geology,' Mildred admitted. 'I took the first test yesterday. It wasn't pretty. My father told me to get a tutor. That's my problem.'

"With the confidence of the mature sophomore, a quality of non-arrogant self-confidence that the voters in this state would soon recognize as the hallmark of a fine politician, John said, 'I took that course last year. I got an A. In fact, I set the curve. I've got a heavy schedule this semester and in the fraternity, but I'd be happy to take a shot at helping you.'

"Mildred, tall and slender and striking, looked up at John, two steps above. She was impressed with his directness, even his bookish persona. She smiled. 'You'll be taking on a challenging project,' she warned him.

"'I'll give it my best,' he replied. 'The library, say around seven?'

"That encounter led to a better understanding of both sedimentary rocks and each other. Two years later, Mildred and John were married at the university chapel. That was forty-nine years ago, just one year short of half a century."

Frantz paused a moment, smiled at the congregation and placed both hands firmly on the lectern, as if he were about to level with them.

"My friends, when you think about it, this touching story really summarizes the life of John Billington. He came upon a 'constituent,' he offered his help, he was taken up on that offer, and he delivered. And, of course, the story has a happy ending, because he was rewarded brilliantly for that willingness to help others; he was rewarded with the love of his life. I think we can all take a lesson from the life of John Billington. If you are always willing to help others, the rewards will come; you don't even have to think about them."

"And Mildred," Frantz continued with a twinkle in his eye, "I'll bet to this day you even still remember a little bit about geology."

Laura glanced down the pew to see her mother nodding her head, her eyes bright with tears.

———————

As the service ended, Mildred, nearly six feet tall and almost as imposing as the night she and John were married, maintained her gracious demeanor, accepting each of the congregants with respect and attention. Mourners passed, offering their condolences and admiration for the partnership she and the senator shared through all the vicissitudes of private and political life. Blessed with five beautiful daughters, their life had been a partnership of love, family, and politics.

Sensing her mother's fatigue, Gwen gently took her by the arm and led her to a waiting limousine.

"Dear Gwen," Mildred admonished, "these friends have come to pay their respects to Father and to see us. We can't leave them standing in line."

Laura wondered whether her mother was as haunted as she was that the driver who had taken her husband had so far gone undetected. The city, county, and state law enforcement agencies were all on the case and, since Billington was a former federal official, so was the FBI.

The limousine took them a mile to The Lakes Country Club for the reception. Her oldest sister, Gwen, told Laura that their mother normally came here to take the Cycle exercises, giving her mind an hour to take flight, to ponder and imagine. With her daily walks and attention to a low-fat diet, they helped maintain her strength and energy.

But Gwen said these last two days had drained Mildred. She had arrived at the Columbus Clinic directly behind the ambulance, had been at her husband's side as he was lifted on the gurney and wheeled into the emergency room. Twenty hours later, still in her bloodstained blouse and jeans, she listened as the doctor told her John had passed.

As much as possible, Suzanne and Cissy had relieved her of the burdens of notification and preparation. But when they all returned to the house from the hospital, grief engulfed her. She was inconsolable, her sobbing interrupted by heaving and shaking. Dr. Neff, her longtime doctor, arrived to comfort her and, finally, to administer a sedative that sent her into fitful sleep.

On Tuesday morning, the six women flew in a chartered Saberliner to Tallahassee. The senator's coffin had been placed in the rear baggage area. The selection of aircraft was fitting—the same one Billington had flown hundreds of hours as governor, including the flight from the capital to Key West in June of 1980, when he first encountered Tony.

At the state hanger of the Tallahassee Municipal Airport, the passengers and crew stood on the tarmac while the body was removed and placed in a hearse for the drive to the state capitol. Following protocol, the family stood at the main entrance to the marble rotunda as the coffin was placed on a bier for the twenty-four hours of public viewing.

For Mildred, the next hours were a gray blur. At the invitation of Governor Dorothy Ramirez and still under the effects of sedation, she retired to one of the guest rooms of the governor's mansion. The ornate Persian rug in the foyer, the portrait of Andrew Jackson by the dining room entrance, and the silver punch bowl she had saved from expropriation by the U.S. Navy were all reminders of happy years.

A delegation of Senate colleagues who had flown from Washington joined another throng gathered at the oldest church in Tallahassee, the white antebellum First Presbyterian. Reverend Frantz again presided. This time the same muted-green-and-blue-kilted piper was joined by the Florida A&M University choir for "Amazing Grace."

Except for "America the Beautiful" and the piper, Billington had left most of the planning and preparation for the hereafter to Mildred. She had decided they would be buried in Tallahassee amongst the oak trees of a cemetery downhill from the mansion. On many summer evenings they had strolled there, hand in hand, absorbing the soft breeze from the nearby gulf and the two hundred years of history locked in the headstones. Billington had made only one other request: that their plots be as close as possible to a former Senate colleague renowned for his storytelling. John had joked that he could listen to his tales through eternity and would never hear the same one twice.

The family filled the first two graveside rows of wooden folding chairs under a green tent. The public stood behind. Tony bowed his head as the final prayer was intoned and Mrs. Billington was assisted from her seat to a limousine for the short drive back to the mansion.

Tony fell in behind the five daughters walking up the hill to the reception. As Laura waited for others to pass at the corner across from her former home, her glance caught Tony's notice. Laura was distinguished from her sisters not only by the style of her dress but also by her demeanor. It was as if she came from a different family. She walked with the pace and crossing step of a runway model.

They did not have the opportunity to speak until the reception was nearing its end. When most of the guests had gone, Tony made his way toward the Florida room that he knew had been Mrs. Billington's dream. She paid the personal and political cost of the criticism for spending more than $100,000 of taxpayers' money on what one legislator described as the First Lady's "play pretty."

Tony approached Laura. "My name is Tony Ramos. I was a staff assistant to your father when he chaired the Joint Inquiry on 9/11. He had an enormous influence on my life. He always treated us as colleagues and gave us his full respect. We admired him greatly and uniformly felt the year under his influence and leadership was one of the most formative experiences of our lives. Please accept my condolences."

"Thank you," Laura replied as if a queen addressing her subject. "He had many admirers."

Kendall gave Tony a soft hug and said, "I know he would have appreciated your being here today."

"I was supposed to be with him in The Lakes this weekend. He had invited me last Tuesday. I'm not sure why."

Kendall asked, "Did you have any idea?"

"You must have known Mark Block, who asked that I extend his sympathy and regrets that he was unable to be here. Mark thought it probably had something to do with the Saudis. Your father was never satisfied with the way the White House kid-gloved their role in 9/11, and last week he wrote an op-ed in the *New York Times* suggesting they might be working on the bomb. I honestly don't know what he had in mind."

Noticing her mother sitting alone in the adjacent living room, Kendall excused herself. Laura motioned for Tony to take the vacated seat. "For the last several years my father and I had what you could call a distant relationship."

"The senator occasionally mentioned an estranged daughter," Tony said.

"I'm surprised he didn't call me worse. He objected to my politics and lifestyle. I had long since rejected his liberalism and domineering paternalism."

"Senator Billington was a strong man. He was comfortable in his own skin, but respected the views of others. That wasn't the case between the two of you?"

Laura glanced down to check the buttoning of her blouse. "Not quite. But, although we were at the opposite ends of the political spectrum, I admired the genuineness of his commitments, wrongheaded as they were. It was his excessive control that broke our father-daughter relationship."

She rose to look at a portrait of her father that hung with those of the other former occupants of the mansion. Turning back to Tony, she said, "Now the family is of one mind in our determination to find my father's killers. You said you were in intelligence. Do you have a hunch?"

"No. I'm a State Department research analyst and spend most of my time following Afghanistan. If you are looking for a Sherlock Holmes, I'm not your man."

He noticed the remaining guests were standing as Mrs. Billington expressed the family's gratitude. Two of the middle daughters, Cissy and Suzanne, took her by the forearm and helped her toward the guest quarters. She held back in the Florida room to speak with Laura and Tony. Those remaining filed out the front door and into the saltwater breeze the Billingtons had so enjoyed.

At the guest room door Mildred Billington took Laura's hands, "Laura, we've hardly spoken. I hope you'll be here tomorrow."

"Mother, this has been a very stressful few weeks. I've got to be in London day after tomorrow, so I can only stay until midday."

With a sharp nod of her head Kendall directed Laura to the mansion's front lawn. Amidst the magnolias and pine trees, Kendall released her frustration. "Where do you get off treating your mother with such disrespect? You may be a celebrity in your chic London circle, but here you're a member of this family, and you have no right to treat us so cavalierly. We've all had just about enough of your disdainful mouth and pompous manner."

"Listen, Kendall," Laura shot back, "I didn't cause any of this, I didn't ask Daddy to freeze me out for ten years, I'm not the one who's making judgments all the time—"

"I, I, I. It's always about you, isn't it Laura? And it's always been that way. God forbid either Mom or Dad should show interest in one of us—you always had to grab the limelight. You know what? You've been sucking all the air out of the room long enough. If you want to leave, then just get the hell out."

"As usual, you're misconstruing everything I've been saying."

"Yeah? Well, maybe listen to someone else's opinion for once in your life. And another thing: your father was a fine man; not perfect, but he always considered himself a public servant, and no one can say he wasn't totally involved with the needs of his constituents and the needs of this family. You only wallow in vanity and whatever will advance your overweening ambition."

"Whatever you say, Sis," Laura responded wearily.

"I remember the first year we were here. It was the night before the execution of the first death warrant Daddy signed. It was a very difficult time for all of us with crowds for and against his decision straining against the fence over there." Kendall gestured to the wrought iron enclosure that encircled the perimeter of the mansion. "He wanted to treat it with as much dignity as possible. And there you were on the balcony with a rope tied around your Barbie doll's neck, jerking it up and down, taunting the crowd. You got what you wanted—your AP picture in every newspaper in the state. But the price was humiliation for your father."

Inwardly, Laura cringed at the memory.

"He should have beaten your ass right then and there. If he wasn't such a gentleman, maybe he could have knocked some sense into you before it was too late. And if on this day of remembrance of our father you cannot rise above self-absorption, go back to London tonight, and as far as I am concerned I hope it will be the last time I will be in your presence."

With an angry toss of her brunette hair, Kendall strode back to the Florida room, where her mother was concluding her conversation with Tony.

"I have something for you," Mildred said. "My husband was looking forward to your visit on Friday." A stifled sob interrupted her speech. "But he was worried that something might keep him from giving you his thoughts, so he prepared this envelope and asked that I give it to you if he were unable to."

Mrs. Billington turned to the side table behind her and lifted a brown envelope, handing it to Tony.

Exhaustion and pain were etched in her eyes and the dark shadows under them. "Please excuse me, but I am very tired." She turned to Laura, who had silently followed Kendall. "I'll see you in the morning."

As they left the parlor, Laura asked Tony, "Are you free for dinner?"

"I have a 10:20 back to Washington."

"Mico's is close. I have a rental car."

Even in midsummer, Tallahassee is a political place, and Mico's a gathering spot. When Tony went up to the maître d', he was told the wait would be at least an hour.

That was when Laura stepped forward. "I'm Laura Billington, the photographer, and daughter of Governor Billington, who was buried today. I'm sure you can accommodate us."

Three minutes later, when they were seated at a back table, Tony ordered a Chilean chardonnay and red snapper.

After Laura selected a gulf shrimp salad, Tony asked, "What was all that back at the mansion between you and your sister?"

Laura's expression was a strange mixture of exasperation and regret. "Although she's next to me, the youngest, Kendall has always been the family enforcer, calling us all to task for our sins and maintaining sisterly discipline. Apparently, I haven't been disciplined enough, haven't been sufficiently punished for my sins."

"Those sins being? . . ."

"Disrespect of my parents, particularly my father; placing my own life and career ahead of the family; having the temerity to question Daddy's politics and values; and generally being a narcissistic bitch."

Tony nodded sympathetically. "And how much of it is true?"

"Probably all of it," Laura replied with a rueful smile. But then a quick change of expression suggested that she had put the matter behind her. "So, Tony," she said, "you've told me what you don't do; so what is your job at State?"

"My job is analyzing information—everything from the newspaper to wiretap intercepts—and trying to find a theme to better understand an ongoing situation, like Afghanistan, or what might occur in Pakistan if the Taliban or al-Qaeda were to take control. I'm not a hero from a John Le Carré novel or James Bond movie."

"Do you ever long for the action side?" Laura asked.

"I think I got most of that out of my system in the army. At least my mother hopes so."

Laura was silent for some moments, then asked, "Tony, is it pos—possible there's some connection between those papers my mother gave you and someone's motivation to shut my father up?"

"I . . . I just don't know," Tony replied as their eyes met.

"I wish there were some way we could know for sure," she said. "I wish . . . I wish there were something I could do myself. I'm not saying I didn't deserve what Kendall threw at me back there, but I do want to honor my father's legacy and memory, whatever she thinks."

Tony hesitated, working the thought over in his mind before he finally said, "Laura, there may be something you could do."

Glancing around to make sure no other diner was eavesdropping, she whispered, "What?"

Leaning over the table, Tony replied, "The only players your father specifically identified, in my personal talks with him and in the *New York Times* op-ed, were the Saudis. You have a unique kind of access to world leaders, from Vladimir Putin to the king of Thailand. If you could get inside the Saudi tent—and be pretty goddamned careful about it—you might learn something valuable."

"I live in Mayfair, three blocks from the Saudi embassy," she said without a stumble. With an exciting assurance she added, "I'm sure I could wrangle an invitation there."

"I was thinking of one of the palaces in the kingdom. Could you arrange a photographic session?"

"You mean, *inside* Saudi Arabia? Are you serious?"

Tony nodded. "*Very* serious."

JULY 23–24

Tallahassee ✶ Airborne to Washington, D.C.

Laura drove Tony to the airport for the last flight to Atlanta and on to Washington. Curbside, she stuttered, "Tony, I don't, I mean, I didn't have the same relationship with my father you did. But, possibly, we might be able to, able to find a way to collaborate, you trying to answer his questions, and I'll try to help, I don't know how, in locating his killer."

She got out of the car, met Tony on the sidewalk, and continued, "I wasn't the son he wanted as his last child. I failed to live up to my sisters. I know all that. And I can live with it. But I'm not such an outcast bitch that I don't want justice for the killer of my father." She was silent for a moment, then added, "And it's not just to prove to my siblings that I cared about him."

"I believe you," Tony said. "And maybe we can work together on this. Okay?"

"Okay," she responded, almost meekly.

He gave her a tentative hug and left through the automatic doors.

————————

The flight to Atlanta was delayed, forcing Tony to dash from the arrival gate to the airport subway and on to the Washington-bound departure at the far end of concourse B. He was the last passenger to board. Before stowing his briefcase, he removed the package Mrs. Billington had given him almost five hours earlier.

As the plane pulled back from its gate, Tony unclasped the manila envelope. Two smaller, white envelopes fell out, the first inscribed "For Your Eyes Only," the other "Travel Documents." Tony tore the flap open on the latter first. Enclosed was a Delta sleeve with four open tickets that together constituted a round-the-world trip from Washington Dulles to Kuala Lumpur and back.

The plane had lifted into the starless sky when Tony opened the other envelope. In it were a handwritten note on Billington's stationery, three single-spaced computer-printed pages, and, rolling out as he turned the envelope upside-down, two .45 caliber shells, wrapped in a wrinkled copy of the *New York Times* op-ed and held together with a rubber band. The note read:

> *Tony, in recent weeks I have become increasingly concerned that*
> *something untoward is in store for me. Initially, it was a series of*

abusive and threatening telephone calls. After almost forty years in politics I was prepared for them and didn't report to the police, and for fear of her overreaction, did not mention them to Mildred. On Monday while I was in the office, these two cartridges were left on the driver's seat of my Buick. I didn't feel I had sufficient evidence to go to the police, but this combination of circumstances prompted my call to Mark.

I would have preferred to discuss my apprehensions with you personally. As you now have this in your hands, that preference will not be honored.

This envelope contains my assessment of the strategic position of our nation and the world. I hope it will provide a context for your travels and mission.

I believe this undertaking is of the greatest significance to our nation, Tony, and regret that I will not be at your side. I have every confidence you will contribute answers to the secrets that threaten the security of America.

Thank you,
John Billington

Tony turned to the typed pages.

To: Tony Ramos
From: John Billington
Date: July 15
Re: The Remaining Secrets of 9/11

At the conclusion of our investigation in December of 2002 and the issuance of the final nonclassified report in July of 2003, three unanswered questions remained:

What was the nature and extent of participation by the Kingdom and entities of Saudi Arabia in the preparation for and execution of 9/11?

What are the will and capabilities of the Kingdom to assist in future attacks within the United States?

Why has the present and prior Administration engaged in such a comprehensive, sustained, and, to date, largely successful cover-up to keep the answer to those questions from the American people?

These questions represent the "keys to the Kingdom." If we can answer them, we will have gone a long way toward furthering American security and justice.

This we know:

In the weeks after the conclusion of the First Persian Gulf War in 1991, the Saudi royal family became intensely concerned with developments disclosed by the war and its aftermath:

∞ *Before the First Persian Gulf War, Osama bin Laden had been on amicable terms with the Kingdom, and his family had benefited from the largesse of the royal family. After Iraq's 1990 invasion of Kuwait, he offered his Afghanistan war–hardened mujahideen to defend the Kingdom and thus avoid the necessity of foreign troops on sacred ground. He was rebuffed. This resulted in bin Laden's departure from the Kingdom and his subsequent threats to topple the royal family.*

∞ *The war, and particularly the stationing of large numbers of U.S. and other foreign troops in Saudi Arabia, was seen by many Islamic clerics and followers as a sacrilege.*

These concerns caused the Kingdom to pursue two post–Persian Gulf War complementary strategies:

The Kingdom increased its support of madrassas, extremist religious schools, and other Wahhabist institutions. It continued to condone private support to extremists, including through a shadowy organization called the Golden Chain—composed of some of Saudi Arabia's wealthiest private citizens who since the 1980s have dedicated their wealth to advancing extremist causes and practices.

Concerned that youthful Saudis might initiate activities that ran counter to the interests of the regime, even lead a revolution similar to Iran's, the Kingdom established a network of agents to monitor the university-age Saudi population, both within the country and abroad, especially the more than 5,000 young people in the United States.

Two of these agents were active in San Diego: Omar al-Harbi and his successor in training, Ahmad al-Otaibi. Beginning in January 2000, they extended their monitoring of Saudi students in San Diego to the provision of a support network and financing conduit for two of the future 9/11 hijackers.

This covert financial support, which included funds diverted from charitable accounts maintained by the wife of the Saudi ambassador to the U.S., Mahmood al-Rasheed, points most directly to an Administration cover-up. The final report of the Joint Inquiry came to over eight hundred pages. When the declassification process was completed, one chapter of twenty-eight pages was totally censored. This was the chapter relating to the Saudi role in financing the terrorists.

With these facts in mind, the arc of events during the 1990s and beyond can be seen in a new light:

∞ *In 1994, although Osama bin Laden had broken with the Kingdom over its toleration of foreign troops, Saudi Kingdom funding for the activities of al-Qaeda began to increase. This facilitated bin Laden's relocation from the Sudan to Afghanistan, where, with the tolerance of the Taliban government, al-Qaeda established its headquarters and a series of training camps to provide its new recruits with the skills of terrorism.*

∞ *In August of 1998, al-Qaeda executed a plan two years in the preparation. Simultaneous attacks were launched against U.S. embassies in Kenya and Tanzania. More than two hundred Americans, Kenyans, and Tanzanians were killed, and more than five thousand injured. Emboldened by this slaughter and what Osama bin Laden considered the anemic U.S. response, al-Qaeda commenced planning for a major attack on U.S. soil. Aware of the difficulties this would entail, bin Laden threatened the Kingdom with civil strife if it did not make its network of agents in the U.S. available to support and conceal the al-Qaeda*

*operatives. I do not conclude that the Saudi royal family was
aware of the specific purposes of al-Qaeda operatives being in
the U.S.; rather, such assistance was demanded and acquiesced
to, with no explanation of bin Laden's intentions demanded by
the Kingdom.*

Tony read the balance of the memo, a Baedeker of the venues and
personalities that had set the stage for 9/11. Billington concluded:

*Tony, in addition to the airline arrangements, I have deposited
$100,000 in your name in an account at the United National Bank.
Ms. Sheila Gonzalez is aware you will be contacting her to receive my
further instructions. I trust this will be sufficient to cover your expenses and serve as an expression of my appreciation for your efforts.*

*I have advised only two other people of your mission. Of course,
Mildred, to whom I am entrusting these communiqués. Also, Senator John Stoner, my closest colleague in the Senate and, you will recall, a member of the committee during the 9/11 inquiry. Upon
completion of this mission, deliver your report to him. Senator
Stoner will treat your information with full discretion and place it in
the hands of those who can use it to enhance our national security.*

*Tony, I have great respect for your professionalism. I am confi-
dent you will use your talents and creativity effectively in the search
for these answers.*

Again, thank you, and buena suerte,

John Billington

Tony folded the memo and replaced it in the envelope. He could feel
the presence of the senator. It was not nostalgia, but rather an emotional
attachment founded on respect and the sense that the baton of responsibility, and its risks, had been passed.

Was Billington so close to exploding the secrets of 9/11 that he recognized his life was at risk? Tony wondered. Who placed the cartridges
in Billington's car? Could the Saudis, or our own government, have

been at the wheel of the Ford pickup? Could clues to the answers be found in the far-flung destinations on Billington's list?

Tony wasn't a homicide detective. He knew he couldn't hunt down Billington's killer. But he could attempt to find the answers to his old friend's questions. It was what he had prepared to do all his adult life.

The flight attendant announced they would land at Washington Reagan in twenty minutes. Tony closed his eyes.

JULY 24

Washington, D.C.

"Detective Hidalgo Martinez?"

"Here."

"My name is Tony Ramos. I was a friend and former staffer of Senator Billington. The family has told me you are the Miami-Dade Police detective on the case. I have some information."

"Mr. Ramos, what do you do?"

"I grew up in Hialeah," Tony told Martinez to give him some local credibility. "For the last ten years I've been an analyst at the State Department's Bureau of Intelligence and Research."

"Um, that sounds like an interesting job. But what can I do for you?"

Tony told him about the .45 caliber shells Billington had discovered in his Buick and how the senator had included them in the packet of materials he had prepared for Tony the day before his death.

"Mr. Ramos, to keep the chain of custody intact, I'm going to ask the D.C. police to retrieve the evidence and relay it to me."

"That's no problem."

"Thanks, if we have further questions, expect another call."

"Any leads?"

"We're working it hard. That's all I can say."

At five minutes before nine, Tony was seated in the anteroom of Assistant Secretary of State William Talbott, across the desk from his assistant,

Florence Wilkens. They were the only two in the office. Ms. Wilkens was casually straightening her desk, with none of the harried appearance of the previous Tuesday. Tony took this as a good time to strike.

"Ms. Wilkens, I've about reached my tenth year of State Department service. How do I submit an application for fifteen days of personal leave?"

Rising and looking down at Tony, she said, "I don't need to tell you this is a busy time. You are aware that personal leave even after your period of service is discretionary. You submit to your immediate supervisor for final approval by Ambassador Talbott."

"Yes, yes," he sighed.

The interoffice box on Ms. Wilkens's desk buzzed.

"The ambassador is ready to see you now."

Talbott was standing at the door as Tony approached. His smile and open arms signaled his pleasure. "Tony, your work on the Afghanistan testimony was first-rate. Even some of the old bull elephants like Rosenbach were impressed."

"Thank you. I'm glad to see you so energized."

"At last, maybe we're getting their attention."

As Tony took his seat, his eyes scanned the case of Talbott's official and personal books. Photographs and memorabilia were displayed in front of the volumes: a photo with his mother on the Nile when she was ambassador to Egypt in the Carter administration; his Yale and Fletcher diplomas; a group picture of the ambassador and staff in front of the Shwedagon Pagoda, at his first ambassadorial posting, Myanmar. It was there, Tony recalled, that Talbott had distinguished himself with the Foreign Service. During a military counterattack against pro-democracy protestors and with communications down, he had arranged and paid for safe passage to Bangkok for all of the embassy dependents.

"Mr. Ambassador," Tony asked, "do you think there's still a chance to turn things around? Can we still win?"

Talbott walked to the window overlooking the Kennedy Center and the Potomac. "I honestly don't know. A major component of the answer is how you define victory. If it's like the British in the nineteenth century or the Soviets in the 1980s, to invade and occupy, or even to achieve our lofty idea of 'nation building,' the answer is no."

He turned to face Tony, all the while pacing in front of his desk. "In my judgment Afghanistan is no longer the primary concern. It's how its fate will affect the stability of Pakistan, the place that will fundamentally determine the future of Central Asia. That's the game, and that's what the public, the press, and much of the Congress, just don't seem to get.

"No matter how we may feel about it, very few people give a hoot about the welfare of the Afghan people. Assuming we had the capability to do so, there are not enough Americans, even in the White House or Capitol, who understand enough or care enough about the people of Afghanistan and their future to stay the course and do what would be necessary to win. If you read the book or saw the movie about Texas congressman Charlie Wilson and his role in the Afghan war against the Soviets, you know that after the Soviets were pushed out, our failure to stay engaged in postwar recovery contributed to turning the country over to the Taliban. Even when we went in, in October 2001, it was all about revenge against al-Qaeda and their partners in crime, the Taliban.

"So I come back to the 'core value': It's all about Pakistan. If our operations in Afghanistan contribute to salvaging Pakistan, the answer is maybe."

"Is that because of the Paks' military doctrine?"

"Yes, but with a reverse spin."

Tony rose, moving to the side of Talbott's desk. He studied the worn acrylic map of Central Asia the ambassador kept on his desk. Tony had spent much of his professional life analyzing the tense relations between Pakistan and India. Pakistan has less than a fifth of the population, is a third the size of its eastern neighbor, and is only 350 kilometers from east to west. Ever since there was a Pakistani state its military leadership has prepared for an Indian ground attack. Central to its avoidance of being overwhelmed by India's vastly larger army is the concept of strategic depth. If and when an Indian assault were to begin, Pakistan's military would fall back to the west, behind the Toba Kakar Range and make its stand in Afghanistan. That necessitates a relationship with whoever is running Afghanistan and an understanding that it would acquiesce in such an occupation of its territory.

Since 1998, the strategy had been augmented by a firm resolve to use the first-strike option of Pakistan's nuclear weapons.

"What do you mean by 'reverse spin'?" Tony asked.

"If Afghanistan falls to the Taliban or anyone else, Pakistan will either embrace the winner and turn its back on us, or if it feels its relations with the victor are such that Afghanistan is not a secure fallback, attempt to dissuade any invasion by India by ratcheting up the threats of a first-strike nuclear attack." Talbott drew a long breath before concluding, "Or both."

He stepped back, sunlight illuminating the detail in his tweed jacket, then took a seat on the corner of the same desk his great-grandfather had used when he was secretary of war under President Wilson. He handed a communiqué to Tony. "If you want some rain on an otherwise sunny day, here's this morning's cable from Kabul. It puts numbers to the linkage between massive increases in Afghan poppy production and the arms it finances for the Taliban. This cable reports that in the last year, Afghanistan grew more poppies for opium than any year in history. Tony, this is the cancer that could kill whatever support is left for this war. We've got to figure out a way to convince our people."

Tony listened with knowing attentiveness. He had been there.

During his first full winter in Afghanistan, his unit of four Americans and two Afghans had been deployed to Kunduz, in the northeastern sector of the country. Long before the Silk Road became a trade route from Europe to Asia, Kunduz served as an exchange point for slaves, weapons, and goods, both legal and illicit. Tony and Amal were assigned to monitor one of Kunduz's southern neighborhoods.

The bittersweet odor of freshly cut poppies permeated the street. Amal cleared his nostrils with a muted sneeze and cloud of frozen air. "My friend, do you know what is on the other side of that wall?"

"I'm not sure. I've smelled my share of pot and coca in Hialeah, but that's new."

"For the Taliban. They store the poppies here until the roads are open and they can take it over the hills to Tajikistan and on to Russia and Europe. Back down that same road comes the ammo the poppies buy."

In the shadows of the early nightfall at this high plain and latitude, Tony circled the two-story, mud-covered concrete structure. He noted a single entrance. Two soldiers in worn Taliban uniforms guarded semi-trailer-sized wooden doors on the south wall. Tony likened this to an out-of-position opponent on the tennis court and reacted accordingly.

With Amal, he retreated to the rabbit warren of side-street huts. It was there they had hidden their motorbikes with Negil, a sympathizer to the Northern Alliance cause and their designated advisor on all things Kunduz. Tony secured four empty water canteens from the bikes' saddlebags and, applying a technique he had learned in the streets of Hialeah, sucked at his bike's gas intake until he had started a flow sufficient to fill them. Prepared, the three waited for the moonless night to descend.

This time with Amal and Negil, Tony again circled the building until he came upon the guard station. One man leaned against the wall while the other sat, snoring, on the muddy sidewalk. From across the street, Negil kept a sharp eye for intruders. With a thumb up, he signaled the way was clear. Neither guard was aware they were in danger until Amal had driven his knife deep into the chest wall of the leaner and Tony had almost beheaded the snorer before removing the chain of keys from his belt.

They opened the lock and one of the doors. With Negil's help, they dragged both bodies into the open space behind the doors.

Tony flipped on his flashlight. From a central corridor he noted rows of canvas bags emitting the distinctive stench of poppy, which penetrated the four-hundred-square-meter enclosure. With their canisters, Tony and Amal sprinkled fuel throughout the warehouse. Negil followed, igniting with his plastic cigarette lighter what was initially a stuttering flame. As the last drop of gasoline was drained, the empty cans were tossed on top of the heap, and the three closed the doors behind them, the beginnings of a conflagration were in place.

Tony and Amal exchanged the traditional Pashtun kisses with Negil and mounted their bikes for a return to the Taloqan base camp. They could smell and see the tower of fire and smoke ascending into the black sky.

———————

Tony refocused his attention on Talbott. He admired what the ambassador stood for. Talbott was a pragmatist in a State Department politicized by ideologues. He represented judgment and experience with the world as it is, not how some theoretician thinks it should be. Tony looked up. "Mr. Ambassador, are we ready to commit more troops?"

"This administration may have less than six months to go, and its primary—maybe only—objective is to avoid defeat in Iraq on its watch. That's why we went back in.

"The commandant of the Marine Corps has been urging that his troops be withdrawn from Iraq; the 'take and hold' strategy which we have reinstituted there is incompatible with Marine Corps doctrine. The general wants his troops redeployed to Afghanistan where the marines can do what marines are trained to do: fight the enemy in the field.

"The commandant is right that our strategy in Iraq has become a political tactic to establish some semblance of the stability that has eluded us ever since we took out Saddam, at least until the election here is over. He was told by the civilian politicians at the Pentagon not 'No,' but 'Hell no.'"

Talbott leaned back into the leather chair. "Maybe the Congress will light a fire. As with the condemned man and the gallows, nothing so fixes the mind of a politician as the prospect of being booted by the voters. They are going to be on the line in November, and I don't think they want a Central Asian crisis on their hands."

He turned his chair to face the window, as if contemplating the late-morning rain cloud. Tony waited for any further comments or instructions, then excused himself and walked to his cubbyhole.

He continued his review of the cable traffic from Afghanistan and re-turned two calls from the CIA station in Kabul. The chief of station was a veteran of Central Asia, Randy Crest. They had first met in 2002 when Tony traveled to the Khyber Pass border region with Senators Billington and Stoner. Crest was running a covert operation out of Peshawar into Afghanistan. After two days with Crest, Billington told Tony he was as close to James Bond as any CIA agent he had ever met.

Crest now captured the situation as plainly as Tony had ever heard it. "Ramos, we are in deep shit," he shouted into a distorted and crack-ling encrypted telephone line. "The Taliban kicked off the spring with a few small actions. Now they're rolling us. Most of their bloody work is to the south, where we're the weakest. We just don't have the numbers to cover the country, and with a few exceptions the NATOs won't take their asses to where they might get them blown off. We might get lucky and hold on until the winter, but I doubt it. And where the hell are the marines? Sitting in Fallujah playing policeman again. Shit."

The phone rang. It was Ms. Wilkens. "Mr. Ramos, Mr. Talbott wants you in his office immediately."

With only the most cursory recognition of Tony's presence, Talbott handed him three cables from Kabul, then turned back to poring over the plastic map, his attention focused on the southern region of Afghanistan, pockmarked with the swirls and slashes of a grease pen.

Tony scanned the cables. A full-scale attack had been launched against Kandahar.

> Our general doesn't think he can hold. The U.S. Army units east of Kandahar have retreated to establish a defensive perimeter around the city center. A battalion of Canadian infantry left its position on the northern outskirts of the city and is reporting seventeen dead and over fifty wounded. Due to heavy rain, air support was limited and unreliable. Afghanistan president Karzai issued a call for NATO reinforcements.

Slumped in his chair, Tony watched a Fox News special bulletin on one of the four television monitors on Talbott's west wall. Interrupted at a White House black-tie dinner for the president of Argentina, the U.S. president expressed his extreme distress, but reiterated that the United States would not contribute to the additional forces requested by President Karzai. "The primary responsibility of the United States is to bring stability and democracy to Iraq," he said. "To accomplish those objectives the United States cannot redeploy soldiers or marines from there to Afghanistan. I call on our NATO allies to respond with additional troops, and not under the limitations on engagement that have hindered the effectiveness of those national units and contributed to the possible loss of Kandahar."

The ambassador's face was ashen. "Tony, the southern provinces are lost. Unless we immediately—I mean tonight—begin the transition of troops from Iraq to what is left of Afghanistan, it will all be gone."

"But, Mr. Ambassador, the president just announced on television there will be no more U.S. troops."

"I know. Somehow he must be persuaded he cannot take the consequences of defeat. Our only chance is the secretary. Prepare the best case you can. I'll give it to her to present to the president tonight. If anyone can get to him, it's her."

JULY 24–25
Washington, D.C.

The secretary of state sent a typewritten note through her assistant that it would be quite impossible for her to meet with Ambassador Talbott. In her precise hand she had postscripted that the president had already announced his position on the fall of Kandahar and that she considered it to be wise and appropriate and would not attempt to intervene.

As he packed his briefcase in preparation for ending the day, seven hours later than he started the process, Tony was irate. *She doesn't deserve to be hanging with the likes of Thomas Jefferson and George Marshall. If she truly believes the president is wise, she's a fool. If it's just for pretense, she is a disgrace. If she knows it is a continuation of one of the worst national security decisions in the nation's history, she is traitorous for not saying so and resigning.*

It was well after 2:00 a.m. when Tony parked his Mustang in an alley lot behind his Capitol Hill townhouse. He had lived on the Hill since leaving the tour, and three years later had bought this two-story, twenty-foot-wide house on Seventh Street. He normally showered before sleep, but tonight he was too tired. He dropped his suit pants and coat and tie on the wooden barrel chair next to the bed and slipped under the sheets. He slept naked. His head was on the pillow when the BlackBerry rang.

"Oh crap," he muttered. "Ramos here. Who's there?"

"Tony, this is Laura. I'm calling from London. I hope I didn't wake you."

"No, Laura, I'm always up at three in the morning. It's my favorite time of day."

Laura laughed, "And I trust I'm your favorite kind of woman?"

Turning on his right side, Tony slipped the question. "That's a little weightier than I'm able to handle at this hour. But I sure as hell hope you've got something important to talk about."

Still cheery, Laura continued, "I've been working on a plan and I need some advice."

"It couldn't wait till morning; *my* morning?"

"When I get an idea, I like to get right at it."

Tony sighed. "Well, now that we're all awake, what've you got?"

"You know what my father thought of the Saudis and 9/11. I've got an idea."

"What are you talking about?"

"You said I needed to get inside the palace, right?"

"I also said it was going to be tough to do."

"Well, last night I was at the Saudi embassy, so I've made that much progress. One of the political attachés mentioned the king would be celebrating his eighty-fifth birthday in December. Putting on my best femme fatale mask, I suggested it would be 'marvelous' if I could announce this to the world with his portrait in *Vanity Fair*."

"Laura," Tony said as he stood. "I know I suggested back in Tallahassee that you go undercover. But I want you to understand the ground rules. The Saudis are ultrasexists. And this could be dangerous as hell. If their fingerprints are on your dad's murder, they'll go to any lengths to keep it under wraps."

"Tony, you've told me that before. And—and remember it was your idea about getting inside the palace. I think I can do it, with a reasonable chance of success."

"But you have to consider the consequences of failure; they're not pretty."

"I've been in tight situations before, same as you."

"Probably not quite the same," Tony said.

"Look, Tony, we have a job to do. Do you want to complete my father's mission or don't you?"

"Of course I do."

"Then this is not the time for you to—what was it Thatcher used to say?—go wobbly."

Tony had no response.

JULY 25–26
Washington, D.C.

Tony slept past his 6:30 alarm. While eating his breakfast of Smart Start cereal with banana and skim milk, he looked again at the contents of the two envelopes given to him by Mrs. Billington and contemplated the logistics.

Riyadh and Kuala Lumpur would require almost round-the-world travel. San Diego was just across the continent. Tony was feeling the hormones of competitive tennis; he wanted the game to start. He figured it would take ten days to do the Riyadh and Kuala Lumpur legs, but San Diego—that could be a weekend. Maybe, if things didn't collapse any further in Afghanistan, he could get an OK for a one-night trip.

As upbeat as Talbott had been on Thursday morning, his haggard, unshaven face, rumpled pants, and discarded jacket bespoke a man who'd spent the night at his desk.

"Tony," he said, "I've given it one more shot with the secretary. Her schedule people say she'll be at the Argentine embassy until noon and then a luncheon with her party's senators. She wouldn't budge."

"Mr. Ambassador, maybe we should see if any of the folks on the Hill want a real-time assessment of the situation."

Talbott raised his eyebrows. "That's already been taken care of. The president's national security advisor has been dispatched to tell them the only thing to do is to cajole the Europeans to send more of their troops into the meat grinder, and now let's talk about our victories in Iran and the ones since we got back into Iraq."

"If there is anything else I can do, I'll be at my desk monitoring the cable traffic." There was another matter Tony wished to mention, but judged this was not the time.

The following morning, he asked Talbott if the situation in Afghanistan was subdued by the second week in August, could he be approved for a weekend trip to San Diego. Talbott responded as if he wanted to be on the same flight. "You've earned it," he said.

Back in his office, passing the time until it was nine on the West Coast, Tony reread the relevant portion of John Billington's memo.

San Diego: Of the various places the hijackers lived before 9/11, we know the most about Nawaf al-Hazmi and Khalid al-Mihdhar, the two who lived from early February of 2000 until the end of that year in the suburb of Lemon Grove. Information on them is central to understanding the full role of the Saudi government and entities in the run-up to 9/11.

Teresa McKenzie, an investigative reporter for the San Diego Union-Tribune, *has written extensively and insightfully on the nexus between the FBI, the hijackers, and the infrastructure of Saudi confederates in San Diego. She was one of the few able to do*

what our inquiry and the 9/11 Commission were denied: talk di-
rectly with the most important figure still living in the United States,
Samrat Nasir.

    Samrat Nasir, age eighty-one, is a retired professor of nuclear
physics, an Indian by birth, and a Muslim. For much of 2000 he was
a paid asset of the FBI and the landlord of al-Hazmi and al-Mihdhar.

When he figured she'd be in her office, Tony called Teresa McKenzie. She answered on the fourth ring. "This is Terri McKenzie, *Union-Tribune.*"

"Ms. McKenzie, my name is Tony Ramos. I'm with the State Department and in 2002 was detailed to Senator Billington's staff investigating 9/11. He asked me to call you."

"Wasn't he killed?"

"Yes, a hit and run; probably intentional. Senator Billington prepared background materials for me, and your name was at the top of the list."

"I'm flattered, I think. What kind of a list?"

"The senator felt there were some unresolved questions about 9/11 and thought you might be helpful in finding the answers. I'm trying to schedule a trip to San Diego in the next three weeks. If I'm able to do so, would you meet with me to discuss his concerns?"

"I'm covering a major fraudulent importation trial, but let me know when you—"

"Fraudulent importation? What's that all about?"

"Some Russians allegedly were trying to get mislabeled, banned chemical or biological substances into the country and were caught down at the Tijuana border crossing. A lot of the trial is being held in the judge's chambers since it involves classified information. Still, it's been more interesting than the everyday corruption trials where I spend most of my time. And, yes. You let me know when you will be here, and I'll try to be helpful."

"Thanks." Tony paused. "And, I have a second request. The senator also has urged me to meet with a Dr. Samrat Nasir, and you are one of the few people who know him. Could you help me set up a meeting?"

"Mr. Ramos," Terri spoke with what sounded like barely suppressed exasperation, "I don't know you, and Professor Nasir is a very private person. Let's meet first. We'll take one step at a time from there."

"I understand and hope to see you soon," Tony concluded.

JULY 26

Miami International Airport

"Mr. Ramon Diaz, please."

Sergeant Whitten held for a response.

"Hola, Ramon aquí."

"Mr. Diaz, this is Sergeant Whitten from the airport police office."

"I didn't expect to hear from you again. Have you found my truck, or should I start looking for it in Haiti?"

"No, but we do have a lead."

"What kind of lead?"

"Detective Longo was reviewing the video from the surveillance camera at 3P in the garage. He spotted two men on Saturday night, just about eight hours after you left your SUV. These guys were removing the license plate from a black SUV. Longo says he could read three numbers and the letter M from the tag and it matches up with the plate number you called in. After they screwed it off your vehicle, they did the same to the car next door and switched them. It looks like they punched out the steering lock and jump-started your SUV and pulled off."

"Sergeant, it's a truck."

"I'm sorry for the confusion."

"Then what?"

"The only thing we know for sure is that they ran the gate at the toll, which triggered the toll camera. We have a clear take on the plate they put on your vehicle and a fuzzy shot through the windshield of the driver and his passenger."

For the first time in almost a week, Diaz was feeling some satisfaction. "So what are you doing now?"

"Well," Whitten said, "we have an all-points out on the van with the bogus plates. The Nissan with your plates is still in the garage."

"Mr. Sergeant, it's a Ford F-150 truck, not a van or sissified SUV."

"Damn it! My head's all screwed up tonight. Where was I? Oh yeah, the Nissan with your truck plates—did I get it right this time?—is still in the garage. We've sent the images to the FDLE—"

"What's that?" Ramon interrupted.

"The Florida Department of Law Enforcement. They have equipment to make the pictures clearer, and maybe they'll be able to tell who it is. Any questions?"

Hearing none, Whitten concluded, "If we pick up anything, I'll keep you in the loop. It may be a month or more before we have a report from FDLE. Those lab guys stay pretty busy and it's complicated stuff. You ever watch *CSI: Miami*?"

"No."

"Well, you ought to. You'll learn something about what we're doing to find your car."

"Thanks," Ramon offered, "but it's a truck."

JULY 29–AUGUST 2

Washington, D.C. ★ San Diego

Washington isn't quite like Paris, where the national government virtually shuts down in August, but it's close. Congress and its entire staff, hangers-on, and the ubiquitous lobbyists circling the Capitol have left. The president is at his farm. Even with two wars to fight, the Pentagon and the State Department are at a noticeably slower pace. Tony figured this was the time to strike.

Five days after he had submitted his request to travel to San Diego, over the following weekend he received an email from Ms. Wilkens:

> *Mr. Ramos, the Ambassador has approved your request to be*
> *away from your station August 1–2. He has directed that you main-*

tain contact with the Departmental duty officer and be prepared to return upon his request to do so.

The Ambassador requests a briefing upon your return.

Florence Wilkens

Tony called Terri McKenzie that afternoon. He left a voicemail message that he would be arriving late on Friday evening and would hope to meet with her the following day. With a slight stumble, he mentioned his continued interest in seeing Professor Nasir. She returned his call the following morning.

"Mr. Ramos, I can meet you on Saturday for lunch at the Sundeck Restaurant; it's at the downtown, old navy pier."

"That's great," Tony said enthusiastically.

Before he could continue, Terri said, "I want to meet you before I make a decision on any arrangements with Professor Nasir."

"I'll take my chances. See you on Saturday."

Tony had kept his overnight bag packed and stuffed into his gym locker. At five on a hot Friday afternoon, he was on State's shuttle to Dulles. With the ticket provided by Billington, Tony departed at 7:15 p.m. on United 236 to San Diego.

By the time the seat belt light was off, he'd finished the *Times* and laid it on the empty middle seat. When the attendant passed by, he asked her for black coffee. While reflecting on the senator's assignment, Tony recalled the conversation with Carol more than a week earlier on the ride in from Dulles to her apartment. Could there be any connection between the Saudi tentacles in Southern California before 9/11 and the kingdom's behavior with the Brits a decade earlier? It seemed far-fetched, but Tony had learned early in his career not to dismiss any possibility out of hand.

As Tony's coffee arrived, his mind transitioned from the Saudis in San Diego to his professional passion. The Belfer Center at Harvard's

Kennedy School of Government had produced a series of open-source papers on U.S. options in Afghanistan and Pakistan. He spent the rest of the flight absorbed.

The Sundeck was a San Diego landmark. South of the retired World War II aircraft carrier USS *Midway,* the architecture of the restaurant was reminiscent of a Napoleonic quartered hat plopped on a dredged sand pile. Sundeck captured the laid-back spirit of San Diego when it had been a sleepy navy town down the road from LA.

Terri was waiting at an ocean-side table when Tony arrived, ten minutes early. While showing the effects of a late night in the newsroom, she was still pretty eye-turning in a tropical floral-design cotton wrap.

The introductory formalities went well. Terri and Tony were both in their thirties, shared Latino Hispanic heritage and working-class roots, an interest in running and tennis, and a curiosity to unravel the remaining secrets of 9/11. Over a lunch of seared ahi tuna for him and taco salad for her, Tony explained why Billington thought Professor Nasir was an important thread in that unraveling.

"There was only one involuntary subpoena issued during the almost yearlong 9/11 investigation. And that was for Professor Nasir."

Terri's journalistic curiosity rose. "What do you mean by involuntary?"

"There were people who were willing to testify, but to avoid the wrath of higher-ups, they wanted the cover of a subpoena requiring them to do it. The inquiry committee voted to send Nasir the real thing."

"I was reporting on the Saudis in San Diego in 2002 and I don't recall the professor going to D.C.," Terri observed.

"You're right. When the Senate got Nasir's subpoena from the court it was on a Friday afternoon. Time was running short to complete the inquiry, and Billington was anxious to have it served over the weekend. The only agency that could serve it was the FBI because it had Nasir in protective custody and only it knew where he was. Billington was reaching out to hand the paper to a bureau attorney. He folded his arms and backed away until his rear end was against the wall of the committee's office. Billington was in his face when he said he would deliver the professor on Monday if he didn't have to serve the subpoena."

"Did he do it?"

"Hell no. On Monday he said he had orders from the director of the FBI herself not to accept the subpoena."

"What was the director's excuse?"

"She told Billington the bureau had to protect the integrity of the assets program," Tony answered. "Given the fact that its asset had just lived with two of the hijackers, one for more than six months, there didn't seem to be much of a program to protect. Billington told me later his failure to force the bureau to deliver Nasir was the single biggest blunder of the investigation. I think that's why he put so much importance on my talking with Professor Nasir."

Tony looked for some sign of acceptance from Terri. Seeing none, he asked, "So have I passed the test to meet with the professor?"

Terri reached her hands across the table, touching Tony's. Tony noticed she wore no rings, although there was an indentation on her left ring finger. "You're making progress. Let me ask you a couple of questions and give you some background."

"I'm an open book," Tony offered. "What do you want to know?"

"Don't get too D.C. suave," Terri said laughing, maneuvering her hands back to her side of the table. "You're trying to convince me you have a legitimate reason to meet one of the most protected and protective men in America."

Tony displayed his first hint of irritation. "Billington went through this routine with the director and the little shit from the FBI. Are you in the suppression of evidence business too?"

"No, but I do know something about protection of sources. In this case, Nasir is over eighty and tires in the afternoon. How long will you need?"

"No more than two hours."

"Keep it to an hour. He's just returned from Jeddah. For the past several years he's resumed his practice of regular visits to Saudi Arabia, and the travel is very draining. He is sensitive and keeps the purpose of his trips to himself. He hasn't even confided in me. Can you stay away from that?"

"Okay."

"Nasir has been wounded by the way he was treated by the FBI. He considered himself loyal and beneficial to the bureau, and became the scapegoat for its bungling."

"I'll maneuver around his emotions."

Terri rose from the table. Tony watched her walk to the porch over the water, talking on her phone. Her posture, balanced against the railing, was that of a feline purring for attention. She smiled, stored her phone, and returned to the table.

"If you can come now, he can see us at two." She reached into her purse and removed her car keys.

Tony paid the bill with his personal credit card. He pulled back Terri's chair. Together they walked out to the piercing midday sun of summer. Tony opened the car door and Terri slid into her silver Acura coupe.

During the thirty-minute drive east, Terri slowed through a neighborhood of subdivision homes. It reminded Tony of Hialeah.

"This is where I grew up," she explained as she pointed to a single-story home on a corner lot. "My parents came from Mexico thirty years ago when I was a baby. They never had much money but believed devoutly in the American dream and that education was the key to the dream. I was able to get a scholarship to San Diego State and, with that and living at home, scratched out a degree in political science and a minor in English."

Tony turned to her, feeling more at ease. Her life story could have been his sister's.

"How did you get into journalism?"

"Luck. My first job offer out of college was with a weekly in this area of San Diego. There'd been a lot of local government corruption, which eventually put a congressman in jail for bribery. I covered that and guess the people at the *Union-Trib* liked what I wrote. Then I got lucky again when Lemon Grove became a hotbed of 9/11 intrigue."

Terri pulled into an open space in front of a postwar two-story wood house with a Mediterranean red-tile roof. "Here we are."

Tony was surprised that even the water-starved lawn was overgrown. The exterior was years beyond needing a paint job. Tony thought his father would have liked to have sold the professor some siding. As they walked up the sidewalk, an elderly, dusty-complexioned man stood on the highest step.

Terri turned to Tony and said, "Dr. Nasir, this is the gentleman I mentioned on the phone."

AUGUST 2

San Diego

Tony and the professor shook hands. "Dr. Nasir, I have been waiting several years to meet you."

Nasir led them through the living room darkened by drawn curtains. Even in the dim light, the heavily carved furniture reflected the wear of years of use. The room was dominated by two wall-length bookcases that held what appeared to be personal photographs and an eclectic combination of science texts and books in Arabic. Tony could see no novels or volumes of poetry in English.

In the enclosed patio on the far side of the house, Dr. Nasir motioned for his guests to sit. He offered tea from an intricately inlaid teapot.

"It is my honor to have you in my home," he began, his painfully slow pace and occasional blurring of final syllables betraying his weariness. "I have been away for almost a month, and when I return I miss the clutter and the voices of the young men who used to live with me."

Sensing his exhaustion, Terri moved through the social niceties. "Mr. Ramos and I appreciate your hospitality and willingness to meet on such short notice, and we respect your circumstances. If you don't mind, he would like to ask a few questions."

"Certainly, Teresa," Nasir said as he turned to face Tony.

Tony concisely laid the predicate with his Joint Inquiry experience and asked the first question.

"Could you tell me about Omar al-Harbi?"

"He had been an agent of the Saudi government since he arrived in San Diego in the late 1990s," Nasir replied. "His gregarious personality and religious fidelity made him well suited for monitoring the Saudi community, especially the college students in San Diego."

Nasir rose and walked to the bookshelf, where he retrieved a photograph. Resuming his seat, he said, "This was al-Harbi when he first came to Lemon Grove in about the summer of 1998."

Tony studied the black-and-white photo of a smiling, burly, black-bearded man and a woman dressed in a white *abaya*.

Nasir continued: "Al-Harbi's income was generous—principally from a Saudi consulting firm, Ercan. It was generally known that he got a paycheck but seldom showed up for work. The manager of Ercan had threatened to fire him, but the rumor was he was told if he did so, Ercan would lose all its Saudi contracts."

Tony leaned in closer as the elderly man went on. "In the aftermath of my bitter and financially disastrous divorce in 1999, I began the practice of taking in young Muslim men as boarders. It was partially for the income, but more for the companionship. I assume because of these tenants, the FBI offered me the job of monitoring Muslim youth, especially Saudi students. My assignment was essentially the same as what al-Harbi did for the kingdom, except I was doing so for your country."

Shortly after he acceded to al-Harbi's request that he take in al-Hazmi and al-Mihdhar as boarders, Nasir said, he noticed their distinctly non-Muslim behavior—late nights at local strip clubs, al-Hazmi going so far as to solicit Nasir's assistance in arranging a marriage with a Mexican dancer.

Tony asked for details of Nasir's relationship with the FBI.

"All of these sacrilegious acts I reported to my agent in charge, Mr. Rick Kelly. He noted it in his book but never asked for additional information or follow-up," he explained with a tone of perplexity and frustration.

"After 9/11, the FBI took me to a house near the Mexican border for the worst four years of my life."

Nodding toward Terri, he said, "I first read her name in the *Union-Tribune* when she reported that people in Washington wanted to talk with me, but no one ever came. I remember after I had been held for a year, a lawyer I had not seen before or since came and said not to be concerned, he would keep them away from me."

"I'm not sure I understand," Tony said. "Who were these 'people in Washington'?"

"I wrote a series in 2003," Terri explained. "Although I never could get conclusive evidence, I suspected the lawyer was retained and paid by the FBI to frustrate the subpoena the Billington committee had issued."

So our inquiry was the "people in Washington" whom the FBI-secured lawyer was protecting Nasir from, Tony thought.

"The whole thing was deplorable," Terri commented. "He has been a naturalized American citizen for thirty years."

Dr. Nasir became noticeably more engaged, more agitated. His body moved as if on a pivot from Tony to Terri, his heavy eyebrows arched for emphasis. "I am not the first person to be used by your government. In the early seventies, I had a very bright graduate student from Chile, Jorge Echeverria. Upon graduation Jorge returned to Chile to found a company that manufactured explosives for the mining industry there. When Pinochet came to power and Chile was rendered an international pariah, the general vowed to become independent of foreign sources for military supplies, and Jorge's firm expanded into ammunition. Ironically, when the U.S. began supplying Iran during its war with Iraq, to hide American complicity, many of the military materials were purchased from these very Chilean munitions merchants. Jorge's outfit provided cluster bombs. The U.S. Marine officer in charge complimented the effectiveness of Jorge's bombs."

The professor paused for a sip of tea, touched his lips with a napkin. "When this whole scheme was exposed—I believe you called it Iran-contra—the death of civilians from Jorge's bombs was publicized. Like me, Jorge became the scapegoat, despite the fact he was told he was helping the U.S. government. With great fanfare, he was ostracized, stripped of his U.S. visa, and denied entry for life."

Tears began to well in his eyes as Nasir's head dropped to his chest. "Jorge called me about four years ago. He had been diagnosed with prostate cancer and the best treatment was in Houston. He asked for my help in securing a humanitarian visa. I called on our Senator Goldstein to help. Jorge was denied. Last August, while I was away, I received a message from his widow that, after years of suffering, he had mercifully passed.

"That is the way your country treats its friends. That is the way it has treated me. I tried to be a loyal citizen of your nation, a country I used to love. After four years held out of my home and against my wishes, your Mr. Kelly told me I was no longer of any value to the FBI and gave me a check for $100,000. That was the end."

To let the old man collect himself, Tony asked permission to use the guest bathroom. When he returned, Nasir's eyes were red, moist, and he had slumped back in his chair.

"Doctor, this will be my last question," Tony said, with a furtive look to Terri. "And I hope it is not too intrusive. Terri has mentioned that you had been visiting Saudi Arabia since the end of the First Persian Gulf War, then suspended your travel for six years, and now you are going again. Could you tell me the purpose of the trips?"

Enveloped by the upholstered chair, Nasir looked at the ceiling of his patio. He could not have missed seeing the twists of peeling paint that scarred the surface. His head and eyes dropped until he was looking directly into Tony's dark eyes.

"In the final year before my retirement, I was asked by a colleague if I would visit the kingdom to discuss possible involvement in a scientific project within my professional expertise. Curious, and frankly anxious to supplement my pension, I agreed."

Tony leaned forward, "Dr. Nasir, what was the nature of the project?"

Terri gave Tony a stern glance. Before she could intervene, for the first time since their arrival the professor evinced a smile. "Mr. Ramos, I respect your governmental position. You must understand that I am not at liberty to disclose details of my employment with the kingdom.

I can say I worked on the project for almost seven years, finally becoming disconcerted as to its direction. When the divorce was final, I left the project, returned permanently to my home, and shortly thereafter began my work with the FBI."

"You said that was about 1999?"

"Yes."

"Did your agent in charge or any other FBI official question you as to your repeated trips to Saudi Arabia?"

In an increasingly strained voice, Nasir replied, "I told them about the trips, I remember giving them the airline tickets from my last one in 1999. Mr. Kelly didn't seem to care."

The doctor asked to suspend the interview for a few minutes and walked to the kitchen, returning with a plate of nan khatai cookies. He explained how these had been his mother's favorite in their Bombay home, and then continued. "After I was released by the FBI, my financial condition was worse than it had been in 1999. The kingdom urged me to rejoin the project. It was only to be for a few months and I accepted. Because of a setback several years ago, the project was extended but now is on track and approaching its final stages."

Tony rose. "Thank you. Your hospitality is very much appreciated, Dr. Nasir."

With a halting step, Nasir accompanied them to the front door. He waved as Tony closed the driver's door for Terri and climbed into the passenger's seat.

Tony thanked Terri for arranging the meeting with Dr. Nasir. "He gave me some exceptionally candid information and insights. But the thing he said which most struck me was his reference to the United States as 'your country.'"

"I had the same reaction," Terri agreed. "That a highly educated intellectual who has been a naturalized American for decades would disassociate himself like that speaks volumes about the state of our relationship with the Muslim world."

"Well, it shouldn't be all that surprising. Our standing in the world in general has taken a pounding with Guantanamo, Abu Ghraib, allegations of torture, and all the rest, not to mention the flap over putting the mosque near Ground Zero and that minister in Florida threatening to burn Korans on the anniversary of 9/11. And Terri, your profession hasn't done us any favors by focusing on the superficial minutiae of foreign relations and underreporting things like those that will shape our future."

Terri demurred, and followed a right-lane sign announcing it was five miles to the airport.

After additional moments of silence that Tony interpreted as his punishment for having gone over the line, he said, "OK, we've gotten that off our chests. Before we get to the terminal—you've told me your life story up to your job with the newspaper. What's happened since then?"

With the same directness she would give to a newspaper story, she related, "I married John McKenzie four years after we graduated from San Diego State. It was a shock for the Martinez family. Before me no one had ever married a non-Latino. The first three years were the forever honeymoon. But after our first child was stillborn, everything changed. We both felt responsible. A year later we separated, and five years to the day after we were married, the divorce became final."

Tony said, "I'm sorry. I hope you find a new happiness."

Terri eased the Acura into an open slot on the departure level. Removing his overnight bag from the trunk, Tony took her hand. "I have a lot to thank Senator Billington for, and you've given me an additional reason."

With a slight hand squeeze, Tony moved to the revolving door and the gate beyond.

AUGUST 2

Long Beach

Less than seventy-five miles to the north, as Tony's United flight was taxiing to the runway, a blue and gold Gulfstream 550 was touching down at the Long Beach municipal airport.

Laura had taken full advantage of its spacious accommodations. After sleeping over the Atlantic to well north of James Bay, she had had ample time for a rejuvenating workout and a warm shower. She stepped off the aircraft as if walking across from her flat to the Dorchester for afternoon tea.

She emerged from the back of a black Peninsular Mercedes and was directed to the front door of The Pacific restaurant. It was less than three blocks from the firm's headquarters and the only five-star restaurant in Long Beach. Jeralewski was waiting at a table.

He made some perfunctory recommendations for the dinner fare and waited patiently while the waiter took their orders. As soon as the young man had collected their menus, Jeralewski leaned slightly forward and said, "Ms. Billington, I want you to become a Peninsular associate."

"I'm sorry?"

"It's an arrangement we have with a select few individuals who can provide us with—shall we say—'strategic' information."

"What kind of strategic information?"

"First, let me say we are aware of your regrettable financial challenges."

"How—how—?" Laura's stammer quickly asserted itself.

Jeralewski waved her off with a flick of his hand. "We make it our business to know things. Though I suspect when the story hits the gossip circuit, it will be difficult for most people to fathom how someone of your celebrity and earning power has managed to get herself fifteen million dollars in the hole."

Laura could feel herself begin to tremble.

"Be that as it may," the chief executive continued, "we are prepared to buy the note you signed before such an eventuality takes place. If the services you perform for us are sufficiently, shall we say, 'valuable,' . . . we might be persuaded, in the fullness of time, to cancel the note and consider the matter resolved."

Laura struggled not to stammer. "What—services?"

"Ms. Billington, your profession and the exceptional celebrity you have achieved through its practice have given you access to many of the world's most important persons. In turn, those are the people who frequently have access to information our firm would find useful."

Laura bristled. "I am an artist. This is a matter of professional integrity."

Jeralewski leaned back and sighed, as if he were trying to make a simple point to a rather slow child. "It is also a matter of fifteen million dollars. You will have to decide how you wish to balance the two."

"What—what—specifically are you—?"

"Well, to begin with, you have befriended a young man, Tony Ramos by name."

She felt as if she had just been stripped naked. She wondered how long they had been watching her.

"We are interested in knowing this Mr. Ramos better, and believe you could be of material assistance."

"What—what would you want to know, Mr. Jeralewski?" she asked.

"At present, whatever you can tell us. Based on that, we might perhaps give you more 'directed' assignments. And please call me Roland."

AUGUST 4
Washington, D.C.

Senator Billington had directed that Tony report the results of his farflung inquiries to Senator John Stoner. Although his San Diego stop was only the first of Tony's assignments, he felt he should use his experiences there as an opportunity to reconnect with Senator Stoner and share what he had found.

Stoner's career had paralleled Billington's. Both had served as governor of their states and moved directly to the United States Senate. Their shared interests included intelligence. When Billington retired, Stoner became chair of the Senate Select Committee on Intelligence.

Tony walked the seven blocks from his townhouse to the Hart Senate Office Building. The edifice was a product of more than a century of competition between the White House and the two houses of Congress. President Theodore Roosevelt built a new wing on the White House without congressional authorization or appropriation. Feeling hurt and ignored, the congressional leaders responded by building the first office buildings for the House of Representatives and the Senate.

In the 1960s, a modest addition to the White House led to the erection of the brutally massive Rayburn Building on the House side. Hart's clean and marbled exterior and the Calder sculpture *Mountains and Clouds* in the soaring atrium were the Senate's bid for parity.

Senator Stoner was waiting for Tony at the door to his elegant suite. The interior decoration indicated that the senator maintained his family's interest in modern art and his own in the native quilts and handicraft of the rural state he represented.

He greeted Tony with the warmth of family members long separated.

Stoner was the tallest member of the Senate; his hair almost brushed the doorframe as he escorted Tony. "It's so good to see you," he declared, motioning Tony to the white sofa. "Have a seat, my friend."

After they sat down and Tony gave him a quick update on his life, Stoner said, "Well, you've covered everything that isn't personal."

"I didn't want to waste your time," Tony responded.

"Horseshit! Is there a special woman?"

Tony was taken off guard and slightly embarrassed. "There is one I've been seeing since March. I hope it will amount to something."

"Okay. Let me know if you need me to impress her on your behalf with my well-documented charm. Now, what else can I do for you?"

"I have some troubling questions Senator Billington surfaced and presented to me just before he was killed."

Tony paused to allow Stoner to reflect on the tragedy of his friend and colleague's death. Tony recounted the telephone call the day before Billington's hit-and-run death. He shared the memo transferred to him by Mrs. Billington.

As Stoner read, Tony stood and walked over to the window with a panoramic view of the Capitol. As many years as he had been living and working in its shadow, the building still filled him with emotion. The events since Billington's death had sharpened his patriotic impulses.

With Stoner having read Billington's memo, Tony related his San Diego experiences and the disclosures of Professor Nasir.

"Senator, of the three questions on Senator Billington's mind, what I learned on Saturday points to deeper Saudi involvement than either the congressional or the 9/11 Commission investigators unearthed. And the reason for those failures to detect seems to be a cover-up by our government."

"What were your take-aways for those points?"

"Professor Nasir confirmed that al-Harbi was an agent of the kingdom, his income came from sources with close ties to the kingdom, and he was the principal interlocutory with Hazmi and Mihdhar while they were in Southern California."

"Do you have any primary-source evidence from al-Harbi?"

"No sir, but I hope to meet with him in Riyadh in September."

Stoner leaned back on the ornate rural-fashion sofa pillows. "Could I tag along?"

"As you like."

The senator sighed. "With the last days of the congressional session and my reelection campaign, I'll have to pass. But I'm anxious to hear what you find out."

"Of course. The second take-away was that the cover-up that kept us in the dark was not just the result of individual incompetence or deceit. That Nasir had simultaneously been a paid asset of the FBI and the landlord of Hazmi and Mihdhar, and that both inquiries were denied access to the professor, was a systematic withholding; I suspect the order came from the top."

"You mean," Stoner hesitated as the significance of his yet unasked question sank in, "the White House?"

"Yes."

"Apart from the professor's trips to Saudi Arabia, which are a mystery to me, what you have unearthed is exactly what Billington and I thought had happened. You could be on the road to answering the secrets the Joint Inquiry could not. Where are you going from here?"

"To complete Senator Billington's itinerary. Assuming events in Afghanistan allow it, I hope to be in Riyadh and Kuala Lumpur early next month."

Stoner stood and paced the lush carpet. "Let me give you some unsolicited advice. Avoid the ambassadors in both places. They're political appointees due to their money and hard-wired neo-con views of the world. Both are very loyal and will not take well to your nosing around." Stoner removed a Senate business card from his coat pocket and scribbled on the back. "These are my personal numbers and email address. If you have any difficulties, contact me."

As Tony prepared to leave, Stoner placed his hand on his shoulder. "Tony, what you're doing is very important to the security of the nation and very dangerous for you. Let me help wherever I can. And when you complete this next stage of your mission, let's talk again."

"Senator, I look forward to that." With a handshake, Tony left the building and started walking in the bright midday sunlight.

By noon, Tony was at his Truman Building office. By 4:30, he was down to the telephone messages. At the top of the pile was one from Carol Watson.

"Carol, how are you?"

"Tony, we've got some issues."

Surprised, he asked, "After the night we had last Monday, what do you mean with a comment like that?"

"Well, to start with, that was then and today is two weeks later, and I have hardly heard your voice."

Attracted by the rising volume of Tony's voice, Ben Brewster leaned in the partially opened doorway.

Tony waved him away and continued, "Look, Carol, you know how overloaded I've been in the office. Plus I had to go to Tallahassee for Senator Billington's funeral and San Diego to find some of the answers to his questions."

"And that's another thing: you could have clued me in on your schedule instead of me having to find out from the bureau's receptionist. And, finally, you said you would find out why Justice had suddenly gotten so interested in this case. Tony, I know how important the senator was in your life. I appreciate that. I'm sorry he was killed in the accident. But it's totally unacceptable for you to fly across the country, not even tell me you're going, and leave me hanging without the information you promised to deliver."

Struggling to keep his temper in check, Tony slowly stated, "Senator Billington was one of the most influential men in my life. Given that, what he was working on, and the circumstances of his death, I owe him my respect and best efforts to get the answers to his questions. And, yes, I haven't had time to do any checking on Justice, but I promise you my failure is no signal that it was just a slam-bam-thank-you-ma'am night."

There was no reply. Tony continued in a quieter and warmer voice, "Carol, I think I'll get out of here by nine. Could I meet you then?"

The phone went dead.

Now aware that Brewster was still eavesdropping from the doorjamb, Tony exploded, "Get the fuck out of here, Brewster; this is none of your damn business!"

With a satisfied sneer, Brewster backed away. "You could be right, or, Mr. Ramos, you could be wrong."

AUGUST 12
Washington, D.C.

Tony had not seen Carol for three weeks. It was not for lack of trying. He had called her every day, even sent roses on her August 10 birthday.

At his regular tennis match with Mark, it was obvious after four points that Tony had never played worse.

"What the hell is your problem?" Mark inquired across the net.

"I'm just getting warmed up," Tony replied without conviction.

Mark lowered his racquet and motioned Tony over to the net. "Take it from Uncle Mark: there are only three areas of major concern in life—work, health, and love. I know you too well to think that work would get in the way of your game. So it has to be one of the other two. So, which one? Are you okay?"

Tony wiped his already sweat-soaked forehead with his towel. "Yeah, I'm fine."

"Okay then, what's the name of the young lady in question?"

"Carol."

"Near the end of July, if memory serves, you had ridden her hard and she was pining for you to saddle up again. Did I miss something?"

"Same problem we had to begin with, I think. She's pissed off because I didn't pay enough attention to her the next few days, didn't tell her I was going to San Diego, didn't break what was left of my dick to finish a project she gave me."

"Hurtful, very hurtful," Mark consoled. "But you won't make any progress in your love life if you lay it—so to speak—on her."

"What do you mean by that?"

"You just ate her up in bed. So she thought you actually were crazy in love with her. Then you got what you wanted and . . . Verdad, amigo?"

"You're right. I'm a jerk. So what do I do now?"

"Well, let us give this some consideration, my boy. Is there anything you've noticed about Carol that could be a clue?"

"I don't think so. Everything about her's a mystery. Like why someone who has a rose tattooed on her boob was so old-fashioned about sex."

"Okay, so she's a girl of contradictions. That's sexy in and of itself. Who, or what, does she most care about, excluding you, of course?"

"Nothing materialistic that I can see. She's a pretty simple Tennessee country girl. There's almost nothing in her style you would call fancy or even sophisticated."

"Then what's the one thing that most stands out in your mind about the way she dresses, carries herself, or the way her apartment's decorated?"

"I like the way she dresses. It shows off her body well, but only in a classy way."

"What about where she lives?"

"The one thing that stands out in her apartment is that nothing stands out . . . except, except, a framed photograph of herself, an older couple, and a young girl."

"Any idea who they are?"

"I've assumed the couple was her parents. I have no idea about the girl; could be a niece."

"Whoever, it must be somebody Carol cares about. She wouldn't have her picture with her parents padded with a child who wasn't special. Tony, why don't you do an end run? Instead of a gift for Carol, get something for the girl. It just might lead her to give you a second chance."

"Hell, my tactics haven't worked, so I might as well try yours."

On the way to the Truman Building, Tony was pondering what that personal something should be. He thought he was good at a lot of things, but playing Romeo was not one of them.

As he was leaving the building at 5:30, he had a thought.

He walked up 17th Street to a jewelry shop he'd passed on his way to work but never stopped in. Browsing over the counter he saw a golden pendant like the one his younger sister used to wear. It was embossed with a single word: "Love." The gold was real and the cost more than Tony would normally consider, but this situation called for extreme measures.

Back to the Truman garage before 6:30, he drove faster than usual through the early evening traffic to Carol's apartment building. He considered calling her on his cell, but reviewed his strategy and decided to proceed unannounced.

At Carol's' front door he gently wrapped with his signature two shorts, pause, and a final short. No Carol. Tony rang the unit buzzer once, twice, a third time. No Carol.

Turning to leave, he almost fell into her, her arms filled with grocery bags.

"Well, and to what might I attribute your being here?" she asked.

"I missed your birthday party; the invitation must have gotten lost in the mail. So I came a couple of days late, just to show my respects."

"You lied last week and you're at it again."

Tony felt his tension rising. "Come on, Carol, I told you I was an asshole. What more do you want me to do?"

Across the hall the door to Apartment 444 opened. A man in his sixties looked out, scanning Tony with a disapproving stare.

"All I want you to do is leave," Carol enunciated each word distinctly. She placed the bags on the floor and turned to unlock the door.

With the door opened she stooped to pick up the groceries. Tony grabbed three of the bags. With a slight stumble on the entrance throw rug, he came in after her, bumping the door shut with his behind.

The occupant of 444 muttered and shook his head, turned from the hallway to his apartment.

Inside, Carol ignored Tony as she placed the groceries in the wood-paneled kitchen cabinet and the Maytag fridge. Then she turned to Tony, still standing by the door.

"Well, that was a nice performance for the neighbors. It's probably the most action the old geezer has seen since he moved here." Carol's eyes glared. "Now get the hell out of my place."

Tony took a step toward her. "For Christ's sake, give me a second chance."

"I did; that was our performance in the shower. And then, once you satisfied yourself, you started ignoring me again."

"I wasn't ignoring you, Carol."

"Well, you can see how I might mistake it for ignoring me. Most girls consider not calling the next day after first sex to be ignoring, but—"

"I have a present I would like to give you; for someone I think you do care for deeply."

Carol was silent. She looked at him warily. Tony went to the coffee table and reached for the photograph of Carol, the elderly couple, and the young girl. From his inside coat pocket he extracted a small square box wrapped in gold paper, secured by a red ribbon and bow.

Turning the photograph to Carol, he said, "I don't know who this girl is, but she must mean a great deal to you. This is a gift for her. I hope you'll accept it."

Carol removed the wrapping and opened the lid of the box. Upon seeing the pendant, her eyes moistened and tears began to form.

Tony reached out and embraced her. With no reserve, she clung to him, dampening his blue shirt collar.

She slowly pulled away and moved toward the bathroom. Tony had an erotic urge as he watched her from behind. In ten minutes she returned, her eyes still reddened but otherwise collected, her face clean and dry. "My choice is to eat alone or with you. If you don't mind ham and sweet potatoes, I'll give you a little bit of another chance."

As they sat on the sofa together, Carol reached out to hold Tony's left hand. "That was very thoughtful. Whatever its inspiration, you could not have touched me more."

"Since it was the only picture in the apartment, I assumed the girl must have a special place in your heart."

Carol used the remainder of a bottle of pinot noir with dinner, and afterward opened one of Graham port she had bought with no special purpose in mind. The hallway confrontation, even the three weeks in the cold, began to fade. They embraced, fondled. Tony rose, pulled her up after him, and guided her to the bedroom.

More than an hour later, Tony was asleep, Carol savoring their reunion lovemaking. Tony awoke and turning toward her, spotted the rose, the only interruption to her lithe nude body.

"Tell me about it," he whispered, circling the area with the tip of his finger.

He thought he sensed her wincing, but then she moved the rose to Tony's lips. He nuzzled, kissed, and touched it with his tongue.

"This is part of my life I want you to know; that I didn't want you, or anyone, to know before. It will explain why what you did tonight was so special."

Carol leaned back on her pillow, her left hand stroking Tony's sinuous hairless chest. "I grew up in Spring Hill, Tennessee. When I was young it was the typical quiet southern town, with traditional values and expectations. For a girl, that meant being good in the Biblical way, graduating from high school, marrying a star of the football team, and having lots of babies."

"That doesn't sound much different from Hialeah."

"Well, Spring Hill changed when I was in junior high school. My daddy, who had worked on his father's farm, got a job at the new Saturn plant. We had some money for once and a new car, a Saturn of course. I began to run with a faster crowd—lots of them had come from out of town for work. I had my first love with a boy six years older than me. He was James Dean handsome and played lead guitar in a punk band. He owned me."

Tony placed his head next to her left breast. "We did some wild things together," she continued. "One night after a gig that had more pot than music, and while we were stoned out of our minds, we had the same rose tattoo—he on his chest, mine . . . here. When I woke up the next morning, I saw it and prayed it would go away." She rotated slightly so Tony was only an eyelash away from the rose. "The tattoo isn't the only result of this wild period. By the time I was eighteen he made me pregnant. I didn't know what to do. He told me that if I didn't get an abortion, he would leave me forever. My father said killing babies was against God's word. I had the baby. She's the little girl in the picture—when Suzie was five."

"What happened to her father?"

"He did what he said he would. He left. I had been accepted at Middle Tennessee; my dad had saved enough to pay to send me. I skipped the first semester to be with Suzie, then left her with my parents, who loved her to death, just like she was their child. I was really sad when I got there—Prozac sad. I was thinking of Suzie all the time, couldn't concentrate on my studies, and the thought of going out with boys disgusted me."

That explains a lot, Tony realized.

"Anyway, by the second year I met a young female accounting professor. I had always been good at math; she took me on as a project, and five years later I had an accounting degree and passed the CPA exams. I got a job with Price Waterhouse in Charlotte. When I was thirty-two I got the chance to come here to Treasury, which takes me up to the Marine Corps Marathon and meeting you."

"How often do you get to be with Suzie?" Tony asked.

"As often as I can. She's almost as old as I was when I went wild, and I don't want her to relive my mistakes. But I know I can't be a single mom with what I'm doing here."

She slipped out of bed and headed toward the bathroom. Carol returned in cotton pajamas and slipped back in the sheets.

"OK, I've just given you my life story. I'm really not interested in yours, at least not tonight. What I do want to know is what you've found out about the DOJ investigation."

"I tried to get some information from Ben Brewster, but he stonewalled. I expect to be following up on Billington's leads in Riyadh and Kuala Lumpur as soon as I can get there, whenever in hell that will be."

Carol pulled her legs up to her chin. "Do you see any connection to what I'm doing with BAE?"

"Not yet."

Carol flipped off the nightstand lamp. "We've had enough for tonight. You can stay or go; your choice."

SEPTEMBER 1
Belle Glade, Florida

Francois Malaux had taken the opportunity afforded by the Labor Day hiatus from his work preparing sugarcane fields for the next year's crop to spend some time fishing with his son. With eight-year-old Alain, he stood on the bank of the main drainage canal linking eastern Lake Okeechobee to the Atlantic Ocean.

Summer was well settled over south Florida. Francois's green T-shirt was soaked through, and even his toughened bare feet stung with the heat of the limestone embankment. All father and son had to show for the first two hours were a batch of hand-sized bream and a single small-mouth bass. They tried a new spot a hundred yards to the west.

Alain arched his cane pole with a sideways sling. The hook, followed by the sinker and bobber, plopped into the still, murky black water. When the bobber was floating on the surface, he felt a twinge. As his father had taught him, he jerked the pole upward to set the hook. It bent almost in half.

"Daddy, Daddy, I have a really big one!" the boy exclaimed. Pulling the pole in all directions, Alain was unable to raise the catch. The line was stretched tight.

"Hold down, Alain," his father cautioned. "We've lost four lines already and we'll be headed home if this one goes."

He took the pole and manipulated it in a more cautious, controlled manner. Frustrated, he said, "It's stuck, maybe under a rock. I'll try to get it unstuck."

Francois cleared his pockets, making a neat pile of his wallet, coins, and a full pack of cigarettes. Wading into the canal, he followed the path of the line. He reached down, then submerged, disappearing from his frightened son's view. He came up again, shaking the water from his near–shoulder length hair. He shouted with a grin that exposed his pearl white front teeth, "It's a truck you caught! It won't taste too good, but it did give up your line."

Disappointed by their bad luck, they sat by the edge of the road. After a few minutes, they saw a Florida Highway Patrol car in the distance from the west. Waving it down, Francois led the trooper to the site of the sunken vehicle. The young trooper asked for the cane pole.

Taking off his patent leather shoes and rolling up his taupe uniform pants, he swashed into the canal almost up to his knees. Poking and maneuvering with the pole, he pinged the object below the surface, feeling out its surface and shape.

Returning to shore, he said, "Yeah, it's a truck, all right. I'll call the station and ask them to send a dive team and a wrecker. This sure as hell isn't the way you want to end a holiday weekend."

Francois nodded and told his son to collect their gear.

———

It was almost dark when a highway patrol SUV arrived with three men.

"Sam, Randy, suit up. We've only got half an hour of light, so scout it out for any human remains," instructed Walter, the crew chief.

Sam and Randy stood on the side of the vehicle screened from traffic as they stripped to their Speedos and pulled on black wet suits.

With Walter's assistance they attached and tested the regulators and shoved their feet into cumbersome, tightly drawn fins. With Sam leading the way, they trundled down the incline and into the water, then disappeared, a trail of bubbles marking the path to the submerged vehicle.

Less than ten minutes later, they reemerged from the dark water.

"Well," Walter called out, "what did you find?"

Randy answered, "There's no body in there. Best I could see, it's a Ford 150 and looks as if it's been here for a while." He held up a webbed sack. "I was able to get this out of the glove compartment."

On the embankment, Walter opened the sack. Out fell a flashlight and, in a plastic bag, a wad of papers and a cardboard box partially filled with .45 caliber bullets.

SEPTEMBER 4−6

Washington, D.C. ★ Minneapolis ★ Airborne,
JFK to Riyadh, Kingdom of Saudi Arabia

At last, the summer was giving way to the first signs of fall. The Redskins would open the season on Sunday. The sidewalk in front of Tony's townhouse, which since Memorial Day had been crowded with Capitol tourists, was back to the regulars. As had been true since Genghis Khan, in Afghanistan the warriors were preparing to retreat from the field to the cave for the winter.

When he reached his desk at 8:40, Tony found a note from Ms. Wilkens.

> *Mr. Ramos, your application for personal leave has been approved by Ambassador Talbott. He has directed that you submit a detailed itinerary of your travels, including contact points throughout. The Ambassador wishes to see you at ten o'clock.*
> *Florence Wilkens*

The good news was marred by Ben Brewster. He leaned his bulbous body around the doorjamb like the jowls of a pig into a trough. The button above his belt buckle had come undone, exposing a wad of hairy fat.

"Get your fat ass out of my office," Tony ordered. "I'm going to be away from you for two weeks and I've got work to do."

"I promise you this won't be a Cuban joke, as much as you like them. In fact, I've got some advice for you."

"I can only imagine. Have a seat, but don't get used to it."

The standard GSA office chair secured Brewster's core with a substantial perimeter hanging over. "I understand you're going to Saudi Arabia to try to get the answers to some questions for the late Senator Billington."

Tony suddenly looked up. "How do you know about that?"

Brewster dismissed the question with a wave of his hand. "We're in the intelligence business, remember? Anyway, I know that territory like you do Afghanistan. My advice: stay home."

"That's not going to happen," Tony said, still shaken that Brewster knew about his trip. "Next piece of advice?"

Brewster leaned back. "At least listen to what I have to say. First, it's dangerous as hell."

"Do you think Afghanistan is Disney World?"

Brewster's voice rose in register and urgency. "Going on a personal mission means going without diplomatic protection. If you get crossways with the Saudis, it's likely your handsome head will be separated from your studly body. Think of all the female broken hearts when that happens."

"I'd rather not, but que será será."

"Second, you are not going to learn anything. The 9/11 Commission looked into all of Billington's fantasies and rejected them. They hardly got a footnote in the final report."

"Billington put that in the same bucket as all the other cover-ups orchestrated by the White House."

"Third, if there is anything to be learned, you won't do it as a lone ranger. Billington's interpretation of the events leading up to and surrounding 9/11 made a lot of official people uncomfortable, and since most of the ambassadors in that part of the planet are political appointees, not only won't you get any help, they'll be trying to take you out with their own version of a roadside bomb."

Tony recalled the same caution from Senator Stoner.

"Benny Boy, though you might find the premise difficult to swallow, I'm no fool and I know what I signed up for."

"My last shot is out of concern for my old and dear friend, you."

"This one I'm really anticipating."

"And I hate being called 'Benny.'"

"I take small pleasures where I can find them," Tony remarked.

Brewster waved him off dismissively. "In spite of what the presidential polls look like nine weeks out, our guy is closing in and I think will pull it out. If he does, his gang isn't going to be out to advance the career of a Foreign Service officer who was trying to dredge up mud from the past. In spite of its stresses and late nights, this is a pretty good job. You don't want to be discredited and on the streets as of next January."

"I'll take my chances," Tony said looking at his watch. "Time's up. Now please get the hell out of my office." As Brewster slammed the door behind him, Tony's BlackBerry hummed.

"Hello, this is Tony Ramos."

"Hi, it's Laura. I'm in Minneapolis. Hope I didn't wake you this time."

"No, I'm on the job. What are you doing there?"

"The convention's wrapping up tomorrow, and I've been contracted to take the senator's photograph for *Time*."

"Good for you," Tony said perfunctorily.

"I didn't call to talk politics. I wanted to tell you the Saudis accepted my offer and invited me to take the royal family photograph. I'll be off from London to Jeddah in about a week."

"Great. But remember, Laura, this is dangerous stuff."

"Yeah, yeah, I know what you've told me. But I'm a big girl. I can take care of myself."

"I know you think you can, but—"

"Just tell me what you want me to do over there."

"It's not that simple. Before you leave London, I'll give you some specifics. But we're going to have to play it by ear, because what I want you to do is get to someone inside the royal court and use your celebrity and charm to get a lead on information we haven't been able to surface so far."

"What kind of information?"

"As a for-instance, I heard in San Diego the king is cranking up a big science project. True? If so, what for and how far along is it? Does it have any military significance? That's the kind of thing we need. I'll call you with more."

"I'll be at my apartment on Monday. Call me in the morning, London time." She hung up.

As Tony passed Ms. Wilkens's desk, he thanked her for expediting his leave request.

"Don't thank me. It's all the ambassador's fault." Uncharacteristically, she smiled as Tony passed into Talbott's office.

The ambassador was more refreshed and energetic than Tony had seen him in a long time.

"No U.S. or NATO casualties in Afghanistan this past week. The Taliban seems to be moving back to its base camps, at least for now. And I was able to recharge my batteries on the Vineyard over Labor Day weekend. So all in all, not a bad week. I hope you were able to get some time off."

"Not much, but I'll see some different territory next week. Thank you for the leave."

Talbott invited Tony to sit and eased into his desk chair. "I know you're going to Riyadh for John Billington. I doubt the people he'll send you to see will be the most virtuous in Saudi society."

He opened a file on his desk. "Tony, INR is not in the intelligence collection business, but you will have some unusual access in Saudi Arabia and Malaysia. The department would like some second- and third-source confirmation on issues that are probably not on Billington's list but you know better than anybody—our darkest nightmares: that all of Central Asia will collapse into the hands of the Taliban and bin Laden. While you are doing your work for Billington, consider two lines of questions in Riyadh: We haven't had much success in shutting down the Saudi money flow into Afghanistan. There's been a lingering suspicion that much of it is coming out of the Golden Chain in Jeddah."

Tony perked up. "When I was in San Diego in August, Nasir used the same phrase. But he was referring to the ownership of Ercan, a company where al-Harbi, the Saudi agent in Southern California, was a no-show employee." He considered all of this for a moment and then added, "That . . . is . . . very interesting."

Talbott raised his glasses to his forehead. "The second area is the Saudis' assessment of the situation in Afghanistan. Raise both issues with your colleague Rizzo and backdoor it to al-Dossari."

Talbott leaned back in his leather chair, glancing at the books in his official library. "Tony, when you're in Kuala Lumpur, find out what their intelligence knows about the Indians' take on Pakistan. The Malaysians' intel is good, and they legitimately feel we embarrassed them about the al-Qaeda meeting there in January of 2000. They've been close to the Indians and might have a take on how New Delhi calculates the possibility of a Pakistani collapse, and what would be India's response."

Tony removed the notebook from his coat pocket and entered the ambassador's requests. "I'll get what I can. If there's anything else I can do, you know where to reach me."

As he reached into his left-side desk drawer Talbott said, "One more thing." He placed a Glock 26 pistol and a package of Velcro on his desk. "With what the senator and I are asking you to do, there is a possibility you'll need this. I assume a former special ops member knows how to use it."

"Well, I don't think it's necessary, but, yes, I think I can handle it."

"Ms. Wilkens will have the paperwork prepared that will make you legal."

Holding and rotating the light personal handgun, Tony said, "Mr. Ambassador, thank you, I guess."

"Thank you, Tony. When you get back we'll have moved you into your new office down the hall."

"Thanks, but . . . "

"You've been here ten years and you've done superior work. I think it's about time. Although it looks over our scenic parking lot, I'm sure you'll find it comfortable. The only drawback is, you'll be farther from your friend Ben Brewster."

Rising, Tony shook hands with Talbott. "I'll try to live with the disappointment. I'll have a full brief when I get back."

The Saturday morning brunch at Eastern Market was a tradition for Capitol Hill aficionados. Carol had spent the night before at Tony's, and at shortly before nine they walked the five blocks to the nineteenth-century market east of the Capitol. Tony's standard was two eggs over light on a three-stack of buttermilk pancakes. Carol settled for yogurt in preparation for the October Marine Corps Marathon.

Sitting on the benches abutting C Street, Tony thought his personal life had never been better. "It's going to be tough being halfway around the world from you," he said, "even for a few days."

"At least I'll be busy in the Caymans while you're away."

"Is that a follow-up to Zurich?"

"Primarily. The department has gotten the green light from the Anglo-Cayman Bank to open up the accounts of transactions involving BAE's money shuffled back from Zurich and where that money went from the Caymans. I don't anticipate the stonewalling I got initially at Zurich-Alliance; at least I'm hoping I won't."

"What else do you expect to be doing there?"

"Well, I've been told there is an eight-mile beach with lots of macho men. Just in case you revert back to form, I want to have some options in place."

Tony smiled and reached out for Carol's hand. "That's good planning. I expect to be back on the 13th. But assuming you don't fall head over heels for some of that meatloaf on the beach, will you hold space on your dance card open?"

"If you're a good boy," she promised.

———————

Tony had scheduled a Saturday afternoon flight on Saudi Arabian Airlines from JFK, to arrive in Riyadh on Sunday morning. That would give him time to recuperate from jet lag and have a late dinner with Jonathan Rizzo, a colleague in the INR on temporary-duty assignment to the embassy.

Once airborne, he opened Billington's memo and reviewed the relevant section.

> *Riyadh, Kingdom of Saudi Arabia:*
>
> *My suspicion is that the agents of the Kingdom who facilitated the 9/11 hijackers reached throughout the United States, but we know they emanated from Riyadh. Two of those agents were based in Southern California.*
>
> *Hamza al-Dossari was the officer for Islamic and cultural affairs in the Kingdom's Los Angeles consulate in January 2000. While it is reported there were numerous contacts with al-Hazmi and al-Mihdhar in January of 2000, what al-Dossari knew of the purposes of their mission is still a secret. His relationship to Omar al-Harbi is even more so.*
>
> *Al-Harbi, while living in San Diego, was described by the FBI in 1999 as an agent of the Saudi Kingdom. His portfolio was to monitor Saudi students attending colleges and universities in Southern California. From January to December of 2000, al-Harbi was the principal patron and protector and a significant financer of al-Hazmi and al-Mihdhar.*

From INR sources Tony had augmented the senator's memo.

> *Hamza al-Dossari has lived in Riyadh since he was declared persona non grata for alleged terrorist-related activities, terminated from the*

L.A. consular position he held 1998–2003, and deported from the
U.S. in May 2003. He has a desk job at the foreign ministry, feels iso-
lated, without a future, and is hostile to the Kingdom ...

Omar al-Harbi separated or has been separated from Kingdom
employment. His employment or pension status is unknown. ... Like
al-Dossari, al-Harbi feels abused and used, in his case both by the
Kingdom and the U.S.

High over the north Atlantic, Tony stretched his blanket over the vacant seats on either side of him and asked the attendant to awaken him for dinner.

SEPTEMBER 7–8
Riyadh, Saudi Arabia

Tony shook off the muscle stiffness from the nearly twelve-hour flight with a brisk walk from the Golden Tulip Hotel around Riyadh's al-Dirah district. During his two years on the professional tour, it had been his habit to arrive at the site of the tournament a day early so his body could acclimate to the time zone and his mind could focus on the nuances of the new environment.

This was his first visit to Riyadh. In the stark contrast of modern office towers scattered among ancient buildings, their perpendicular corners anchored by spires from which came periodic prayer calls, Tony abandoned any pretense of direction and meandered from the modern boulevards to narrow, heavily shadowed alleys. The acrid smells of lamb barbequing on an overhanging patio melded with the heavy smoke from the narghiles in street-side cafés. Women in black burkas and veils strolled in groups of twos and threes, stepping into the gutter when men approached on the cobblestone walk. In the distance Tony heard the roar of a crowd.

At the end of the block, he turned left and entered a portal opening onto a sunlit square about the size of ten tennis courts. On the far side was an ornate three-story structure, its front inscribed with classic Arabic script identifying it as the palace of the provincial governor. From the upper balcony an elderly man dressed in silken robes solemnly observed the activities below.

In the center of the square was a platform, two meters above the ground. Ten wooden steps led up the side of the rectangular structure. Five rows of men encircled it and prevented Tony from drawing closer.

The murmuring of the gathered became a rising wave. What appeared to be a college-age youth, hands bound behind his back and a black-and-white scarf tied over his eyes, was being pulled up the steps. He resisted, tripped, and fell to his knees on the last step. Three men in military camouflage uniforms dragged him to the center of the stage. The noise from the crowd grew louder.

The youth was positioned in a squat, head pressed between his knees. A football lineman–sized figure, the details of his physique hidden by a loose black shirt and his face covered with the desert equivalent of a ski mask, emerged from among the functionaries assembled on the rear of the platform. He walked with assurance to the far side of the youth. He was cradling a curved sword more than a meter in length.

The youth had given up the struggle. Even if Tony had understood colloquial Saudi Arabic, the youth's garbled utterances would have been indecipherable. His robes were stained with his own urine.

The burly man planted his feet at a distance equal to the sword's length. Slowly he raised the blade over the center of his body as gracefully as the backswing of the most accomplished golfer, arched his back, and brought the weapon forward, accelerating as it neared impact.

The head of the youth fell between his legs, spewing deep red blood as it rolled over the front edge into the crowd. Amid shouts of exaltation, the onlookers surged forward to shake the hand of the executioner.

Tony felt his abdomen tremble. Lowering his head toward his now sweat-soaked chest, he turned away, his initial walking steps morphing into a jog until he reached the Golden Tulip.

He washed himself first in the shower stall and then soaked in the elaborate two-person bathtub. It took the better part of an hour before he could deflect his mind from what he had witnessed in the square, and ordered his sleep-deprived body into a near-coma.

He slept through his six o'clock wristwatch alarm, and it was almost seven when he rolled over to look at the bedside clock. Drowsily he recalled his dinner appointment with Jonathan Rizzo in the lobby bar in half an hour.

At the appointed time he stepped off the elevator into a lobby mixed with time zone–blurred men and others with the voices and body language of weekend celebrants. Tony spotted Jonathan sitting at one of the tables that separated the bar from the concierge desk. They embraced as old, long-separated friends. Jonathan led the way into the darker interior of the lounge. He ordered Chivas Regal and Tony, seeing no tropical options on the bar list, did the same.

The two friends reconnected over tales of their interwoven experiences as intelligence officers. Both had come into the State Department in the summer of 2000, Jonathan from graduate studies at Fletcher, and Tony having been eliminated in the second round at Monaco, his last pro tennis tournament. After the mandatory introductory training and six months of Arabic language school at Monterey, they were assigned to the Central Asia desk of INR. In a childhood bout with measles, Rizzo had suffered hearing loss that necessitated an aid in his right ear. This handicap had affected his ability to fully capture Arabic; thus his speech was distorted. Except for Tony's sixteen months with Senator Billington, both had been desk-bound analysts until Rizzo was detailed to Riyadh to work on classified issues between Pakistan and Saudi Arabia.

"Tony, before we order another round," Jonathan advised, "we should go to your room. I don't know what you or your friend Billington have been doing, but it's making some serious waves out here in Riyadh. Better we talk in a less public place. I've got a bottle from the embassy exchange. We won't die of thirst."

In Tony's room, Jonathan poured the scotch and Tony added a splash of water. Jonathan turned the television to an Argentine-Brazilian soccer match and raised the volume. They sat on the facing sides of the room's twin beds, speaking in a whisper with Jonathan's right ear tilted toward Tony.

Tony detailed the beheading.

"That's the way they do it here: swift, public, and violent."

"What's the point?" Tony asked.

"The place you stumbled into is known in Riyadh as Chop-Chop Square. The kingdom and its religion believe in maximum punishment as maximum deterrence. What distinguishes this culture is the number of criminal acts that carry the death penalty. The kingdom is committed to public violence for its chilling effect on deviant behavior and dissent."

"Do you have any idea what that poor bastard might have lost his head for?"

"Who knows? There's been an increase in sentences for people—did you say he looked to be in his twenties?"

"Yes."

"Probably for acts the kingdom considers threatening. Whenever there's an uptick in anti-royal behavior, the executioner comes out. Since Iraq almost caved and we had to send our troops back in, the princes have been concerned that an emboldened al-Qaeda might surface. I don't know, you could have witnessed the last moments of a suspected bin Laden follower."

"Will we ever find out?"

"Oh, yes. Part of the chill is to broadcast the bloodiest details on national radio and TV. It'll be in the papers tomorrow."

Tony and Jonathan took a full swallow from their hotel glasses. Tony went to the bathroom.

When he returned, Jonathan was reading a paper he had sequestered in his inside coat pocket. "There are at least three pieces of intelligence relevant to the current situation in Saudi Arabia that could be helpful to you," he offered in an even more guarded tone. "With the avalanche of dollars from the run-up in oil prices, the Saudis have increased their support of extremist factions. We have not been able to confirm he is a beneficiary, but there have been sightings of Osama bin Laden in Jeddah."

Tony straightened. "Are you serious? And none of this has been re-ported publicly?"

"Way too sensitive for this administration."

"God damn, I hope we have better sources than we did before we started the war in Iraq."

"We do. Since we started to let more Americans of Arab ancestry into the agency, our intelligence has dramatically improved. Also, we have vetted assets within the palace and, more recently, two foreign NOCs."

Tony was familiar with the increasing use in this part of the world of nonofficial cover assets, such as businessmen or professionals who had a second job: spying for the United States.

"The king was stunned by the renewal of terrorist attacks, especially against the royal family. It's been over two years since the attack on the oil facilities at Aramco. The response to that was typically Saudi: con-flicted. An increase in enforcement, as you witnessed this morning, coupled with an effort at reconciliation."

Jonathan walked to the door and cracked it open. He stuck his head into the hallway. When satisfied, he resumed his seat on the bed. "Now it looks like a third way is again on the table: capitulation. As you know from the congressional inquiry, two years before the attack, bin Laden threatened the kingdom with revolution unless al-Qaeda's operatives were given access to and support from the Saudis' agents in the U.S. The old king capitulated. We're not sure what the ask is this time, but we're concerned the current king will also give in. That's why we're tak-ing to ground the rumors about Osama.

"And the monarchy is determined to proceed with a world-class uni-versity within the kingdom, probably on the Red Sea. For a couple of years there was resistance from the scholars they tried to recruit. The king has sweetened the pot and pledged to Western style inside the uni-versity community. They could never have attracted female faculty or spouses if what you saw here in Riyadh was to be the standard of living."

"Jonathan," Tony interrupted, "isn't this modernization exactly what we've been encouraging the kingdom to do?"

"Could be. The stated reason for the university is to establish an intellectual underpinning for a post-oil society. That would be a good
thing. But our sources are convinced it's to support projects that will
strengthen the Saudis' military capabilities. One of the reasons I am
here is to sniff out whether the Saudis are getting any help from the
Pakistanis, like the North Koreans and Libya did. Finally, sources have
told us that Saudi Arabia was somehow complicit in the Syrian nuclear
site the Israelis took out a few years ago."

"Ambassador Talbott asked me to find what the king's courtiers are
saying about Afghanistan."

"This is highly sensitive, as you may have gathered from the reticence
in my cables. But the Saudis are very concerned that the war is lost.
When that happens it will have regional destabilizing consequences. I
know a lot about their apprehension over the future of Pakistan. To say
they are apoplectic is no exaggeration. They're watching closely what
NATO and we are doing. The king is astonished that we have been so
slow to see the collapse and put more troops in.

"You've read the cable traffic on Iran sending bags of money to
Afghanistan. They are not the only ones. The king has directed the government to redouble support to the Karzai government, while the
Golden Chain pours money into al-Qaeda. As seen from the palace,
that's how far conditions there have deteriorated. From the outside, it
underscores just how conflicted the kingdom has become."

Jonathan rose and pulled on his suit coat. "Tomorrow, I'll try to get
appointments for you with al-Dossari and al-Harbi. Both have been
mostly under the radar since their return to Saudi Arabia."

Still seated, Tony asked, "Thank you, but I have another request.
After I finish tomorrow I want to go to Jeddah. Could you help make
some introductions?"

"Maybe; depends. But I thought you had to be in KL. Why are you
staying around? Want to see more beheadings?"

"No, but I do want to see if I can find out what's going on in Jeddah,
all the rumors about a secret science project. Maybe I can get something on the Golden Chain. If I go tomorrow, I can fly from Jeddah to

Kuala Lumpur on Wednesday night and will only be a day behind on my schedule."

Jonathan shrugged. "Whatever you want. I'll give you a call before nine in the morning."

Tony walked Jonathan to the elevator. They shook hands; the door closed and Jonathan departed.

In ten minutes Tony was in a deep sleep.

———————

Tony took breakfast at 7:30 in the Golden Tulip coffee shop. The hotel had provided a courtesy copy of the English-language *Arabian Post*. Below the fold was a picture of Hassan al-Nami. His deep-set eyes peered above a flattened nose and trace of a smile. The accompanying story described his beheading at the provincial governor's palace. The twenty-three-year-old had been executed for treasonous acts against the kingdom. Hassan was identified as the younger brother of Ahmad Abdullah al-Nami, one of the September 11 hijackers. Men who had witnessed the execution were quoted as praising the king and the executioner for their faithful discharge of the will and law of Allah.

Tony returned to his room. At 8:30 Jonathan called. "You have a meeting with al-Dossari at ten at his office in the foreign ministry. And at one with al-Harbi at his flat in the new development west of the central district. That should give you enough time to catch the six o'clock flight to Jeddah. I'm working on the arrangements in Jeddah. Call after you finish with al-Harbi."

Jonathan paused for emphasis. "You have my number, if you need me please—and I mean this as an order—call."

SEPTEMBER 8
Riyadh

The foreign ministry was within walking distance of the Golden Tulip. A royal palace during the interwar period, it had retained its imperial appearance and dominated a courtyard square ten times the size of the site of the beheading. Three sides of the courtyard were devoted to commerce and culinary pleasures.

Tony arrived precisely at 9:50. He was ushered into the office of the assistant to the deputy minister for consular affairs. The floor was covered with a dreary abrash-hue rug, upon which was placed a rectangular two-meter *surya* prayer rug. On the wall behind the credenza hung the only visual distraction, the shield of the Kingdom of Saudi Arabia.

Tony was standing by the courtyard window when al-Dossari arrived. He had studied his résumé and photographs in the bureau's files. He was taller than Tony had expected, an inch above himself. Al-Dossari showed the wear of the past few years. In the photo taken in 2001 at the King Fahad Mosque in Los Angeles, through his clerical robes and headdress he projected the solemn power and confidence of the mosque's prayer leader. Now, in his business-casual white cotton garb, beneath his uncovered head, half-moons of flesh hung under his clouded eyes.

Al-Dossari reached out for a Western handclasp. Amid these pedestrian surroundings, the jeweled golden ring he wore on his right middle finger, granted for distinguished service to the crown, bespoke a career of promise aborted.

"I am honored by your visit. Please have a seat," al-Dossari offered. "I must say I have been deficient of serious guests."

Tony had wondered why the meeting was held at the Foreign Ministry. Given Jonathan's precautions, the openness was surprising. He soon learned the reason. Al-Dossari demonstrated no inclination to be forthcoming to Tony's inquiries. To Billington's questions on al-Dossari's relationship with al-Harbi in January 2000, the answers were rote. "I was in the service of the king. His communications will be granted the necessary confidentiality."

When Tony transitioned to U.S. foreign policy in the Middle East al-Dossari was more open.

"Your war in Iraq was seen here, in Cairo, and in Damascus as a war on Islam. Your incompetence has saved you from yourselves. If you had succeeded in your first attempt to establish a government in Baghdad that was truly representative of the people, it would surely have been extremist, even more closely lashed to Iran than what you have now. It would have had a cascading effect across the region, a wave of ayatollahs." Al-Dossari's face showed its first hint of expression, a lifted brow with three horizontal furrows. Leaning forward, "Is that what you want?"

Tony said, "Of course not, but I will admit our actions in Iraq have not been characterized by strategic thought."

Tony recalled a speech Senator Billington had delivered to the Council on Foreign Relations shortly before his retirement. In the question-and-answer session, he was asked to explain his opposition to the Iraq war. Repeating much of what he had said in his Senate speech in October 2003, he elaborated:

"In September, the Senate Intelligence Committee took a break from the 9/11 inquiry to drill down on the rationale for a war with Iraq. The administration had largely abandoned some of its previous justifications, like a close link between bin Laden and Saddam Hussein before 9/11, and was focused on Iraq's weapons of mass destruction. The director of the CIA brought to a closed hearing several white-covered three-ring binders, each holding descriptions—ground-level and satellite photographs and even street addresses—of some 550 sites in Iraq where weapons of mass destruction were being produced or stored. It was pretty damn impressive . . . until, until I asked the question, Where did you get all this detailed, highly specific information?

"The director's answer: 'From the exiles.'

"That sounded fishy to me. I knew that most of the exiles had been out of the country a decade or more. Beyond that, they had a clear conflict of interest. Their primary objective was to regain control of Iraq, and the only way that was going to happen was if and when they could enter Baghdad following the exhaust fumes of an invading U.S. tank. The exiles had a vested interest in exciting America to war.

"So I asked who has the United States had on the ground to verify the reports we were receiving from the exiles? Who was knocking on the door or looking through the window of those 550 buildings to determine if, in fact, they were harboring weapons of mass destruction?

"The answer was zero." Tony recalled that Billington held up his right hand, thumb to index finger forming an O, to drive the point home. He then continued, "No one with our interest as their principal concern had given a confirming second opinion. Nobody.

"That's when I concluded the White House was not adhering to a sound strategic policy in Iraq. Rather, we and the American people were being subjected to a massive con game with enormous adverse consequences. That was when, and why, I decided to vote no."

Al-Dossari's chuckle snapped Tony out of his reverie. "Not in the least have your actions in Iraq been characterized by strategic thought. And it is even more empty and disastrous in Iran and Afghanistan. When you invaded Iraq, there was no nuclear program in Iran. Today, I've heard five thousand centrifuges are spinning. That's what your stance of being too pure to talk to Tehran has achieved."

From his most recent briefing, Tony knew the number of Iranian centrifuges was considerably lower, either because of technical lapses on the part of the Iranians, effective reverse engineering by Western suppliers, or manipulation by intelligence hackers. He lowered his valuation of Saudi intelligence a notch.

"We don't believe even your belated recognition of the seriousness of the consequences in Afghanistan is going to avoid a defeat by a thousand cuts. May Allah help us when that occurs. You are fools, and unless His Highness acts to protect the kingdom, we will be the victims of your stupidity."

Tony realized that al-Dossari had essentially confirmed what Jonathan had represented as the projections of Saudi elites, only with a sharper point and a twist of the rhetorical sword.

Tony glanced at his notes. A scribbling from the meeting with Professor Nasir caught his eye. "I have been curious about a Saudi organization known as the Golden Chain. Could you provide me with any information on its current status and activities?"

Al-Dossari turned to the window and the crowds he could see in the courtyard below. He paused as if surprised by the question and unsure of the answer. "The Golden Chain has a history going back more than twenty years. It was originally founded in Jeddah by a group of wealthy men, many of whom, like the bin Laden family, had long ties with the kingdom. Its purpose was to preserve traditional religious and social norms."

"Could you elaborate?"

"The original initiatives were to support institutions such as orthodox mosques and madrassas, to protect women, and to advocate within the monarchy for a less Westernized orientation. By the conclusion of the war you refer to as Persian Gulf, there was concern among the non–royal family members of the aristocracy that the king was becoming too compliant with the wishes of foreigners. Your country, Mr. Ramos, was at the top of the list."

"Excuse me but how did the Golden Chain become identified with bin Laden?"

"Initially through the influence of his family. When he returned from the Sudan in 1993, Osama ingratiated himself with the founders of the Golden Chain and urged a more aggressive course of action. This led to the transition of an affiliate of the organization, al-Qaeda, which in English would be loosely translated as 'the platform,' from a financier of the terrorist plots of others into an active terrorist operator with the Chain's support and financial backing. The increasingly violent acts of al-Qaeda caused it to be renounced by the king, forcing bin Laden to seek refuge in Afghanistan and ... and, you know the story from there."

Tony felt he was being detoured from his initial question. "But what is the current situation with the Golden Chain?"

"It has been less visible. The perception is that the leadership has backed away from overt support of what might be considered activities hostile to the king and has sought opportunities to collaborate."

"Could you tell me what some of those forms of collaboration might be?"

Al-Dossari lifted his shoulders as if relieving soreness in his upper back. "Of course, I cannot be too explicit, but I believe substantial financing has been directed toward the new university and the science programs it will undertake. Beyond that I am not sure."

Tony rose. It was his sense that he had gone as far as al-Dossari would allow.

"Thank you for your courtesies and time. Should you return to the United States I hope I will have the opportunity to reciprocate."

Al-Dossari, now also standing, bowed before observing, "I doubt such an opportunity will become available to me. May I be of assistance to you during the balance of your stay in the kingdom?"

"Thank you for your courtesy. My plans are to be in the kingdom only until Wednesday. Should the occasion arise, rest assured I will accept."

On the curbside, Tony observed one of the many anomalies of Riyadh. Directly across the street from the ministry was a Starbucks flanked by a rug merchant and a traditional coffee and smoke café. He chose the latter.

He ordered the domestic coffee. It was heavier than the espresso served in Hialeah. Seated, he punched in Laura's London apartment.

"Laura, Tony. Are you ready to leave?"

"No. I've had some complications here. One of my former clients, Alexandros Metaxas, now the prime minister of Greece, is in town and has asked me to lunch. He is such a dear it's impossible to say no. I've secured the king's consent to delay the shoot a day."

"Give the prime minister my best wishes. I'll give you a call about eight London time tomorrow morning."

"OK, be safe."

"Same to you."

SEPTEMBER 8

Riyadh

Tony hailed a cab. He gave the driver al-Harbi's address and settled into the backseat. It was a twenty-minute ride through the center of the city and into the northwestern suburbs. In contrast to the al-Dirah district surrounding the Golden Tulip, the suburbs were an arid version of those he had seen in Singapore—thirty-story apartment towers separated by open spaces where children were playing under their female protector's attentive eyes. The apartment buildings, steel structures covered with stucco, appeared like thornless white cacti springing up from the sand.

Al-Harbi's flat was on the twenty-third floor, reached by exiting the elevator on the twenty-second and walking up a flight of concrete stairs. In San Diego, al-Harbi had the reputation of an outgoing, hospitable man with a penchant for videotaping all the guests at his frequent parties. He confirmed that promise with a warm welcome, introduction to his wife, and invitation to the balcony overlooking Riyadh. In passing through the living room with a television flickering in the far corner, Tony observed the expected Arabic furniture and floor coverings, but also walls filled with colorful photographs of the family in Southern California.

Mrs. al-Harbi served the two men coffee, fruits, and meat wrapped in grape leaves. As they stood by the railing, al-Harbi reminisced about his experiences in San Diego, the story evolving from joy upon arrival to bitterness at his departure through Great Britain back here. He said he had been abused by the Americans who had sullied his name, but also by his own country, which had failed to shield him.

Al-Harbi's eyes misted as he recounted his experiences in Birmingham, England.

"The days after September 11 were difficult for Saudis in the United Kingdom. Our family had been living in Birmingham since we left San Diego in June of 2001. Suddenly, you felt everyone was looking at you with suspicion. You can imagine how I felt when two men with Scotland Yard credentials confronted my wife, Manal, at the front door of our flat. They pushed by her, pulled me up from my kitchen chair, told me I was being detained, handcuffed me behind my back, and with no further explanation to Manal, dragged me out."

Tony suggested the two of them sit. Al-Harbi declined and continued: "At the Scotland Yard jail I was told that the Americans, the FBI, had asked that I be held as a potential terrorist and under British law I could be detained for a week with no grounds for detention, no lawyer, no rights. Every day I expected the Americans to show up and begin the interrogation. Knowing what I do now about American interrogations I don't know what they would have done with me. But they never came."

"Never came?" asked Tony.

"Never. When the week was up, Scotland Yard drove me back to my place. No 'I'm sorry' or 'We apologize'; just a goodbye at my front door and they were gone. It had been an anxious week for me but nothing like what it had been for my wife and children. The kids had been taunted in school—Firas, our youngest, assaulted by a schoolyard bully. Manal was spit on in the grocery store, told 'her kind' had no home in England."

Al-Harbi's eyes turned down. The embarrassment and shame of years earlier were still intense. He inhaled, raising his head as he released the air. "There was a chance to clear my name and the suspicion that entrapped Saudis living in the West. In July of 2003, long after I was back here in Saudi Arabia, a report was released on September 11. There was a section—sometimes it is referred to as the twenty-seven pages—purportedly on the complicity of the Saudis with bin Laden and the hijackers. Only a few people know its contents, because that part of the report was treated as a U.S. state secret. My government protested, urging that this section of the report be released as the only way our people and government could be cleared. Our foreign minister asked for a meeting with your president, and without waiting for a reply, he and a senior counselor to the king boarded a plane to Washington. Before the plane had landed, the president announced he would refuse to meet with them. The two men feigned outrage. Mahmood al-Rasheed, our ambassador, lamented the inability of the Saudis to defend the nation's honor and drove the foreign minister and the king's counselor back to Andrews Air Force Base."

After a pause, al-Harbi concluded the tale with a question. "Was anybody deceived by such behavior?"

"Yes, almost everybody," Tony replied. "Your king was pretending to be offended, and our president boasted that he was defending national security. My friend Senator Billington saw this as just another chapter in the U.S.-Saudi cover-up. The surprising thing is that this third-rate soap opera got by most of the U.S. press and virtually all the American public."

The afternoon heat was becoming oppressive. Al-Harbi suggested they adjourn to the living room. There, Tony began the questioning. He thought the directness, the absence of al-Dossari's circuitous responses, gave credibility to what al-Harbi was recounting.

In 1995, while he was an auditor with the Saudi Civil Aviation Authority, al-Harbi was recruited to serve as an agent of the kingdom, monitoring the activities of Saudi college students. With approximately twenty others, he was given six months' training in the craft of clandestine personal surveillance, a crash course to enhance his English, and an overview of American culture. He was reassigned by the Civil Aviation Authority in the summer of 1996 to a shell position with the CAA's U.S. office and two years later transferred to a "ghost" job at Ercan, a Saudi subcontractor to the aviation authority in San Diego.

"What do you mean by 'ghost'?" Tony asked, seeking confirmation for what Billington had written and he had heard from Nasir.

"I never showed up except to get my paycheck and allowances."

Al-Harbi didn't know how many of the other trainees had been placed in the United States, but it was his impression that most had shared his English-language and American-culture training.

"When I left for Birmingham, I was replaced by Ahmad al-Otaibi, who I had mentored in San Diego. He had received similar preparation in Saudi Arabia. He left after 9/11. I have been told al-Otaibi's current successor went through the same courses we had but also had an intelligence background. The kingdom seems to be continuing a policy of surveillance, but with enhanced capability to take on other assignments."

Al-Harbi confirmed the January 2000 meeting with al-Dossari at the kingdom's Los Angeles consulate. At that meeting he was told by al-Dossari that two Saudi men on an unknown mission were in Los

Angeles and the consul had been directed to provide them with sanctuary and support for an indeterminate time. The two would be having lunch at the Mediterranean Restaurant at one o'clock that afternoon. Al-Harbi and his traveling companion, who was waiting in the lobby of the consulate, were to meet them and urge them to relocate in San Diego. When the two Saudi men agreed to do so, arrangements were made for al-Harbi's monthly allowance at Ercan to be increased by an amount thought to be sufficient to cover their expenses while they were living in San Diego. Several weeks later al-Harbi determined the amount was not adequate for their lifestyle plus flying lessons, and additional funds were made available through an account at the Saudi embassy under the control of the wife of the ambassador.

"I was not given a voice in the decision to place these two men, al-Hazmi and al-Mihdhar, under my supervision. It was a distraction from my surveillance responsibilities. And they did not conduct themselves as followers of Allah."

Al-Harbi confirmed Professor Nasir's description of the two men's inability to control their vices. "They both became regulars at the strip clubs of San Diego. And they weren't any better at what they were here to do. Both took flying lessons, but they were so inept—their trainer called them 'dumb and dumber'—they were pulled out of the flight school."

Tony glanced at his watch. It was approaching 2:30. "How did Professor Nasir get involved?"

"Both, particularly al-Hazmi, were—what is the English word?—finicky. He didn't like the apartment I had found and paid for. He had heard of the professor who took in young Saudi men as boarders and demanded to move. Al-Mihdhar was a boarder at Professor Nasir's home for only a few weeks. He was recalled to Yemen to recruit additional hijackers, the ones Americans call the muscle men. Al-Hazmi stayed seven months. I was unaware Professor Nasir had become a paid informant for the FBI. If I knew then what I know now I would never have let them stay."

Tony asked, "I've heard rumors of an organization called the Golden Chain. While you were in San Diego did you have any awareness of such a group?"

"Well, one of its members owned Ercan, so I assume he was aware of what I was up to. Occasionally, there were wire transfers to al-Hazmi from Jeddah, which I suspected, but had no evidence, were from the Golden Chain. It is very rich."

"One final question, please," Tony requested. "I understand you were questioned by representatives of what we in the U.S. called the 9/11 Commission—correct?"

"In late 2003 or early 2004, I did talk with a man from the commission, but only under the condition there be a member of the Saudi intelligence service in the room at all times. His questions were not all that deep; not like yours."

"What were some of the questions?"

"It's been a long time, but as I remember, they were mainly about my assignments before al-Hazmi and al-Mihdhar arrived. How many students was I monitoring? Did I detect any activities that could have been threatening to the kingdom? What did I do with that information? None related to 9/11. I got the sense he wanted to say he had interviewed me but without going to the places your questions have."

Tony thanked al-Harbi and his wife. He was returning to the television as Tony closed the door and began the first steps down the staircase.

In an alcove on the ground floor Tony called Jonathan on his encrypted BlackBerry.

"Tony, are you secure?"

Hesitating slightly, Tony answered, "Yes."

"Our lead foreign NOC in Jeddah is Jaime Sayfie, designation 100 407 3672 88. Ask for Petra. Tell him Micca sent you." Tony's cell went dead.

SEPTEMBER 9

Tallahassee

"Detective Martinez, look, I'm doing the best I can to get your stuff processed," Keith Whitten, an agitated Florida Department of Law Enforcement lab technician, barked.

Detective Hidalgo Martinez of the Miami-Dade Police Department had been around too long to be put off by bureaucratic whining. "Keith, that's not good enough. We're all under pressure. I've been on this case from the beginning. I was at the wall as the ambulance was leaving; the blood was still oozing on the sidewalk. Now it's been almost eight weeks since the senator was run over, and I get regular calls from a *Herald* reporter, 'When are you going to make an arrest in the Billington murder case?' And then my boss gets the same question from the Billington family, and he asks me the same question. My question to you is, Where are you with the evidence we've sent?"

Whitten examined the inventory on his desk at the FDLE's forensic laboratory. "We've wrapped up the work on the paint chips from the right front fender of the truck the highway patrol dragged out of the canal. They're a match to the scrapes on the wall in The Lakes. I'm satisfied the truck was the vehicle that ran down the senator."

"What about the identification of the owner of the F-150?" Martinez asked.

"Mixed bag. The VIN number on the truck's engine block is registered to Tropical Nursery in Redlands. The license tag is more complicated. The tag that was pulled out of the water doesn't match the VIN number or the tag that was on the truck when it left the airport parking garage."

"These guys were real pros," Martinez commented. "They knew that there would be a BOLO out for a vehicle with the Nissan tag. So somewhere between the airport garage and the canal they swiped the tag from an honest-to-God F-150 and slapped it on the stolen truck."

"One place the pros screwed up was after the collision," Whitten observed. "They ran a red light at 154th Street and the Palmetto Expressway. The intersection cameras there got a clean shot at the rear of the truck. The plate was the one taken from the Nissan at the parking garage, so they rode around with the potentially incriminating plates from Saturday until at least Tuesday morning. The forward camera got a shot of the passenger and driver, and it may tell us something."

"Any idea as to who these guys are?" Martinez asked.

"We're working on it. We've sent the garage and red light photos to the FBI for more advanced photo analysis. You know about budget cuts in Miami-Dade; we've had the same here and our enhancement equipment is out-of-date. Most times, the FBI takes forever to do photo enhancement, but given that the victim was a former U.S. senator, maybe they'll give us a break."

"What about the ammo box?"

"Now there we made some progress. The bar code on the box told us it was distributed by a wholesaler in El Segundo, California, and the retail sale was at a San Diego gun shop this past June. We sent a request to the San Diego PD asking for an inquiry at the shop. But they're in worse financial shape than we are, and it could be a long time before the request works its way up the SDPD's food chain."

"And the bullets?"

"Standard S&W .45s. Our lab is looking at the particulates to see if they give us a trail. No report so far."

"Anything on the two I sent you from the intelligence guy?"

"Well, these two are from the same lot as those in the ammo box. I'd suspect they came from that box. And surprisingly, we got something from the *Times* op-ed in which the bullets were wrapped. The newspaper stock on which the *Times* printed this is from the printing shop that does Southern California distribution. So we've got double confirmation as to where the bullets came from."

Detective Martinez had no further questions. "Good job, Keith. I know you're under a lot of strain, and I do appreciate you getting on this so quick. When you get any more information let me know ASAP. And please give the FDLE commissioner my best wishes from down here deep in the swamps."

SEPTEMBER 9

Jeddah, Saudi Arabia

Calling on the BlackBerry from his room in the Jeddah Hilton, Tony said, "Petra, please. This is a friend of Micca."

"Micca has alerted me to your arrival. Come to 93 Il Abogado at 8:30. It's about twenty minutes from your hotel. Look for a black Land Rover."

The address was the parking lot of a strip shopping center. Tony spotted the vehicle as he was paying the taxicab driver. Covered in mustard-hued sand, the door panel on the driver's side was painted in white Arabic lettering: Gulf Engineering—Dubai, UAE. The driver waved Tony to the passenger's seat. He exchanged introductions with Jaime and Jamal Sayfie, both late twenties, dressed in grey overalls embossed with the Gulf Engineering name and logo, an oil-drilling rig.

Jaime maneuvered the vehicle onto a four-lane concrete highway, heading south. A kilometer beyond the center, Tony asked, "Is this clean?"

"We swept it this morning."

"OK. I'm here because I've been told by several sources there is a clandestine science project under way in Jeddah. Do you know anything about it?"

"Somewhat," Jaime answered as he slowed to reach for a file on the backseat. "Our firm has been providing specialty metals in the kingdom since 1995. A year ago we became a service provider to the Prince Sultan Research Center."

Tony had great admiration for non-official-cover spies. Most spooks had an official affiliation, commonly as an innocuous diplomat at an embassy. If they were busted for their real job, the worst that could happen would be declaration as a persona non grata and deportation. NOCs had no such protection. If a businessperson or professional was also assisting an intelligence agency on the side, his sanction could be the loss of his head.

"As foreign NOCs gathering sensitive information in another country for a third without any diplomatic or other cover, you're doing the most dangerous job in the intelligence business. How did you get involved?"

Settling into the left lane and accelerating to one hundred kilometers per hour, Jaime answered, "Our family has been in metallurgy since after the Great War. We started in our home country of Yemen and migrated to Dubai in 1991."

"What caused you to leave?" Tony asked.

"We had a good business there milling parts for businesses in the oil and gas industry, particularly the Americans. Then, after the war in Kuwait, radical groups began to take control in Yemen. When my older brother was killed as a bystander to a firefight and my cousin Jamal here," motioning to the man in the rear, "lost part of his leg, the whole family decided to leave. We were able to continue to do business with our former customers from our new base in Dubai."

Tony turned and saw three one-by-one-meter wooden boxes in the backseat next to Jamal and in the far back of the vehicle. "And what are those for?"

"They're going to the Prince Sultan Center. You'll see what for."

Approaching the Red Sea port district of Jeddah, Jaime swung on to a narrow two-lane road through warehouses and industrial buildings. He parked the Land Rover near a storefront with the same designation as on its door panel.

"What are we doing here?" Tony asked.

"Changing you into a Gulf uniform," Jamal answered from the rear seat.

In the small office, Tony was handed a cardboard box with a uniform, soiled like those worn by Jaime and Jamal, white socks, and well-broken-in, over-the-ankle lace-up work boots. He replaced his khaki pants, golf shirt, and loafers with the Gulf uniform and boots, folding and placing his own in the box. Tony removed the wallet from the overalls' rear pocket and, noting the identification cards, was impressed with a quite acceptable likeness of himself and his new name, Khalid Khoury. Now that he was properly dressed, Jaime instructed Tony as to his work assignments.

Back on the highway Tony asked, "How did you get in this business?"

"Last year, the manager of one of our customers, Union Oil of Houston, told us about a project under way here in Jeddah. He said it required a considerable amount of special metal fabrication and that he had recommended us. We were contacted by a representative of the Saudi Ministry of Defense and Aviation. He must have checked us out, because a week later he offered us a contract and we've been working for them ever since."

"Okay. But what about your present job as NOCs?"

"The situation in Yemen continued to deteriorate. Al-Qaeda was even more a force there than in Afghanistan. It wasn't a coincidence that the attack on the U.S. destroyer in 2000 took place in Aden. After al-Qaeda affiliated with a local gang that adopted the name al-Qaeda on the Arabian Peninsula, it was getting an ever greater pile of pounds from the Saudis."

"What does that have to do with what you are doing now?" Tony asked.

"About the time of the failed bomb attempt over Detroit, our payment checks stopped coming from the ministry and instead were from a Jeddah organization called the Golden Chain. We knew it was a big part of the money flowing to bin Laden in Yemen. We were offended by the relationship and figured there was something more than science going on at the center. It was shortly after that first Golden Chain check that I walked into the U.S. consulate in Jeddah."

———

The Prince Sultan Research Center was hidden in a grove of cedar trees on the far side of an abandoned military air base twenty-five kilometers from the city center. It was surrounded by a five-meter-high fence topped with concertina wire. Jaime stopped at the security gate. Five armed soldiers dressed in the ubiquitous camouflage military fatigues encircled the vehicle. The tallest one, with the single gold bar of a master sergeant, commanded the three to exit the Land Rover. The other four soldiers, in a well-practiced routine, examined the undercarriage of the vehicle with a mirror on a pole, opened the hood and inspected the engine, and recorded the license tag, ministry permit, and block numbers. As the sergeant inspected their papers, he asked, "What is your mission?"

Pointing to the three wooden boxes, Jaime offered, "To deliver and install this shipment of recast parts."

The sergeant stared at Tony. "Khoury. Lebanese?"

"Yemeni."

"My records do not indicate you have been here previously. What is your purpose?"

In his best Arabic, Tony responded as he had been rehearsed to do, "This order required my particular expertise with forming vacuum tubes. I have come from Dubai to deliver and assist in their installation."

Apparently satisfied, the sergeant returned to the security hut, placed a call, listened, and waved them through.

Circling the perimeter of the otherwise abandoned military air base, they passed twelve warehouse-like structures. When they reached the one designated E, Jaime said, "That's where we have been working. The crew from the main plant would bring us devices to be reworked or replaced. Today is the first time we have been given access to the hanger." He nodded toward a three-story concrete semi-cylindrical structure the size of two American football fields.

"I'm not sure why, but it may be that they are close to completion of the project and need the repairs to be done on-site to save time."

In front of the hanger were five rows of military aircraft. Tony assumed these were mothballed, reduced to service as a spare parts inventory. In the back row were nine of the BAE Tornados. He wondered if the kingdom was ready for another round of under-the-rug payouts.

As the three were unbuckling their seat belts Jamal admonished, "Talk only if absolutely necessary inside the facility. If there are questions, they will be answered later."

Approaching the main entrance, each man carrying one of the wooden boxes, Tony noticed Jamal walked with a distinct limp. Passing a bronze sign designating the facility as the Prince Sultan Research and Development Center and dated 1992, they entered. The clearance process was even more demanding than at the gate: the boxes were taken into a separate room for inspection while the men were strip-searched by civilian security and fingerprinted, which caused Tony a "the game is up" moment until Jaime signaled his would be accepted; then they waited twenty-three minutes for the documents to be validated.

With an escort, they were led into a cavernous room, built to house Saudi military aircraft, now filled with fifty-five rows of what looked like silver hot-water heaters, each four meters high. There was a slight background noise, similar to a room air conditioner. Tony could see a half-dozen men in white maintenance suits with green stitching monitoring the instrumentation on each device and recording it in a hand-held electronic wand.

Following a list held by Jaime, they moved to the first device necessitating their attention. At station 47-EG Jaime and Jamal verified that the equipment was not operating and had been disconnected from its electrical source. Applying the rudimentary instruction he had received in the office, Tony unscrewed the front panel, carefully slid the vacuum tube through the opening, and placed it on a ceramic-covered workbench. With the confidence of one who did this for a living, he removed a cigarette pack–sized container from the tube, appeared to inspect it with meticulous attention, replaced it with a similar packet from the wooden box, then reinserted the tube and reattached the cover.

For five hours the two Gulf technicians and Tony repeated this process in multiple variations eighteen times. As Jaime made the required notations on the final individual log, and with their wooden boxes now filled with metallurgical items to be returned to the Dubai headquarters for rehabilitation, they went through an exit clearance.

"You do this every day?" Tony asked Jamal, now seated in his original rear position in the Land Rover.

"Three or four times a week, but this was a new experience gaining access to the hanger, and we've got another assignment for tomorrow. Will you be with us?"

"Yes. What will we be doing?"

"I think it has something to do with shipping materials. I do know we will be making a delivery to the military side of the King Abdulaziz Airport."

"Can I ask some questions now?"

"Shoot."

"What in the hell were we doing in there?"

"The last stage of nuclear enrichment. As you probably know, in its natural state uranium is enriched at between three and five percent. To be optimally useful for a bomb, it should be eighty-five to ninety. Those machines, the centrifuges, do the job. You just saw 5,185 of them at work, plus the 19 disabled we put back on line."

"How much of the strong stuff can they spit out?"

"When all of them are at peak, about ten kilograms per month. The ministry is holding about four hundred kilograms, enough for six bombs. Tomorrow will be the first time to my knowledge any of it has been relocated."

"Where is it going?"

"That's what we may find out tomorrow," Jaime replied as they turned off the highway to Gulf Engineering's office.

Tony had to make a call. He went into the men's restroom—what he determined was a secure facility, due in large part to the wrenching odor from the open toilet hole. He began to breathe in gulps through his mouth.

He dialed Laura's London apartment.

"Ms. Billington, please."

He was greeted with a pert and officious female voice.

"I am sorry to inform you that Ms. Billington left for the midday flight to Jeddah over three hours ago. I suspect she has departed. May I take a message?"

Skipping the question, Tony asked, "Do you know when she will arrive in Jeddah?"

"Might I inquire, who are you?"

"Tony Ramos, a friend of Ms. Billington and her late father."

"Oh yes, she was expecting your call before she left. Ms. Billington was disconcerted she had not heard from you."

"When will Ms. Billington's flight get to Jeddah?"

"Eleven-fifteen this evening."

"And where may I ask is she staying?"

"Mr. Ramos, you know that is a question I cannot answer."

"Thank you," with one last gulp of air through his mouth followed by a three-blow sneeze, Tony returned to the main office.

With an understanding to meet at the Gulf Engineering headquarters at 8:15 the following morning and an offer to be dropped off and picked up at the hotel, Tony gathered his wrinkled clothing and walked to the Land Rover.

SEPTEMBER 9–10
Jeddah

Having napped, showered, and shaved, Tony was in the best condition his circumstances would allow as he waited for British Air 1104 at the main terminal of the King Abdulaziz Airport shortly before eleven. When the 767 was parked at its gate, he observed through the airport's glass wall a limousine waiting at the front exit ramp. Laura and five people Tony did not recognize, and a sixth he did, got off the aircraft and entered the Bentley. He watched as it drove to the VIP arrival terminal. He walked the half mile to the exquisitely fitted palace used solely at the invitation of the king for royalty and foreign dignitaries.

Laura noticed him as she stood on the curbside, having completed the always turgid passport process. When Tony was within earshot, she called over, "Where in the hell were you this morning? I waited two hours for your call and almost missed this flight."

Now standing close, Tony explained: "I was on a mission of high importance. I'll give you the specifics later when we're under more accommodating circumstances," and he rotated his head at the persons nearby who were listening to their overheated conversation.

"I'll call you at six in the morning. And I won't be late. Where do I call?"

Laura snapped, "The Imperial, and make it at five."

Concerned he might fail Laura again and with only four hours sleep available, Tony set his Casio alarm and a travel clock and asked the hotel for a 4:50 wake-up call. At the precise strike of 5:00 he called.

"Laura, Tony."

She got right to the point. "What do you want me to do in Jeddah?"

"Four things," he answered her in kind. "From what I learned, there's a lot of smoke around the kingdom working to get the bomb. I need second-source verification. See what you can find out. Is it happening, how far along are they, who knows about it, what are the Saudis' intentions, if and when they get it?"

"Second, there have been alleged sightings of bin Laden or a surrogate in Jeddah. Try to confirm these, and if true, why is he here?"

"That will be an interesting challenge. Do you think he'll invite me to take his photograph in the cave?"

Tony didn't respond. "Third, there is an organization based in Jeddah called the Golden Chain."

"If that's an upscale jewelry salon, Jeddah may be more interesting than I thought."

"Not quite. It's made up of superwealthy Saudis who have been giving support to 'traditional values' and bin Laden. What I was up to yesterday may have had its fingerprints. The Golden Chain is supposed to be involved with science projects at a new university. Whatever . . . See what you can find out.

"Finally, the thing that has most confounded me is overreaction to your father. It's reasonable to expect the Saudis were pissed at him for always ripping their drawers, but outright murder is way over the top. Did he know something more than he let on? Remember that op-ed in the *Times*? Was he just fantasizing, or had he stumbled onto a plot he never disclosed? Was this the reason for his premonition and preparations for his own death?"

"So how do you propose for me to get all this?" Laura stuttered.

"Remember what I told you; it's just old-fashioned spy craft: identify someone on the inside and convince him to give or get you the information you want. But it *is* dangerous. If you want to reconsider, now's the time."

"Tony," she stammered, "remember—remember what I told you in Tallahassee. I want to help find the bastards who killed my father."

"Don't do anything stupid. Even if you follow my precautions, I can't write an insurance policy, but your odds will be a damn sight better. Any other questions?" Tony waited; no answer.

Jamal collected Tony and his overnight travel bag at 8:00. By 8:30, with Jaime, they were on their way back to the Price Sultan Research Center, this time in a four-door Toyota flatbed truck. Again, they were subjected to gate and entrance clearance. Tony had erroneously thought that since they had been through this less than twenty-two hours earlier, it would be less intrusive. To the contrary, it was more so, and when Tony was required to complete a form with additional information on his security status, he thought his short tenure as a metallurgical technician might be coming to an end, along with his freedom or life.

But what he came up with was enough to get all three cleared. This time they were led out of the hanger and around to the rear loading dock.

On a pinewood pallet sat five canisters that looked to Tony like kegs at a Georgetown undergraduate beer blast, though they did not have a tap or a Bud or Miller's designation. Rather, painted pea green, a thermometer-like tube filled with an almond-colored liquid was attached at the top and bottom of each canister.

Jamal and Jaime inspected the canisters with an instrument that emitted a clicking sound. Tony gave enough serious attention and support to avoid being suspicious. Inspections completed, the canisters were placed in plastic containers protected by four-inch-thick padding. The pallet and canisters were gently lifted onto the rear of the Toyota, where they were firmly secured and covered with a tarpaulin held in place by steel rope straps.

In less than an hour the truck was backing into a ramp at the military cargo bay at King Abdulaziz. An air force colonel inspected the containers and attached transit documents to each. He directed the Gulf Engineering employees to deliver them to a Dessault Falcon waiting on the tarmac.

As he placed the five plastic containers on the diagonal conveyor belt that would lift them into the cargo hold, Tony discreetly glanced at the manifest. The destination: Quetta, Islamic Republic of Pakistan.

As they returned to the military-side parking area, they noticed a Nissan with the insignia of the Saudi Ministry of Interior parked in front of and perpendicular to the Toyota. Two men waited, their dark-haired arms casually resting on the automobile's open window frames. Tony thought the one in the passenger seat looked familiar.

Jaime leaned over the driver, "Excuse me, officer, but that's our truck and we've got to take it to the next job."

The men emerged and stood by the left front fender. Dressed in the olive drab uniforms of the ministry with sleeves rolled above the elbow, both possessed biceps toned in the gym and guts betraying equal fidelity to the food table.

The taller turned toward Tony. "And, as I asked you yesterday, who are you?"

Although yesterday he had been in the Royal Army fatigues, Tony recognized him as the master sergeant at the entrance gate who had questioned his nationality. "Yemeni," he answered, for the second time.

"I don't think so. There is no Khalid Khoury of Yemeni ancestry registered in the employ of Gulf Engineering."

"There must be some mistake," Jaime asserted. "He is recently in the kingdom; he relocated from the UAE precisely so his special skills could be at the service of the king."

"Lying bastard," the tall man lashed out, unholstering his Luger. "Justin," he ordered, pointing the handgun at his subordinate, "you herd those two in the truck; that one drives—you know, the gimp—and you, Khalid," he said with a smirk, "in the back. You keep 'em under your gun and don't be weak-kneed about using it."

He turned to Jaime. "Get your ass in the driver's seat of our car and don't give me an excuse to send you to Allah."

With all in their assigned places, the faux sergeant kept his dark steel weapon aimed at Jaime's hairline as he directed the Toyota to lead to the central office of the Ministry of Interior.

The truck, followed by the Nissan, pulled out of King Abdulaziz onto the main highway headed south. In the Toyota the men sat silently as it entered the heavy midmorning traffic. The open windows allowed the thick layer of petroleum discharge to invade the cabin. Tony leaned forward, his head touching the back of the seat. His hands dangled beneath him as he unloosened the rawhide shoestrings on his workman's boots. Justin glowered and swung his weapon so it pointed at Tony's left eye. The truck jolted as Jamal jerked toward the curb to open a space for a petroleum tanker. The move momentarily alarmed and distracted Justin. "Foreign slime, can't you keep this pile of shit on the road? It won't be long before you won't be able to keep your head connected to . . . " Those were Justin's last words. With the wrist control of a drop shot at the net, Tony looped the double band of laces over the man's head and around his neck. A sharp crack preceded an instant protrusion from the back of Justin's neck just below the back panel of his ministry cap, which Tony, from his training in close combat, recognized as the second cervical vertebra. He gurgled as he slumped down. The cap tumbled from his head to the floorboard.

Seeing a commercial road to the left, Tony barked at Jamal to take it. With the gravitational force of a roller coaster, the right-side wheels off the pavement, he executed the turn. The turn completed, the Toyota slammed onto the asphalt. The force caused Tony's single travel bag to bang into his chest. He unsnapped the locks and removed his Black-Berry and a black plastic box that shielded the Glock.

The Nissan reacted to what was occurring ahead with an even more harrowing swerve. Over the noise of the wind swirl and traffic, Tony could hear the tall man cursing and berating Jaime to overtake the truck. "Jamal, stay in the right lane and let them close the gap," Tony directed before assuming a horizontal position, his head against the left rear door.

By the external noise, punctuated by the sergeant's booming and profane voice, Tony judged the vehicles were parallel. He eased to the base of the window and fired two shots at point-blank range into the sergeant's ear. A trickle of blood flowed over his jaw. Looking to the rear,

Tony saw no sign that the altercations had drawn attention. He told Jamal to continue driving to the west, stay within the speed limit, and avoid attracting notice.

Tony punched in Jonathan Rizzo's number. Speaking in agitated Arabic, he barked, "We're in a hell of a situation, but may just have a chance of coming out alive."

"Tony," Jonathan's voice was uneven, with sound dropping out. "I'm having a hard time making you out. Tell me what you want me to do, and say it in English."

"I'm with the NOCs, who have earned their keep today. We're in two vehicles on road 25A north of Jeddah, and for starters need a place to get off the road and out of sight."

"We have a safe house. It's more a safe cow barn, about twenty-five kilometers from where I think you are. Stay on the line and I'll talk you in."

Tony relayed Jonathan's instructions and turned and waved for Jaime to follow. Satisfied they were headed in the right direction, Tony continued. "Jonathan, the three of us have got to get the hell out of this place as fast and as unnoticed as possible. I can't abandon these guys or they'll be the next on the execution block."

"The agency keeps a Lear Jet with long legs based undercover at Il Kani airport. I could have it there thirty minutes after nightfall with enough fuel to drop them in Dubai and take you to KL."

"Sounds OK, but I don't feel comfortable trying to hide out in the barn all afternoon. I imagine when the big kahunas find two of their men and a vehicle missing, it'll be an all-hands-on-deck manhunt."

"I'll see what I can do. Wait at the barn for further info."

Tony jumped out and rolled back the wooden barn door. The stench of decaying cow manure was intense. After parking their vehicles at the far end of the barn, the three did a quick search. The source of the foul odor was banked against the north outside wall. Jamal located the toolshed and extracted two snow removal–type stubby shovels. He and

Jaime burrowed a hole in the dark-brown pile while Tony removed the two bodies from the truck and Nissan. He dragged both, Justin first, by the feet into the now adequately sized pit, which was then re-covered. "This violates just about every burial tenet of the faith," Jamal observed, "but at least they won't be cold."

Tony walked through the pasture that had once been home to the bovines. Their water source was now a green scum–covered mud hole hidden four meters below the field's surface. With a fallen and forlorn tree limb he found, he probed the scum and determined the hole was at least five meters deep.

Approaching from the north over a tree line, Tony heard the thump-thump-thump of a helicopter. Flattened against the far side of a date palm, Tony saw the black Sikorsky circle the field, hover over the barn, bank, and continue south.

In fifteen minutes the pounding of the helicopter was replaced by the high whine of the Nissan. With Jaime at the wheel gunning the engine to full throttle before releasing the brakes for a fifty-meter spurt, the vehicle flew over the edge and at a thirty-degree angle disappeared into the sludge of the mud hole. Jaime emerged exhilarated at the experience, soaked in cow shit. The Nissan released its last bubbles to the surface.

As Jamal hosed Jaime down from the barnyard faucet, Tony called Rizzo.

"OK," he said, "it's 1615 and you're an hour from Il Kani. I'll have the Lear Jet there at 1730 with hot engines. Come directly to planeside and load on. Any questions?"

"We won't be late. Thanks, I owe you a big one."

It was 1727 when the Toyota, with Jamal at the wheel and Tony and Jaime riding shotgun at the two rear windows, rolled through the unmanned entrance to Il Kani, another abandoned military air base. The white with blue trim Lear was touching down at the far end of the field. Jamal bumped over the neglected runway toward what he estimated would be the loading site.

The aircraft decelerated at the far end, turned 180 degrees, and halted. The three were fixated on the descending passenger ramp as the first burst of automatic weapon fire shredded the asphalt behind the left front tire. Tony and Jaime returned fire with their underwhelming handguns.

Closing on the Lear, Jamal spun the truck in front of the aircraft so it would not be in the line of gunfire from the rapidly approaching Hummer. "Get out with whatever you've got to take and run like hell," he commanded. Following Jamal's mandate, in a squat sprint Tony and Jaime reached the ramp.

With less than thirty meters separating them, Jamal jammed the gas pedal and surged the Toyota toward the Hummer. The incoming machine-gun fusillade turned exclusively to the truck, shattering its front windscreen and strewing jagged glass over the hood and front seat. In less than two seconds the Hummer and Toyota collided nose to nose.

As Jaime took the first step up the narrow stairs, a fireball erupted upward and the windblast shook the Lear Jet. The aircraft was rolling forward when Tony glanced in horror at the clouds of fire rising from the vehicles, now totally engulfed in flame. The Lear rocked as it struggled to reach critical airspeed. At six hundred feet, the plane turning to the east, Tony looked for the last time as the two vehicles exploded in an orange blast.

SEPTEMBER 10
Jeddah

Laura Billington was assisted into the van by Jason, the newest member of her crew. Bringing on the retired MI5 agent was the first of Tony's precautions to protect her. With the driver and Walid, the assigned royal aide, Laura and her entourage left the Imperial Hotel by the sun's first rays for the twenty-minute drive from the Biblical Jeddah walls, through the new portside city, to the King Saud Bridge. As part of a massive reclamation project to create a deepwater port by extending the natural shoreline farther into the Red Sea, two isolated islands to-taling about fifty acres were created. The summer palace is connected to the shore by a three-hundred-foot-long grand boulevard planted in an allée of giant date palms. At the portal points and intersections were elaborate inlaid stone designs of khatim, eight-pointed stars represent-ing the seals of the prophets.

The palace was aesthetically subordinate to the elegant gardens. In the Arabic tradition, fountains and constantly flowing water—the Is-lamic symbol of purity and provider of a cool oasis in the sweltering heat—were the most conspicuous features. The garden was integrated with meandering paths framed by plants, shrubbery, and shade trees. Laura, in a demure headscarf and black abaya, spent two hours in it as-sessing possible exterior locations for the royal portrait. Walid assisted with suggestions and the placement of the lights and equipment.

It was ten o'clock, with the temperature topping one hundred, when Walid invited Laura and her associates to enter the palace. They passed through the foyer, which was decorated to mimic an ornate Bedouin desert tent, skirted a small anteroom where four women wearing black burkas were conversing, and finally entered a previously male-only waiting room. Walid excused himself.

The room had a twenty-foot ceiling. Several men were standing, with a few more slouched against the wall, resting on colorful pillows. After ninety more minutes of waiting, a palace functionary arrived with documents to be filled out.

"We are here at the invitation of the king," Laura declared. "Could you determine when we will be permitted to continue the preparation for our work?"

"It will be when it pleases the king, madam. He will inform me when that time has arrived." He turned his back to Laura and exited through a wooden double door.

She thought back to another of Tony's warnings: *The Saudis are ultrasexists.*

Her tedium was relieved by the increasing number of men in white cotton robes and sandals who filled the waiting room. Although unable to understand Arabic, Laura could tell by body language and response that the dismissive treatment she was experiencing was standard.

One man caught her attention. Surrounded by a circulating audience of attentive acolytes, he seemed vaguely and strangely familiar. Almost a head taller than any of the others and clean-shaven, he listened closely before responding in soft, short declarations. The same functionary who had delivered Laura's paperwork appeared, rising on his toes to whisper in the tall man's ear. Together they strode toward the waiting room's rear exit. Laura noticed with interest that one of the four women fell in behind the tall man as they disappeared into an adjoining chamber.

There was another man, perhaps about her own age (she found it difficult to assess the chronology of Arab males). Through his thick, gold-rimmed bifocals, he appeared to notice her and crossed the room. He wore the uniform white cotton robe, sandals, and black-and-white patterned headdress. He approached Laura, careful not to make any contact.

"Madame," he said, "could you be Ms. Billington of London?"

"I am," she replied.

"If I may introduce myself, my name is Zaid al Swainee, a grandson of King Khalid Ibn Abdul Aziz. The family is most pleased you have offered to photograph His Highness. We have seen your work, most recently the portrait of Queen Elizabeth. You are very talented."

"I am most appreciative of your observations. It was an honor to receive the invitation of His Highness. Few have the distinction of being in his presence. It had been my intention to assist in my minor way to allow the world a deeper appreciation of his essence."

"Had been?" Zaid asked, removing his glasses.

Laura nodded, feigning great sadness.

"What could have dissuaded you? You have come so far."

"Your Royal Highness, with my colleagues, I have been waiting for four hours. Other than the drudgery of forms, we have had no hospitality extended. Our time is valuable; we have come at the king's solicitation. Apparently we will not be received and thus are preparing to return to our hotel and take the evening flight to London."

"Madame, please desist while I determine your status. Will you give me that opportunity?"

"Yes, but not for long."

Twenty minutes passed. Zaid returned. "The Steward of the Two Noble Sanctuaries has had an unexpected conference which necessitates that your work be delayed until tomorrow at ten. I regret this inconvenience and would be honored at the opportunity to show you our city and share dinner."

"Are you confident tomorrow will not be a repetition of today?"

"May Allah strike me down if it were not true. I have arranged for your colleagues to leave their equipment and I will guarantee its safety. At your convenience we can leave."

Zaid held open the door of a red Alfa Romeo convertible for Laura. Leaving the shoreside end of the King Saud Bridge, he turned toward the corniche that paralleled the Red Sea and the modern buildings of the new Jeddah. In the next two hours, with the convertible's roof down and the gentle wind blowing through her hair, Zaid introduced Laura to one of the world's most fabled and ancient cities. The tour concluded as Zaid eased the Alfa into the entrance of the Imperial Hotel.

At twelve stories, it was a fusion of traditional and European design and materials. Designed by the same French architect who had overseen the restoration of important holy sites in the kingdom, its exterior was clad in local sandstone highlighted by mandarin marble.

Leaving the convertible with a valet, Zaid assisted Laura into the Imperial's lobby, which was dominated by an oasis pool surrounded by date palms. In a private parlor adjacent to but screened from the public lounge, he joined her on a burgundy leather couch and ordered a Maker's Mark for her and a scotch and water for himself. As he finished his second glass, he said, "It was a personal honor to be with you and share a fresh vision of my city through your aesthetic eyes. When one spends much of his life in one place, there is a tendency to become numb to the details."

It was time to press her advantage. "Zaid," Laura said, moving closer to him. "It is a handsome city and you bring its history and culture to life. But, I, I would like to know more about you. What is it like to be the grandson of one of the most powerful men in the world?"

"I'm a long way from the king. My father is the fifth of seven sons, and I am the twenty-third grandson in succession. Whatever my capabilities, I will never be king, will never be a serious member of the kingdom's leadership. I am approaching forty and still awaiting my first assignment. Last week I was told that the position I had sought, ambassador to Singapore, was going to another, younger grandson."

Laura placed her hand on his, mentally calculating the effect she was having.

"I am confident," he continued, "that I can be successful, but the opportunity to demonstrate that is slipping away. Sometimes I feel trapped." He had finished his third scotch when he said, "I wish I had your freedom."

"Freedom always seems more appealing from afar," Laura said. "There is an American country song that says, 'Freedom's just another word for nothing left to lose.' Your access to the innermost secrets of the kingdom would be only a dream for me. I can record the powerful, but only at a distance, and am sometimes treated with the disdain you observed."

Zaid ordered another round. Laura declined, motioning to her still half-filled glass. "Zaid, you are too modest. Tell me about yourself, your experiences, what one can learn living on the inside of the most powerful monarchy in the world."

He dropped his head and lifted it upward, smiling. "I have had some, but my experiences with women have been limited, especially women of your status. I want you to overcome the bitterness caused by your treatment earlier today. If my insights on the royal court would contribute to that, I will be as open as discretion will permit, but please interrupt if I become boring."

Laura lifted the amber tumbler from the waiter's tray, placing it in his hand. "Zaid, your courtesies and candor have erased any ill feeling. Your charm is mesmerizing. The least of my concerns is that you will become a bore. Please tell me more." Yes, she was having the desired effect.

Leaning back, he sipped from his fourth scotch. "I mentioned in the car the time when Americans came to meet with the king. The Persian Gulf War had just ended. It had been a great fright to the family; without help from America the Iraqis could have overwhelmed our kingdom. You would have thought the king would have been appreciative, gracious. Rather, he was afire with scorn and indignation."

"I remember that period as a teenager," Laura said. "What was the reason for the king's anger?"

"He confronted the Americans with the information our agents in Baghdad had uncovered. Saddam Hussein was within a few months of completing a nuclear weapons program, and the Americans, without our knowledge, certainly without our consent, had been assisting him for seven years."

"Assisting Saddam? How?"

"By the fourth year the war against Iran was going badly for Iraq. Saddam was deploying chemical weapons against the waves of Iranian troops invading his country, and also against the Kurds and other internal rebels. An envoy from your country told the Iraqis America might reconsider and soften its policy against providing dual-use materials."

"What does 'dual use' mean?"

"Items that have a commercial use but could also be utilized militarily, like parts for industrial or medical application, but that can be used in electronic isotope separators or centrifuges—critical technologies for speeding up the production of highly enriched uranium. Saddam was desperate to do so, and with assistance from your country, he did." Zaid took a drink of his scotch.

"Saddam thought this would turn the tide of war, either by actually using nuclear weapons or just the Iranians' awareness that he had that capability. Only Saddam's stupid invasion of Kuwait and humiliating defeat kept him from realizing his goal. I was a young man. I will never forget the king's outrage at your country's perfidy. But . . . "

Laura looked at him quizzically. "Our relations today, even after the events of 9/11, seem to be as strong as they were at the end of World War II. How was His Royal Highness placated?"

Zaid called the waiter and ordered another scotch. "My English is not the best, so I am not sure of the word 'placated.' He gave the Americans the challenge of providing to our kingdom the same level of assistance it had extended to Saddam."

"The same assistance?" Laura said as she stiffened. "The king knows us well enough to understand that no American official would consider such a proposal. It would be contrary to our treaty commitments and a rank betrayal of Israel."

"That's what I remember the Americans saying. But the king asked them to explain why those same restraints had not kept them from assisting Saddam. There was no answer."

The drink was poured and glasses clinked before Zaid continued. "The Americans withdrew with assurances they would return with an answer to the king's demand."

"So?" Laura left her question dangling.

Zaid moved to close the remaining space between them. "Why don't we have dinner in your suite, where we can continue in the privacy this topic requires?"

"I would like that," Laura said with a sultry smile. Zaid drained his glass.

From the balcony of the twelfth-floor penthouse, Jeddah spread out before them. The bright lights of the city center escalated toward the south and the new portside sector, dimmed to candle strength toward the traditional neighborhoods at the foothills, and faded to black in the mountains beyond. The salt-tinged breeze off the Red Sea had a bite of fall. Laura suggested they return to the living room and commence dinner.

Zaid lifted a Leica from the penthouse coffee table. Rotating the camera to observe all the functions, he asked Laura, "Could you show me how to use this?"

"Certainly. This is not what I will be using tomorrow. I keep the Leica nearby for unexpected opportunities. We will start the lesson after dinner."

Zaid nodded with pleasure.

After lentil shurba and an assortment of Arabian appetizers, the main course of grilled lamb was served. Zaid resumed his recollections. "In about a month the Americans returned. I was not allowed into this meeting, but my older brother described it to me. The Americans said they would honor the king's request for assistance, but there would be conditions. The king would commit to keep any weapons or materials secure, and none would be removed from the king's personal control without the explicit approval of the Americans. The Americans de-manded that this, this—what would I call it, partnership? Yes, partner-ship would not be disclosed to any parties—the king committing to protect the secrecy of the program in the kingdom and the Americans in your country."

As the plates were being removed, Laura inquired, "Were there other conditions?"

Zaid leaned back in his stately chair. "I fear this is all becoming very tedious. You had indicated after dinner there might be a beginner's les-son in photography from the ultimate professor. Could we commence?"

"As you wish, Your Highness," she said rising. "You are so fascinating. I have spent my life freezing life and its emotions. You breathe life into them. I want to hear every detail—but after I have had the honor of in-troducing you to what has meant so much in my life. Before doing so I ask your indulgence if I slip out of these work clothes."

Zaid nodded assent and Laura disappeared into her bedroom.

In ten minutes she returned in a rose-blush shimmering silk robe, loosened to expose her breasts to the edge of the nipple. She was pre-ceded by the seductive fragrance of Dior's J'adore. Folding both legs under her, Laura eased into the lushly pillowed sofa, gesturing Zaid to her side.

She instructed him on the basics of shutter adjustment, lighting, and framing the subject. "The best instructor," Laura said, "is actual expe-rience. I will be your model."

He grasped the camera firmly and pointed the lens at Laura.

As each set of frames was completed, Laura rotated to emphasize the variety of her allures: her facial features, careful to provide maximum exposure to what she considered to be her more seductive, right side; stretching full length, delicately lifting her gown to expose her thighs.

"You are so thoughtful and such a gifted student. You caress the camera as you would a beautiful woman. Would it interfere, if I were to ask a few more questions drawing on your personal reservoir of experiences?"

"Of course not, if my esteemed teacher will allow me to complete her first assignment while I respond."

As Laura settled herself in another pose, she asked again, "Were there any other conditions on the partnership between the king and the Americans?"

"There were other conditions. My brother described the king as distraught with the Americans' demand that the kingdom pay them, through a banking scheme to be devised, what amounted to more than three billion pounds, to be paid in less than two years. Remember the prewar price of oil had been less than twenty dollars a barrel. Three billion pounds, even for His Highness, was a staggering sum."

Laura rotated her pelvis and thrust her hip at the camera. The pace of Zaid's photo snapping accelerated. The tension within him between the provocative woman and his recitation of history produced thinness in his voice.

"When the king objected, the Americans said they knew of funds the kingdom was receiving from another source that would easily cover their demand."

"What did the king say?" Laura asked as she posed for what would be the final scene, a nonchalant declension of her décolletage to uncover her left breast.

After the final exposure, Zaid turned his head toward the balcony, gathered himself, and continued. "He was reticent, questioning whether the Americans could maintain confidentiality with funds of this magnitude flowing into their treasury in a matter of months. The American my brother described as having an accent from your South, assured His Highness these payments would not be publicly accounted for; they would be held in a private trust. My brother told me neither side wanted to put the partnership in writing, so they shook hands and pledged their honor to the completion of the transaction."

Laura re-covered herself, bringing her knees together hard against her abdomen. "And was it, the partnership, consummated?" She emphasized the last word.

Stretching to return the Leica to its original position, Zaid said, "My dear, I fear you have moved from past history to current actions of the king. That is a place I cannot go."

Laura's lips curled into a pout. She intercepted Zaid's now empty but still extended hand and placed it over her left breast. "I thought our new attachment was going so well, with much more to come. Now that you have ended our photographic seminar, is that the end of the evening?"

Zaid moved his hand to the loose knot that held her robe in place and pulled.

With her right hand Laura fended him off while with her left she struggled to hold her robe together. Flirtatiously melding her born southern and acquired aristocratic voices, Laura said, "Zaid, you are a very handsome and intelligent man and, beginning this evening, a promising photographer, with me as your model and muse. I want to know you better."

Zaid released his hold as she continued, "But I am tired, and tomorrow I will have to be at my best for the session with your grandfather and the family. I will be staying over until noon on Friday. Could we continue your intriguing recollections tomorrow evening and conclude the fascinating suspense story you have spun for me thus far?"

Zaid nuzzled her neck, which Laura interpreted as a yes.

"And, Zaid, add to those treats the first viewing of your photographic talents. With your permission we might explore undiscovered regions of your artistic potential. I will be more alert with a good night's sleep and my mission to His Majesty complete."

She rose, taking Zaid's hand lightly, and led him to the door. He took her in his arms and with scotch-tinged words said, "I am disappointed that we cannot deepen our friendship here, tonight. But I am gratified that you have come and will respect your wishes. Tomorrow evening will be special for me, and I hope for you as well."

He tightened his embrace and lingered over a strong kiss on Laura's open lips.

As Zaid was straightening his shirt, Laura arched her neck for a final kiss. "I am also anticipating a very special tomorrow."

She waited until she heard the elevator begin its descent. She returned to the main room and placed a call on her iPhone.

"Mr. Jeralewski, please."

SEPTEMBER 10–11

George Town, Grand Cayman Island

Carol's American Airlines flight arrived from Miami at eleven. The plane was less than half filled, and Owen Roberts International Airport was virtually empty. George Town was as laid back in September as Zermatt was bustling in July.

When she stepped outside the airport, even wearing her stylish Ray-Bans, she had to shield her eyes from the blazing sun. There was no line for the Toyota taxis at the airport. With her overnight and laptop bags in hand, she hailed the nearest of them and directed the driver to the Anglo-Cayman Bank.

Another taxi, occupied and waiting in the short-term parking lot across from the terminal, moved in behind Carol's, far enough away to be hidden by two intervening vehicles, but sufficiently close to maintain visual contact.

Hector Nuñez, an elderly Afro-Caribbean, neatly dressed in a black suit, stiff collar, and narrow sky-blue tie adorned with the Anglo-Cayman emblem, a dolphin rising from the sea, greeted her as she eased from the rear seat.

The occupant in the following taxi noted the time and the description of her host.

"Ms. Watson?" Nuñez said as he nodded respectfully.

"Thank you, yes," she said. "I have an appointment with Mr. Rawls at noon. Would it be possible that you might store my luggage until later in the day?"

Nuñez escorted her into the cool lobby, cleared her with the receptionist, offered a seat on a tropical upholstered sofa, and left with Carol's bags. After ten minutes, Carol noticed that she and the receptionist were the only persons in the lobby. No one else had entered or exited during her wait. At noon she was told that Mr. Rawls would meet her in the third-floor conference room.

Mr. Rawls, shoulders moderately stooped from his six-foot height and looking every one of his sixty-two years, was standing by the elevator door. He welcomed Carol in a thick Scottish accent and led her to a spacious conference room overlooking the harbor.

"Ms. Watson, we are honored by your presence. Our friends in Zurich have alerted us to your inquiries there, and I hope we have the information you are seeking."

"It's pretty straightforward," she replied. "On the instructions of my government, I am auditing a flow of funds that reached your institution from October of 1991 to October of 1992. From the records at Zurich-Alliance, Anglo-Cayman received substantial transfers during that thirteen-month period. I am tasked to determine the subsequent disposition of those funds from your bank."

Rawls motioned Carol to a corner seat and took the chair at the head of the table. With a noticeable quiver calling greater attention to his accent, he explained, "That was the period in which we were converting and automating our systems. I fear there are some gaps, such as records and data transitioned to our main office in London and not fully retrieved." Reaching into his briefcase, he handed her a mixed stack of computer-generated spreadsheets and manual ledgers. "I hope you will find what you desire in these. Would you care for lunch while you are reviewing these documents?"

"Very thoughtful, thanks. A chicken or turkey sandwich with unsweetened ice tea would be fine."

Rising to depart, Rawls said, "This room is yours as long as you care to use it. I can be reached at extension 308."

It took less than an hour for Carol to eat her lunch and reprise her first-day reactions in Zurich. What she had been given was the counterpart of the disbursements from Zurich-Alliance to Anglo-Cayman, but no new information.

She was still stuck only one step beyond what the British Serious Fraud investigators had found and the *Guardian* disclosed. Carol dialed extension 308. "Mr. Rawls, I need to speak with you as soon as possible."

Looking more earnest than at noon, Rawls entered the office. Carol explained that what she had been provided did not advance her inquiry.

"I regret your displeasure." Rawls apologized. "The records you are seeking must be among those missing. I will contact our office in London. Unfortunately, as it is now almost eight in the evening there, it will be tomorrow before our colleagues can commence the search."

"Mr. Rawls, in all honesty, I am more than displeased," Carol declared in an edged southern accent. "This bank has known for more than three weeks what I wanted to review; clearance had been granted by your executives in London. This is a matter of extreme urgency, and my government will be highly disappointed that your institution is so unprepared to be responsive."

Carol withheld what she knew, that 250 million British pounds would be an enormous transaction for Anglo-Cayman, requiring the knowledge and approval of the highest echelons of the bank in London and the Caymans. Mr. Rawls was lying.

"Ms. Watson, I apologize for any inconvenience. We who represent the Queen's interest in the remainder of the colonial empire strive to maintain the highest standards. I will beseech the London office to expedite your request and will urge clearance from the Foreign and Commonwealth Office be facilitated."

"Why is that a concern?" Carol asked.

"From your first inquiry in August, we recognized the sensitivity of your request and have kept our colonial ministers advised. Certainly you and your government can appreciate the appropriateness, no, the necessity of doing so."

"I can't, and doubt that my superiors at Justice or the Treasury will be very understanding." Folding the papers Rawls had given her, Carol rose. "I'll be back at 8:30 in the morning and trust you will have more and positive information from London."

An hour later, in her room at the Grand Cayman Marriott Beach Resort, Carol received a call.

"Ms. Watson, this is Hector Nuñez. I need to talk with you."

"Why, Mr. Nuñez?"

"Mr. Rawls did not tell you the whole truth."

"What do you mean by that?"

"The documents you came to audit are in the bank, but not in the files Mr. Rawls gave to you. I know where they are located."

"How do you know this?"

"It will be better for all if we say no more on that subject."

"Can we meet tonight?"

"Come at nine this evening to the parking lot across from the hotel, next to the Stern's Jewelry. I'll be waiting in a white Hyundai Sonata."

"I'll be there at nine," Carol confirmed.

As Nuñez disconnected she heard a slight hum in the background.

She arrived ten minutes early and, not seeing a white Sonata, slipped into Stern's. As she entered she noticed a man step behind a curtain in the rear of the elegant store. All that could be seen of him was two large and squat feet strapped in sandals covered with sand.

Carol couldn't enjoy browsing at the upscale store. She could not concentrate on the bracelet she was considering for Suzie as she furtively and repeatedly glanced at the curtain. The sandaled man was now seated with his hairy, heavy legs exposed to midcalf.

At nine, through the pane of glass separating the store from the sidewalk, she saw the headlights of a sedan that fit Nuñez's description. She walked to the passenger's side. Nuñez motioned for her to enter.

He couldn't avoid noticing Carol's distress. "Ms. Watson, is there something bothering you?"

Carol nibbled at her lower lip. "There was a man at Stern's who looked eerily familiar. As soon as I came through the door he slipped into one of the cubicles where they show the really expensive jewelry. He was still sitting there when I left."

Nuñez consoled her: "He was probably just one of those rich Americans picking out something for his girlfriend."

Carol wasn't convinced but wanted to put the concern behind her. As Hector pulled out of the lot, she asked him why he had offered his assistance.

"First, as an internal auditor of the bank I have had access to the email traffic surrounding your arrival. In one of the bank's communiqués with the Home Ministry, a Mr. Tony Ramos, formerly of Guanabacoa, Cuba, was stated to be your—in English I think you would say your colleague in this inquiry. That name was familiar, so I checked further and determined he was the grandson of an old friend from our hometown."

"How was that?" Carol asked.

"I am also from Guanabacoa. Mr. Ramos's grandfather and I played baseball together. During the war, when it was hard for American teams to fill their rosters, they picked up some Afro-Cuban players. His grandfather and I were two of those. We played a season and a half with the Kansas City Monarchs of the Negro National League. You become close far from home."

"And how did you get from Guanabacoa to here?"

"After I quit playing baseball, I went to work at a bank. I started as a cashier, and after a few years I was the head teller, and then Fidel came. Most of my friends, like the Ramos family, went north to Miami. And after the Bay of Pigs, I decided to go south where I thought I could find a better job, and have been in the Caymans and at this bank for over forty-five years."

"Mr. Nuñez, that is a very uplifting personal story, but I'm still not sure why you took the risk of helping me."

"Ms. Watson, I don't like women to be made to seem inferior."

"And was that happening to me?"

"Indeed. I know you work for the U.S. Treasury and used to be at Price Waterhouse, so you must be very smart. I know what it takes to be a bank auditor, and I don't think a bank officer would have tried to deceive a man the way you were treated." Nuñez maneuvered the Sonata into a parking space behind Anglo-Cayman in an otherwise empty lot. "I'll show you how that was later."

He held Carol's door as she eased from the car. Nuñez had the codes to open the rear door of the bank. He introduced Carol as the new auditor to the drowsy security officer, Granville Meldrum, who nodded and dropped back to sleep.

Nuñez led Carol down a flight of stairs into the back office of the bank, where the courtesies and amenities of the executive suites were converted into profitable business. He opened a final set of electronically secured double doors, exposing a file room no more than thirty feet square. "This is where the information you have come for is kept. These are Anglo-Cayman's special clients' files."

From a shelf labeled "Diplomatic," Nuñez removed a file notated "Mahmood al-Rasheed" and handed it to Carol. "I'll be back in thirty minutes," he said.

In less than fifteen, Carol discovered that 3.25 billion pounds had come into that account from Zurich-Alliance in the period from October 1991 to October 1992, in increments of 250 million pounds per month. She spent the balance of the time trying to figure out where it had gone. Carol's alternative hypotheses were that BAE's pounds were washed through a British colonial bank to obtain even greater control and confidentiality than a Swiss bank would provide, or the pounds were being spread to additional princes whom al-Rasheed wanted to keep undisclosed.

Her analysis undercut both of those theories. Mahmood al-Rasheed's accounts indicated that each month, within a day of receipt, 2 million pounds were wired to his account at the Riggs Bank in Washington, D.C. The remaining 248 million pounds were sent to a numbered account at the Empire Bank of Commerce in New York City.

When Nuñez returned he was carrying yet another file. This one was titled "Accounts." It contained the names of the holders of the numbered accounts in two dozen banks in Europe and the United States. The account into which 3.224 billion pounds had been transferred was held by the Peninsular Partners.

Realizing she was unlikely to get her hands on this material again, Carol took copious notes. To assure an evidence trail, Nuñez assented to Carol's request to allow her to copy the most significant of the bank records.

It was after eleven when Nuñez returned the files to their original location, leaving no evidence of removal. With a perfunctory nod to Meldrum, Hector and Carol walked toward the Sonata. There was now a second car in the lot.

As Nuñez turned onto Eastern Avenue, the second car followed. Nuñez pushed the gas pedal to ten miles over the speed limit.

"What's the rush?" Carol asked.

"We're being followed."

Carol turned and peered into the high beams of the trailing car. It kept pace until Hector turned into the Marriott's circular drive, whereupon it continued north along the beachfront road.

Standing by the front of the Sonata, Carol asked in a hushed voice, "Who do you think that was?"

"No idea. From the front plates I can tell it was a rental, so it could be almost anybody. I do know you should be very careful. What time is your flight?"

"Five-thirty tomorrow afternoon."

"I suggest you leave as soon as you can," Nuñez advised.

Carol nodded and thanked Hector profusely. "I would have been frustrated and lost without your assistance. I am deeply indebted."

"It is always a pleasure to help a good person. Two requests: Please give Mr. Ramos my best wishes. His namesake was a fine infielder and an even better friend. And be safe."

"I will and look forward to seeing you tomorrow."

"Igualmente."

Carol strode across the tile lobby, waited until there was an empty elevator, ascended to the fifth floor, opened the door to 522, scanned the room, entered, and locked the door behind her with the dead bolt and the chain.

After a restless night, each slightest sound waking her, Carol canceled her plans for a jog down the soft white-sand beach. In her room she ate her accustomed breakfast of orange juice, bran cereal, and coffee, dressed, packed, and was walking through the main door of Anglo-Cayman as it opened at 8:30.

Mr. Rawls was on the other side of the stately entrance. "Ms. Watson, I regret to say we have not heard back from the London office, but I'm sure we will before the end of the business day in London."

Carol smiled. "I appreciate your efforts, but I have all the information I expect to secure and have changed my airline reservation to the eleven-thirty flight to Miami."

Surprised, Rawls continued. "Ms. Watson, please tell your supervisors at the Treasury that we did all within our capacity and the time available."

"I certainly will fully inform them of the level of assistance provided to our inquiry."

Confused by the turn of events, Rawls retreated toward the elevator. Carol stopped him with a final request. "Mr. Nuñez was very gracious during my work at Anglo-Cayman. I would like to express my thanks before leaving."

"I wish that were possible, but Mr. Nuñez has apparently been delayed. It is quite unusual. Punctuality and dedication to duty are two of his many positive characteristics. I will give him your regards when he arrives."

SEPTEMBER 10−11
Kuala Lumpur, Kingdom of Malaysia

On the second leg of the flight from Il Kani to Kuala Lumpur, Tony had concentrated on encrypted cables Jonathan had emailed to his Black-Berry, as well as Billington's memo and his own notes and reflections.

There was sufficient dual-source confirmation now to sustain a strong inference as to the old man's speculations. He was right that the San Diego scheme was managed and supported directly by the Saudi diplomatic and intelligence services. What was in this for the Saudis was not so clear.

Hamza al-Dossari's description of the mid-1990s recruitment and training of future Saudi agents supported Billington's belief that al-Dossari was not the only overseer of Saudi students. And his observation that the agents were now being drawn not from bookkeepers but from the Saudi intelligence corps raised additional questions. What Tony didn't know was whether other 9/11 plotters had received support from Saudi agents similar to that al-Dossari had afforded al-Hazmi and al-Mihdhar. Even more important, was the infrastructure still in place for future use? If so, these trained agents would allow the Saudis to provide assistance to whomever and in whatever form the kingdom would direct.

The secret of U.S involvement in covering up the Saudi role was still that—a secret. It was inexplicable that a president with such an off-the-chart public approval rating as he had after 9/11 would have sheltered the Saudis. Al-Dossari's lament about the clumsiness with which the Saudis' attempt to extricate themselves from suspicion had been staged further obscured their motivation and the president's possible com-plicity. Maybe there would be some answers at this last stop.

Tony reread Senator Billington's memo:

Kuala Lumpur, Kingdom of Malaysia
Chapter One of the 9/11 plot began in Kuala Lumpur. On January
4, 2000, a summit of terrorists was held at a suburban condominium.

Both the plot to attack a U.S. naval vessel, which matured into the
attack on the USS Cole in October of 2000, and 9/11 were prod-
ucts of this summit. The two living people most knowledgeable of the
summit and its aftermath are:

Yazid Sonji—a Malaysian businessman trained there and in
the United States as a microbiologist, and a convert to Muslim
extremism—complied with a request from Osama bin Laden to
make his second home available for the meeting. He was detained
for five years after 9/11 by the Malaysian Interior Ministry at an
undisclosed location, but eventually was released and is now re-
puted to continue his close ties to bin Laden.

Colonel Tan Row was the Malaysian intelligence officer charged
with surveillance of Sonji's condo. He might be the key to explaining
why the Malays and the CIA were unable to gather enough infor-
mation to interdict the plot at its first stage.

———

Tony awoke shortly before seven in his forgettable Kuala Lumpur hotel room, showered, dressed in the seersucker suit that had steamed in the shower overnight, knotted the tie purchased in the Dubai airport duty-free (maroon silk with a pattern of tiny white Indian-style elephants) and left for his first appointment.

In less than fifteen minutes his taxi had arrived at the One Center Tower. Kuala Lumpur was a city of new high-rise office buildings, including the Petronas Towers, which had only recently lost bragging rights as the tallest buildings in the world.

Today was September 11, and as long as he lived, Tony knew he would not be able to banish from his mind the image of those towers much closer to home that once had held those bragging rights. That was the existential, defining moment for his generation. And everything in his professional life, it seemed, was dedicated to stopping that from happening again. *If at all possible.*

Tony took the elevator to the twentieth floor. The door opened to the reception room of Opal Enterprises. He introduced himself to the male attendant and was directed to a sofa facing a picture window with a panoramic view of the city. Whatever its political shortcomings, he thought, no one could be unimpressed by the energy and dynamism of the place Noel Coward once lampooned in the lyrics to "Mad Dogs and Englishmen."

The attendant approached Tony, informing him that Mr. Sonji was ready to meet with him.

Sonji remained seated as Tony entered. Almost twice Tony's age, he showed the strain of his five years of detention. His seething anger was underscored as he eschewed traditional Asian politeness and protocol during their introductory meeting.

"Mr. Ramos, I appreciate your punctuality." He motioned with his left hand toward the chair on the opposite side of the intricately carved Malay desk. "Since I have been able to return to my private work and passions, each day has been congested from years of absence. Today will be a particularly demanding one. I must depart in an hour, so I would ask we dispense with formalities."

Sonji rose, turning his back to examine a memento hanging on the rear wall. Tony's attention was drawn to the testimonials to Sonji's accomplishments. He especially noted a yellowing formal photograph of Sonji and four other men in front of what appeared to be a pharmaceutical plant. The most diminutive of the group was at the far left of the assemblage; Tony recognized him as Professor Nasir. When Sonji turned to face him, he exposed the far side of the wall, decorated with his academic recognitions and diplomas, most prominent among them a doctorate from the University of California at San Diego.

Leaning forward on the desk, supported by his fully extended fingers, he continued, "Mr. Ramos, I know the purpose of your visit. My colleagues elsewhere have informed me of your inquiries." His voice raised a half octave as he announced, "I have no interest in your intrusive questions."

Rising to his full height of just under five feet, nine, Sonji continued, "The only reason I accepted your request to meet was to convey a message to you and the country I assume you represent. These issues you have raised have long been closed by your own government. Your attempts to disinter them will only strain the few positive relationships your country retains and make it all the more difficult to rebuild its credibility in the world." He paused, looking down as if staring into the grave of America's indiscretions.

Tony spoke: "Mr. Sonji, I can assure you I am not here as a representative of my government. I am a Foreign Service officer in the State Department and my superiors are aware of my travels. But I am here as a private citizen attempting to answer questions that have confounded many of my people. I am in hopes you will be of assistance in doing so."

"I shall not," Sonji interrupted. "My relations with your country have been extremely hurtful. I labored to complete my education against the prejudice and insolence of most of those with whom I was required to associate. The hostility toward my religion was palpable, isolating me from all but those who shared it. The arrogance of undeserved superiority, the condescension towards me and others from non-Caucasian ancestry, has left a permanent scar."

He resumed his seat. "When I returned to my home after five years in yours, my senses were more attuned to the changes that had occurred here, the extent to which American secularity was confronting and diluting our religious traditions. I fought against this perversion, militarily and politically. This brought me in contact with Osama bin Laden, a young man who had given up the pleasures of an opulent life in Saudi Arabia for the battlefields of Afghanistan."

Tony broke in. "You know bin Laden, personally?"

"He is one of my closest friends," Sonji said, reaching into his desk drawer. He withdrew a Pashtun knife, encased in a goatskin sheath. "This was his gift to me in 2000 for the use of my condominium by his people. Osama bin Laden represented the will to protect our values, the capability of triumphing over the Russians and the Americans. He has become my friend and idol, as he has to millions who uphold the faith. When he asks for my help—and that incident in January of this new century is by no means the only time he has done so—I attempt to be as forthcoming as possible. And, I assure you, I will continue to do so."

"Could you describe your present relationship with Mr. bin Laden?" Tony asked.

"In respect to him I will not. Let me only say that what he has accomplished is only a modest reflection of what the future holds. Even now, with the will of Allah, he is preparing for more spectacular actions, actions which will bring you heathens to your knees."

Tony rose. It was clear the interview was over.

Curbside, Tony hailed a cab and gave the driver the address of the Malaysian intelligence agency, approximately forty kilometers distant.

As he gazed down twenty stories and watched Tony enter the taxi, Sonji pushed a button on his console telephone. In a calm voice he said, "Anthony, order the container of 43B medical devices to be placed with DHL and forwarded to our Hong Kong representative on the 6:55 Malaysia Airlines flight."

SEPTEMBER 11
Jeddah

King Khalid Ibn Abdul Aziz was forty minutes late for the photo shoot. At almost eighty-five, he showed the effects of a decade of declining health. Within the last fortnight he had been hospitalized for a recurrence of what was speculated to be a persistent heart abnormality. The *Economist*, which Laura had read on the flight from London, reported that His Highness's decline had weakened his government through unsteady decision making and widening fissures within the court as factions among the next generation positioned themselves in anticipation of the king's demise. The splits had been accentuated by the passing of the heir apparent to the throne, Crown Prince Sultan, in June.

Zaid, who was no part of the palace intrigues, met Laura and her colleagues.

Like a U.S. president in his last year in office, the king was thought to be burnishing his legacy. Photographs by the internationally acclaimed Laura Billington would give a face to that legacy.

Laura and her staff were ready. Tony's advice again proved valuable. The king had a reputation for vanity, and lack of punctuality was a serious offense. Obviously, the same standard did not apply in reverse. In the royal chambers to which Laura had been denied access a day earlier, her suggestions to the king as to positions and demeanor were silently deferred to. After ninety minutes, the king was pleased.

The next photographs were with King Abdul Aziz and the recently designated heir apparent, Crown Prince Nayef. Through an aide, His Highness directed that the shoot be extended into the afternoon to include designated other members of the royal family.

Zaid was not one of those selected, but he hovered in the background, offering Laura advice and information on some of the lesser-known family members. By four, the family, Laura, and her weary crew were more than satisfied with the quality of the photos.

During breaks, she wandered into the room in which she had spent so much time the previous day, but didn't see the tall, beardless man this time. Laura did not escape the scrutiny of the woman in a black burka who had trailed him into the rear chamber of the palace the day before. From the chamber entrance she had an unobstructed view of Laura and her revolving royal photographic subjects. For her, Laura was a dream. As a young girl in Bombay, she had aspired to be an international journalist. It had happened only at the periphery. Laura was the embodiment of what might have been. Not that she was without pride in what had been achieved: the respect, if not the understanding, that her beliefs had at long last received. But she was disconsolate at what she had heard in the palace chamber. As influential as her leader had been, he was preparing to take a new, more indiscriminately violent course. She was worried for herself and her people—all of them, but mostly Mamata.

She rose as the king and the tall man approached. Anxious not to lose her place behind her leader, she soon disappeared into the adoring crowd.

Zaid dutifully assisted Laura and her crew in folding up the equipment and even helped place the light stands, deflectors, and other photographic equipment in the Toyota van.

With the shoot completed, Zaid and Laura departed in his Alfa Romeo for the Imperial Hotel.

As the attentive waiter was placing the first round of Maker's Mark and Chivas Regal on the glass tabletop, Laura slipped Zaid his printed photos from the night before. His pleasure and arousal were obvious. "A successful photographer must be able to relate intimately with the subject. I can see that you certainly possess that talent," Laura oozed.

"I am very much looking forward to further hands-on lessons from you," Zaid replied.

After a second round of Maker's Mark and scotch on the rocks at the bar and a minimalist dinner in the palatial five-star restaurant, Laura and Zaid took the elevator to Laura's penthouse suite.

They both traded the clothing they had worn during the day for the Imperial's maroon-and-gold bathrobes. Zaid continued to drink as Laura plied him with questions, commencing with the one he'd deflected the night before.

"You described the meeting with the Americans, I believe it was in 1991, at which a partnership was established. Can you tell me if it went forward?"

"I appreciate the manner in which you have reframed your question. And the answer is yes, it appears so. Shortly after the meeting with His Highness, a former military air base was converted into a research center. Scientists from the United States and Europe, and India too, started to arrive. In a few months, cargo containers of equipment were being delivered to the center weekly."

"Thank you, Zaid. It appears our relationship has reconnected."

He smiled as he took another sip of scotch.

"One more question: just before his murder, my father had written in an article about the possibility Saudi Arabia was developing a nuclear weapon. Do you think he had some inside intelligence, and was that why he was killed?"

With apparent candor, Zaid declared ignorance.

Laura reached out her toes and stroked Zaid's feet. He nuzzled her breasts, then pulled back.

"Zaid, yesterday I saw a tall, beardless man in the reception room of the palace. I looked for him today, but never saw him."

"The man you saw was Osama bin Laden," Zaid replied with the barely obscured pride of one with special knowledge.

"What!"

"Yes," Zaid said calmly. "Osama bin Laden. To maintain some anonymity for one of the best-known persons on the planet, he has shaven his beard and is approaching His Majesty with a very humble appearance."

"It can't possibly be bin Laden. We keep hearing that since 9/11 he's been hiding out in caves somewhere along the Afghan-Pakistani border."

Zaid spread his hands indulgently. "That may be what is given out, and your people may very well believe it. But the fact remains, that man you saw was Osama."

Laura stiffened. "That's—that's just—incredible. Anyway, I thought he was the sworn enemy of the king and had tried to assassinate Prince al-Faisal. Why would His Royal Highness have tolerated him in the palace? It makes no sense."

"My grandfather is first of all committed to the safety and well-being of the nation and the House of Saud. As he has done before, he will deal with whomever he must to ensure that."

Laura's head was spinning. "What's he doing here in Jeddah?"

"Like your father, but no doubt with more evidence, Osama has reason to believe the kingdom has processed a sufficient amount of nuclear material for several bombs. He is here to—what is your expression?— to do business."

"That's even more unbelievable." She strained to keep herself from stammering. "How could the kingdom have come so far so fast? From what I understand, Iran has been working on a nuclear weapon much longer than you and still hasn't been successful with even one."

Zaid's smile was midway between sardonic and smug. "My dear, we have better partners than the ayatollah."

Was he being honest or just trying to impress her? Laura wondered. If he was telling the truth, his revelation was earth-shattering. It was time for the full-court press. She poured another inch and a half of Chivas into his glass, and then slipped to the floor, deftly allowing her robe to reveal a little more. Zaid leaned forward and reached within to fondle her breasts.

Laura put her hand on top of his while discreetly tightening her robe. "Zaid, we've been tracking bin Laden for more than ten years and in the most god-awful places. Are you saying that while we're doing all that, he has open access to the palace and comes and goes as he pleases? How could the king have not told us, his most faithful ally? If the U.S. doesn't know of bin Laden's presence and reason to be in the kingdom, who does?"

"I do," said Zaid, trying to underplay his satisfaction with his own omniscience. "Before the 9/11 attacks, His Royal Highness was in the same position. Osama demanded access to the kingdom's agents in the U.S. to provide security and support for the operatives who would soon be inserted in your country. The king capitulated rather than face an al-Qaeda-led civil insurrection. Now, in exchange for a commitment not to turn the kingdom into another Iran by unleashing his operatives—twenty thousand in the kingdom, and only Allah knows, how many in the gulf region—Osama wants enough nuclear material for three or four bombs. This would consummate—I like your word, Ms. Billington—his long-standing goal of acquiring weapons of mass destruction. The king seems to think that if Osama does not receive what he requests, he is willing and able to carry out his threat."

Laura stood. "Zaid, you can't be serious. That would be a global catas—catas—catastrophe. It would be the end of the kingdom—a rank betrayal of the U.S. and your other friends."

"The king is losing faith in the capability and reliability of your nation. And we have other friends."

Suddenly, she had an idea. "Zaid, darling," she said in her most kittenish voice, "if I give you my Leica, do you think you could get some photos of him?"

"Well, I don't know—"

"It's small and discreet. No one would have to know, and you could practice your 'candid' photography. What Henri Cartier-Bresson did on the streets of Paris, you could do in the halls of power of the Middle East!"

"But how would I—"

"The trick is to always look as if you're photographing something else. You can practice on me, here in the hotel room. I can make it *interesting* for you," she promised.

"Well, how can I refuse such an offer? But first, we will relax."

Rising, Zaid wrapped his arms around Laura's waist. He gently guided her toward the adjacent maroon-and-gold-tiled bathroom and its steam shower.

Zaid adjusted the temperature of the steam to 120 degrees.

Seated on the marble shower bench, they slumped against the walls. Zaid's eyes were closed when he felt Laura stroking his groin. He reacted with a start, then pleasure. Laura rotated to a sitting position on his knees and began caressing his graying chest hairs, around the back of his neck, to his now aroused nipples.

He started to rise, touching Laura's genitals with his organ.

"Not yet, Zaid," she said, "enjoy this moment."

As she spoke, the doorbell rang, followed by three sharp knocks. Laura looked up apprehensively.

"I will get it," Zaid said, then toweled himself off and pulled on his robe. With his hair matted and glistening, he closed the bathroom door behind him and went to the front door.

Naked and dripping, Laura cracked the bathroom door. Through the narrow opening, she saw two men in uniform and heard one of them tell Zaid, "We are agents of the Ministry of Interior. We have instructions from His Highness that you are to come with us to the palace. Now."

Zaid closed the hotel room door and returned to the steaming bathroom. "Laura, my grandfather has called for me and I must go. I will return when I have fulfilled his wishes." He gave her a lingering kiss on her lips. "And then I will serve ours."

As he hastily dressed in the bedroom, Laura wrapped herself in the hotel robe, went to her backpack, and retrieved one of her Leica M9s. She inserted a freshly formatted memory card and handed the camera to Zaid.

"Don't forget this," she said. "You might even see him at the palace tonight. I can't wait to see the results."

"And I cannot wait to show them to you," Zaid replied, accepting the camera.

He kissed her again.

The door closed. Laura heard the elevator engage.

She waited for an hour before placing a call to Tony. She left a voice message to return her call at 9:30 the following morning.

With no word from Zaid but still trembling from his revelation and the promise of photos to prove it, Laura returned to the bathroom, completed her shower alone, and fell into the empty bed. Despite her anxiety, it was not long before exhaustion overtook her and she fell into a dreamless sleep.

SEPTEMBER 11

Kuala Lumpur

As befitted his position in the Royal Malaysian Intelligence Corps, the Kor Risik DiRaja, Colonel Tan Row was meticulous. His answers to each of Tony's questions were thoughtful, considered. He consulted his personal log before commenting.

"December 3, 1999, was the first contact I had with your station chief at the time, Mr. Richard Brandon." The colonel leaned forward so Tony could verify the date from the logbook.

"So that was the first time you were aware that a meeting of al-Qaeda operatives was to be held at the Evergreen condominium. Did Mr. Brandon make any specific request for intelligence assistance from the Special Branch of the Royal Malaysian Police?"

The colonel adjusted his glasses higher on his nose and studiously reviewed his precise handwritten inscriptions. "My notes state that he requested our service in placing a listening device in unit 703."

"Was this an unusual request between intelligence agencies?"

"As you know from your experience with the intelligence community, dating from World War II there has been a special relationship among the English-speaking nations. Without explicit permission, one such country's intelligence service will not collect information on, or in, another, but will respond to requests for assistance. Your country has honored this understanding. Sometimes, as in Latin America, you have defended this agreement against hostile words from several of your allies who think of it as yet another example of Anglo exclusivity. Malaysia is not a full participant in the relationship, but as a former British colony, we have liaison status. No, I would not say this was unusual, and we were prepared to be helpful."

Although it occurred before he was with State, the incident to which Colonel Row referred was well known to Tony. In December of 1994 President Clinton convened a meeting of all the heads of government of the Americas, with the notable exception of Fidel Castro, for a hemispheric summit in Miami. It had been almost thirty years since any significant number of hemispheric leaders had sat together. It was a signal occasion for the resurgence of democracy and liberalized trade. Expectations were high.

Prior to the meeting and without clearance from the appropriate officials at the White House or the Department of State, the FBI secured a warrant allowing it to wiretap all but one of the presidents and prime ministers in attendance. NBC broke the story on its *Nightly News* several days after the conference had concluded. The heads of state whose private conversations had been intercepted were indignant. The U.S. ambassadors throughout Latin America and the Caribbean had hell to pay. The cauldrons grew hotter when these national leaders learned that their only colleague to escape surveillance was the prime minister of Canada. All the goodwill the summit was intended to engender was washed out to sea.

"Prepared?"

Colonel Tan Row, trained as a military officer, had spent the last fifteen years in the Kor Risik DiRaja. He combined the discipline and dominant personality of a colonel with the political nuance of a diplomat. Like most military men who led intelligence services, including those in the United States, he wore the uniform. Colonel Row filled it well, his elongated, Western-shaped head and hazel eyes sitting atop a sinuously lean Chinese body. He personified the blending of genetics and culture that prevailed in much of the upper classes of his country.

"We had the personnel with the technical competence to conduct the installation of the intercept, but not the equipment that would be required in this particular venue. Our interior oral collection device is the standard MR-16."

The colonel opened a desk drawer and removed an oval-shaped object half the size of a digital wristwatch. "This is what we would normally use, and the performance has been quite satisfactory. However, it is not without its limitations. A clever technician with materials easily obtained on the Internet can infuse a space of over seven square meters and garble the transmission.

"We have long been familiar with the owner of unit 703 at the Evergreen, Mr. Yazid Sonji, and knew of his propensity for the utmost care in security matters. Assuming he had taken precautions to avoid interference with his activities, we needed more specialized interception devices than were in our inventory, and requested Mr. Brandon to make them available to us."

This piece of information was not in Tony's detailed briefing book. There had been no indication of Mr. Sonji's security precautions. He was taken off guard by the colonel's response. *Damn,* Tony thought, *if I had known that three hours ago, I would have asked Sonji why he felt he was so vulnerable.*

The colonel continued: "Mr. Brandon said that was quite impossible. He had three other drug or money-laundering cases running and all his people and support were committed. I restated our willingness to be of assistance, but noted our limitations under the circumstances."

Tony winced. Early in his career with the INR bureau, he had been in the CIA auditorium at Langley, Virginia, and heard then-director George Tenet sound the trumpet: "We are at war with al-Qaeda." Tenet followed with a memo to the entire American intelligence community:

"We must now enter a new phase in our efforts against bin Laden. Our work to date has been remarkable and in some instances heroic; yet each day we all acknowledge that retaliation is inevitable and that its scope may be far larger than we have previously experienced... We are at war. I want no resources or people spared in this effort, either inside the CIA or in the larger intelligence community."

A year later the National Security Agency had intercepted communications from Osama bin Laden describing the convening in Kuala Lumpur of his most experienced terrorist operatives. Included were those who had blown up two United States embassies in Africa. *Our agency chief here cannot get his goddamned ass or assets into the meeting,* Tony had thought. *Obviously, no one was listening to George's trumpet blast.*

Tony refocused on the colonel's tanned face. "So there was no intercept of the conversations that would take place four weeks later?"

"I regret, no. Who could have prophesied the horrendous consequences of that failure?"

Tony turned the page of his briefing memo. The colonel's corner office had grown noticeably darker in the shadow of a thunderstorm that had arisen during Tony's taxi ride from Mr. Sonji's downtown office to the elevated suburbs where the Kor Risik DiRaja had its headquarters. The campus was a former British officers' quarters with five two- and three-story buildings surrounding a lush parade ground. The British preferred to locate their elite installations out of the city and above the stifling tropic summer heat. The thunder became more intrusive.

"Colonel, Mr. Sonji had been a biologist and engineering graduate student at the University of California, San Diego. Are you aware of any continuing relationships he has had with the university or his former colleagues?"

"No. Mr. Sonji has become increasingly estranged from his American experience. Since his religious conversion he has been hostile, even violent, toward your country. To our knowledge the only person with whom he has maintained a connection is a former professor, an Indian who shares Mr. Sonji's religious fervor."

The colonel rose from his desk and walked to a black cabinet from which he removed a file. Scanning the pages as he retook his seat, he paused and, when he appeared to be satisfied, said, "Yes, his name is Professor Samrat Nasir. My notes, which are now over three years outdated, state that in retirement Nasir continues to live in San Diego, although he has business arrangements in Saudi Arabia and frequently visits there. On at least two occasions, our intelligence indicates, he met with Mr. Sonji in Jeddah."

Tony was more than displeased. *Why in the hell didn't we know that? What is our station in Riyadh doing if we missed those two getting together? It doesn't look like we've learned much from 9/11.*

"Going forward to January 4, 2000, I understand that while there was not an oral intercept, there were photographs taken of the fourteen men who attended. Are you aware of their distribution?" Tony asked.

Without consulting his notes the colonel replied, "Yes. Our officers took over twenty rolls of film. We kept the originals and submitted copies to your CIA. We had expected the CIA station to reciprocate, but instead, Mr. Brandon urged us to turn over our own copies, stating that this was a highly sensitive case and the agency wanted custody of all the intelligence. Of course, our procedures required that we maintain our own photographs, which we did. We did ask Mr. Brandon what his distribution would be, and he said there would be none. It was wholly an agency matter. Professionally I was surprised that he didn't consider it appropriate to share this information within your government, but sometimes your procedures are murky."

"Colonel, could you indulge me one final question? Your service has the reputation of maintaining a close liaison with your Indian counterpart. How does New Delhi assess the situation in Pakistan?"

"Well, of course, I will have to be cautious in speculating on what one nation feels about the circumstances of yet another. But it is our feeling the Indians believe the Pakistanis are in desperate circumstances. The continuing violence—such as the Mumbai assault, two attacks on India's embassy in Kabul with indications of Pakistani intelligence involvement, and last week's attack on the Islamabad Marriott hotel—are indicative of the unraveling of the Pakistani government's control. Despite its representations, New Delhi is very concerned with the security of Pakistan's nuclear stockpile. As long as the weapons were under the control of the Pakistani military, Indian intelligence calculated the chances of proliferation were minimal. But with the current state of instability India is disturbed, very disturbed. Some unsolicited advice: your government needs to take all steps to reassure India you are committed to the security of Pakistan's nuclear weapons, even if it means you will take direct control of the warheads."

Tony turned to look out the window that faced the colonel. The storm had arrived. Rain was coming down at a forty-five-degree angle. Glancing at his Casio watch, Tony saw that he was already twenty minutes behind the time he should have left for the Kuala Lumpur International Airport. In the late afternoon, as he knew from past experience, the traffic would be deadlocked, and the storm would make for a drenching run to the cab and a damp and slow ride to the airport.

"Colonel, I am very appreciative of your willingness to receive me and the valuable information you have provided. If at any time I or the Department of State could be of assistance, please give us the opportunity to do so."

The colonel directed Tony to the door and walked with him through security at the main entrance to the intelligence service. "Mr. Ramos, you are on an important mission for both our countries. I am pleased to have provided what I trust you will find to be reliable information. While we have been spared the hideous attacks you suffered on September 11, we have lived with a radicalized minority for more than a decade. We are comrades in this war."

A police guard opened the heavy wooden door. The burst of wind-driven rain blew him back, twisting his blue slicker around his thighs. As the colonel gave Tony a parting handshake, the guard opened a black Oxford Street umbrella and motioned for Tony to follow to the lone taxi waiting at curbside.

Tony tossed in his single bag and slid his rain-soaked body into the backseat of the Toyota Corolla cab, waved thanks to the rapidly retreating police officer and directed the driver to the Malaysia Airlines terminal.

Leaving the compound, Tony noticed a Sony advertisement digital clock on top of an office building. It read 5:02. It would be close. Tony began the mental preparation for his arrival and the preboarding procedures.

Kuala Lumpur's was part of the new generation of Southeast Asian airports. Stimulated by surging international commerce and a nascent tourist sector, Malaysia had made a 3.5 billion–dollar investment in a state-of-the-art terminal. Built on a former rubber plantation, the main terminal's soaring, peaked roofline created the appearance of giant tents in the desert. Its glass and marble surfaces glistened. But Tony did not have the time or inclination to focus on the architectural design. It was exactly one hour before departure, and his cab was caught in the jam of vehicles two blocks from the inclined entry to the airport.

The rain had ceased. The sun roared out from behind the clouds. What a few minutes ago had been a showerhead at full blast was now a steam room. Tony grabbed his travel-worn Samsonite bag, tugged at the driver's shoulder to stop, gave him the fare and tip, ripped open the door, and commenced the last five hundred meters at his former-athlete speed and agility. The Malaysia Airline insignia beckoned like a mirage, visible and almost within reach.

It was 6:06 by the terminal clock when Tony passed through the glass-and-steel revolving door seeking the first Malaysia Airline staff member he could locate. Unlike most of their American counterparts, airlines in this part of the world still made service a central component of their passenger relationships.

Tony's potential rescuer, according to the identification badge on her navy-blue uniform, was Ms. Lim. Stopping momentarily to catch his breath and shake off the last remnants of rain from his clothing, Tony asked Ms. Lim for assistance in boarding Malaysia flight 9724 to Hong Kong. She looked at him and the documents he gave her in polite disbelief.

"Mr. Ramos, it is quite impossible. The flight has been closed for more than twenty minutes; all of the luggage has passed through security and entered into the aircraft. Could I help you with arrangements for a later flight?"

Tony's mind flew backward—Riyadh, Jeddah, Dubai, and now Kuala Lumpur. The mere idea of another extension was too much. Without responding to Ms. Lim and her offer of future assistance, he had another idea. Maybe the embassy could contact the airline and get an approval to board despite his late arrival. With Ms. Lim's help he located an airline phone. Tony made the call.

"This is Tony Ramos of the INR bureau and I need help. Could you please connect me with Mr. Blair Roberts?" The operator rang the extension of the deputy chief of mission.

Moments passed. "I am sorry, but Mr. Roberts is not answering. His secretary says that he has left the building for the day."

Tony moved to plan B. "Could I speak with Ambassador Singletary?" He did not know the ambassador other than by reputation, which wasn't very positive.

Singletary, a California private-equity capitalist and major party fund-raiser when selected, was part of a mounting wave of political appointments to ambassadorial positions. There had always been some non–Foreign Service ambassadors representing America. Traditionally, these political appointments were limited to prestige posts such as the Court of St. James in London or locations where whoever the ambassador was would not make much difference. The first President Bush appointed a political crony from Nevada as ambassador to the Bahamas. When pressed for his credentials, the new appointee said, "I love golf and they have a lot of nice golf courses and good fishing."

"This is Ambassador Singletary."

"Thank you, Mr. Ambassador, my name is Tony Ramos and I am with the INR bureau. I apologize calling you for help, but my friend and former colleague in the bureau, Mr. Roberts, is not available. Briefly, today I have been taking interviews, and due to an unexpected extension of my final session and the severity of the thunderstorm, I arrived late for my 6:55 Malaysia Airlines flight to Hong Kong."

Tony paused to catch his breath before continuing, "Without your help I am not going to make it. I would greatly appreciate your intervening with the airline."

There was silence on the line.

"Mr. Ramos, I don't know who you think you are, but according to cables we have received from Riyadh, you are using your INR credentials to carry out a set of personal interviews in furtherance of your own agenda, whatever that may be. It is quite unprofessional and unacceptable for you to use the expectations created by your official position with the department and your diplomatic passport to stir up unwarranted suspicions as to the actions of your government. Let me be plain, Mr. Ramos: I don't give a damn when you get back to the United States, if ever. You can rot here, for all I care. And please know that among your superiors are people who are aware of your misuse of office. I certainly hope and anticipate that the most severe sanctions will follow."

A wave of anxiety settled over Tony as he heard the phone receiver slam down. The embassy calls had consumed over ten minutes, and no results—at least no results likely to have a good effect on Tony's timely return to the United States or his career path at the State Department.

There was no plan C, beyond accepting Ms. Lim's offer of assistance with a future flight.

Tony looked down the concourse. He noticed a neon sign for The Prop, a bar on the mezzanine level and outside the security zone. He took the escalator, walked past a mall of retail shops and local and international fast-food outlets, seated himself on a steel-and-leather barstool, and ordered a Singapore sling. Under a propeller from a vintage Pan American clipper, he selected a spot at the bar with an unobstructed view of the runways.

———————

More than a thousand meters beyond Tony's range of vision, on the perimeter sidewalk outside the cargo warehouse of the Kuala Lumpur International Airport, a man with a furled umbrella under his left arm gazed at the main east-west runway. Due no doubt to the recent thunderstorm, it was unusually congested, with eleven aircraft in line awaiting authorization to taxi toward the takeoff point. The storm had left its signature in the form of a heavy mist that hovered over and partially obscured the tarmac, further delaying flight operations.

The man glanced at his watch. It was 7:12. He calculated that Malaysia 9724, ninth in the queue, would not be airborne for at least another thirty-five minutes. He went inside to confirm for the second time that his package of medical devices had been delivered by DHL and placed on the aircraft. Reassured, he took a cup of green tea and relieved himself in the WC before returning to the exterior of the warehouse.

———————

By 7:39, the last of the aircraft in front of Malaysia 9724 had completed its takeoff roll and was lifting into the sky. As Tony watched, the flight he so much wanted to be on was moving into position at the head of runway L14.

The Boeing 777-300 started its takeoff run. Although he had grown up in a Hialeah neighborhood, north of the Miami airport, and for all of his youth had watched airplanes of all descriptions take off and land, it was still a source of mystery how these Goliaths could break their bonds with earth.

The plane moved at a steadily increasing rate of speed until it reached 174 knots. The main gear was off the runway and the undercarriage was withdrawing inside the fuselage. The aircraft crossed the fence at the southeast corner of the field and commenced a slow turn to the right.

As Tony rose from his stool and began to gather his still-damp coat and suitcase, he glanced back and noticed a thin stream of black smoke flowing from the underbelly of the Malaysia plane. It was making a tighter turn than required for a departure route. He could see a red glow emitting from the passenger windows over the right wing. The nose of the 777 was straining to elevate itself, while the mass of the aircraft was descending.

The right wing dipped, exposing a gash in the composite material. Suddenly, the nose shook violently as the Boeing lost its flight speed and stalled and the right wingtip dropped as if it were an arrowhead pointed to the ground.

A flaming object of the same proportions as a human being spilled into the air five hundred feet above the runway. A second and third tumbled out. According to the subsequent Malaysian Aviation Authority report, 9724 was in flight for fifty-one seconds before its right wing slashed through twenty-two automobiles parked in the distant lot of the airport, and the 777 cartwheeled and came to rest on the motorway that formed the airport's western perimeter. An explosion of flame, higher than the control tower, engulfed the fallen aircraft.

Two seconds later, the sound of the explosion, the last to be heard of Malaysia 9724, reached the cargo warehouse. Returning to the lobby of the cargo terminal, his umbrella tucked under his left arm, the man took out his Nokia. A smile of satisfaction crossed his lips as he began to recite his observations.

It took an additional half second for the explosion to resonate in Tony's ears as he stood facing the window wall of The Prop bar on the mezzanine of the airport. After the initial shock of the crash itself, the realization slammed into Tony's brain: *My God! It was me they were after. That plane went down because I was supposed to be on it!*

At a goat pasture in Afghanistan he had been shot at by the Taliban, and he had had a near-death experience at Il Kani Air Base, but this was of a totally different order. Who would want him dead so much that they were willing to slaughter several hundred innocents? Who had been denied their bloody objective by the most fortuitous combination of circumstances?

As he took deep breaths to compose himself and slow his superaccelerated heart rate, Tony recollected what had brought him to this window in an airport bar halfway round the world from home.

Feverishly, he punched numbers into his BlackBerry. He waited interminable seconds, only to reach a voice mail.

"Carol. I've just—an airplane . . . You're in danger! Call Ambassador Talbott. Now!"

SEPTEMBER 12

Jeddah ✶ London

Laura slept until 9:00 a.m., a rare indulgence. She checked her phone messages and was disappointed that there were no calls from Zaid or Tony. She couldn't get the revelation about bin Laden out of her head. Could there possibly be anything to it? Was it her duty to immediately contact the American consulate in Jeddah? While applying her lipstick she decided she wouldn't do anything until she could get through to Tony and tell him. He'd know what to do.

She dressed in her travel casual and met the crew in the lobby. At noon she proceeded through the minimal airport security and bought an *International Herald Tribune* and the local *Post*. She folded them into her travel bag for airborne reading.

Thirty minutes later, settled into her first-class seat, Laura opened the *Post*. Above the fold was a photograph of an airliner in flames, spiraling to the ground. The photographer in her instinctively marveled that someone could have captured the shot at that moment of highest drama. Then the human being caught up as she read the headline that screamed that 331 persons had perished. Below the fold, there was more tragedy: a three-column picture of a broken body on a dimly lit curbside. Even in the photo's graininess, there was something about the body that . . .

Laura blanched as she read the opening paragraph: "Prince Zaid al Swainee, grandson of King Khalid Ibn Abdul Aziz, was found dead on the sidewalk in the rear of the Imperial Hotel last night. The police are investigating the cause of death. Preliminary indications are that Prince Zaid fell from an as-yet-undetermined site in the hotel. A damaged Leica camera was found near the body. Police speculate that the Prince was leaning out the window to take a photograph, lost his balance, and fell. A police spokesman said the camera's memory card would be examined in an effort to confirm this theory."

Laura ordered a double Maker's Mark and downed it in a single gulp. She was haunted by the newspaper photos, anguished at what they threatened for her. During the seven-hour flight to Heathrow she composed her plan.

As the wheels touched the runway she called Roland Jeralewski.

"I am highly incensed," he snapped.

"What possibly—possibly," Laura stumbled. "What are you talking about?"

"Ms. Billington, we are paying you a hundred thousand dollars a month for information. It has been almost twenty-four hours since you came into possession of the most important information to Peninsular and the world. And you have not shared a word with us."

Aware of the man seated to her left, Laura moved the cell phone to her lips. "Mr. Jeralewski, I have been communicating at every opportunity when there is credible intelligence. You may know that my source, Zaid al Swainee, died last night under questionable circumstances. This has been my first secure chance to do so."

The phone was silent. And then, "An important reason for Peninsular's success has been our reputation of being first to access world-changing developments. Being twenty-four hours late is for losers. Of course we knew of al Swainee's fall; we didn't have to wait for the morning newspaper. Do you think only the Saudi Ministry of Interior was monitoring your conversation? This was a test of your judgment and reliability. Ms. Billington, your results are woefully inadequate."

Laura was enraged. Even more, she suddenly felt threatened. Ignoring the man rising from his seat to accept his blue blazer from the flight attendant, she said in a stern, steady voice, "Mr. Jeralewski, I resign my position with Peninsular, effective immediately."

"Ms. Billington, I do not believe you understand your position. After reaching our agreement on August 2, Peninsular has purchased your promissory note for the sum of fifteen million dollars. The terms are callable on thirty days' notice. Are you prepared in that time frame to discharge your obligation?"

As the first-class passengers began to file out, Laura muttered, "I'll call you later."

Inside Terminal 4, Laura's second call was to Tony. She got his voice mail.

"Tony, it's Friday afternoon at three o'clock Greenwich. I'm at Heathrow. I think I may be in major trouble. I'll be on the next plane to Dulles. For God's sake, be there!"

SEPTEMBER 12

George Town

Since his wife had died of cancer four years earlier, Hector Nuñez lived alone. Through the rewards of diligence, positions of increasing responsibility, and a mortgage loan from Anglo-Cayman, he had been able to purchase a modest one-story house in a subdivision south of the airport. The traditional Caribbean clapboard cottage was elevated two feet above grade to protect it from the periodic tidal surges.

On this second day of Nuñez's failure to report for duty, Mr. Rawls dispatched a bank security officer to check on his whereabouts. Rounding the corner of Nuñez's street, Officer Granville Meldrum noticed nothing out of the ordinary. The white Sonata was parked in its accustomed place under the roof of a detached open garage. Other than two days of uncollected newspapers, the lawn was as impeccably clean as Nuñez was known to keep it.

A neighbor noticed Meldrum parked in the driveway and walked from his home directly across the street to the driver's side.

"Is there a problem?"

"I don't know," Meldrum said. "For the last two days Mr. Nuñez has not reported for work, which is very unusual for him. Have you seen him in the neighborhood?"

"The last time was Wednesday night when he came home at almost midnight. I know that because I was watching *The Jay Leno Show*. I think he's the funniest man on TV."

"Did you see or hear anything unusual?" Meldrum probed.

"No, I didn't."

"We're worried about him." Handing the neighbor his business card, Meldrum concluded, "If you learn anything, I would appreciate a call."

"Sure."

Meldrum climbed up the four front steps and knocked on the white wooden-frame screen door. No response. He was surprised the door was unlocked and swung open with a slight push. He walked across the living room, trailed by the reverberating sound of his hard-soled shoes on the bare pine floor, and through each of the other four rooms. Nothing appeared to be out of order.

Meldrum stepped through the unsecured rear door. His first hint that something was amiss was the pungent odor of a decaying carcass. He scanned the rear yard. There was nothing there but a couple of pairs of pajamas, underwear, and undershirts flapping in the sea breeze on the clothesline.

As Meldrum circled the cottage the odor grew more intense. Stooping to look in the crawl space under the floorboards, he saw a rug rolled up like a bale of hay. Stretching out, he was able to grab a corner and pull the rug toward the lawn. The weight was obviously more than that of a floor covering. The smell became noxious.

The neighbor from across the street reappeared.

"Can I help?"

"You surely can. Kneel down and pull the other side of this rug. Be careful; it's damn heavy and stinks."

Together Meldrum and the Good Samaritan neighbor were able to pull the full rug from under the house. They unrolled the bloodstained aqua carpet, exposing first an arm and then the full body of Hector Nuñez.

The right side of his head, neck, and shoulder was covered with co-agulated blood. Meldrum diverted his eyes; he felt his breakfast was on the verge of ejection.

Gathering himself, he called the island emergency service. After a terse explanation of the circumstances he was assured assistance was being dispatched.

In ten minutes a red-and-white E-One EMS vehicle was in the Nuñez driveway.

―――――――

While the paramedics moved the corpse to the van, the accompanying police officer began gathering information for his report. After debriefing the neighbor, he turned to Meldrum. When the full set of questions relating to the crime scene had been asked, he began a more general inquiry.

"Mr. Meldrum, you are also an employee at Anglo-Cayman Bank?"

"Yes, for twenty-three years."

"And you had known Mr. Nuñez as a fellow employee?"

"Yes."

"Do you have any knowledge as to his whereabouts in the last thirty-six hours?"

"Yes. I saw him on Wednesday evening in the area of the bank vaults. It was roughly ten to eleven at night."

"Was he alone?"

The inquiry was interrupted by the return of the lead paramedic.

"Inspector, while we were moving Mr. Nuñez from the gurney to the van, these fell out of the rug." He opened his palm to disclose two .45 caliber bullet casings.

The inspector placed them in a plastic evidence bag and marked the identification tag. "Good work. When we get back to the station I want to take a full statement on how you found these."

"It won't be a very long full statement."

Again turning to Meldrum, the police inspector asked a second time, "Was he alone?"

"No. He was with a younger woman—a very attractive young woman—who he introduced to me as a new auditor at the bank."

"Do you know her name?"

"No, but she and Mr. Nuñez left together in his car," pointing toward the Sonata.

"Interesting," the police inspector mumbled. "She may have been the last person to see Nuñez alive."

SEPTEMBER 12–14

Airborne, Kuala Lumpur to Washington, D.C.

The Kuala Lumpur International Airport had been closed for twelve hours since the crash. After he had gathered himself and found an airport Hyatt in which to rest in preparation for the grueling flights back to Washington, Tony called Carol.

"I know you're going to hate me for this, and please, please don't think it means I'm ignoring you, but you've got to give me a one-day rain check on our date."

As soon as she heard his voice, she broke into a flood of hysterical sobbing.

"Girls don't usually get that upset when I have to postpone a date," Tony said drily.

"Tony, how can you joke? When I got your email about having to change your schedule, I was sure you were on that plane that exploded. And then you never answered your cell." Her voice was still shaky.

"I was going to send you another email when I got bumped from the flight, but I was so preoccupied with getting out of the country . . . "

"So—so that is the plane you were supposed to be on?"

"Yeah—it is—was," Tony said, finally allowing himself to confront the enormity of what had happened and the capriciousness of fate.

"But you're all right? Tell me you're all right," Carol insisted. "It's been the lead story on CNN all morning."

"I'm OK, Carol. Really. Did you get my voice mail?"

"There was something garbled but I couldn't tell what it was. That must be the one you're talking about. What did it say?"

"I wanted you to call Ambassador Talbott right away."

"Why?"

Tony suddenly had a change of heart. As shaken up as Carol was, he couldn't upset her further by saying he thought she might be in danger, just as he was. He would take care of it himself—contact Talbott directly and have him get her some protection.

"It doesn't matter anymore," Tony said. "It can wait." He quickly changed the subject. "So, did you get in any beach time in the Caymans?"

"I never even got close to the hotel pool. I was going to jog on the beach, but something happened that made me think that wasn't a very good idea."

"What was that?"

She was beginning to calm down now. "Let's wait until we're together. There is some good news; what I stumbled on in the bowels of the bank was unbelievable."

"I guess we'll have a lot of tales to share. And I can't wait to share your—tale, I mean . . . "

"You and your nasty mind. Why do I love you?"

"We'll rediscover that on Sunday. I love you."

———————

Given his utter physical and mental exhaustion, Tony thought he'd be able to sleep on the plane, but he was so keyed up he couldn't close his eyes, even with a succession of stiff drinks. During the four-hour layover at Hong Kong's Chek Lap Kok Airport for Cathay Pacific 6120, Tony listened to his voice mails. He tried to return Laura's messages, but her cell was off. She must already be on the flight to Dulles. He left her a message to stay at one of the Dulles airport hotels and he would call when he got to the States.

––––––––––

Almost fifteen hours later, now in Los Angeles, he awoke her at the Dulles Marriott.

"Laura, this is Tony. I'm in L.A."

"Tony, I read about the terrible accident in Kuala Lumpur and was horrified you might be on that flight. Are you okay?"

"I'm okay, but not because I didn't bust my butt to be on it."

"God. Tony, take care of yourself."

"Laura, I'm doing the best I can. Could you meet my L.A. flight at Dulles? It'll be early, around 6:50."

"Yes. I want full details and the chance to be with you alone."

––––––––––

Laura met Tony outside the United arrivals area at Dulles. Together they took a taxi into the city. During the forty-five-minute drive, she told him of what she had learned from Zaid before his demise less than forty-eight hours earlier.

After summarizing Zaid's description of the 1991 meetings between the king and the Americans and the partnership they formed, she zeroed in on bin Laden. "He seems to intimidate the king. His physical stature is dominating; he has achieved his status not by privileged birth, but by heroic actions, at least that is the way they are seen among his believers; and by his willingness to do what he says—there is no subterfuge or guile. The king certainly gave him exceptional deference."

"But what about the nukes?"

"Zaid said bin Laden has had weapons of mass destruction as his Holy Grail since long before 9/11. You remember the biological weapons lab we wrapped up after the 2001 invasion of Kandahar? According to the *Times,* it had been active since the early nineties and bin Laden was close to having a device. If it hasn't already happened, I'm convinced he will and soon."

Reflecting on the containers moving up the conveyor belt at the Jeddah airport, Tony offered, "I think it already has."

Tony listened attentively as Laura gave him an expurgated version of her short relationship with Zaid. "I gave him a Leica so he could photograph bin Laden unobtrusively. That would have cinched it."

"It sure would have," Tony lamented.

He told the taxi driver to drop Laura at his place to get some sleep. No such luck for him; he had a command performance with Talbott at ten.

"In the meantime," Tony added, "say nothing to anyone. We have to assume that Zaid's fall or push, or whatever it was, means you are at risk."

"What about you and your exploding airplane?"

"Let's try to stay rational here, Laura."

———

In Talbott's office, the atmosphere was gloomy. The Taliban was on the verge of retaking Kabul, President Karzai had fled to Bangladesh, and the civil unrest in Pakistan had intensified. The beginning of what was supposed to be preparation for the winter lull had turned violent.

At the end of this bleak report, Talbott asked all but Tony to leave. Once the two were alone, Tony related what he had heard and his experiences in Riyadh, Jeddah, and Kuala Lumpur, and what Laura had told him from the palace: the suggestion that there was American complicity and the likelihood that weapons-grade nuclear material had been transferred to Osama bin Laden. Talbott was not surprised that the Saudis had an advanced nuclear program. He had long suspected a Saudi tie to the A. Q. Khan Pakistani nuclear network, but he was incredulous that the United States was involved and shocked and outraged that the Saudis could be negotiating with bin Laden. Talbott immediately called the secretary of state's office to request an urgent meeting.

———

Within an hour, Talbott and Tony were in the seventh-floor office of the secretary of state. Talbott deferred to Tony to brief the secretary. She seemed distracted, not connecting with the severity of the information.

When Tony concluded, the secretary, without a deliberative moment, said, "With all due respect to the dead, al Swainee is not credible. Upon learning of his death under somewhat suspicious circumstances, our embassy cabled me that he was a marginalized member of the royal family, taken to self-delusion about his influence, and self-destructive in his behavior."

Rising from her chair, the secretary continued: "Saudi Arabia is our ally in the war on terror, and we have committed to protect the kingdom, especially since 9/11. There is absolutely no evidence of U.S. support for a Saudi nuclear initiative. My predecessor urged the British to close down the BAE investigation, which might have raised suspicions as to illicit involvements with the Saudis by both our governments, and the attorney general took steps to assure we had that matter under our control. The most absurd suggestion is that the king would collaborate with Osama bin Laden, much less that he has visited Saudi Arabia since 9/11."

"With respect, Madam Secretary," Tony said, "we have direct testimony. As I just explained . . . "

"This is the rambling of a drunkard with an inferiority complex who was trying to impress an attractive female celebrity. And, Mr. Ramos, is it possible you have been deceived by a ruse?" She looked directly at Tony, "With your limited—would it be correct to say, nonexistent?—experience in intelligence craft, you would be an easy target."

"I was in Special Forces," Tony pointed out.

"Not the same," the secretary declared. "Do you have any documentary evidence to support your claim about bin Laden in Riyadh?"

"We were going to get it from Zaid, but then, as you know . . . "

"So the answer is no."

Tony nodded.

"And if you think this administration is going to jeopardize this alliance over hearsay and innuendo, you ought to resign from the State Department right now. I will not have that kind of gossip and rumor-mongering going on under my watch, I can assure you."

She rose, staring down at the ambassador and Tony. "I want both of you to clearly understand what I am about to say. You are never again to discuss this. And Mr. Ramos, I am classifying your information as national security top secret. Tell Ms. Billington she is under the same mandate. The presidential election is in seven weeks. In case you haven't noticed, our candidate has closed the margin to less than four points. But he cannot tolerate dealing with this incendiary rumor."

Walking to and opening the door from her office to the lobby, she concluded, "If you encounter any further drivel about these bizarre allegations, bring them to my attention, and my attention only. Thank you."

As they walked back to his office, Talbott's generally unshakeable diplomatic mien had turned purple. "Everything in this city is politics, not politics as in Socrates, but politics as in power. I feel as if I don't even belong here anymore."

Talbott stepped into an alcove, joined by Tony and the bust of John Jay. "This is beyond politics. The lives of millions of people are at risk; the ability of the world to live together with something like peace. Avoiding this nuclear Armageddon may be the last chance for civilization, and she's talking about making us look better for the election in November."

The two men reached Talbott's office. He closed the door as soon as they were inside.

"Tony, what you have uncovered is the single most important threat to the world today. The potential is cataclysmic, and the time to avoid the ultimate calamity is short. We don't have time to go through bureaucratic niceties. I want you to take this as your own and only assignment until it is contained."

"Contained?"

"Contained by locating and destroying the nuclear material before bin Laden can use it against us."

While Tony paused to assimilate what Talbott had said, the ambassador continued: "And you will be alone. I don't trust the FBI, the CIA, the Department of Homeland Security, and certainly not the leadership of this department. They might use anything you came up with to frustrate, not facilitate, your mission."

As a veteran of INR, Tony was fully aware of the politicization of the government. If the leadership of America's national security policy would withhold action when the nation was at extreme risk, what was his responsibility? It was glaringly clear.

"I understand the rules of engagement," Tony assured him. He was in personal and professional conflict. Tomorrow was the night for the delayed reunion with Carol. But he wanted to squeeze Laura for more of her Jeddah-derived intelligence. Juggling relationships with two women was something he thought he had given up with his pro tennis career.

"Carol, I hope you are in a good mood. I'm asking for another twenty-four hours. I've been in meetings all morning with Talbott, and I still have some debriefing to do on Saudi Arabia and Kuala Lumpur. Would you still take me in if it were Monday instead of tomorrow night?"

Carol did not disguise her disappointment. "I've got the ingredients for the most delectable paella a girl from Tennessee has ever cooked. And I bought tropical lingerie in the Caymans."

"Even without the enticements there is no place I would rather be. But . . . " Tony stalled, "I'll make it up to you. I promise."

Laura waited until it was after nine on Sunday morning in Long Beach to breach Tony's directive. From the rear of his first-floor kitchen, she called Jeralewski.

"Are you better today?"

"No," Jeralewski said gruffly. "And it isn't going to be any better for you. I've started the process to call your note."

All of the characteristics that had caused her to be called the bitch wolf of the camera poured out. "The worst day in my life was when I set foot in your office."

"No, no, Ms. Billington. That is yet to come. I discern you fail to appreciate your circumstances." Jeralewski paused to let his words have their intended effect. "I control your future. As a sanction to you and a message to others, it is my intention to crush it."

Stung, Laura screamed, "You—you are—you conniving, dirt-around-white-collar scum. You have sold your country for three billion pieces of gold and now you are trying to take me down with you. You bastard."

Calmly, Jeralewski responded, "Your peripatetic boyfriend has been vomiting the spew you gave him from Jeddah to the secretary of state and God knows who else. Madam Secretary has called her boss and told him what is coming."

"And why would he care?"

"Because this close to an election, no one wants to open up a Pandora's box full of the most volatile issues we face—Democrat or Republican. The law of unintended consequences is just too harrowing. No one knows who will be struck by collateral damage."

Laura placed her phone on the kitchen's wooden countertop. She breathed deeply. In a considered voice, she said, "Roland, I think you have blown this out of perspective. Let me suggest that rather than searching for a scapegoat you would be better served to plan a counteroffensive."

Jeralewski's sneer crept through the wireless transmission. "Rest assured that within Peninsular we are well prepared to do so. Rather than concern yourself about Peninsular, you would be better advised to consider your own self-preservation. You have thirty days to do so, and if it means anything to you, I have accepted your resignation. You are no longer a Peninsular associate."

Tony met Laura at The Monocle restaurant near the Capitol. She had regained her composure after the volcanic discussion with Jeralewski. As she had done throughout her professional career, she had used the intervening hours to plot her personal survival strategy.

Tony was stimulated by the assignment he had been given; he felt a hormonal surge of an intensity totally different from those before his most important tennis matches. Seated at a romantically lighted side table, Laura and Tony diverted from the tension of the past week to more personal matters. They had grown up within ten miles of each other and had many common memories.

———

Later that evening, after a short stop at one of Tony's favorite bars, they walked up 7th Street to Tony's townhouse. Laura slipped out of her dress into jeans and a sweater, while Tony opened a bottle of Finca Abril malbec. With Tony's arm casually around her shoulders, Laura returned to their Jeddah telephone conversation four days earlier.

"Tony, can you tell me where you think this is going?"

He moved his arm and turned to face her. "There's a lot more to learn, but I think there are at least three key players—Osama, the king, and the Americans who made it possible. I suspect some combination of those three is responsible for the hit men who killed your father and Zaid's push from the roof.

"My guess is that the senator's op-ed speculation was overinterpreted and led the kingdom or the Americans, or both, to conclude that he knew too much to be left 'in place.' The question is, Who are those Americans?"

"How are you going to find them?"

"I've got a hunch if we can follow the money trail far enough, we'll close the loop. And we have the right person on the hunt."

"Who's that?"

"Well, it's a forensic accountant at the Treasury Department. Her name is Carol Watson. She's been working a case in which a Brit defense firm has been paying bribe money to Saudis. It may have something to do with their nuke program; we should find out in the next few weeks. Let's wait until she finishes her work."

Clearly dissatisfied, Laura asked about Tony's encounter with the secretary of state. He had enough control to respect the privacy of his and the ambassador's conversation, even if he had lost respect for his leader.

Laura moved toward Tony, flitting in like the hummingbird's approach to the ovule. She stretched her back on the sofa, her head lowered on Tony's lap. Looking up, she asked, "Tony we're in this together—together," she stammered, "to determine who killed my father. If you're unwilling to share with me, our chances of catching the murderers will be close to zero." She began to lift her cashmere Fair Isle sweater. "Remember, we're a team."

"Laura," Tony responded, "do you remember my last piece of advice for your dealings with the Saudis? It was to be prepared to use alcohol and the expectation of sex as a means of extracting information. Methinks you have learned that lesson too well. It's late and we've both had a stressful three days. You can use my bedroom; I'll sleep here."

Without a word she rose frigidly and climbed the eighteen steps to the second-floor bedroom.

Twenty minutes passed. Laura crept back down the stairs and assured herself that Tony was asleep on the sofa. She retrieved her cell phone from her purse and tiptoed toward the bathroom. In the moonlight she mistakenly opened the closet door. She brushed against a woman's summer outfit with a discernable residue of white linen perfume.

"Slut," she muttered.

Now in the bathroom, she punched a key.

"Roland, this is Laura; I have something to tell you."

SEPTEMBER 14
Washington, D.C.

The attorney general of the United States was an angry man. Less than thirty minutes after demanding an immediate meeting with the secretary of the Treasury, he was sitting beneath the chandelier in the secretary's gold-inlaid office adjacent to the White House.

The attorney general was the cabinet member closest to the president. He had served in his state administration and as White House general counsel before moving to the top legal position in the U.S. government. He was a small, intense man with the pugnacious personality of a middle-aged welterweight fighter.

In contrast, the secretary of the Treasury was newly arrived from the upper echelons of Wall Street to the cauldron of Washington politics.

It was understood that his job was to make no waves, keep the economy on keel or at least create that perception through the election, and be an all-purpose cheerleader for the administration's meager economic accomplishments.

"What in the hell are you doing?" the attorney general demanded. "My people have told me that your auditors have been poring over the accounts of a Swiss and Cayman bank and are about to disclose some very sensitive information. Is anybody giving your Treasury people adult supervision?"

The secretary knew without further scolding the attorney general's concerns. He had been briefed by Carol and her supervisor on her findings in Zurich. They were on his schedule for the next day to report on her discoveries at a bank in the Caymans.

"When we were given the assignment of supporting your investigation of the BAE-Saudi connection," he said, "it was my understanding that we were engaged in a serious corruption matter that might have implications for the policy decision to allow BAE to acquire a U.S. defense contractor. We have been doing what we thought you wanted."

"Mr. Secretary, the president was choosing his words with purpose when he labeled our response to 9/11 as a *war on terrorism*. He knew it was necessary to disguise the truth, and a public 'declaration of war' was the means to do so. As Churchill said, 'In wartime, truth is so precious that she should always be attended by a bodyguard of lies.' That certainly includes the precious truth of the Saudi undertaking. Anyone without the highest clearances, including Ms. Watson, has no need to know that truth or its attendant bodyguards."

With visible rage, the secretary stood, towering six inches above the attorney general, and placed his right index finger in the AG's chest. "God damn it, I know you have a different set of rules here, but I am going to do my business. If you didn't want us to be professional, you should never have asked us in. But having done so, we are going to follow this as far as the facts lead and place whatever we find in the hands of the appropriate officials. Mr. Attorney General, it sounds like that will not be you. When the time comes, I will inform you with whom we have shared our conclusions. I think it best you leave."

In his limousine back to the Department of Justice, the attorney general placed a call to the president's chief of staff. "Tom, we have a problem; one hell of a problem. I need to talk with the boss."

SEPTEMBER 14

Long Beach

In the penthouse executive suite of Peninsular Corporation, two men faced each other in a corner office. The older man sat with his legs crossed—the demeanor of one comfortable with the exercise of power and with his own importance.

The more assertive one was almost a generation younger. His supple body was tense, poised on the farthest edge of the sofa. "Mr. Chairman, one might conclude we have lost control. I assure you that is not the case."

With a southern accent tuned at an Ivy League university, the older man offered, "Roland, I am concerned. It seems every week there is yet another crisis. Have we abandoned our principles—to keep our understandings with both partners and clients confidential, to use force only as the last resort?"

The younger man began to pace the serenely patterned carpet. "Mr. Chairman, we have abided by your rules. Our operative in Malaysia clearly overreacted, against all our guidelines. We believe he may have been mentally disturbed to react the way he did, and I assure you, he will not be involved with any future operations."

"A little late, wouldn't you say?"

"Certainly," the younger man said with regret. "He was supposed to follow the model by which the senator and the black man in the Caymans were dealt with—in a much more orderly fashion, with our agents quickly taken out of the country." He sipped from his delicate china teacup. "We have a new matter. The senator's daughter, the photographer Laura Billington, has been enlisted as a Peninsular associate. In Jeddah she received information from a grandson of the king."

"Was that the same young man who tumbled from the Imperial?"

"Yes. He told Ms. Billington enough to impress her, and she, in turn, repeated this tripe to a young analyst at State's INR bureau."

"Is that the same underling you told me was poking around in Saudi Arabia and Malaysia, asking questions about stale 9/11 matters?"

"He is," Jeralewski answered.

"Umpff," he scoffed. "That doesn't sound too serious to me. Do you know what Ms. Billington had been told?"

"About our special program with the kingdom. That His Highness was negotiating with Osama bin Laden to share some of its results. As you know, when we concluded our understandings with the King, he committed that he and his successors would guarantee that none of the project's output would go beyond the control of the royal family without our explicit sanction. King Khalid Ibn Abdul Aziz has broken this solemn understanding."

"God damn," muttered the older man. "I was afraid the old Lion of Arabia would replicate Munich in Riyadh to hold onto power. It appears he has done so with a modern Hitler aspiring to harbor nuclear bombs. Who knows about this?"

"At least Billington, her INR friend Tony Ramos, and probably Ramos's superior, William Talbott. The secretary has spoken to me, and she is blaming us for allowing this to happen and the possible impact it could have on the election."

The older man leaned forward, "In other words, Roland, she will throw us under the bus, if necessary. What was the line from the old *Mission Impossible* show—'The Secretary will disavow any knowledge of your actions'?"

The younger man nodded grimly. "It goes beyond the secretary. We cannot count on any friends we have in government to continue to protect our activities." The younger man paused and glanced out to the Pacific before proceeding. "Ms. Billington is another matter. She is a very difficult, quixotic, self-centered woman. It was for her other qualities, access and creativity, not to mention her financial vulnerability, that we took her on."

"And you are convinced her value overrides her liabilities?"

With his hands clinched behind his head, Roland responded. "Yes. She has made a surprisingly creative observation that might just lead us to resolve several problems at once."

"What time parameters are you contemplating?"

"Our team is analyzing the strategy right now to contain the damage already done. It is not going to be an easy month."

His companion sighed, "The last month before an election never is."

The men rose and walked to the glass wall facing the Pacific.

"At least some of the news is encouraging. The Afghanistan developments have totally rattled the oil market. This afternoon, the cost of a barrel moved from ninety to ninety-eight dollars."

As the younger man escorted the elder to the elevator, they paused for a glimpse of the cable news on the television in the reception room. An intense commentator, with Biblical assurance, intoned, "The death of Pakistani president general Ali Siachen, ambushed in his helicopter, has brought the instability in Central Asia to crisis proportions. Before the smoke from the stricken aircraft had been extinguished, thousands of insurgents were in the streets of Karachi. While the culprit has not been identified, our sources are confirming that Iran is almost certainly involved."

SEPTEMBER 15–16

Washington, D.C.

Tony knocked on Carol's door with his signature two shorts, a pause, and one short. Carol opened it and clung to Tony. He saw her eyes were swollen from crying as she buried her blotchy face in his chest.

Tony lifted her to the sofa, closing the door behind them. Carol was in the professional woman's uniform of just-above-the-knee blue skirt and matching loose blouse. From its wrinkled condition, Tony assumed it was what she had probably worn to the office. He stroked her unkempt blond hair.

"What is it? Has something happened to Suzie?"

"Thank God, no. Tony, somebody killed Hector and I'm responsible." Carol broke into sobs.

Tony was silent, continuing to console her with gentle strokes of his finger through her hair. When she had gathered herself, he asked her if she felt up to telling him what had happened. "To start with, who was Hector?"

"Hector was the sweetest man and he loved your grandfather." Between bursts of tears she described her meeting with Hector Nuñez in George Town, his relationship with Tony's family, his assistance in allowing her to execute her assignment.

"At around three this afternoon an FBI special agent came to my office at the Treasury. He told me Hector had been murdered on the same night he took me to the bank vaults. From what the Cayman police have been able to determine, I may have been the last person to see him alive, except for the person who shot him. The agent asked me a lot of questions and said I would likely have to go back to the Caymans to be a witness. I may even be under suspicion. Tony, I don't know what to do." Carol clutched him as she broke down again.

"The first thing is to pull yourself together. From what you've told me, there is no way you could be a credible suspect. There must have been people who saw you at the Marriott that night. No murderer would wait twelve hours to leave the scene."

Carol interrupted, "And Tony, there is something else. Just like in Zermatt, a man was stalking me in George Town. He hid from me at Stern's and then followed Hector and me when we left the bank. The last thing Hector said to me was to be careful and get out of the Caymans as fast as possible."

"I'll report that tomorrow to Mr. Shorstein," Tony promised. "The best thing for you is to get control back in your life, starting tonight. Why don't you wash up and I'll get supper?"

Carol nodded and walked toward her bathroom. Tony went to the kitchen.

———————

Tony had lived alone long enough to be a pretty fair cook. Looking in the refrigerator, he saw the ingredients for paella, one dish every Cuban child learns to prepare. By the time Carol had gathered herself and dressed in casual jeans and a T-shirt, he had a bowl of the prawns, clams, mussels, calamari, rice Valencia, peppers, onions, and saffron that constituted this Latin standard. He put two plates on her coffee table. The final touch was chilled Adelita, a dry white Spanish wine.

A great deal had happened in both their lives since brunch at the Eastern Market. As they each forked bites of the paella and sipped wine, Tony recounted his trek from Riyadh to Jeddah and on to Kuala Lumpur, his near misses at death, and the briefing he had given Ambassador Talbott, and explained why he was now concerned for Carol's safety. The Cayman stalker was one more reason for apprehension.

"You'll be getting Secret Service attention, including periodic surveillance of this building. If they feel circumstances warrant, they'll provide personal protection, here and escorting you to and from work. Are you okay with it if it comes to that?"

"After what you've been through, my situation is a rose garden. Yes, I am very satisfied. There is one more development, but I'll save that for later."

Carol, now in better emotional control, filled in the details of her brief time in the Caymans, concentrating on what she had found in the vaults and her conviction that without Hector she would have been stonewalled. "Tony, what do you know about Peninsular?"

"It's a huge, very successful and influential private-equity firm. It was established in the 1990s by people with ties to the old administration."

Carol listened thoughtfully.

"And it's your conclusion that the vast majority of the BAE money didn't end up in Jeddah or Riyadh but in Peninsular's bank account in New York?"

"That's what I'm going to tell my boss when I debrief him tomorrow."

"What are you going to recommend he do with this information?" Tony asked.

"First, it's important you keep this undercover. Before tomorrow only three people know I have this information: Mr. Nuñez," Carol paused, "now only you and me.

"Second, the only way to find out where the money went next is to get access to Peninsular's accounts. It might be done through SWIFT and FinCEN records, but that would be difficult. Peninsular is a complex partnership and no doubt has blended these funds with others to conceal the ultimate recipients. It would also take a serious commitment of time and resources. We don't have the former and doubt this administration would make the latter available."

Not hiding his frustration at the tangled web, Tony asked, "So what would you recommend?"

"Given the political context and high profile of several of the Peninsular partners, I will recommend a search warrant to make a preemptive strike on its headquarters. I think I have enough evidence to meet the test of probable cause to convince a magistrate. Then we would have the primary-source records to know where the money went and who might be criminally responsible."

Carol let that hang in the air before she went to her next concern. "Tony, I'm afraid I might lose control again, but I have to tell you about the latest thing that's happened."

Tony held her again. "Don't stress yourself. Tonight isn't the last time we can talk about these things."

"I know, but I want to. I need your advice and help. That special agent told me something else about Hector's murder. In the rug where his body was found there were two .45 caliber cartridges." She looked Tony directly in the eyes. "And I don't think this is a coincidence. When I got back here at about six, these were leaning against my door." Carol reached into her handbag and extracted two .45 caliber casings. "I have no idea . . . what do they mean?"

"Jesus Christ," Tony exclaimed. "Hector wasn't the first person to get this message. This is just what was in the senator's envelope. He'd found them in his car the day before he was run over." Tensely, he recounted the events Billington had laid out in his memo of mid-July. "He thought they were a sign he was being watched. Tomorrow morning, in addition to Shorstein I'll report to the D.C. police and the FBI guy. And I'm also going to call Talbott and ask him to call the Treasury secretary to beef up the Secret Service protection. In the meantime . . . "

Tony began rolling up his right pants leg. Below the knee was the Glock 26 he had used in Jeddah. It was attached to his calf with a Velcro wrap. "Since I was given permission to take on Billington's secrets, Talbott has insisted I carry this. You take it. Have you ever used a handgun?"

"Growing up in rural Tennessee, learning to shoot was a rite of passage; didn't make any difference if you were a boy or a girl."

"Carol, I never want to impose myself on you, particularly with what you're dealing with. I'd had an idea what tonight would be like—some plans that have been on my mind since Jeddah. But if you'd rather, I can certainly understand if you want to be alone."

She looked at him with a tenderness he had not detected before. "I suspect I've had the same steamy plans. I may be allowing other parts of my anatomy to control my brain, but I need to be with you tonight." Carol lifted her T-shirt over her head. She was not wearing a bra.

It took half an hour and increasingly intimate foreplay to change the atmosphere from anxiety to passion. Tony lifted Carol and carried her into the kitchen.

Tony and Carol had developed their own techniques of sexual athleticism, but this was the first time amid the remainder of paella. Tony partially unzipped Carol's jeans. He was further stimulated at finding no undergarments. As she leaned back against the sink, Tony rotated against her, initially through his jeans, and as they slipped progressively lower, down to bare flesh.

Carol wrapped her fingers around Tony's shoulders. "Be gentle," she whispered. Both naked, Tony again carried her to the bedroom and two hours of aggressive lovemaking.

At 7:00 a.m. Tony dressed in one of the suits he stored in Carol's closet, took the elevator to the basement, and drove up the incline and out into the noisy, early-morning traffic on Connecticut Avenue.

Carol was emerging from her dreams when she heard what sounded like Tony's signal knock on her door. Surprised but pleased, she went naked to the door, opened it slightly, and instantly tried to push it closed. The silencer of a Beretta blocked her attempt.

Fleeing to the bedroom, she grasped Tony's handgun and fired it at the full-bearded man in a denim maintenance uniform standing in front of her. Her shot hit the doorframe.

The first blast from the Berretta struck Carol in the crotch. Blood spurted as from a fountain.

The man stood over Carol, her diamond-blue eyes aflame with panic and pain. He admired and was aroused by her bloody, supple body. With a faint smile he fired three shots into her breasts, and then, as a final flourish, one between her blue eyes.

Exiting by the same stairwell he had climbed less than ten minutes before, he walked to the side street and left in a waiting Dodge.

SEPTEMBER 16–18

Washington, D.C. ★ *Maxwell Air Force Base, Montgomery, Alabama*

In his new office after his morning workout at the Senate gym, showered and suited, Tony checked with the State Department's security officer and was given the name of Detective Randall Larsen at the District of Columbia Police Department.

"What was that address again?" the detective asked.

"3201 Connecticut Avenue, Apartment 441," Tony repeated.

"OK. What's your report?"

"Last evening while visiting with a lady friend at that address, Ms. Carol Watson, she told me that while she was on a Treasury assignment in the Caymans she was stalked by an unidentified man and, on returning to her apartment yesterday afternoon, she had found two .45 caliber cartridges in front of her door. She gave them to me and I have them here in my office."

"We get a lot of suspicious incident reports here, but I've got to say that is a first."

"Not to me," Tony responded. "One of my former bosses, Senator John Billington, retired back to Florida, discovered two similar casings in his car and the next morning was killed in a hit-and-run being investigated by the Miami-Dade Police as a homicide."

"I'll check that out. What was Ms. Watson's reaction?"

"Disturbed. No, I would say frightened."

"Understandable."

"I told her to be especially careful and I promised to call the D.C. police and report. And, Detective Larsen, there's another piece to this puzzle: Ms. Watson is a forensic accountant for the Treasury Department. Last week she was reviewing bank records in the Caymans. On two occasions Ms. Watson felt she was being stalked. She was informed yesterday by an FBI special agent that an employee at the bank who was particularly helpful was murdered and that two .45 casings were found with his body. As soon as we hang up I'm going to call him and tell him that Carol has now gotten the same gift."

"OK, I'll call her for more details. And, Mr. Ramos, keep the cartridges in a safe place where they won't be misplaced or altered. It is important we maintain the chain of evidence. I'm sending officer Lindsay Neas to collect them."

"Thank you, Detective."

Tony next called the FBI special agent and left a voice message that Carol had also been the recipient of two .45 shells. John Oxtoby took Tony's message about the stalker and promised to inform Samuel Shorstein. He seemed more convinced now that her suspicions were credible than he had been almost two months earlier.

For much of the three days since receiving Talbott's mandate to contain the bombs Osama bin Laden appeared capable of possessing, Tony had focused on identifying the right questions and the beginnings of the answers. The United States had devoted years and more than a trillion dollars to the search for bin Laden, with no success. He had at most weeks, possibly days. And he was alone. From the White House to Foggy Bottom, the U.S. leadership seemed committed to a "Don't blame me" cover-up.

The first question was obvious: assuming bin Laden has access to weapons-grade nuclear material, where and how would he most likely use it?

After talking to his sources, Tony was convinced that the best thinking on the subject was located at the Counterproliferation Center at Maxwell Air Force Base, near Montgomery, Alabama. Concerned that operating too openly in his office would bring him to the attention of the secretary's henchmen, Tony waited until he had completed his work on Wednesday and left for a prearranged meeting at Maxwell the following day.

Tony was met at the Montgomery Municipal Airport by Chief Master Sergeant Willis Rankin, an Air Force escort. He had been a combat controller, parachuting in ahead of the 82nd Airborne. Sergeant Rankin was no stranger to the battlefield: Vietnam, Grenada, Panama, and Iraq in 1990–91 and during the last eight years, three tours in Afghanistan. On the thirty-minute drive to Maxwell in an Air Force's GMC van they talked about Rankin's recently completed fifteen-month deployment.

"I thought we were making progress until early last July," Rankin offered.

"What kind of progress?" Tony asked.

"Well, the number of attacks was down and the Afghans, like the Sunnis in Iraq, seemed to see us as the likely winners and were joining our side."

"And, what happened?"

"Then all hell broke loose. Even our base in Bagram was taking mortar fire, and more of the civilian Afghanis were no-shows because of the threat of roadside bombs on the way to work, and what I guess was an uptick in Taliban intimidation in the villages. And these were the same villages we had retaken just a couple of months earlier."

Stopped at a traffic light, Rankin squinted into the late-morning light. "I shouldn't be saying this, but if you have a chance to tell somebody with influence in Washington what a noncom in the field thinks: it's over. If we had moved even a year ago to get more troops, and I guess they would have come from the troops just sent back to Iraq, it could have made a difference. Those villages would have had some marines embedded with the locals, and they would not have been so scared. Let me tell you, these Taliban play for keeps. They cut the heads off your neighbors' sons and rape your daughters. That's not something many locals will stand up to."

As he accelerated, Rankin became more agitated. "From my grunt viewpoint, it's too late now. Even if the president wanted to do something different, wanted to send in more troops, it won't happen. The Taliban will wait us out. They have a saying: 'The Americans have all the watches; we have all the time.' I signed up for the Air Force during Vietnam. Afghanistan has the same smell. We need to figure out how we're going to get out without more of ours getting themselves killed. My service time is almost over, this is my last enlistment, but that's what I think."

———

Colonel Eleanor Hill met the van as it stopped in front of building H. Dressed in her blue uniform and modest jewelry, she was every bit of five feet, ten inches a military professional.

Offering her hand she said, "Mr. Ramos, I am honored you would come from Washington to meet with me. I trust my comments and those of my colleagues will be worth the effort."

Colonel Hill was the officer recommended to Tony as the most knowledgeable on Osama bin Laden and nuclear bombs. A twenty-five-year veteran of the Air Force and for the last eight years director of planning at the center, Hill had been identified by the small circle of experts in nonproliferation as having a unique grasp of the technology, policy, and geopolitics of weapons of mass destruction, especially nuclear. She had also been strongly recommended by Mark Block, who was aware of Senator Billington's high opinion of her and their frequent consultations.

Her office was two hundred square feet of military standard order. Other than a photograph of her parents and a younger sister and her Air Force Academy diploma, there were no personal effects.

Colonel Hill had prepared for Tony's visit. After introductory preliminaries of remembering the senator and expressing shock at the brutality of his death, she turned to the matter at hand.

"Consistently since bin Laden returned to Saudi Arabia from the Sudan, there have been reliable indicators of his future behavior. He does what he says he will do; his words make a difference." Reaching into her desk drawer she withdrew a binder. "There are those who think his bombasts are just that, over-the-top egotism. We think he is serious, including this recently re-released version of his pre-9/11 fatwa." Looking down she read:

> The ruling to kill the Americans and their allies—civilians and military—is an individual duty for every Muslim who can do it in any country in which it is possible to do it, in order to liberate the al-Aqsa Mosque and the holy Mecca Mosque from their grip, and in order for their armies to move out of all the lands of Islam, defeated and unable to threaten any Muslim. This is in accordance with the words of Almighty God, "and fight the pagan all together as they fight you all together," and "fight them until there is no more tumult or oppression, and there prevail justice and faith in God."

"His dramatic flair is also expressed in detailed, exhaustive preparations toward the goal of making each future attack more lethal than those before. The track record of U.S. deaths is five in the African embassies, seventeen seamen on the USS *Cole*, and three thousand in New

York City, the Pentagon, and Pennsylvania. He is determined that the next attack will exceed the number of deaths on 9/11."

His notebook open, Tony made notes on the colonel's briefing.

She continued, "Maybe his best-known characteristic is tenacity. If the first attack failed to accomplish the mission—on the World Trade Center in 1993 or on the USS *The Sullivans* at Aden in January 2000— he will retarget for a future operation. He knows his limitations. He does not use force for the traditional reasons of expansion of empire or personal vanity. His goal is chaos—to paralyze the emotional spinal column of the world by inflicting terror, a self-absorbed fear freezing people with the question, 'What will happen to me?'"

She walked Tony through additional instances in which each of these characteristics was illustrated. "Applying these predictors of future behavior to the facts as you think them to be, bin Laden would use his nuclear material to create several weapons. The number and size would be a function of the amount of nuclear material he controlled. Assuming it was sufficient for at least two or three smaller blasts—for instance, the size of the ones tested by the Pakistanis more than ten years ago, and one weapon significantly larger than the Hiroshima bomb—this is what we believe would be his plan for utilizing the bombs and have so advised the Pentagon: The smaller ones would be used against targets proximate to bin Laden's base of operations so as to reduce the risk involved in extensive transportation. If he were to use one or both in another country, he would look for the most porous international border crossing to reduce the chance of detection. If bin Laden had unsuccessfully or, by his standards, inadequately attacked a target before, it would be prioritized. He would select a target for maximum global emotional impact and instability, and high kill rate."

She paused for a sip of water. "These smaller weapon attacks would be done in a particular sequence, such as on the first Friday of successive months, so as to enhance the apprehension of another attack. After each of these blasts he is likely to make demands, demands he knows we could not or would not meet. After the first bomb it might be the removal of all international troops from Iraq and Afghanistan in thirty days; after the second, a repeat of the first demand and also that all foreign aid to Israel be halted and the Israelis evacuate the occupied territories within another thirty days. Or he might not make any demands at all—merely show he is in control.

"The final attack, using a weapon twice as powerful as the previous ones, perhaps more so, would be aimed at us."

Tony was stunned with what he had heard. "Twice the previous two?"

Colonel Hill nodded. "That would be two to three times Hiroshima and Nagasaki. At Hiroshima, the initial blast killed seventy thousand; at Nagasaki, forty thousand. You can do the math.

"Bin Laden would use the first weapon shortly after he has it in his possession. He would not hold it like the North Koreans, whose goal is to warehouse enough nuclear weapons to deter an enemy. His capability to securely store the weapons is limited; the sooner it is used, the less the danger."

"Convert that into a calendar prediction," Tony requested.

"Assuming it is weaponized on receipt or he has the capacity to weaponize it, such as with the designs of A. Q. Khan . . . "

Tony's mind flashed back to Ambassador Talbott's comments on Sunday. "You mean the Pakistani?"

"Yes, designs Khan provided to the North Koreans—no more than ten days."

Tony thought, *Mission Impossible has become a hell of a lot tougher.*

"I don't think any of the three or four bombs he might have would be delivered on top of a missile. We have no reason to suspect he has access to such a device, but if he did, it would require more time than bin Laden is prepared to wait. But more important, only a fool would send the bomb with his signature on the means of delivery. And whatever you think of him, bin Laden is no fool."

Tony interrupted. "Isn't our Star Wars defense based on the assumption that a missile would be the most likely means of delivering the weapon?"

"Mr. Ramos, I am providing you with our best intelligence analysis, not what is politically correct. If the United States is truly committed to a policy of deterrence through maximum retaliation, and our commander-in-chief has repeatedly said we are, the use of a missile with a 'return address' would be the ultimate irrationality."

"Have you told that to the Pentagon?"

"To the uniformed leadership, yes; to the civilians, no. It's not what they want to hear."

Tony nodded acceptance of what Colonel Hill had said, and she continued: "Rather, it would be more conventional, a truck or a cargo container. That very conventionality would be an element of its capacity to inflict chaos through trauma."

"I don't want to be argumentative, but won't it be difficult for a bunch of reformed Bedouins living in a cave to almost overnight acquire the logistical sophistication to, for instance, place an enabled nuclear device on a transoceanic cargo ship?"

"The old al-Qaeda was able to plan and execute 9/11. The new, the post-9/11, al-Qaeda is more like a franchise than the hierarchical organization bin Laden led when he had a sanctuary in Afghanistan. General Motors has become McDonald's. Most likely, the attacks would be carried out through a franchisee, like al-Qaeda on the Arabian Peninsula or al-Shabaab in Somalia, with al-Qaeda Central providing financial and operational support and the weapon. Decentralization makes al-Qaeda more violent, more nimble, able to anticipate and plan around local defenses."

For two hours, Tony continued to explore the colonel's projections and analysis, challenging her assumptions. She invited three members of her policy unit to help answer Tony's questions. Satisfied that Colonel Hill was the real thing, he left her office confident he had the answer to Question One but staggered by the challenges of Question Two: Where are the weapons and how can they be contained within, what—days? hours?

Sergeant Rankin was waiting to drive Tony back to the airport. Tony climbed in the front passenger seat.

As they drove, Tony turned to Rankin. "Sergeant, I've spent a lot of my intelligence career analyzing and trying to understand Afghanistan because it was the place from which al-Qaeda launched its attack against us. I concluded that the war in Iraq was a distraction from completing the mission there. In the last couple of years I've altered my analysis. My assessment was that the stability of Afghanistan was fundamental to our new national security priority, Pakistan."

Tony paused to look out the window at this modern city that had been the first capital of the old Confederacy. "I've been thinking about what you said this morning, what I just heard from Colonel Hill, and what I learned in Saudi Arabia and Malaysia. Maybe events have circled back with a new end point. We need to get our focus back on al-Qaeda. The reality is that only a few—probably less than a hundred—al-Qaeda operatives are still in Afghanistan. But the war in Afghanistan is soaking up most of our capabilities, and you've got a better read on where the war is going than the president and the generals. As we fight it, not just in the north of the country—which is already gone—but eventually all of Afghanistan will be lost. And while we are nailed down there, al-Qaeda is getting stronger. I'm thinking we need a strategy for cutting our losses and refocusing like a laser on al-Qaeda in Pakistan and the other places it has established a beachhead, beginning with Somalia and Yemen."

"Thank you, sir," Rankin responded.

Tony's BlackBerry rang.

"Tony, this is Mark."

"Yes, my friend, next Tuesday morning is a go, but this time let's go over to the new courts by the south Capitol metro station. I've got a new friend, Air Force sergeant Rankin, who has given me some very valuable insights as to what is happening on the ground in Afghanistan."

Rankin's eyes were locked on the airport traffic, as a smile of appreciation rippled across his face.

"I'll tell you about it after I beat your ass."

"Tony, this is serious. Are you sitting down?"

"Solid. In the shotgun seat of an Air Force van in Montgomery."

"Tony, Carol was killed. The *Post* is just getting the story up on its website, but what they say is that the D.C. cops were contacting her on a report of suspicious activity and found her shot to death in her apartment. They're not releasing any further information until the medical examiner is finished."

Tony's face drained. He felt the air suddenly disappear from his lungs so completely that he gagged, then coughed to recover. He slumped in his seat and moaned.

"You all right, Mr. Ramos?" Sergeant Rankin asked.

Tony did not answer. He could hear Mark calling his name on the BlackBerry he had dropped to the van's floorboard. Tears, an extremely rare phenomenon for Tony, began to roll down his face.

But then some instinctive force kicked in, learned and cultivated in his special ops days. He knew he couldn't give in to his grief, not just yet. He had to focus, figure out what to do next. He retrieved the phone and said, "Mark, would you meet me at Reagan? I'll be there about 7:30 on a Delta flight from Atlanta. Find out as much as you can. And would you get me Carol's parents' number? They're still living in Spring Hill." Tony's voice broke. "That's all I can do now."

SEPTEMBER 19

New Delhi, India ✶ *Islamabad, Pakistan* ✶ *Longitude 71°7'51.16" East, Latitude 34°9'18.24" North*

The Indian prime minister was hosting a reception at the official residence for eight prominent European Union business leaders. With the politeness and refinement of a seasoned political leader, the prime minister chided his guests for their procrastination in following the Americans' example of surging investment in India. As he recited the comparative economic statistics on investment and trade, an aide delivered a message.

Displeased with the interruption, the prime minister glanced at the note and blanched, a charge of anxiety stiffening his body. Barely able to speak, he muttered to the Europeans, "I have been informed that a device—apparently nuclear—has been detonated in Mumbai. That is all we know as of this moment. I regret I must excuse myself."

Maulana Fazullah, the new president of Pakistan, who had taken power in the aftermath of the assassination of President Ali Siachen and the ensuing civil eruption, read an email message from New Delhi. The statement, issued by the Indian prime minister within the previous hour, read: "The nation extends its deepest condolences to the thousands of our fellow citizens who have lost their lives in the dastardly attack on Mumbai this day. Their grieving families should know that every resource of our government will be deployed to identify the murderers and bring them to the sternest justice. It is far too early for a final judgment. Yet the relationship between this horrid act and the seizure of power in Pakistan by an extremist and rogue regime is all too apparent to ignore. For the security of the nation, I have placed our military on full alert and have ordered the deployment of twenty-five divisions of the Army to the Pakistani border. Until further notification, the security of the homeland is at Stage Red."

For a man who had known much violence and bloodshed, Fazullah was stunned. He directed that a call be placed to the Indian prime minister and was informed that there was no emergency, no fail-safe, communication protocol between India and Pakistan.

Turning to the joint chiefs of the Pakistani military services, newly designated following the execution of their predecessors, Fazullah proclaimed, "With Allah as my witness, our hands are clean. We have taken no hostile action against the Indians. But we must protect ourselves. Exercise your authority for our ultimate defense, and ready our missiles for deployment. Command the army to prepare to confront our enemy."

At the same time, west-northwest of Pakistan's capital city, the tall man with the stubble of beard was ebullient.

"Even though we committed only the smallest of our three nuclear devices, praise be to Allah, we have accomplished all of our objectives. We have eliminated over sixty-thousand of the infidels, twenty times 9/11. Our new partners in Mumbai followed our plan and implemented the attack without a flaw. The idea of using an ambulance as the means of delivering our device was brilliant—learned from our brethren in London—using a modern Trojan horse to gain unobstructed access to our target. The Indians have misread the evidence and are now massing for an attack on Pakistan. The chaos of war is within our reach. The terror of the world is reflected in every nation that has gone to the highest level of alert; the economies of the developed world are teetering. With our oil now at $108 a barrel, our brothers will be able to mount even greater assaults against the enemy. There is panic as to where the next nuclear device will be utilized."

After a pause sufficient to indicate the leader had concluded his remarks, a younger man using a PowerPoint presentation on an LG screen said, "Our wise leader has directed that the balance of our material be conserved for two additional attacks. He has commanded that the third attack be on the greatest infidel and with the most force. Our leader has determined that on October 10 our second device will be deployed. He will soon inform us as to the target of this attack, thanks be to Allah."

In the rear of the cave, the only woman in attendance, dressed in a black burka, listened attentively. Her despair over the prospects of indiscriminate violence had now solidified. While many marveled at the ability of arguably the best-known man on earth to avoid detection, she reflected on the changes this isolated and bizarre life had inflicted on him. She had known him when he was the young warrior defending the sovereignty and religion of ancient peoples under assault by a modern industrialized army. He was charismatic, intuitive, romantic; she had personally experienced all of these traits. Now, he was frequently withdrawn, moody, short-tempered, detached.

Where would this lead? Who would be the next victims? And for what purpose? Is Mamata safe?

SEPTEMBER 19

Washington, D.C.

Tony was transfixed by the television images from Mumbai. The central business and financial sections were flattened. It reminded him of the pictures of Nagasaki after the bomb that ended the war. Five hours after the explosion, the surrounding ring of the destroyed city was still in flames. Scenes of terrified people fleeing were intercut with those of the Indian army mobilizing for a run to the Pakistan border, and others of the new Pakistani president denouncing the accusation made against his government.

A thoroughly depressing day became more so as Tony met the Watson family at the arrival area of Reagan Airport's concourse A. As this was the first time he had met them and Tony wasn't confident he would be recognized, he held a handmade cardboard sign with the single word "Watson."

Fred and Sarah Watson looked considerably older than their late fifties. Their clothes were worn and rumpled as if they had thrown them on with no attention to appearance. Their eyes were reddened and betrayed the shock of what they had first heard from the police the previous day. Exhaustion was reflected in their shuffling gaits as they pulled black wheeled bags.

Surprise was also evident as they turned into the main terminal and first saw Tony's face. They addressed him with solemnity.

"Mr. Ramos, we appreciate your call. Carol was very fond of you and ... " Mrs. Watson was interrupted by a muted sob.

"Carol was the most important person in my life. I loved her deeply. You have every right to be very proud of the daughter you raised. I just can't believe that ... " He couldn't finish his sentence, but from their eyes, the Watsons seemed to understand.

Nor was there a verbal response from either of them. Tony led them to the parking garage where he had parked Mark Block's Lexus sedan. Tony had calculated his Mustang was neither large enough nor the right style for the situation.

Between the airport and the Mallory Funeral Home, the conversation was sparse, centering on the few details known about Carol's death.

"The police have calculated the time of death as between 6:30 and 7:30 yesterday morning," Tony detailed. "They say it was instantaneous, so she didn't suffer. As of this afternoon, they didn't have a suspect but were saying they had several leads. I'm sorry, but that's all I know."

At Mallory Funeral Home there were decisions to make, ones that overwhelm families, for which they are almost always unprepared. Carol's body was mutilated beyond consideration of an open casket. The Watsons declined the invitation for a personal viewing. Although it was contrary to the tradition and their literal reading of the Bible, Fred and Sarah decided on cremation. Jonah Mallory told them the police and coroner had not completed their last examinations and it would probably be Monday at the earliest before the body could be seen to. Tony comforted the Watsons and shared their regret that the commencement of the healing process would be delayed over the weekend. When the arrangements were completed there would be a small, simple service for her D.C. friends and colleagues, with a fuller memorial service in Spring Hill later.

Shaken as he was, Tony had one professional task to perform. Back at his office after hours, he called Samuel Shorstein. This time he was able to reach the principal himself. Shorstein was aware of Carol's murder.

"While I was with her she told me of her disclosures from the Cayman bank," Tony said. "As Carol had done in Zurich, she took meticulous notes and copied pages of the bank's records. I assume these were taken by the D.C. police in their examination of her apartment."

"I asked the police to hold these for our officers' review," Shorstein said. "They'll be forwarded to the secretary of the Treasury and the FBI investigators. They are potentially very important in our BAE inquiry. And, I would think, as additional evidence in Ms. Watson's homicide. It sounds as if the police are building a very strong case."

Tony concluded, "I hope so."

It was half past six when Tony left the Truman Building and returned to his townhouse. Detective Randall Larsen was parked in front, waiting in his unmarked police car.

SEPTEMBER 19
Washington, D.C.

Seated in Tony's cramped living room, Detective Larsen was brutally direct. "Mr. Ramos, we consider you to be a primary suspect in the rape and murder of Carol Watson."

Tony had to drain his accumulated supply of restraint—what Ernest Hemingway had defined as courage, grace under pressure—to maintain a semblance of composure.

"Mr. Larsen," Tony declared in a steady voice, "I loved Carol. I would have never done anything to harm her—"

"Before you go further," Larsen interrupted, "I am obligated to inform you of your rights as a criminal suspect." He removed his wallet and extracted a credit card–sized piece of plastic. Placing silver-rimmed glasses on his nose, the officer read:

"You have the right to remain silent and refuse to answer questions. Do you understand?" Tony nodded yes.

"Anything you say may be used against you in a court of law. Do you understand?" Tony grimaced before nodding.

"You have the right to consult an attorney before speaking to the police and have an attorney present during questioning now or in the future. Do you understand?" Tony's head moved vertically.

"If you cannot afford an attorney, one will be appointed for you before any questioning if you wish. Do you understand?" Tony twisted in his chair before assenting.

"If you decide to answer questions now without an attorney present you will still have the right to stop answering at any time until you talk to an attorney. Do you understand?"

Tony spoke for the first time. "Yes."

"Knowing and understanding your rights as I have explained them to you, are you willing to answer my questions?"

Tony leaned back against the cushions. His mind was grappling with the reality that this was happening to him. Finally he said, "I want to make a call."

As he was exiting the living room he picked up the remote and clicked on his Samsung. CNN appeared. "Give me a couple of minutes to get my head straight."

On the kitchen wall phone, Tony punched in Mark Block's number. When the Flatbush Avenue accent penetrated his ear, Tony whispered, "Mark, I'm screwed."

"What's the problem, amigo?"

"The D.C. police detective, Randall Larsen, told me I'm a primary suspect in Carol's murder . . . murder and rape. He just read me my Miranda rights."

Tony could sense the intensifying of emotions as Mark was taking it all in. It made him temporarily mute. "Have you told him anything?" he finally asked.

"Only that I didn't kill Carol. I figured that was pretty safe."

"Tony, the only thing you are to say to Larsen is that you will consult your attorney before making any further statement."

"And what then?" Tony asked.

"I'm one hell of an attorney if you're in trouble with the IRS, but this is at another level. One of my partners is a former D.C. prosecutor. I'm going to bring her in. Before the cops will talk with us, I'll need you to sign an engagement agreement with our firm to be your lawyers."

"Mark, this ain't the only trouble I'm in. Next week I plan on leaving town for a very sensitive assignment Talbott has just handed me. How will this interfere?"

"Well, if you're in jail—"

"That's very reassuring," Tony responded.

"I'll contact my partner and try to set a meeting with Larsen tonight."

"Mark, I'm scared."

"Tony, you would be less than human if you didn't feel exactly that way. Try to get some sleep. Tell Larsen you won't talk with anyone until you have a lawyer."

"OK," was all Tony could muster.

Returning to the living room, Tony told Larsen of his decision.

Larsen shrugged and began stuffing papers back in his briefcase. "Here is my card. You might want to share it with your lawyer. Tell him to contact me in the next eighteen hours. Until I've talked with him, stay close." He looked up at Tony. "Mr. Ramos, we have sent the two .45s we picked up at your office to the police in Miami for matching. Haven't heard anything back. Thanks again for being a good citizen."

"Yeah, right," Tony replied.

"And, on another matter," Larsen offered, "I heard from that FBI special agent on the murder case in the Caymans. The police down there have sent the .45s to the bureau lab in Quantico. We're coordinating with Miami and the FDLE to determine if there's a match. Thanks for that one too."

As the detective rose to leave, both men turned to the Samsung, where the breathless young woman on the 7:30 p.m. segment of CNN was reporting, "In the wake of the first hostile nuclear detonation since the end of World War II, the situation between India and Pakistan continues to grow more tense . . . "

SEPTEMBER 19

Washington, D.C.

A call-waiting message from Mark Block was on Detective Larsen's phone when he returned to his office at 8:50. After phoning his wife to alert her that this would be another late night, Larsen called.

"Mr. Block, this is Detective Larsen returning your call."

"Thank you, Detective. Mr. Tony Ramos has retained me to represent him in the matter you discussed earlier this evening. I would like to meet with you tonight."

"Mr. Block, could we put that off until in the morning? I have an ass-high in-box to unload before I can call it a day, and I'll be better prepared to review the Watson file then than tonight."

"I respect your commitments. But my client has an unusually demanding assignment from the State Department, and it is imperative we bring this assertion of his involvement in the death of Ms. Watson to a resolution as soon as possible. I don't contemplate taking more than thirty minutes of your time."

Glancing at the digital wall clock, Larsen relented. "If you can get here by ten o'clock you'll have thirty."

"I'm on the way."

Mark was only five minutes late when he arrived at the D Street station, accompanied by Stephanie Toothaker. She was holding the document Tony had signed twenty minutes earlier.

Standing across the metal desk from Detective Larsen, Mark introduced Ms. Toothaker and handed him the agreement. Larsen scanned it and waved for the two attorneys to take seats in his pine office chairs.

Mark opened. "Thank you for meeting with us at this hour. It isn't relevant to your investigation, but as I said earlier, Mr. Ramos is carrying a very heavy portfolio at the State Department. It is important to him and the department that we get to the bottom of this as soon as possible."

"When rape and murder are the charges, it's generally considered more than trivial," the detective drily observed.

"What are the status of the investigation and my client's alleged involvement?"

Larsen leaned back with his glasses held in place by the tip of his nose. He leafed through the thin file before answering. "Ms. Watson was shot five times in her apartment on September 18 at approximately 7:00 a.m. Her body was found on the floor next to her bed twelve hours later by Officer Neas, who had been dispatched to discuss two .45 caliber casings that had been left at her front door the previous night. The body was transferred to the medical examiner, where it is undergoing analysis."

"Has she made any determination?"

"Beyond the time of the incident, she has made a tentative finding that Ms. Watson was raped before she was killed."

"What was the basis for the rape determination?"

Larsen glanced at Stephanie before proceeding; she was professionally focused. He continued, "The nature of the homicide. Except for the head shot, all the shots were fired at her breasts or sexual organs, which might support the theory that this was the conclusion of sexual predation."

Stephanie inquired, "Was there any physical evidence?"

"Although her sexual organs were compromised by the location of the wound, there was evidence of a forced entry of her vagina. There was blood and a large discharge of semen on the bedsheets, indications of multiple entries. We have sent the specimens to the lab for analysis. It is likely we will request a sample from your client."

Mark glanced at Stephanie. "It is our client's intention to be as cooperative as possible."

"That's appreciated," Larsen continued. "Mr. Ramos is a suspect because he had a continuing relationship with Ms. Watson and appears to be the last person in the apartment prior to the murder. Ms. Watson was on a watch list for another matter, and the Secret Service officer on duty outside her apartment noted Mr. Ramos's Mustang leaving the garage at 7:05. I hope to have further evidence when I interview him, other apartment owners at The Greenwich, and Mr. Ramos's colleagues at the State Department."

Mark pulled up his left sleeve and noted that the interview with Detective Larsen had gone ten minutes beyond the thirty minutes promised.

SEPTEMBER 22
Washington, D.C.

"No, Ms. Toothaker, we have not heard from the San Diego Police Department."

Stephanie slid the telephone console across the desk, closer to Tony so he could better hear the conversation. "Detective Martinez, when did you send them the photos from the FBI lab?"

"Let me check." There was an extended pause on the Miami side of the call. "They were sent west by the FDLE lab in Tallahassee on August 29. I was honestly surprised we could get that fast a turnaround from the Feds. I guess it helps to be a senator, even a dead one. I'd been in contact with the SDPD, telling them to expect the photos since we figured the gun shop where the box of .45 shells was sold would be the first place to go to determine if someone could put a name to the face."

"That's disappointing. I guess that means they haven't had a chance to check with the gun shop about the box's bar code?"

"No, actually an Officer Wyllie did that. The manager of the Lock & Load gun shop confirmed the box had been sold at his store in late June. He had a vague remembrance of the man who bought it; said he recalled he had a black beard and looked a little scary. That's a strange thing for a gun shop manager to say about a customer. Maybe when he sees the photos it'll jog his memory some more."

"Detective Martinez, Mr. Ramos and I appreciate your efforts. Please let us know when you hear anything further. Thank you."

Stephanie punched off her office phone and turned to Tony. "We're making progress, but time is not on our side. Any ideas about how to jack up the San Diego police?"

"Maybe." Tony scanned through the phone directory of his Black-Berry and rang up a number with a 619 area code.

"Could I speak to Ms. McKenzie, please?" Tony nervously twisted his Georgetown Class of 1996 ring.

Stephanie's phone rang. She turned her back on Tony and leaned down to listen to her call.

"Terri, thank you for taking the call." Almost thirty seconds elapsed before Tony said, "I'm sorry I haven't gotten back to you since I left. I know it's inexcusable but I've been on the road."

Another sixty seconds of Tony holding the phone, looking painfully at the back of Stephanie's head. Then, "OK, I'm an asshole. We agree.

Now, can I ask a favor?" Without waiting for a response Tony continued, "I need some help from the San Diego PD. I'll explain later why; just believe me, it's important. A Miami-Dade police detective, Luis Martinez, has sent to an Officer Wyllie of the SDPD some photographs of a man involved in the hit-and-run homicide of Senator Billington. It's urgent that Wyllie take them to the Lock & Load gun shop to see if the manager there can make a positive identification. Could you call Wyllie and ask as a special favor if he would do so ASAP and report back to Detective Martinez?"

Tony leaned forward in his chair. For the first time in two days he smiled and said, "Terri, I really appreciate this. I'll figure out some reason to be back in San Diego soon and thank you personally. You're the greatest."

Tony and Stephanie completed their conversations simultaneously. Stephanie said, "I've got some bad news. That was Detective Larsen. He said the semen samples match with yours. He also gave me the quickie version of interviews he's completed with two witnesses. Both described recent confrontations between you and Ms. Watson. Larsen wants you to come to the station."

Tony's body language was that of a man run over by a locomotive.

"Tony," Stephanie said as she laid a comforting hand on his shoulder, "let me take care of this. I've got some work to do at the office. Meet me at the station at five."

———————

Stephanie and Tony arrived at D.C. police headquarters at 4:45. Detective Larsen was interviewing a witness concerning another case. They waited in the lobby, where a stream of the capital city's population flowed by: a distraught mother looking for her missing daughter; an intoxicated or mentally challenged older man occasionally punctuating his mumblings to himself with the right and left hooks of a washed-up fighter; a young couple sitting beside each other holding hands. Tony knew that each one of these people had a story to tell; they probably thought he had one too.

Larsen waved them into his office.

"Mr. Ramos, the medical officer indicates it was your semen she removed from Ms. Watson's vagina."

Tony glanced at Stephanie. She nodded affirmatively.

"Ms. Watson and I have been living together since mid-August, sometimes at her place and on the weekends at mine on Capitol Hill. And, yes, we had intercourse Monday night."

"Mr. Ramos, the exam showed tearing of the vulva, which would be consistent with a forced entry. Did Ms. Watson consent to intercourse?"

Stephanie interrupted, "Detective, I am going to ask my client not to answer that question until I have had an opportunity to review the report."

"That's certainly your right. Now, Mr. Ramos, Mr. Franklin Sands has apartment 444 at the Greenwich, directly across the hallway from Ms. Watson. He has signed a witness affidavit that on August 12, you and Ms. Watson had a loud—his term was 'spitting match.' He remembered the date because two nights before was Ms. Watson's birthday and she had invited him to the party. He said he doesn't get many invitations from beautiful young women and he was glad to go. Mr. Sands says you pushed yourself into her apartment and he stayed up for an hour with his door cracked open in case he heard a racket and needed to call the police."

"Again, Mr. Larsen, I want to read the report," Stephanie said.

"Okay, the last piece is Mr. Benjamin Brewster, who was especially helpful. He said that in early August—he couldn't recall the exact date—he overheard an office telephone conversation in which you were screaming profanities at Ms. Watson. He said it was very disturbing to the other female employees in the vicinity. Mr. Brewster went on to say your display was consistent with your reputation as an amateur and professional tennis player. He compared you to—what's the name of the guy in the car rental TV ads?—Jim McEnroe?"

"It's John," Stephanie corrected. "I want to read that report, too, before my client comments. Is there anything else?"

"No, but frankly that makes your client not just a suspect, but now the main suspect in the rape and murder of Ms. Carol Watson."

"Before you go too far down that track, let me share a few other matters," Stephanie offered. "I understand that the forensics lab has determined the bullets that killed Ms. Watson were S&W .45s from a Beretta. Right?"

"That's correct," Larsen confirmed.

"The handgun that Mr. Ramos was authorized by the State Department to carry was a Glock 26, which, of course, fires a .37 millimeter round. Can I assume you are satisfied Mr. Ramos's weapon was not the murder weapon?"

"It wasn't the Glock, but I can't say that was the only handgun Mr. Ramos had access to."

"If we could determine the origin of the .45 casings used in the homicide of Ms. Watson and the identity of the person who purchased those and the Beretta, would you be prepared to reconsider your assessment?" Stephanie asked.

"Do you have that information?"

"Not now, but I hope to soon."

"How soon?"

"Forty-eight hours." Tony looked at Stephanie with dismay.

Detective Larsen waited for Stephanie to continue and, failing to do so, said, "There is one other matter I should tell you about. Mr. Ramos, your superior, Ambassador Talbott, called me on your behalf. He gave you a strong character reference and, within the limits of its classified nature, told me of the assignment you have been given. What I'm going to do is to leave this matter where it is; you are the primary suspect, but we are not going to lock you up at this time. I'll be continuing to gather evidence, and urge you to bring to my attention anything you find as soon as possible." Looking at his watch, he concluded, "It's 5:30 on Monday. I want to hear from you by this time on Wednesday. Ms. Toothaker, will you produce your client by then?"

"Yes, and we will have more information."

SEPTEMBER 23

San Diego

Terri McKenzie was waiting in her Acura on the arrival level of San Diego airport. She recognized Stephanie Toothaker from the description she'd received from her the night before.

Stephanie placed her overnight case in the trunk and slipped into the passenger seat. "Tony speaks so highly of you."

Terri laughed as she accelerated away from the terminal. "We've only spent one day together, yet I had a hissy fit when he didn't call until he needed something."

"That's part of why I thought I should get out here and explain the lay of the land before you got in deeper."

As Terri looked on expectantly, Stephanie told her the story of Tony and Carol, including Tony's status as the prime suspect in her rape-murder. "There may not be enough evidence for a beyond-a-reasonable-doubt conviction, but he is damn close to being charged, arrested, and put in the D.C. jail. And this comes at a very inconvenient time—a critical time—for Tony and the U.S."

As they neared El Cajon, east of San Diego, Terri remained silent. Her only visible emotion was a tightening of her hands on the steering wheel. Finally, "Do you think he's guilty?"

"That's not a fair question. My job is to defend my client. Honestly, I don't know. He sure doesn't seem the type, but in my business, you get cynical about what you see. I guess yours too."

Terri nodded.

"The evidence is strong, but what we're going to be doing today will go a long way in determining if it's conclusive. Tony's best—maybe only—shot to avoid arrest is to find a credible alternative as the real killer."

Lock & Load was located on the west end of a neighborhood shopping center.

Terri pulled into a parking space in front of the store, and she and Stephanie entered. San Diego police detective Stu Wyllie was waiting on them. He was a decade older than the two women and gave off the aura of mature assurance, like Clint Eastwood in his later movies. Wyllie had seen enough sides of human behavior to tolerate it with a wry smile and few words.

He led the way to a solitary rear corner of the shop where he opened an oversized beige envelope. He extracted ten black-and-white photographs, each focused on a Ford F-150. Starting from the top, he displayed and explained them.

"The photos are in order of the date and time they were taken. These two were taken about midnight on July 12 in the Miami airport garage. The camera didn't have a good angle, and there's not much to see except an oblique corner of the license plate.

"The next two were taken by the tollbooth cameras when the truck was driven through. The two men are reasonably discernable, particularly the thick-bearded one in the passenger's seat. The FBI lab guys did a good job on him."

Skipping through the next four, Wyllie came to the last two. "These are the most conclusive. They must have slowed before deciding to run the Palmetto red light, and the camera had a clear shot at their faces attentively looking up. I asked the FBI lab guys to enhance and enlarge these to life size." He turned the last photograph face-up. "And this is what we got. Better than your high school graduation photo, I bet."

———————

Jorge Santos, a thin forty-year-old with a swagger in his step and speech was the owner-manager of Lock & Load. Wyllie identified himself and introduced Terri and Stephanie without title or description.

Santos agreed to examine the photos to determine if any of the persons depicted in them looked familiar. He paused over the tollbooth shots, but couldn't be sure. It was when Wyllie turned over the enlargement that the lights went on.

"Mohammed al-something, or Mohadded; I don't know. He comes in here from time to time, more regularly last summer than any time before or since."

"What did he do when he came in?" Wyllie asked.

"Mainly, he bought ammunition. He used to have a long rifle; he said he took it to Texas to hunt deer and antelopes."

"Did he change his pattern?" Wyllie asked.

"Yeah. Midsummer; I know it was before the Fourth of July because I was off for a couple of weeks starting then. He bought a Beretta and a box of ammo. Most of our handguns are pretty much Saturday night specials, cheap. I remember whenever we sell a top-of-the-line handgun like that Beretta."

"If we had Muhammad in a lineup, could you pick him out of a crowd?"

"I think so."

"Could you look through your sales receipts before July 4 and determine his last name? Be sure the spelling is right—those Arabic ones are easy to confuse."

Santos excused himself and went into his back-room office, closing the heavy security door behind him.

––––––––––

Wyllie looked at his watch. Over ten minutes had elapsed. He waited another ten before unholstering his Glock 23 and opening the office door.

Santos's body was slumped on the floor, behind the steel desk. A towel extended from his mouth, partially obscuring the jagged slash that had ripped open his neck and throat.

Grimly, Wyllie returned to the main room. "I'm afraid we're not going to get any more information from Mr. Santos. He's been murdered." He immediately called the homicide unit and alerted the medical examiner's office.

On the sidewalk, each of the three took his or her time coping with what had just happened. Stephanie said, "I don't know if we have our man, but at least a serious suspect. Officer, since this is a registered gun shop, won't there be a record of the sale in the Bureau of Alcohol, Tobacco, and Firearms file?"

"Yes. ATF should have the name and information on the purchaser of the Beretta. Homicide will be on top of that."

Terri opened the passenger door of the Acura. On her seat were two .45 caliber casings.

SEPTEMBER 22−23
Washington, D.C.

Terri accompanied Stephanie on the red-eye flight back to Dulles. It didn't take much persuasion from Stephanie and Officer Wyllie to convince her she was at risk. The gory memories of that afternoon were haunting. Neither woman was able to release them sufficiently to rest on the five-hour flight.

Sensing a major story, the *Union-Tribune* was quick to grant Terri indefinite leave with pay.

Proceeding directly to Detective Larsen's office, the two exhausted women met Mark Block and Tony in a private interview room at D.C. police headquarters.

Stephanie filled in the details of the murder in San Diego, an event that had made it to page A4 of that morning's *Post*. "Wyllie thinks he will have the name of the Beretta purchaser today. The San Diego police will put on a full-court press to locate whoever that may be."

"We've been doing some investigating here," Mark chimed in. "I've been re-interviewing the State Department personnel Larsen talked to on Saturday. With Ambassador Talbott's assistance, I pulled the phone records of the INR bureau. Tony, your buddy Brewster has made twenty-two calls to the same number in Long Beach since the first of July."

Tony shook his head. "The INR is a place for analytical nerds. But we're around the spooks enough to have some idea of tradecraft. To make that many calls on an office phone for nonofficial business is stupid . . . and illegal. I think I can guess, but who were they to?"

"Peninsular."

"And what was his explanation?"

"Don't know. Brewster's been AWOL all week. We checked his apartment and he seems to have left town."

Detective Larsen called the group into his conference room. Stephanie briefed him on what had happened in San Diego, the photographs,

Santos's preliminary recognition of the suspect, and minutes later, his murder. The two bullet casings in Terri's Acura were the final icing on the cake.

"Have you heard back from the SDPD?" Stephanie asked. Then she added, "On the bullets?"

Larsen responded, "No, but at this point their origin is secondary." His desk phone rang as he was finishing his thought: "What I'm interested in is the identification of the person who bought the Beretta."

He spun his chair so he was facing the rear office wall and hunched over to take the call, leaving the other participants to gaze at each other in silence.

The detective replaced the receiver and, head still down and scribbling notes, slowly rotated to his original position.

Turning to Tony, Larsen said, "Mr. Ramos, it appears as if the Watson case has taken a new twist. That was Officer Wyllie. He says the ATF has given them the name of the man who bought the Beretta, and the homicide unit has been sent to bring him in for questioning. Pending what we hear further from California, I am reducing your status from suspect to person of interest. Ambassador Talbott has taken personal responsibility for your appearance, should it be required. Good luck on Mission Impossible."

SEPTEMBER 24
San Diego

It was late on Wednesday afternoon when Sergeant Hector Alvarez and the ten other officers of the Beta SWAT Squad of the San Diego Police Department drove an unmarked Ford van past a one-story house in a working-class neighborhood across a canyon from the zoo. The lime-green concrete-block structure appeared to be deserted: no cars in the open carport or on the street in front, the grass needing attention, newspapers accumulating on the lawn.

Following departmental protocol, Alvarez parked the van half a block away, on a side street with a clear view of the lime-green house.

In helmets and full body armor, ten SWAT officers arrayed themselves behind the van in two lines of four and six. Alvarez looked down

at his clipboard, then addressed them: "Abdul Muhadded is under suspicion of first-degree murder in the homicide of Jorge Santos on September 23. Muhadded has been implicated in a series of related
homicides. He is armed and considered extremely dangerous. Every
precaution should be taken in executing his arrest warrant. Consistent
with maintaining the security of the operation, occupants of dwellings
within one hundred yards of the target have been advised to vacate until
the operation is complete."

Looking up, Alvarez turned to the six officers constituting the line
on his left. "Team A will enter through the front door, facing on
Fontana Street. The knock-before-entering protocol is waived. On my
command, force the door and enter." Alvarez pointed to a diagram of
the five-room interior of the house that had been distributed to each
officer. Except for the leader of team A, each was assigned a specific
room to enter and control.

Turning to the four on his right he continued, "Team B will control
the rear door and enter on my command or that of the team A leader.

"Alpha Squad is available as backup if needed. Team leaders will call
for help on the open command channel.

"You are authorized to use lethal force at any indication of resistance.
Are there any questions?"

There was the shuffling of veteran warriors anxious to engage, but
no questions.

Each officer made a final check of his M4 automatic weapon and
other equipment. At Alvarez's hand command, team A circled around
the front of the van and moved laterally, flat against the row of houses
facing Fontana between them and their target. Team B moved from
the rear through the backyards of those same houses.

Alvarez remained in the van command post. Through his binoculars he could observe the movement of team A. Now, with their backs
pressed against the wall of the target facing Fontana, the six inched
their way to the door in a cautious, well-practiced procession. The
team leader reached the door; Alvarez radioed the command to enter.

The team A leader inserted a Halligan bar between the lock and
the doorframe, and slammed the bar with a sledgehammer. The door

gave way. From a crouch, M4s at the ready, the SWAT officers burst in.

Even in the almost vacant neighborhood, their efforts did not go unnoticed. From the curtained front window of a house of the same model catty-corner from the one now occupied by team A, Ben Brewster and his olive-skinned, black-bearded companion had an unobstructed view of both teams. When all six had passed through the door, Brewster removed his Motorola cell phone from its holster and punched in a seven-digit number. His right thumb hung over the green SEND key, then pressed.

The bomb had been placed in the front corner bedroom, number 5 on Sergeant Alvarez's diagram, whose walls were first to collapse. With the structural integrity of the building compromised, the enclosure surrounding the front door fell into the lawn and the roof crashed to the terrazzo floor. For a lingering moment the blinding light erased the afternoon shadows. A millisecond later the shattering sound of the blast caused both onlookers to cover their ears with their hands.

Brewster and the bearded man closed the curtains through which they had been watching and left through the rear door.

Brewster, at the wheel of a Toyota Tundra, turning west, spied Sergeant Alvarez running full-tilt, covered like snow by the falling debris, toward the collapsed house. He paused to look at Brewster and the passenger, who raised a Beretta and fired two shots. Alvarez stumbled before crumbling to the pavement.

In less than seven minutes Brewster had turned the Toyota Tundra south onto Interstate 805. Police sirens wailed in the distance. Entering the flow of traffic, he noted a sign that read: Mexico 17 miles.

SEPTEMBER 27

Washington, D.C.

Mark Block was quick to accept the invitation when Tony called and said that he was exhausted and tense and needed to work through his funk on the tennis court. But Tony also had an ulterior motive. Mark was renowned for his memory and the way he applied it to staying in contact with his legion of friends and acquaintances, and Tony needed to tap into that.

In less than an hour of a crisp fall morning, Mark was dispatched 6–1, 6–0. Leaning against his Mustang, Tony generously observed, "You started strong. I calculate that's twenty-four straight wins."

"Actually," Mark corrected, "The number is twenty-three."

Tony accepted the correction and moved on. "It's that steel-trap mind I'm here for. Do you recall that young attorney, Jeff Nussbaum, who worked on the FBI file of the 9/11 investigations? I heard he was somewhere in the Justice Department, but I'm not sure."

"Yeah, Jeff has just been reassigned from the criminal division here in D.C. to the U.S. attorney's office in Los Angeles."

"Is that an up, down, or sidewise move?" Tony inquired.

"Up, I think. The L.A. office has had a lot of problems, like the Chinese spy case."

"What Chinese spy case?" Tony asked.

"It came to be called the Parlor Maid case," Mark explained as they walked to their cars. "This Chinese woman for twenty years lived a triple life. She was allegedly passing national security secrets to the Chinese, including nuclear secrets. For most of this time she was an informant of the FBI, who paid her $1.7 million for her services. And she was the lover of the two FBI agents who were supposed to be her handlers."

"She must have been exhausted," Tony wryly observed.

"I don't know about that, but when she was finally caught and tried in federal court in L.A., the judge threw out most of the charges for prosecutorial misconduct. It was one hell of a put-down and embarrassment for the FBI and the U.S. attorney's office."

"And how did Nussbaum get involved?"

"He was sent out there to fix a leaking ship," Mark said as he opened his car door. "He revved up the FBI, took on the China case as his own, and six months after he arrived, got the conviction, although it was for lesser charges, for which the Parlor Maid only got probation and a ten-thousand-dollar fine. If you still want to talk to him, I can get you his office and cell number."

Rotating into the driver's seat, Tony called out through the open window, "Give me a call when you've got them. You're my man for all seasons."

Tony showered in the State Department gym. Foggy Bottom was unusually active for a Saturday. All the spaces in the executive section of the parking garage were taken. The basement cafeteria was filled as if it were a Tuesday. As Tony walked down the INR bureau hallways toward his new office, the only unfilled cubicle was Brewster's.

There is nothing that fixes the diplomatic mind more than the prospect of a nuclear war, he thought.

By the time he reached his desk and checked voice mail, Mark had left him a message with Jeff Nussbaum's numbers. Tony called Nussbaum's cell. With the three-hour time difference, Tony woke him up.

After the social niceties, Tony outlined his three-part theory that the Saudis and bin Laden had a role in what had happened in Mumbai. The question was, Where was the United States in this? He concisely shared what he had learned from Carol and how he thought what she had found in the bowels of the Cayman bank fit into the larger frame of that U.S. role. A key missing piece was Peninsular. He asked Jeff what the U.S. attorney for central California could do to assist.

Jeff responded, "It's awfully early in the morning. I'll need to get further details and then discuss it with my boss. He's become more and more risk-adverse. It's going to take a solid sales job. Would it be possible for you to come to L.A. next week to brief him?"

"Absolutely. I need to come to San Diego on a related aspect of this puzzle. Could you check if Wednesday would be open?"

"I'll call you first thing Monday."

At the FBI ballistics lab, technician Henry Ashton had an unexpected caller.

"Yes, Madam Director," he said, startled as she walked in the door. "We have received the bullet they dug out from the armor of the San Diego police officer."

In her intense, nothing-but-the-facts voice, she asked, "And what results?"

"None, so far. I haven't gotten to that one yet. On regular order it will be another week."

"Mr. Ashton, this is not regular order. Senator John Stoner, the chair of our authorizing committee, has asked me to expedite this analysis. He says it may be related to the murder of Senator Billington. Could it be out the door by two o'clock?"

"Yes, ma'am."

"Thank you," she responded, and left as abruptly as she had come in.

SEPTEMBER 27

Ramallah, West Bank

Although there are other contestants, most connoisseurs of olive oil rank the rich and amber liquid from Ramallah as the best in the world. In spite of all the difficulties and constraints on production agriculture in the West Bank, a freshly processed lot of olive oil was stacked on the warehouse loading dock ready to be placed in a twenty-foot ocean cargo container.

Two rows of pallets, each holding six boxes, each box filled with twelve two-liter cans, had been lifted into place by a Komatsu frontloader. Two hours of carefully placing the pallets in precise vertical columns to optimize the space in the container had left it almost half full. The loading crew was happy the warehouse manager had declared a thirty-minute respite.

The three men left the stuffy facility to go over the small hill that separated the olive grove from the warehouse and share midmorning coffee and stories of their conquests.

With the laborers gone, a Hyundai van with four young, athletic-looking men stopped beside the truck on which the cargo container had been placed. With the hill and truck shielding them from view, the men lifted a box twice the size of a steamer trunk to the dock and then placed it against the cartons of olive oil midway in the container. After securely connecting wires extending from the box to wires that snaked across the floor to a panel on the port side of the container, the quartet maneuvered additional pallets until all semblance of their other work had been buried.

When the workers returned, the Hyundai had departed. They were curious but pleasantly surprised that someone had completed a part of their labor. When the cargo container had been filled to the maximum allowable weight, the rear doors were closed, sealed with an international transport medallion, and embossed with a sticker: Unit W42408, *Petronius*, Port of Aden, Arab Republic of Yemen.

SEPTEMBER 28–30

San Diego

"Terri, this is Tony."

Terri responded in a throaty but empathic voice, "Thank you, Tony, for calling. I've been thinking about you a lot and all you've been going through. Are you okay?"

"Better than I was yesterday."

"How so?"

"This morning Detective Larsen called to say there was a match between the signature on the bullet that killed Carol and the one that was pulled from Sergeant Alvarez's armor. Larsen said this was enough evidence that the same Beretta fired both, and that exonerates me. So, Terri, you're talking to a free and cleared man."

"Well, then, while we're at it, I have some good news and bad news."

"Give me the good news first."

"It looks like Sergeant Alvarez is going to make it. He was removed from intensive care a couple of days ago and has been able to make a positive identification of the man who shot him from the Toyota. It was the same bastard who killed Billington and probably Santos."

"That's damn good news. What's the bad?"

"They still haven't caught the two shits. The SDPD thinks they're hiding out in Tijuana or farther south."

"I wish I could help. But maybe you can help me with a job supposed to be closer to my skill sets."

"Let me guess," Terri offered. "Anything to do with Professor Nasir?"

"Can't put one over on a first-rate investigative reporter. I need advice on how to prevent a second, third, and possibly fourth Mumbai. The old man is my best pick to be able to provide it."

"I'll see what I can do. When do you want to meet?"

"Tomorrow, as early as possible."

"You're fast. I'll let you know by noon."

The answer was yes. At ten o'clock the following evening, Tony arrived on the same United flight he had taken five weeks earlier. This time Terri met him at the terminal. The drive to the Marriott was a strategy session on how to secure the professor's counsel and help, but without the delay for considered judgment that frequently encumbered academic or governmental decision making. By the time Terri's Acura stopped at the hotel entrance, they had a plan.

Professor Nasir was noticeably more rested and energetic than at Tony's first meeting with him. He greeted Terri, even Tony, with more genuine warmth, offering them a full breakfast of Indian delicacies before bringing them out to the patio.

One thing that had not changed was the deteriorating status of the professor's home. Unlike the first visit, this time Nasir felt comfortable in mentioning his surroundings. "I regret the conditions in which I am receiving you. This house bespeaks my financial situation, which is in worse shape than after my divorce, or even after my FBI detention, for which I apologize. But I have some prospects for improvement."

Terri offered a quizzical expression.

Nasir deferred explaining. "I'd rather wait until they move from promise to reality. But I don't think you came here, Mr. Ramos, all the way from Washington, to discuss my economic status. How can I be of assistance?"

Seizing the opening and receiving a supporting nod from Terri, Tony proceeded to lay out what he knew and suspected: the Saudi realization of the objective for which Nasir had labored for more than ten years—acquisition of nuclear capability; the still befogged role of the United States in the Saudis' accomplishment; the king's agreement to share a portion of the material with Osama bin Laden; the fragile situation in Afghanistan and Pakistan's collapse into extremist rule; and within a fortnight, a nuclear explosion killing tens of thousands in the professor's home country.

"We are confident this is not the only attack," Tony stated. "We suspect less than twenty-five percent of bin Laden's nuclear material was used in the attack on Mumbai. Professor, the world is coming apart with fear, and you are one of the few who has the capability of helping us avoid further, more horrific disasters."

The professor was clearly moved by the murder of so many of his own people, especially the children.

"I have been carrying a heavy burden on my heart," he said. "Neither the religion of my birth nor the one I now profess would countenance such killings. Let me first purge my soul."

He described a meeting to which he had been invited at the Jeddah palace of the king of Saudi Arabia in February 1991. The king confronted his American counterparts with the knowledge that the Americans had provided materials and scientific assistance to Saddam Hussein in his pursuit of a nuclear device during the 1980s. Only late reversals in the war with Iran and the incredibly stupid decision to invade Kuwait had prevented successful completion of the project and Iraq's emergence as a nuclear state. The king was emphatic in his condemnation of the Americans for having allowed this to occur and, more so, for doing it without consulting him, supposedly America's closest Arab ally.

Nasir became almost theatrical as he dramatized the king forsaking his broken English and expressing his feelings in torrid and profanity-laced Arabic. The king insisted that if the Americans did not extend the same assistance to him as they had to Saddam, he would trumpet to the world the Americans' duplicity and cancel the special relationship that had been in place since World War II whereby Saudi Arabia assured the United States of a stable supply of petroleum and the United States gave the kingdom its security shield. Reverting to English, the king said, "You know of the help we have recently received from the British with its Tornados; we are not without other friends."

Nasir returned to San Diego during the spring of 1991. At the urging of the science advisor to the king, who said the Americans had capitulated, Nasir agreed to accept a royal appointment.

"I had been invited in February because of my scientific background and religious beliefs," the professor told Tony. "In June I was given the opportunity to be the agent of the king in establishing the project and overseeing the subsequent flow of scientists and equipment to make it a success.

"But the assignment was not without its toll. Due in large part to seven years of extended separation from my wife and the strains of the working arrangement, by 1998 my marriage of over forty years was crumbling. It was bitter and dispiriting. I knew I would have to withdraw from the project until my personal circumstances were stabilized. After the divorce I was depressed and heavily indebted."

Sensing the professor was becoming overwrought, Terri asked if he would prefer to suspend for a while the recitation of what were obviously painful experiences. He shook his head and continued on.

"It was during this period that I found some degree of financial balance in the arrangement with the FBI and solace in the fellowship of young Arab men who came to San Diego to study and, as we now know, for other purposes.

"In 2005, when I was unfairly terminated by the FBI, I was contacted by the kingdom and encouraged to assist in the conclusion of the project. The king was alarmed at the instability the Americans had unleashed with their ill-advised invasion of Iraq and their failure to maintain a focus on Afghanistan and Pakistan. He was anxious to expedite the project's completion.

"My chief contribution was in the evaluation of alternative delivery systems for the weapon. We never considered a missile; only a fool would send a nuclear device with his name painted on the side of a missile. The king had an understanding with the president of Syria to test various techniques. That, of course, came to an end when the Israelis found out about it and blew up all our test equipment—the Americans having told us the Iranians were the Judas, attempting to distract the Israelis into thinking the target was an ayatollah nuclear enrichment site. Fortunately our project was sufficiently advanced that the Israelis' mistaken attack was only a minor annoyance."

Nasir fell silent, his chin falling to his chest. While he left the patio to use the bathroom, Terri filled his cup with coffee, sugar, and half-and-half. When he returned he sat and gathered himself, sipped from the cup, and continued.

"I left the kingdom's service for the second time this summer. The threats from bin Laden to unleash a revolution if his desires for nuclear material were not met, and the king's acquiescence, drove me away. I warned the king's advisors that he was repeating the mistakes of 1999, when he compromised with bin Laden and allowed al-Qaeda to use the Saudi support infrastructure—such as my friend al-Harbi provided here in San Diego—to protect and assist the hijackers. My plea was that without a protector for the kingdom in the White House, the consequences of arming bin Laden with nuclear material would bring down the wrath of the Americans, not another cover-up. All my protestations were rebuffed. I have never understood why."

The professor paused. Tony respectfully waited until he realized Nasir was expecting the next request. "Professor, more than ever, I appreciate your centrality to arresting, or at least limiting, the worldwide bloody hemorrhage the convergence of events from Mumbai to Washington could inflict. How would you advise me, and what are you willing to do, to put your words into action?"

It was several long moments before Nasir spoke. The full light of late morning penetrated the heavy curtains in the nearby living room. Terri was squirming in anticipation as he spoke.

"You need to identify a person close to bin Laden who could dissuade him from continuing on the path of annihilation or, more likely, failing that, would give you credible information on his plans. Don't depend on your CIA to find such a brave soul. Your confidence in the agency was misplaced in 2002 in Iraq, and it will be again if you rely on it to determine wherever 'Osama bin Forgotten' is hiding and what his next intentions are.

"Give me twenty-four hours and I will have a recommendation."

OCTOBER 1−2

San Diego ★ Los Angeles

With an eagerness Tony was just beginning to recognize, Terri offered her car and wanted to go with him to Los Angeles.

He had checked out of the Marriott earlier in the morning in anticipation of spending the night in L.A. At Pacific Beach, they stopped at Terri's apartment, where she pulled together the bare necessities for an overnight trip.

The 125-mile journey would almost exactly retrace the route al-Harbi and his travelling companion had taken in January 2000. Terri and Tony speculated about what a different world it would have been if the events that journey facilitated, 9/11 and its aftermath, had never happened.

They shared a restrained pleasure in the just-completed meeting with Professor Nasir. As they had planned, allowing him to work through his own guilt from his complicity in a tragedy that had inflicted so much pain on his country and city of birth was personally therapeutic. The request Tony made for his advice and help gave him an outlet, an avenue of redemption in the form of a chance to cut short another, even greater loss of life. Yet while they respected the sincerity of Professor Nasir's intentions and the wisdom of his advice, he had yet to deliver. Maybe in a few hours he would.

The slightly more than three hours it took to drive up the I-5 gave them a chance to unburden and sort out some of their feelings. After a quick stop at a Burger King, the confessionals began.

"I think about Carol every night," Tony admitted. "No question she was a professional and good at what she did, but at the core she was soft and insecure. Her over-the-top reaction to my trip to Billington's funeral was just one signal. From what I learned of her parents, particularly that she had never told them who I was, it had to go against a lot of what she was raised to believe—the idea of getting together with an African American, and a Cuban one to boot."

"Tony," Terri said as she pulled her legs under her on the car seat, "you are too locked into your own past. Times and standards of tolerance have changed. I can say that from my own life experience as a Mexican girl growing up in the barrio."

"It's different," Tony rejoined. "You could see it in the faces of the Watsons the first time they saw me at Reagan Airport. Even with mourning hearts and souls and their mouths shut, I could hear them wondering what that black man was doing to their beautiful daughter."

"Well, that's over," Terri consoled as she gently stroked his leg. "How are you dealing with Carol now?"

"It's hard for me to believe it's only been two weeks. I guess the reality is starting to set in. When Mark told me she was dead, I couldn't believe it. I was even more stunned when Detective Larsen said I was the prime suspect in her murder.

"It got so complicated so quickly. Have you ever had the feeling that you were watching a movie and at the same time were one of the actors? That's what it's been like for me."

"I can only imagine," Terri said.

"I knew the truth. I also knew how incriminating the circumstances appeared. I could go from saving the world from another Mumbai to being in prison for the rest of my life."

He slowed and moved into the left lane. Stopping, Tony snapped on the emergency light and turned to her. "Terri, I will never be able to repay you for what you did to get to the truth."

Wordlessly, she reached over and gave Tony a kiss on the cheek.

"I know it sounds strange, but in a way, Talbott's assignment is a gift. It forces me to do something other than wallow in my own grief. It's given me the hope that I'll find some purpose for Carol's life and," he choked, "her death."

Tony reclined in his seat, his head pressed against the headrest and his eyes squeezed tight. He remained that way for several minutes. Eventually regaining his composure, he restarted the car and continued north.

———

From the 101 in L.A., he took the Wilshire exit for the crosstown slog to the La Mar condominiums. James Levy, a Georgetown classmate and tennis teammate who had ridden the Southern California real estate tide to a minifortune and was now trying to hold on, had offered the unit to Tony for his L.A. stay.

It was 7:30 when Tony parked in the underground garage. Together he and Terri rode the elevator to the thirty-third floor.

Unit 3302 was the embodiment of Levy's successes. More than twenty-five hundred square feet of elegance stretched over two floors with a panoramic view of Century City and the L.A. Country Club golf course. Furnishings represented the eclectic tastes of a top Beverly Hills decorator.

Terri and Tony were both weary. She showered first in the top-level bathroom. As she prepared to step out she admired her lean muscled body projected on the mirrored stall.

On the stopover at her apartment, one of the necessities she'd chosen was a transparent negligee. She didn't want him to have any mixed signals about her desires tonight.

Tony waited in the opulent, first-level living room. He put down the Chivas as Terri slithered down the stairs.

Rising, he wrapped her in a gentle embrace, his hands clasped behind her lower back. They kissed, their lips lingering.

Tony released his hold, picked up the scotch, and moved alone to the floor-to-ceiling glass window looking out on the sea of early evening lights.

Turning, he gazed at her for several moments. "Terri, you are beautiful."

She looked down demurely, while savoring the tingling sensation in her thighs. He took a full swallow of his drink and moved toward the flowered sofa in the center of the room.

He motioned her to the sofa, and as he put his right arm around her shoulders, she began nibbling, nuzzling his ear as Tony continued. "I've been thinking about our conversation in the car. Maybe one of the things that affected my relationship with Carol was that we became too physical too soon."

Terri pulled back. Her tongue withdrew and went dry.

"We both wanted to say with our bodies that our distinctly different backgrounds, upbringing, color—didn't count. But of course they did. If we had not rushed our decision to live together, maybe she wouldn't have been in the position she was that Tuesday morning. I don't want to repeat that mistake with you. Do you understand?"

"No," Terri admitted, "but I respect you. I don't know if we can have a successful relationship, but I want to give us the best chance to find out."

Tony raised his hands to her cheeks and gave her an affectionate kiss. They disengaged.

"You may not believe it, but this is harder for me than for you."

"I don't know about that," Terri responded, "but I'll follow your pace. I'll take the master suite upstairs. You use the second bedroom down here."

———————

Tony and Terri were sitting in the L.A. office of the U.S. Attorney for the Central District of California, on the sixth floor of the Federal Building at 11000 Wilshire Boulevard. She was reading the *L.A. Times*. He was reviewing notes for his imminent presentation.

Jeff Nussbaum rushed into the reception room, exhibiting the same high energy as he had when he was a linebacker for Brown. Rep tie askew, the thinning hair atop his six foot, two frame even more untamed than the last time Tony had seen him, Jeff shook hands with Terri and waved Tony to follow him into his office.

Tony noticed that Jeff's office was on the same floor as the U.S. attorney, a sure sign he was on the career fast track. Following up on Mark's comments, Tony had studied Google news on the Chinese spy case and now congratulated Jeff for his doggedness.

"But we didn't reserve thirty minutes with the boss to discuss this; he already knows more about that than he would want." Looking at his watch, Jeff took Tony by the arm into the adjoining office. "Make it as sharp and clean as you can."

Jeff introduced Tony to Randolph Edgar. His reputation as a straight-down-the-line prosecutor had been fogged by the China case and recurring newspapers' speculation that he was considering a run for governor when the president left office.

Tony had prepared PowerPoint slides that explained the situation in heightened granularity, beyond what he had told Jeff the previous Saturday. "Sir, I attempt to avoid overdramatization, but these facts cry out that thousands, maybe millions, of lives are at stake and that Americans are the most at risk. There are still many missing pieces to the puzzle, but the picture is beginning to fill in."

Tony divulged what he had learned the previous day in San Diego. "It is urgent that we know what role the Peninsular group has been, and is, playing. We need to know and we need to know now."

Tony was deflated when Edgar responded, "This is a very sensitive matter. I'll have to send it up the flagpole and let you know the higher-ups' decision as to where to go."

Terri dropped Tony at LAX and headed back down to San Diego. The departing kiss was warm but not as passionate as the night before. Waiting at gate D-40 for Delta 78 back to Dulles, Tony received a call from the professor. "Mr. Ramos, I have considered the alternatives and would recommend a mutual friend of mine and bin Laden's, Mr. Yazid Sonji of Kuala Lumpur. I believe you have made his acquaintance."

OCTOBER 3
Port of Aden, Yemen

The twenty-foot container of Ramallah olive oil had arrived at the port of Aden by truck. For three days the cargo was parked on the sprawling and dusty landside lot awaiting the arrival of the *Petronius,* the newest ship in the fleet of the Greek maritime titan Aristotle Stephanous.

Ships like this 195,000-ton product of the Chinese shipbuilding yard south of Shanghai had long since eclipsed the size capable of traversing the Panama Canal. Its life would be spent transporting fifteen thousand containers per trip from the Middle East and Asia to the U.S. West Coast and returning with a new load.

Aristotle Stephanous himself had come to launch its maiden Pacific crossing. From his position near the site where, almost to the day, years earlier, an al-Qaeda suicide squad had attacked the destroyer USS *Cole,* Stephanous watched as the Ramallah container was lifted 140 feet above the dock and placed in Bay 13 slot K7.

Three hours later he was proud but vaguely discontented as his newest prize eased into the Gulf of Aden. From his lavish stateroom, he viewed the receding port.

OCTOBER 10
Aramco Oil Facilities, Eastern Saudi Arabia

In the interminable game driven by security, economics, and national pride through which the supply of petroleum from the world's largest producer was managed, the faucets should have been at full throttle. A day earlier, West Texas light crude had sold for $119 a barrel. The global thirst for oil, the absence of any intention on the part of the largest customer to institute a policy of energy restraint, and the uncertainties unleashed at the Indian-Pakistani border had daily pushed the oil market to new highs.

Luke Simmons had a central role in reopening the faucet. An expatriate for twenty-three years from Lubbock, Texas, he was responsible for the second-largest oil-processing facility in the kingdom, which prepared petroleum for the long journey to the refineries in the consuming nations of the world.

Operations had been down for fifty hours. Luke worked without rest to bring the massive plant back on line. As he inspected the valves in the most confounding unit of the plant, he felt a strong gust of hot wind on his back. Before he could turn, he was knocked from his feet and enveloped in a hundred tons of collapsing steel and concrete.

The cloud could be seen from Riyadh, three hundred kilometers to the west, and from Abu Dhabi, almost twice that distance to the east. Petroleum was spewing like a thousand Old Faithfuls, settling over the dead body of Luke and his as yet uncounted colleagues.

The news reached halfway around the world. Fox interrupted its ten o'clock political roundtable to announce the consequences:

"The disruption occasioned by the nuclear attack on Saudi Arabia's largest oil production center has driven the price of oil in overnight trading to $135 a barrel. Oil experts have identified the obvious—the primary beneficiary is Iran."

OCTOBER 11

Long Beach

The older man wasted no time on pleasantries as he paced across the ornate carpeting. "Well, it seems to be over. Our misjudgments and the actions of people we trusted have taken us to the endgame. Roland, what do you think we should do?"

Roland Jeralewski stared silently at the Pacific for several moments. He turned to the older man with tears in his eyes. "Mr. Chairman, I agree with your assessment. As successful as we've been in maintaining our distance and covert status, with what has happened in Mumbai and Aramco, those temporary victories are almost certainly going to be stripped away."

"So what happens next?" the older man asked grimly.

"I believe the next attack will be on our homeland. Since the early weeks after that tragic Tuesday in 2001, our friends in the White House have given as their ultimate defense for continuing the disastrous policies in Iraq and Afghanistan that the U.S. has avoided another attack. In my opinion, the fundamental reason for this is not that the terrorist enemies have been weakened; by every standard they are stronger. Rather, it is what bin Laden says. He has consistently followed the strategy that in order to maximize global chaos through terror, every attack must be more lethal than the last. Up until September 19, he had not demonstrated the capability to exceed 9/11. Now he has done it twice. There is no question in my mind that the U.S. is next, and sooner rather than later."

Privately pondering the significance of what he had just said, Roland paused to collect himself. "We must do everything in our power to keep that from happening. We must identify the people in our government who can develop a plan outside the official line and join in a common effort to avoid an American apocalypse. That should start with . . . "

The door to Roland's office was flung open.

Jeff Nussbaum and ten officers in uniform entered. "Mr. Jeralewski, I have a search warrant issued by the magistrate for the Central District of California. I would appreciate your cooperation by providing us with your pagers, cell phones, keys to your desk, and computer passwords."

For two men accustomed to command, it was a moment of truth, mixed with unreality. The chairman read the magistrate's document as he had hundreds of others, but none with the personal consequences of this warrant. Jeralewski handed over his iPhone to Nussbaum.

Amidst the confusion of more than a hundred law enforcement officers sealing the offices, herding employees into the conference room, confiscating personal communications devices, and readying for a microscopic search, the television in the reception room broadcast Fox News at noon:

"The young man has utterly failed in his first test of leadership as the presumptive next president of the United States. His twelve hours of silence since the nuclear explosion in the oil center of Saudi Arabia has emboldened our most violent enemies. There are reports of thousands in the streets of Tehran cheering the attack against the Saudi Sunnis. Oil is now selling on the world markets at $163 a barrel."

OCTOBER 13
Washington, D.C.

Tony was met in the State Department lobby by two unscheduled visitors: Roland Jeralewski and Laura Billington.

Having canceled his nine o'clock appointment, Tony led them to the fifth-floor conference room. Jeralewski seemed distantly familiar. Tony had seen photographs of him taken at various Washington high-society festivities. But his eyes were on Laura—why was she here?

All three were too stressed for small talk; Jeralewski took the initiative. Describing what had happened the previous day, in an emotion-choked voice he said to Tony, "Mr. Ramos, my colleagues and I are responsible for what, in retrospect, can only be described as actions contrary to the best interests of our country. The U.S. attorney's office will soon have all the documentation. But there is nothing we can do about the past at this point. What we are here for is to offer our assistance in avoiding even further death and violence."

"You can start by filling me in on what happened," Tony directed.

Jeralewski hesitated, then nodded and began. "Within a month of the conclusion of the Persian Gulf War, while still in government, I attended a meeting with other U.S. officials at the Jeddah residence of the king of Saudi Arabia. He was enraged that our government had given considerable assistance to Saddam Hussein in the fulfillment of his nuclear aspirations. The king demanded the same consideration. We tried to dissuade him, but it became clear he was adamant. We withdrew to Washington for consultations at the highest levels of our government.

"In the course of these discussions, we were informed of an arrangement the king and a British defense contractor, BAE, had reached in 1988. In exchange for the sale of thirty-five-billion pounds' worth of Tornado fighter jets and ancillary equipment, BAE agreed to a more than three-and-a-half-billion-pound 'facilitation fee' to various Saudi officials, principally the Saudi ambassador to the U.S., Mahmood al-Rasheed.

"Realizing that our term in office could terminate in a few months—and it did—we speculated that if the facilitation of seventy-one Tornados was worth over three billion pounds, how much higher was the value of access to the bomb? When we returned to Jeddah, we told the king he would have full U.S. assistance in making his kingdom a nuclear state if he would divert what amounted to ninety percent of the BAE payment to an account we would designate and control."

The information was almost unbelievable, and yet it made perfect sense. Jeralewski was the third confirmation of the 1991 Jeddah palace arrangement, the king's grandson Zaid al Swainee and, two weeks before, Samrat Nasir, having provided the first two. Each participant at that fateful February 1991 meeting had provided an additional perspective. Each contributed to the converging confirmations necessary for an intelligence officer to convert suspicion into truth.

Tony interrupted: "Whatever Saudi ethics might be, would it not be unethical and illegal for the U.S. government to accept such payments? Who is the 'we' in your last sentence?"

"Of course it would," Jeralewski confirmed. "The 'we' was various members of the previous administration, under the cover of Peninsular. The king agreed—over the kicking and screaming of the ambassador, I might add—to the arrangement that other than a pittance for the ambassador, all future payments would be directed to the Peninsular account at a New York bank. The kingdom began the project almost immediately, using U.S. or U.S.-trained scientists and materials provided under the supervision of an American physicist of foreign descent. The flow of funds to our account commenced in October of 1991. Our assistance continued until the project was completed.

"There were, of course, conditions that went along with this arrangement. We insisted that none of the material produced from this project was to go outside the control of the kingdom without our explicit approval. The king concurred. For our part of the bargain we would use all our governmental authority and influence to keep the existence of our agreement and the project secret."

"How successful were the parties in keeping those commitments?" Tony asked.

"Until this summer, the king had kept his part of the bargain. For our side—in spite of the political difficulties after 9/11 caused by the literally dozens of investigations that sniffed around the edges of the project, not only in the U.S. but elsewhere—with the help of our political friends we were able to keep it under cover. Now the king's 'indiscretions' with bin Laden will hurl our agreement into the headlines. I would label it a failure."

Jeralewski's shoulders drooped with the weariness and resignation of a condemned man.

Since the explosion of the 777 in Kuala Lumpur, Tony had suspected there was a greater motivation for the U.S. cover-up of the Saudi involvement in 9/11 than anything Senator Billington had contemplated. This was the first hard confirmation from the U.S. side of the partnership. The puzzle pieces were falling into place.

"Are you saying that the reason for all the 9/11 cover-up had nothing to do with 9/11 itself?"

"The previous administration and, to a slightly lesser extent, this one have been built on secrets, keeping the American people uninformed so they could be manipulated," Jeralewski said. "But the scale of the cover-up was driven by the realization that if the Saudi project and our participation and profit from it had been known, the president would never have survived the next election.

"In Great Britain, internal investigators were about to open up the BAE case. Prime Minister Tony Blair shut it down, saying that relations with an important strategic ally were at risk. Most assumed that was Saudi Arabia. Blair, in fact, was referring to the U.S. and the consequences of the disclosure of the project for our government. With the governments of both countries reeling from the Iraq war, you can imagine what the disclosure of this scheme would have meant on each side of the pond."

"I have a final question. Why is Ms. Billington with you?"

"We had an arrangement by which she provided us with certain 'services.'"

"Services beyond photographic?" Tony inquired.

With obvious irritation, Jeralewski turned to face him. "I think that's enough self-flagellation," he replied curtly. "We're dealing with the reality that millions of lives are at risk. I'm here to ask what I can do to help."

Without a pause Tony said, "I'll get the answer to my question from Ms. Billington later. But to yours, Mr. Jeralewski, it's urgent that I make contact with a U.S.-trained scientist who lives in Kuala Lumpur. I think you might know him: Mr. Yazid Sonji. I need to talk with him as soon as possible, forty-eight hours on the outside. Can you help?"

"Yes, we can."

A solid knock on the conference room door broke the tension. Tony opened it to a young woman in a blue skirt and blouse. "I'm FBI special agent Karen Pugh. I am here to escort Mr. Roland Jeralewski to our headquarters for additional questioning."

Tony nodded his head toward Jeralewski, who rose saying, "Mr. Ramos, I appreciate the opportunity to clarify events." Then he turned to Laura. "Ms. Billington, depending on the duration and outcome of the questioning, I will hope to see you this evening for the flight back to Long Beach." Approaching the still-open door, he added, "Ms. Pugh, I am at your service."

Once Jeralewski was gone, Tony confronted Laura.

"What in the hell were you thinking?"

Taken aback, Laura responded, "And what in the hell are you talking about?"

Tony reached into his coat pocket and handed her a printed email. "This is the road map you sent to Jeralewski on the fourteenth of last month. It lays out the connection between my inquiry and Carol's and the fact that we were sharing information. He was thoughtful enough not to scrub it from his laptop, and the agents found it last night during the wrap-up of the raid on Peninsular."

"Well, it's true, isn't it?" Laura protested.

"True enough to lead to her murder!" Tony shouted back at her.

Laura read the text. Head down, she leaned back on the oaken table. She braced herself with outstretched hands clutching the edge. The look in Tony's eyes said he wanted to physically attack her, to rip out her heart. She involuntarily flinched from the blow she thought was coming.

But instead, he kept up his verbal pounding. "Let me ask you again, Laura Billington: What the hell were you thinking when you handed over Carol to your vicious playmates, who then conveniently arranged for me to be the primary suspect?"

"I was thinking about me. Look—look," Laura stuttered, "for most of my life I'll admit I took care of me first. It's how I learned to survive."

Throughout his tennis career, Tony had struggled to control his emotions while conducting a steady mental dissection of his opponent, probing for his weakness. Laura had just revealed hers, and he was ready to strike, to turn them to his advantage.

"So all that talk about us trusting each other and all you wanted was to bring justice to your father's killers, all of that was just so much bullshit; like apparently everything else about your pathetic life."

To avoid Tony's smoldering gaze, Laura focused on the ceiling. "I was scared. My reputation, my way of life, was crumbling. You are well aware of my profligate lifestyle. I got in over my head. I took on the financial burdens of my friends and associates and succumbed to the temptation to live in the style of my aristocratic clients. I was on the verge of bankruptcy when Jeralewski purchased my note and offered to withhold enforcement if my services to Peninsular were acceptable."

"Services?"

"It wasn't a one-way relationship. I was able to provide Peninsular with information only I had access to. I relayed most of what I learned from Zaid and you."

Tony was stung by this duplicity. He had the urge to beat her, or wrap his strong fingers around her neck and squeeze. He felt as if she had suddenly forced him to question every judgment he'd made in life, to review every trust he'd ever placed in another person. "And that justified murder?"

"Tony, it never occurred to me that this would happen."

"Oh, and what did you think would happen?"

"I'm a competitor, including in sex. I've hated Carol ever since you dissed me in your townhouse and then I smelled her scent in your bedroom closet. Figuring out how to take her out became an obsession, a challenge, but I never meant for her to be physically hurt."

Now in total control of the situation and over his immediate urge to throttle her, Tony could let himself go. "No, of course not! I'm just glad your father doesn't have to see you now. You can't even admit to yourself you caused another person's death. It's all about 'obsession' and 'challenge.' And Laura, Laura, Laura. Are you so self-deluded that you can't call it what it really is: murder?"

Laura began to tear up. She wrapped her arms around herself. She tried to speak, but couldn't get the words out. He'd seen her stutter several times when she was nervous. Maybe he'd finally gotten to her.

Tony was conflicted. Was this the first sign of genuine remorse, or was it just because she had been caught, the regret of a spoiled little girl who wants it all her own way without ever having to face the consequences?

"My brain is trumping my gut."

"What?" Laura asked, surprised at the sharp turn of Tony's interrogation.

Tony turned his back to her, walking to the far corner of the room. "I can't say what it will be, but I think you could be useful."

"Useful?"

He was now looking at her from twenty feet away. "Useful in the same way you were useful to Jeralewski—having inside knowledge and no scruples in using it."

Laura took a step toward him. "Are you saying I can go back to London?"

"That's not my decision to make, but that's what I'm going to recommend to the FBI and the U.S. attorney."

Laura closed the space and reached up to touch Tony's face. "I guess I should be thankful."

"We'll see."

OCTOBER 16

Kuala Lumpur

It had been almost six weeks since Tony was last in Yazid Sonji's office. The world had changed, but not Sonji's arrogance and anger. Even with Professor Nasir and Roland Jeralewski joining him, Sonji was as difficult as he had been on September 11.

Tony had the feeling the conversation from his previous visit had not been completed, just suspended.

"Have you Americans learned anything from your egregious behavior? Your attack on Iraq and your continued occupation of Afghanistan fuel an expanding conflagration in the Muslim world. Now that world, praise be to Allah, is unleashing its hatred, and Osama is again the symbol and instrument. Do not delude yourselves that Mumbai or the oil fields of Arabia were the ultimate targets. They were but appetizers before the ultimate treat, a treat that will soon be deliciously consumed."

Professor Nasir exercised his right of seniority and interrupted, "Yazid, we know and agree with much of your feelings. I can assure you my people in India are even more distraught, and with good reason. But there is nothing any of us can do to rewrite history. We can alter only the future."

With respect, Sonji leaned forward.

"If the world cannot arrest this rage of terror, it is truly the end," the professor continued. "We have all done the calculation. If his pattern is fulfilled, and you know Osama better than almost anyone not in his cave, the next strike will be on October 31."

Sonji glanced at his desk calendar and nodded affirmatively.

The professor frowned and pursued his analysis and prophesy. "All over the world the most irrational actions are being taken. In England they are fleeing from London to the highlands of Scotland. In Japan I am told tunnels are being dug. It is as if six centuries of civilization are being rolled back in a fortnight."

The others sat silently as the professor concluded.

"I doubt that if we could locate him and he agreed to meet, we could convince Osama to desist. What is a more reasonable objective is to identify one who is close to him but may be having qualms about the ever more radical direction of al-Qaeda or, for some other reason, might be willing to give us information on his plans for the use of his remaining nuclear material."

Tony had heard the professor deliver the same analysis when they'd met in his home. Here, it carried even more intensity and persuasiveness.

Sonji was incredulous. "I know how Osama thinks. He considers himself to be a demigod, the living incarnation of Muhammad. This perspective is shared by his inner circle. You are sorely misguided if you think one of them would turn against him. It would be beyond my friendship with Osama, my reason, my ability to do so."

"Yazid," the professor said, "this is not just a matter of humanitarianism or theology. Several of us have served more than one master. So all of you will be aware of my circumstances, I will be serving as a consultant to Yazid's new enterprise."

He turned to Sonji as he said, "And your employee Anthony has been consulting with me. He has told me of the orders you gave after your last meeting with Mr. Ramos and the subsequent murder of 331 innocents on the Malaysian flight to Hong Kong, which you sent him to personally witness and confirm."

Tony was stunned by the revelation and the fact that Nasir had not told him of Sonji's role in his near murder. He muttered, "You goddamned sons of bitches," as Nasir concluded.

"If that were to be made known to the Kor Risik DiRaja, you would be hanged from the tallest gallows in the kingdom. I would suggest that if saving lives is not sufficient to secure your assistance, possibly saving your neck is."

OCTOBER 18

Peshawar, Pakistan

Peshawar, the eastern gate to the Khyber Pass, had been a crossroads for war, trade, and intrigue for two millennia. With Sonji and Nasir

Tony was about to thrust himself into this ancient and ongoing history. Having completed the contact promised, Roland Jeralewski left Kuala Lumpur in the Peninsular Gulfstream to return to the States.

The three men, who had met two days earlier and more than four thousand kilometers to the east, were sitting in the cellar of a mud-thatched house on the western fringe of Peshawar. Joining them was a woman, her *abaya* concealing all but her dark eyes.

The meeting had already run an hour. There was underlying tension. By being alone with unrelated males, the woman was violating the Islamic law of Purdah, the same offense that had caused a nineteen-year-old victim of gang rape in Saudi Arabia to be imprisoned and given two hundred lashes; the same offense for which the three women in the goat yard would have been flogged had Tony and Amal not intervened.

The professor and Sonji had flattered and humored her and appealed to her best instincts of humanity. All to no avail.

Sonji requested that the others leave so that he could talk with the woman alone.

Standing in the brisk midmorning fall breeze, Tony and the professor observed the interplay among the people of this city teetering between the Middle Ages and modernity. A convoy of eighteen-wheel petroleum tankers headed west for Afghanistan was stopped by a leather-skinned, barefoot farmer as he struggled to herd his goats across the road. The combination of circumstances he was observing gave Tony a greater appreciation of the forces that had culminated in the slaughters in his own country, slaughters that had brought him to Peshawar.

Sonji emerged alone. "I have some, but not sufficient information," he said. "As we suspected, the third attack site is America, somewhere on the Pacific Coast. The device is currently at sea on the Greek cargo container vessel *Petronius*. The device is to be detonated from on shore. She does not know by whom or how. She hopes to determine those answers but will need to return to the mountains to do so. It will be at least three more days before she can meet again. She is amazingly self-confident and brave."

Tony replied, "The next attack will be on October 31: thirteen days. Once we know the operational details, it will take time to devise and activate a plan of action. Can she get the information any faster?"

"I doubt it. I intend to stay here until I have the information."

Sonji turned and disappeared into the house. Tony and the professor pondered their options.

Tony broke the silence. "I want to know more about the *Petronius*—where it is, who owns it, how to get access."

Before departing Washington, anticipating the need to communicate from locations outside reliable cellular range, Tony had secured a State Department satellite phone.

"Ambassador Talbott, Tony. I'm in Peshawar with the professor and his former student from Kuala Lumpur. We have what I believe to be reliable intelligence. The bomb is on a Greek cargo ship, the *Petronius*, which is headed for a U.S. Pacific port. I am assuming the arrival date is on or before October 31."

"I'll check on that."

"I have an acquaintance—Laura Billington, the photographer—who has contacts at the top echelons of the Greek government. She might be helpful in gaining access to the *Petronius*. Her London number is . . . "

The phone went dead. Tony tried repeatedly to reconnect, but got no answer.

———

It was noon when Tony's satellite rang. It was Laura.

"I have heard from Secretary Talbott. He told me about the *Petronius* and its cargo. I've talked with Prime Minister Alexandros Metaxas. He's agreed to put me in contact with the owner of the ship, Aristotle Stephanous. I'll attempt to arrange a shoot."

Tony smiled. "You're turning out to be quite a student of spy craft." But the smile was quickly replaced by an expression of intense concern.

"Laura, if you are going to do anything, it has to be now. Call Stephanous. Make up some story about how close you are to the prime minister. The connection with power is the ultimate door-opener in

Athens. Tell him how personally intrigued you are with his life story and his big ships and that you want to show and tell the world about both from the deck of the *Petronius*.

"You're good at making up wild tales, but this is no fictional story and it needs to happen in the next twelve days."

"That's a faster pace than even I am used to, but I'll do my best."

Again, the phone went dead.

OCTOBER 20

Khyber Pass, Pakistan

At Sonji's suggestion, in order to be two hours closer to the woman, the three moved northwest to what had been a nineteenth-century British military officers' encampment on the Afghan border, now converted to a Pakistani patrol station. In these surroundings, the poetry of Rudyard Kipling came vividly to life.

> *When you're wounded and left on Afghanistan's plains,*
> *And the women come out to cut up what remains,*
> *Jest roll to your rifle and blow out your brains*
> *An' go to your Gawd like a soldier.*
> *Go, go, go like a soldier,*
> *Go, go, go like a soldier,*
> *Go, go, go like a soldier,*
> *So-oldier of the Queen!*

In October the sun set early at this latitude; by 6:30 it was midnight black. Tony's satellite phone hummed.

"Tony, Laura. I'm working on the plan."

"Okay, great, but we're down to only ten days," Tony warned.

Even over the static, it was clear Laura was miffed. "Tony, I haven't been lollygagging over tea at the Dorchester. This morning I reached Stephanous in Paris. He's a vain man who feels he is appreciated only for the size of his bank account and not his international importance. I promised him a display in a prestigious international magazine if he would arrange a dramatic setting for his portrait."

Tony cut in, "It sounds like he deserves his pompous reputation."

"The important thing is, he was receptive. Tomorrow morning he's sending his Falcon to Gatwick to collect me and the crew. He hasn't determined the specific logistics but will do so while we're in the air."

Tony was, at last, encouraged. "That's a great start. I'm in the same shape you are—there's more information required to get this job done. I hope to have it inside of three days."

"Do you have any direction for me in the meantime?"

"This is what you need to do: Expect a package to be delivered to the Falcon while it's on the ground at Gatwick. Place it in your equipment bag, wherever Stephanous is not going to discover it. It will contain an electrical box, instructions, and a satellite phone. Stay tuned; the places you're likely to be aren't Washington or London."

Tony's phone hummed with a call waiting. He closed with, "Laura, call me when you have more information, and I'll do the same." He clicked onto the waiting call.

"Tony, this is Talbott. Where in the hell are you?"

Tony started to quote from the opening of Kipling's poem. Talbott was not in the mood for poetry.

"The Indians have concluded it was not Pakistan but bin Laden who blew up Mumbai, but they have already given orders to launch on Karachi. And they don't know if they can pull it back. New Delhi has informed us, but they cannot get through to Islamabad. Stand by for further instructions."

OCTOBER 21

Islamabad, Pakistan

The capital city of Pakistan was in advanced preparation for war. The main intersections were controlled by sandbagged patrol stations. A steady stream of cars and trucks jammed with riders made its way toward the hills north of Islamabad.

Talbott had directed Tony to take a bus during the night from Peshawar to Islamabad in hopes he could arrange a meeting with Maulana Fazullah, for five weeks the president of Pakistan. It was not going to be easy. The new president was consumed with the prospects of imminent war, and the U.S. embassy had been vacated. Tony arrived at the presidential headquarters tired, dirty, and stressed.

After submitting his U.S. State Department INR documents, he requested, in his best Arabic, a meeting with the president. The young lieutenant at the desk was unimpressed, motioning Tony to the already crowded, noisy waiting room. After a half hour with no discernable progress, Tony turned to the crude information brochures the new government had released and that were scattered throughout the room. He was taken with an announcement that under President Fazullah, General Mahmood Ahmed had resumed his former position as head of the Pakistani intelligence service, the ISI.

Tony stepped out into the street and placed a call to Senator Stoner.

Tony had never met Ahmed, but recalled the numerous occasions on which his name and role had arisen in conversations with Senator Billington. He and Stoner had first met Ahmed on an Intelligence Committee tour of primary terrorist sites in August of 2001. Ahmed had been very hospitable and informative in his briefings. He had the reputation of knowing the Taliban and al-Qaeda better than any other non-Afghani. It was Ahmed's responsibility to maintain close ties with Afghanistan, including the current Taliban government, in the event Pakistan were attacked by India and had to retreat beyond the mountains into Afghanistan. A receptive Afghanistan, whatever the character of its government, was a crucial element of Pakistan's defense-in-depth doctrine.

The relationship between Ahmed, Billington, and Stoner had grown to the point that in appreciation for a dinner he had hosted on their final night in Pakistan, the senators had invited the general for breakfast in the U.S. Capitol on his next visit to Washington. That invitation was accepted for September 11, 2001. The coincidence had been one of Senator Billington's most repeated stories.

Billington's fourth-floor Intelligence Committee conference room in the Capitol was no match for the spacious parade ground at the ISI headquarters in Islamabad, nor did the scrambled eggs equal that evening's tribal feast, but the atmosphere was electric in anticipation of an expansive sharing of information and analysis among friends and allies.

Dressed in a blue English business suit rather than his usual olive-brown uniform, General Ahmed reviewed the nuclear standoff with India from the Pakistani perspective. Billington's assessment was that no progress had been made since Pakistan had tested its first nuclear weapons in 1998.

The conversation turned to the topic Ahmed knew as well as any person on earth: the mentality and intentions of the Taliban and the guests it had invited to Afghanistan, al-Qaeda.

"Most people live in three stages of life—the accumulated experiences of the past, the realities of today, and the dreams of tomorrow," the general began. "Most people are aware of their past and fantasize about the future."

He was interrupted when the committee's staff director handed a note to Billington. He scanned it, then read to his guests: "The North Tower of the World Trade Center has been hit by an airplane."

Billington would say later that he was perplexed, but, aware of several other instances when large buildings had been hit by airplanes, was not overly anxious.

The general, with no apparent mental or emotional reaction, continued. "But the primary focus of most humans is on the present—getting along day-to-day. The Taliban and al-Qaeda are different. For them, only the future of paradise after death matters. Any activities of the present are trivial interludes until the ultimate is achieved. The discipline, the norms of behavior that influence everyday life, are irrelevant for those who dismiss the worthiness of today."

A short time later, the staff director returned with another note. This time the color drained from Billington's face as he read it. "A Boeing 757 has hit the South Tower."

The breakfast broke up in distressed confusion. As Billington said, "And the world entered a new era."

Upon returning to Islamabad, Ahmed found his previous value as an intermediary with the Taliban had become an embarrassment to the Siachen government, and he was sacked. It now appeared to Tony that this old general-to-senator relationship might be his opening.

"Senator," Tony said over the garbled satellite phone, "I'm in Islamabad and need your help." He explained his circumstances and the urgency of his meeting with the new president of Pakistan. "If you intercede with General Ahmed, I think you could make it happen."

"I'll call you back within an hour."

Stoner called back forty-five minutes later. "Tony, I have spoken with the general. He will receive you in his office now."

All of Islamabad's taxis having long since taken to the hills, Tony jogged the three kilometers through the turmoil to the ISI headquarters.

He identified himself as staff to Senator Billington and presented his State Department credentials. Having been pre-cleared, he was escorted to General Ahmed's office. Ahmed, although several years older, did not appear much changed from the inscribed photograph Senator Billington had kept behind his desk in the Hart Senate Office Building. Tony thanked the general for seeing him and got down to business.

"General, thirteen hours ago I was informed by my government that the Indians have determined that Osama bin Laden, not the government of Pakistan, was responsible for the nuclear attack on Mumbai. However, based on its assessment of Pakistan's intention to initiate a first strike, India has commenced the process for a nuclear launch on Karachi. Prime Minister Sabha has attempted to communicate with President Fazullah, but has been unable to connect."

Ahmed motioned Tony to join him at his desk. It was cluttered with military maps and satellite photographs of Indian strategic facilities.

Pointing to a cluster of vehicles and support equipment surrounding a launch pad, Ahmed declared, "This is Sriharikota, the Indians' primary rocket base. The presence of this activity is clear evidence they are within hours of the ability to strike. I have so informed our leadership and urged that we strike preemptively."

"General," Tony pleaded, "it is critical to your people and the people of the world that this calamity by miscalculation be stopped. Your president must talk with the prime minister immediately and step back from the most unimaginable consequences of this rush to nuclear destruction."

"Mr. Ramos, I accept the wisdom and urgency of your request, but there is no means of doing so. There has never been the kind of hotline that existed between the leaders of the United States and the USSR during the Cold War. There has been no serious, sustained engagement in over a decade. Regrettably, it is impossible. We have no choice but to ..."

Tony punched in his phone. After an endless twenty seconds, Ambassador Talbott was on the line. "Mr. Ambassador, I'm in the office of the director of the ISI. He informs me there is no channel for communication between his president and the Indian prime minister. It is imperative that this take place; both sides are rushing to be the first to strike. Could you get the prime minister on this line, and I'll give the phone to President Fazullah?"

"Leave the line open," Talbott directed. "Take your phone to the presidential office and I'll contact the Indians."

In General Ahmed's Mercedes, Tony sped through the now almost empty streets to the president's headquarters. As they were racing up the five flights of stairs to the president's office, Talbott's voice resumed. "Tony, I have Prime Minister Sabha on the line."

They continued up the remaining steps to the office of the president of Pakistan. Breathing deeply from the exertion and adrenalin flow, General Ahmed said, "Mr. President, Prime Minister Sabha is holding. I implore you to talk. The future of both our nations depends on your willingness and wisdom." Tony handed the phone to the president.

Tony and the general stood back as President Fazullah and Prime Minister Sabha commenced the first direct conversation between the heads of government of these two neighboring nuclear countries in ten years. From the side of the conversation he could hear, with President Fazullah speaking in his minimal English and red-faced with emotion, it seemed to Tony that it would be a short talk with the worst possible outcome. But after five minutes, the tone quieted. Fazullah was now speaking in Pashtun. With a semblance of a smile, the president handed the phone to Ahmed, who continued in his Sandhurst-influenced English. Eighteen minutes after the conversation began, the parties disengaged.

Ahmed invited Tony into the adjacent office. "Mr. Ramos, the president and the prime minister have agreed to a three-day moratorium under U.S. and U.N. supervision. Since you are here, and through your association with Senator Billington, I consider you to be an honorable man. I suggested you be the observer of our stand-down. The Indians have agreed."

Tony, demanding rather than responding, said, "I must have a ten-minute meeting with your president. Now."

Ahmed returned to the president's office. In three minutes the general ushered Tony into the presidential chambers and withdrew.

"Mr. President, I appreciate your confidence in commissioning me to oversee your activities for the next three days," Tony said. "But, before I can undertake another responsibility, I must complete one for my country."

Tony summarized what he knew of the *Petronius* and the prospect that a third nuclear attack would target the United States in less than ten days. It was imperative that he know the detonation code for the device so that he might secure a reprieve for Americans, as he was facilitating one for Pakistanis and Indians.

"Mr. President, you know Osama bin Laden; I implore you to avert another impending tragedy."

In English, the president replied, "You are a good American. Whatever the world thinks of your leaders, we admire the personal qualities of your people. I will do all in my power to comply with your request."

OCTOBER 24

Islamabad

Sixty hours of the moratorium had passed. Tony had contacted Randy Crest and the former U.S. embassy military liaisons in Islamabad and received their advice on how to carry out his supervisory role. In the hours available to him he had arranged for continuous telephone and Internet linkage between the president and the prime minister, discussed with the new joint chiefs the security arrangements that controlled Pakistan's nuclear stockpile, and personally toured the two northern strategic installations by Pakistani army helicopter. All seemed to be in order and consistent with the president's and prime minister's understanding.

Tony left his satellite phone with President Fazullah's chief of staff, as General Ahmed had provided him a Pakistani replacement. Ahmed was on the phone.

"Mr. Ramos, the president is ready to meet with you in his office."

After checking with the pilots, Tony responded, "General, I can be there in ninety minutes."

At 10:43 p.m., Tony entered the president's reception room. The room, which the previous morning had been crowded and filled with agitated voices, was quiet and empty except for Sonji and the veiled woman.

Sonji spoke first. "Mr. Ramos, the president and, when they realize what you have done, the people of Pakistan are deeply gratified by your intervention on their behalf. Your friendship will be rewarded. When we were together Saturday—it seems a year ago—you met Madam Bakht."

Tony nodded to the woman, dressed in precisely the same manner as when they first met in Peshawar.

Sonji continued: "She has been Osama's principle advisor on the non-Arab media. She had served him loyally since she left her home in India to join in the war to evict the Russians from Afghanistan. Ms. Bakht is the mother of one of Osama's daughters, Mamata. In 2002, when al-Qaeda was forced out of Afghanistan into the tribal areas of this country, Mamata returned to live with her grandparents in Mumbai. She was one of the schoolgirls killed in the September 19 attack."

The woman dropped her head to her black garment. A gasp and sob emerged from beneath her scarf.

"Since Ms. Bakht has been in Pakistan, she has worked with President Fazullah, who was then the al-Qaeda leader in this country. When the president contacted her after your visit Tuesday, she overcame her earlier reluctance and pressed to secure the information and, at substantial personal risk, has done so."

Sonji handed Tony a brown envelope as he and the woman excused themselves from the office.

OCTOBER 27
The U.S. Southwest ★ Los Angeles

Abdul Muhadded and Ben Brewster were on Interstate 15 en route from St. George, Utah to Henderson, Nevada.

Five weeks earlier, as they had sped south, Muhadded had been savoring another period of seclusion and solitude in Mexico. Except for a tranquil interlude in Switzerland, he had spent the time from his earlier successful operations in Florida and Grand Cayman until called to duty in Washington in a quaint village north of Cancún. It was not until the third Tuesday in September that he returned to his San Diego family and responsibilities.

Before reaching the Tijuana border station, Ben convinced him that the risk of detection in attempting to run border security and then not being able to get back into the country were too great. Instead, they diverted over local roads to the east. In Calexico they rented a Kia and dumped the Toyota pickup at an end-of-the-line automotive salvage yard, removed the tags and documents from the glove compartment, and continued toward New Mexico. They were assiduously cautious crossing Arizona, concerned that a minor traffic offense could result in arrest and detention.

During the following weeks they stayed on the move, rarely lingering in one location more than a couple of days. Every two weeks, they discarded their rental car and leased a new one. Muhadded shaved off his beard and took to wearing wraparound Formula One–style sunglasses. He committed to a strict diet that shed a dozen pounds. Brewster's effort to downsize from obese to rotund was less successful; the rich food of the American Southwest added seven pounds to his already generous frame.

Their only close call occurred in the third week, ten miles south of Gallup, New Mexico, when they were pulled over by a New Mexico state patrolman for speeding. The officer submitted all the information he was trained to request, but there were no kick-outs from any of the state or federal law enforcement data banks. He wrote the two a ticket for $175, and they continued on. The ticket was shredded and flushed down the next gas station's toilet.

It hadn't taken Muhadded and Ben Brewster long to bond. By the time they reached the desert south of Las Cruces, Muhadded was feeling the effects of yet another separation from his family and his duties as monitor of Saudi students in San Diego. He had been learning the names of new freshmen and graduate students when he was called for the operation at Lock & Load.

In spite of the increasing number of extraneous assignments and extended absences from home, after three years in San Diego, Muhadded was becoming more comfortable with American culture. He admired the rapidity with which his two primary-grade daughters had learned English and assimilated with other children in the neighborhood.

Through his infrequent civil conversations with Tony, Brewster was aware that Billington's and Carol's killer had an idiosyncratic signature: the placement of two .45 caliber casings in locations where they were certain to be found shortly before each victim's death. This apparent indiscretion from a man Brewster was coming to admire for his judgment drove him to ask, "Muhadded, I don't understand the .45s thing. You're leaving a trail of evidence for the police to track you down. It seems so out of character. What are you doing?"

"Have you ever hunted?"

"I've shot some quail at my uncle's plantation in south Georgia."

"Nothing bigger than a fat little bird?"

"No."

"I don't know about quail, but if you are hunting large animals like pronghorn antelope, there is an understood code of conduct: you don't shoot females; you don't shoot an animal on the ground; you don't shoot until you are sure you have a kill shot—and if you wound an animal, you are responsible for putting it out of its misery. And there are other rules like that. This is what I am talking about."

"What's that have to do with killing humans?"

"There is a code there, too. It is no sport just to hide and kill from ambush. Your prey should be aware he is in danger. That gives him the chance to take evasive action, to try to get away, to make your job more challenging and interesting. Most are like that old senator, no change in routine. The day after I dropped those shells in his car he followed exactly the same walking route as he had the day before. The kill was so easy it almost took away the rush. On the other hand, the girl had gotten a handgun. On purpose I let her fire first. On purpose because I figured I wasn't in much danger. So I guess you could say I do it just for the high I get when I take down a worthy target who knows he—or she—is going to end up in my crosshairs. And I took her out of her misery."

Both were quiet for several minutes. Muhadded broke the silence.

"Ben," he asked, "I know why I am here in this situation, but why are you? Look at what you have given up for the life of a fugitive. What happened?"

"It didn't happen in a single step," Brewster confessed. "It was a series of what, at the time, seemed like unrelated events that came together to change my life."

"That's true for most people," Muhadded commented. "How did it start?"

"I'll admit to having had a privileged life: nurturing and well-off family, whatever financial support was needed, and superior education. I was able to be successful without too much heavy lifting. But I felt I had not been truly tested, so after graduate school at Princeton I looked for something that would challenge me."

"And that was? . . ."

"I applied to Goldman Sachs, but after three rounds of interviews I was rejected. They didn't tell me why, but I suspected they thought I was too patrician and soft for the rough-and-tumble of international investment banking. It was the first time anything like that had happened to me. In hindsight, it was a positive experience. It made me more competitive, more willing to put it on the line with at least an appearance of self-confidence."

"So what did you do with this new insight?"

"I looked around at possibilities in the federal security and intelligence agencies, applied for a few, and was selected by the State Department's INR bureau."

"INR?"

"I don't know how it relates to the intelligence agencies you used to serve, but State does intelligence analysis. After five years as an apprentice I got my break and was given the Saudi Arabian portfolio."

"So you started looking at us at about the same time I was getting prepared to look at you."

"And I hope your side was better at it than mine. The compensation for a young officer was adequate by federal government pay standards, but nothing like what I had been used to. I felt like I was economically deprived, entitled but not compensated. And, as I got deeper into the U.S.-Saudi relationship, particularly studying the classified information from the 9/11 investigations, I became suspicious of the Saudi role. I thought this was of such importance, and might be such a feather in my career cap, that I went around my immediate supervisors and took it directly to the secretary of state herself."

"In my government that would be a very bold move."

"It was with mine, too. She said I was out of my territory. She was aware of the information I had provided; that it was of the highest national security and classification status, and I was not to discuss it further with anyone. Then two strange things happened."

"What?"

"Ten days after the encounter with the secretary I received a call from the Saudi embassy. I was asked to come the following day for a briefing by an embassy counselor."

"Was that an unusual request?"

"Somewhat, but not as strange as the counselor and the subject: the ambassador and my 9/11 suspicions. He made no effort to dissuade me as to the correctness of my speculation; rather, he said it was a matter of great significance to both governments that it remain classified. The ambassador is an unusually suave and persuasive diplomat. He was aware of my financial situation and offered to be of assistance. He indicated there was an organization called the Golden Chain, comprised of distinguished Saudis. He said it was prepared to be helpful, and if I were interested, he would arrange the further details."

"Uh-huh, I see," Muhadded nodded, briefly glancing at Brewster. "I have a position at the Ercan corporation, previously held by Omar al-Harbi. Although it has made no requests for my services, the income from Ercan is what supports me and my family. The owner of Ercan is one of those distinguished Saudis."

Brewster stiffened, silently mulling what Muhadded had just said, then continued: "Ten days after my visit with the ambassador a man called, introducing himself as Roland Jeralewski. He gave a concise résumé, which I didn't need as he was well known in Washington political and defense circles. He said he was calling at the ambassador's request. We arranged to meet for dinner at the Metropolitan Club."

"And he also made you an offer?"

"At dinner Jeralewski said he was there on behalf of his organization—Peninsular Partners—and the Golden Chain . . . "

Abdul interrupted, "Jeralewski, Peninsular of Long Beach?"

"That's their headquarters and he's the head honcho. Why?"

"That is who my supervisor told me to contact in early July and do what I was asked to do. He said the kingdom was in some sort of a partnership with Peninsular. Even for me it has turned out to be pretty damn violent. But, I do what I'm told."

"How many people have you killed on this assignment?"

Muhadded looked at his fingers as if counting. "Starting with the old man in Florida, four plus those San Diego cops. Praise be to Allah, each has gone well, at least for me."

He drove for another ten minutes before he picked up the conversation. "You were talking about your dinner with Jeralewski."

Brewster was jarred by the ease with which Muhadded moved back from murder to a long-ago conversation in a refined, fraternal setting. It took Brewster several moments to recalibrate. "Well, Jeralewski said both Peninsular and the Golden Chain shared the interest of the secretary of state and the Saudi ambassador in keeping my disclosures from others in the bureau and the government and from the American public. He also remarked on the ambassador's distress at my fall from economic comfort to mere adequacy and offered to help, the only requirements being keeping silent about what I suspected to be the truth and reporting back to him with information of interest to him and the entities he represented."

"What kind of help?"

"On the first of each month since that dinner, I have received a check drawn on a numbered bank account for $25,000."

"Who was it from?"

"I never asked," Brewster said coyly, "though I assume it was either Peninsular directly or the Golden Chain."

"You said there were two things that affected you."

"A colleague, Tony Ramos, had the same status I held, and his portfolio was Afghanistan. Due to some connections with a recently deceased ex-senator, he began poking around in my Saudi sand. I attempted to cut him off every way I could think of, but nothing worked."

Brewster paused to make sure Muhadded was following the narrative. "Around this time I was introduced to another Peninsular consultant, Laura Billington . . ."

"*The* Laura Billington, the photographer?"

"That's right. It seems she had some financial issues considerably larger than mine. She tipped off Peninsular about Ramos and the woman from Treasury he was sleeping with, so they were able to set him up as the killer. I thought that would be it for him, but he squirmed out of that one too."

Muhadded cringed. "That's the operation I told you about while we were in San Diego. So that's why you left Washington?"

"Yes, plus the final call from Jeralewski, telling me the monthly retainers would stop. He said Peninsular was under investigation and Golden Chain had informed him that the purpose of a scientific project it supported had been attained. For now, its resources would go to the liberation efforts in Afghanistan and Pakistan. He did offer me a place in San Diego to hang out until the dust settled, and that place turned out to be yours."

OCTOBER 28

Maui, Hawaii

Laura strained to hear over the prop wash from the Italian Agusta A-109 helicopter.

"Tony, please talk slowly and distinctly. The helicopter that's taking us out to the *Petronius* is noisy as hell. Please repeat."

"I'm on my way back from Islamabad," Tony yelled into his cell. "The situation there is stabilized, but very iffy. The Pakistani president, our friend from Kuala Lumpur, and a woman, an extremely courageous woman, have—God knows how—gotten the information. When you open the package you received at Gatwick, you will find detailed instructions attached to the electrical box."

"What's the purpose of the box?" Laura asked.

"It's a remote detonation device. It will activate the bomb if you precisely follow the instructions. Paragraph 8 will direct you to insert a code; you will do it twice—which is DA34M701. Again: DA34M701."

Laura read back the code.

"Laura, I'm headed for Long Beach, where the *Petronius* is supposed to dock. The secretary's finally a believer, and she's given me her plane, so I should be there on Thursday. I'll meet you at the L.A. Port Authority heliport that afternoon. Do you have any questions? You'll be on your own from here on out."

Laura repeated the code one more time, had no questions, hit the END button, and boarded the Agusta to the greetings of Aristotle Stephanous and her three-man crew.

OCTOBER 28

Henderson, Nevada ⋆ *Los Angeles*

After four weeks and 24,200 miles, Muhadded and Brewster were in their second night at the Siesta Motel in Henderson, Nevada. Muhadded received a call on his cell from the Saudi Arabian consultant in Los Angeles.

As he had on numerous occasions, Faroung Barkett, the counselor for political and cultural affairs—the post Hamza al-Dossari had held for four years—was demanding Muhadded come to L.A. for instructions.

They dressed, paid the attendant at the Siesta's front desk, and started the trek to Los Angeles in the Ford Focus they had rented from Alamo the day before.

The meeting with Faroung Barkett was short and to the point. As it was their first and Brewster's recent activities had given him some cachet, Barkett greeted him with civility and apparent respect.

"We are, of course, aware of the service each of you has rendered to our common cause. Your fidelity to that cause has been closely reviewed by our external security agency and confirmed. Mr. Brewster, we are pleased you will be assisting Mr. Muhadded in a critically important assignment."

Turning to Muhadded, the lean, white-robed and sandaled young man continued, "On Thursday evening or, at the latest, early Friday, the Greek cargo vessel *Petronius* will arrive at the port of Long Beach.

Friends and associates of the kingdom are anxious to ascertain the precise docking space for this ship, along with its positioning. As soon as you have secured this information, reply to me at this number."

Handing Muhadded an envelope, he asked, "Do you have any questions?"

Brewster considered asking the reason for this portside intelligence, but thought better of it.

"No," Muhadded replied.

After an hour and a half of mid-afternoon L.A. traffic, Muhadded parked the Ford in front of the Long Beach Port Authority building. Before leaving the consulate he had ascertained that the offices of the Stephanous Shipping Line were on the third floor. He had been given a second envelope with documents.

Behind a mahogany desk a youthful clerk looked up. "May I be of service?"

"We are representatives of the ATR maritime security firm." Muhadded handed over the materials from the second envelope.

The clerk glanced at the forms, nodded, and again looked Muhadded in the eye.

"Several of our clients have shipments on the *Petronius,* which we were told will arrive on the evening of the 30th or the morning of the 31st. To facilitate the transfer of the containers, they want to know the pier that has been assigned."

The clerk squinted at the screen of his Dell desktop. "38A."

"And the positioning?"

"What do you mean?"

"How will the ship be oriented?"

"That's a curious question, but since you asked, the stern will be dockside."

"Thank you. I trust we will see you on Friday."

"Right," the clerk replied, then added idly, "Happy Halloween."

"Thanks. You, too," Brewster said.

He detected a momentary wave of concern on Muhadded's face. He thought he understood, though, when his companion spotted that rarity of postmodern America, a pay phone, on the far side of the Port Authority lobby. Brewster figured he didn't like transmitting vital information, whatever its purpose, wirelessly. He waited while Muhadded called in with the docking instructions.

As he replaced the phone in its cradle, Brewster asked, "What's the matter? It seemed like when that clerk mentioned Halloween, you suddenly got all funky. You're so strict you get bent out of shape at the mention of pagan rituals?"

"It is not that," Muhadded corrected. "It is just that the counselor has asked me to return to his office on Wednesday and to be prepared to report on Thursday and Friday as well. This could mean I will not be able to go trick-or-treating with my daughters. They have put so much effort into their little costumes. It is my favorite American holiday."

OCTOBER 28–29

The Petronius, *Pacific Ocean*

For the first three hours of the flight, the Pacific had been as calm as a bathtub. The pilot and copilot stretched the legs of the Agusta to more than eight hundred kilometers. With the last rays of sunlight fading through the black clouds in the west and reflecting off the now rolling seas beneath them, the chopper reached the illuminated helipad on the rear deck of the *Petronius.*

After four hours of the thud-thud of the Agusta's twin engines in quarters crammed with crew, passengers, and equipment, Laura was fatigued and politely declined Stephanous's offer of dinner. By nine she had retired to her cabin.

Laura was disappointed that the clouds of the previous evening had matured into a rainstorm, which drenched the *Petronius* and slowed the execution of her photographic plan. Drawing on the movie *Titanic,* the centerpiece shot would be from the bridge, with Stephanous at the tip of the bow, his silver mane of hair blowing in the Pacific wind. She thought that kind of pop-culture connection would appeal to his glaring ego. She would now have to wait another day to commence her work.

The *Petronius* was a workhorse. It would soon account for almost one percent of all the cargo traffic crossing the Pacific. But it was not without its elegance: the owner, Aristotle Stephanous, occupied a palatial suite above the bridge. Glass swept around three sides, offering a panoramic view of the ocean. With a gracious flourish, Stephanous re-extended his invitation to Laura to join him there for dinner.

The final containers of electronics and automobile parts had been lifted on board the *Petronius* at the Thai port of Laem Chabang. The supership had also taken on a pallet of local fish, food, and spices. It was from this stash that the gingered shrimp-roll salad was prepared as the appetizer for Stephanous and his guest.

Gazing out on this now tranquil scene, Laura said, "Aristotle, I am deeply gratified that you accepted my call. I have told the prime minister of your courtesy, and he joins me in our appreciation."

Stephanous maintained his focus on the ocean as he took a sip of Cristal champagne. "This engagement is not for me. It has been my practice to concentrate on my love, the business of the seas, and leave the credit and attention to others."

Moving closer, Laura said, "I am honored that you deviated from your pattern of self-effacement. Why did you give me this unique opportunity?"

He turned to her, his deep voice dropping another half octave. "It is my belief that what I am doing is a fundamental contribution to world order. As the people of the globe become more reliant on the goods and services of others, they are more likely to forgo violence as a means of resolving their inevitable disputes."

He rambled on about an incident between Argentina and Chile in which trade relations had deflected a war. "I wish this were true elsewhere, India and Pakistan particularly. To me, the *Petronius* is a symbol of peace."

"And you feel what we will do tomorrow will contribute to that recognition?"

"Through your sensitivity and talent, yes."

A staff of five served a dinner the equal of the best restaurants in Paris. They luxuriated over the lemongrass-accented green curry with fresh prawns and sesame oil–marinated pomelo with ginger ice cream and engaged in sophisticated conversation for two hours.

When the last of the cutlery was removed and the parlor returned to its stately ambiance, the two of them were again alone, resting on the exquisite antique Italian sofa. This time Stephanous closed the distance.

In a voice still deep, but now affected by an evening of heavy champagne and wine consumption, he said, "Laura, I have spoken of my dedication to peace and the humble contribution I believe I am making to its realization among nations."

He paused to drain his glass. "The same is true between humans. Closer contacts are the keys which turn chance meetings into lasting relationships." With that, he slid his right hand under Laura's dress.

She pushed away his hand. "Aristotle, I am here for professional business and, more important, assuring that you are introduced to the world as the Periclean leader of men you are. We will both be together soon; there will be time for us to know each other better."

"Stay and cruise with me to Los Angeles. We still have a day and a half."

With his hand now resting on her knee, Laura said softly, "Aristotle, sadly we have already lost a day. I must get the photographs we will take tomorrow to the publishers by Friday. We have a chance at being in the Christmas editions, the most widely read of the year. I will meet you with the greeting party when you arrive on Friday, and we will celebrate."

As Laura returned to her suite, she withdrew the Gatwick box and read the instructions. They were, as Tony suggested, detailed and complex. When she reached paragraph 8, she carefully entered the code.

OCTOBER 29

Long Beach

"Abdul," Faroung Barkett, the Saudi consular officer, instructed, "when you get to the Long Beach exit, take it to the Hyatt Harborside. You have a room reservation. When you are in the room, call me. Have you followed my directions? Do you understand?"

"Yes and yes," Muhadded said as he maneuvered the Dodge minivan he had rented at Avis in El Segundo into the right lane. Brewster knew he didn't like cell phones. "Will I be able to return to San Diego before sundown tomorrow?"

"If you mean in time for Friday prayers, possibly."

It was after 4:30 when Muhadded turned the van into the hotel parking lot. Following instructions, he and Brewster went to room 2032, overlooking the harbor, and called the consulate.

"Abdul," the same voice said, "within the hour, DHL will deliver a package to your room. Open the container carefully and follow the instruction meticulously. When you have done so, place your Beretta where it is always accessible to you. Replace the items in the DHL box and store it under the bed. Call me at nine in the morning for further instructions."

On the last leg of his trip over the Pacific, from Guam to Los Angeles, Tony reviewed the complicated chess match that was nearing its endgame. Laura was by now on the *Petronius*. Her instructions were to complete the photo shoot by midday, when the ship would still be more than four hundred miles from Los Angeles. She knew what to do from there. If for some reason she was unable to carry out her assignment by noon, the *Petronius* would then be within blast range of the coast, and any attempt to intercept the cargo carried the risk of an onshore conflagration.

That was the basis of Tony's plan B. He composed a terse email to Mark Block. The secretary's 767 was still almost three thousand miles from LAX when Tony received his reply: "Al-Harbi's current successor is Abdul Muhadded. He is driving a Ford Focus with Nevada license plates LV 2267. The Long Beach and Los Angeles police are on the lookout. Buena suerte, Mark."

OCTOBER 30

The Petronius ✶ *Long Beach*

At daybreak, yet another squall had overtaken the *Petronius* from the west.

The bridge was swaying. The lighting technician had hinted to Laura that the shoot be suspended until the afternoon, when smoother seas were projected.

"Damn it, John, we need to get this done now. Tie down the legs of the lighting stand with gaffer tape. Inform Stephanous we'll start in thirty minutes."

On cue, Stephanous took his position at the bow. The increased crosswinds and darts of rain gave his mane of silver hair an even more leonine flourish. In less than an hour Laura had taken sixty-five images from her perch. In another two hours she had collected a sufficient number in the engine room, cargo deck, and crew mess to meet her needs, or at least give the impression that she had. For once, something other than her images and her ego demanded precedence.

Aristotle was a handsome man with an ego and pomposity to match the scale of his newest possession. Laura felt she had captured those qualities. Stephanous was flattered.

———

On the tarmac of the LAX executive air terminal, Tony stretched and twisted his torso, releasing the accumulated tensions of the flight halfway round the world. State had arranged for a limousine. He was surprised to find Mark Block waiting in the backseat.

"What the hell are you doing here?" Tony asked.

"I thought you'd need some backup," Mark said, "and I didn't exactly see a long line offering to help."

"Any leads on Muhadded?"

"He's staying at the Hyatt in Long Beach. The cops are still looking for his car, but think they have a lead from an Avis lot south of here. I've changed your reservation to the Hyatt so you can be near your new closest friend."

"Yeah, I'm considering friending him on Facebook."

"I'm sure he'll be thrilled."

Mark continued, "What's your buddy up to?"

"What do you mean?"

"What never has made sense to me is the Saudis helping bin Laden. Here he blows up Aramco and kills several tens of thousands of Saudis and foreigners. Why are they lending him Muhadded?"

Tony took a sip from his Diet Coke. "He's a known and seasoned professional intelligence officer and assassin. That and the king's long-standing partnership with Peninsular explain why he was detailed to do its dirty work.

"As for al-Qaeda, it's following its old habits, repeating what it did with al-Harbi and the hijackers. Bin Laden asked his allies in Riyadh to task the Saudi consulate to arrange for a trusted operative, and they found him in the same place: San Diego. And you know why Mu-hadded's in Long Beach?"

"I think I do," Mark said. "We'll probably find out for sure in a few hours."

Muhadded had been up since eight when the phone rang. He had dressed, fulfilled his prayer duties, and reread the instructions. He moved the blue-steel Beretta, which had been under his pillow, to the top of the chest of drawers.

"Abdul," the crisp, nearly unaccented voice of the counselor said, "it appears it will be another thirty hours before you will be called upon to execute your highest responsibility, praise be to Allah. I trust it will be completed sufficiently early for you to attend your mosque. For today, at precisely three this afternoon, you should have your equipment at the ready to prepare and practice under the same conditions as you will face on Friday. I'll call you back at ten minutes of three."

"I will be prepared."

In room 2030, Tony and Mark rewound the recorder and replayed the wiretapped conversation. "It looks as if we have the rest of the morning off," Tony said.

With Brewster's assistance, Muhadded had placed the NE wireless triggering instrumentation by the open window. Developed initially to assist utility meter readers working remotely from an office or truck, it had been converted to a lethal detonation device for IEDs in Iraq. Now further enhanced, the NE had a signal reach of more than ten kilometers.

Muhadded moved the wide-angle lens device to point directly at the midsection of Pier 38A of the Port of Long Beach. Even at a distance of five miles, with field binoculars Muhadded could clearly see what would be his target.

He was on the phone to the consulate, making final adjustments, familiarizing himself with the equipment when the door crashed open.

Tony, crouched low to the ground, chin touching his knees, led the way with Mark behind. Muhadded locked his arms together and, using them like a sledgehammer, crushed them into Tony's face, throwing him back into Mark and the two of them into a pile of thrashing arms and legs crashing to the floor next to the king-size bed. Brewster leapt from the bed, on top of the pile. Mark slammed him against the open door, lacerating Brewster's bald skull.

Muhadded spun and reached for the chest of drawers. As his fingers grasped the Beretta, Tony regained his balance and launched his right foot into Muhadded's underarm, knocking him back, sending the chest and pistol to the floor. Tony pirouetted, sliding the weapon with his right foot to Mark. Muhadded snatched the NE, lifting it from the tripod. Tony was able to deflect it by lowering his head and raising his right shoulder into the tripod's arc.

Two bursts of light—the first from outside the hotel balcony was a blinding flash like a line of lightning bolts—the second was from ten feet with a .45 caliber explosive force and discharge. Mark's shot hit Muhadded in the chest. He staggered backward to the balcony's steel railing, crashed through it, and fell twisting in a summersault until his body ripped open the top of the valet station shed 220 feet below. The horrified attendants scattered in full flight from the first burst of light.

Brewster, blood flowing through his eyebrows, grabbed Mark's right wrist, attempting to dislodge the Beretta. Mark wrapped his left arm around Brewster's neck and grounded him with a horse-collar lock, the pistol jammed in his obese torso.

"Back off, Mark," Tony shouted. "I want the bastard alive."

After a buffet luncheon in the owner's dining room, this time open to all of Laura's crew and the pilot and copilot, the captain announced his calculation that the ship was 450 miles from the Port of Long Beach. Once the helicopter was topped off with jet fuel from the *Petronius's* onboard tanks and loaded with photographic equipment, Laura and her three assistants lifted off the helipad while waving to Stephanous, the captain, and the crew. With a slight tremor, Laura snapped on her stopwatch and counted down.

As the Agusta climbed farther from the *Petronius*, Laura distanced herself emotionally. For a lifetime, she acknowledged, she had been preparing for this moment. Her life had been devoted to herself, the feelings of others a matter of indifference. She reflected how, as a teenager, when a boyfriend had dumped her, she had accused her older sister of enticing him away and told her parents that she was a slut. Her own sexual competition had started early. Carol's death, she realized, was probably the first time Laura had truly regretted anything she'd done. The consequences of that murder and her role in it finally moved her to consider and confront some moral and human dimensions of her life. Maybe that was preparation for what she was about to do.

She could see the *Petronius* on the horizon. She could still taste the food and wine they had all just shared, and here she was, about to kill each and every one of them. Laura even had a twinge of regret for deceiving Stephanous. What Tony had accused her of doing to Carol Watson she was about to do to Stephanous. The thousands who would be saved would be unaware of what she had done.

Will there be some higher being who will give absolution? she wondered. *When this is over I want to talk it through with Tony. He understands the calculus of moral trade-offs.*

At fifty-five seconds after liftoff from the deck, which the instructions indicated should be two and a half kilometers, Laura withdrew the box and, carefully following paragraph 8, inserted the code a second time. She waited ten seconds, drew a deep gulp of air into her cactus-dry throat, and firmly pushed the red button.

Laura heard a roar like she had heard as a child in advance of a Florida thunderstorm. The blue skies became red; the helicopter began to swing from side-to-side and then bow to aft. She felt the onset of air sickness. In mounting panic, she glanced down at the instructions. She was trying to convince herself that at this distance the helicopter should be well beyond the blast zone, when a broken rotor blade cracked the cabin window with less than a thousand feet separating them from the water below.

What Tony may have miscalculated or misinterpreted in preparing the instructions was the power of the Ramallah bomb. This was not two, but five times the power of Hiroshima.

The helicopter spun out of control and fell clumsily into the Pacific. Without nautical buoyancy, it quickly sank.

OCTOBER 30–31
Long Beach ✶ Laguna Niguel, California

The Long Beach police and FBI had taken over Muhadded's room as a crime scene and dispatched Brewster to the bureau's downtown detention center.

Until almost midnight Tony was debriefed by the FBI's special terrorism unit. He recounted the events of the last six weeks and, with particular detail, the final twelve hours.

———————

Tony dropped Mark at LAX for his American red-eye to Dulles.

Mark confessed, "That was the first time I killed a man, and I have a feeling I'll be working through it a long time. I know he was a killer with no regard for human life, but, well . . . he was a human being."

"You did what you had to do," Tony counseled.

"Whatever, I am extremely proud of what you have done and that I could be your sidekick for the last act. See you on the court Tuesday, same time, same place."

———————

That night was another sleepless one for Tony. At sunrise, he stood at the balcony for an hour staring at the expanding haze over the western horizon, trying to get his adrenalin-driven emotions to subside. As he was returning to the bedroom, his BlackBerry hummed.

"Hello, Tony Ramos here."

"This is Talbott. Tony, there is no way the world or I can recognize or fully appreciate what you have done. If bin Laden had accomplished his objective, the earth would be in total chaos and panic."

"Thank you, Mr. Ambassador. This has been a once-in-a-lifetime experience."

"Let's hope so," Talbott commented, "for all our sakes."

"And I wouldn't have had it without your confidence in this deskbound analyst's ability to be an on-the-ground operative. I'm not sure I would have trusted me."

"You've got good judgment, Tony. And that holds up whether you're at that desk or out in the 'real world.'"

Tony paused for a moment, then said, "The FBI has asked me to stick around in case it needs a second round of debriefing. They've already got a name for this thing."

"I know: TERRORNUKE. Cute, huh?"

"I guess. May I get an extension of my leave from the office?"

"Of course. And one more item: I'm recommending to the secretary and the director of the INR bureau that a unit be established within INR that will not be geographically structured; rather, it will be tasked to respond to whatever the most immediate and urgent international challenge to the nation happens to be. What you have just been through demonstrates the bureau needs this capacity on a permanent basis. I'd like you to be a part of it. Are you okay with that?"

Without hesitation Tony responded: "That is exactly what I would like to do. And if the secretary balks, there's likely to be a new person in her office when the next administration arrives. Thank you for giving me this chance."

"I like your game plan. I'll keep you up to speed. Is there anything else?"

"There is. What do you know of the status of the search for the Agusta?" Tony asked.

"Because of the radioactive nature of the site, it's been impossible to launch a recovery operation. But there are no false illusions. The helicopter went down in twenty thousand feet—unfortunately, there is no hope of survivors."

Tony was silent. Talbott continued, "I have briefed the White House on your involvement and strongly recommended it make a commendatory statement on your role and valor. They have declined. Hector Sanchez, the officer who has taken Ben Brewster's Saudi portfolio, has given me a public statement and an accompanying private message Riyadh has sent. King Abdul Aziz has implored the president to remain silent as to the kingdom's role, and he has agreed to do so."

"What did the Saudis say?"

"Hold on, I'll read it to you directly." Tony waited while the ambassador searched his emails. "Here it is: 'The worst people in the world have gained access to the worst weapons and have shown again their intention to use them against innocents. The kingdom has been a victim of this brutality. The world is at risk, and we join our American friends in the most aggressive and sustained efforts to halt the carnage and bring the perpetrators to justice.'"

Tony felt a tightening in his gut. "The Saudis know, of course, that's total bullshit."

"I suspect you're right, but I also know the election is next Tuesday and—"

"I don't give a goddamn about the election," Tony shouted into the receiver. "Tens of thousands of people have been killed, starting with Senator Billington, to protect their dirty secret and the political power of the administration. If it requires resigning my position at State, I will not be a party to covering up their bloody laundry."

"That's what I admire in you, Tony. And unless I have already gone first, I'll be at your side."

It took Tony a half hour to settle himself and ponder the future. The first step was to call Senator Billington's widow.

"Mrs. Billington, this is Tony Ramos."

"Tony, I've been so worried about you. Since I saw the television reports of the explosion, I've been able to think of nothing except what you and John had set out to do."

"I can't tell you how much worse this horrid scene would have been were it not for your husband's wisdom and tenacity. I know there is nothing that can ever replace him in your life, but I trust that Mumbai, Aramco, and now, almost, Los Angeles have given added meaning to the significance of his life and death."

Tony could hear her quiet sobs. He waited, then said, "Mrs. Billington, there will be a recovery effort made for Laura, but I would be dishonest to hold out much hope. She and her father are now forever joined in their common commitment to avoid mass death and destruction. I hope that can bring you some solace."

———————

Twelve hours later and less than eight blocks from the Hyatt Harborside, in the executive suite of Peninsular Tower, Roland Jeralewski and the chairman looked out over the Pacific. The cloud was drifting closer. Beneath them in the streets thousands were huddled, ignorant of the causes of what they were experiencing, panicked at the potential consequences.

His eyes never deflecting from the scene to make contact, Jeralewski intoned, "Mr. Chairman, what have we done?"

"We pursued legitimate corporate goals with a sovereign government allied to the United States. It is not for us to try to impose morality—if you could even define it in this context—on the world."

Jeralewski stared directly, incredulously, at the chairman, and then he did what he seldom had done before—refuted him, "No, Mr. Chairman, that's not what we have done. After a life devoted to public service we succumbed to the belief that we had earned special treatment and rewards, that we were entitled. Our weaknesses—arrogance, greed, lust for power—have placed the world at risk. They have surely destroyed us. That is what we have done."

———

FBI agents had driven Sergeant Alvarez and Terri McKenzie to L.A. to confirm the identification of Muhadded's corpse and to brief the officers interrogating Benjamin Brewster. Even with the beard shaven and body mutilated by the gunshot wound and the long fall to the roof of the parking attendants' shed, Alvarez was unflinching in his assertion that the man in the morgue was the man who had tried to kill him. Terri provided background on Brewster's involvement with Peninsular.

———

The sun was setting as Tony and Terri in their Hertz Mustang convertible passed Newport Beach on Highway 1 headed toward Pacific Grove. Terri drove. The extreme tension of the clash with Muhadded and Brewster and the mental exertion of intense interrogation had exhausted Tony's emotional reserve and separated him from his innermost feelings. But now, suddenly, it was as if the wall had lifted, and tears began to roll down his cheeks.

Terri put her hand on his arm and quietly said, "Share it with me. Tell me what you're going through. Maybe I can help."

"I don't know if anyone can," Tony responded.

"At least I can listen."

"I don't know where to begin. I feel as if I've lived an entire lifetime all crammed into the last hundred days. Senator Billington, Jeddah, Brewster, Mumbai, Pakistan, you, of course, Carol, Laura . . . It's like it's all become a halo of bright lights flashing in my brain. Whatever you might think, whatever your training, you're never prepared for this hurricane of unknowns, each one swirling in its own ocean, until they collide."

His last words hung in the ocean air. His head fell back on the headrest. "It all happened so fast . . . I just can't make any sense of it. I loved Carol, I think; I didn't even get the chance to be sure. And she died because of me; Laura, too. And with Laura it all got so twisted. I shouldn't be laying all this on you, especially about Carol and Laura."

"No, Tony, I want you to. If we're going to have a relationship going forward, you need to be able to deal with what's happened and share it. But listen to me: I'm presuming a relationship that hasn't . . . well . . . you know."

He turned his head toward her and looked earnestly for several seconds. Finally, "Yes, Terri . . . there is—it is happening. But I need some time to sort it all out. I don't want to make the same mistakes I did with Carol."

"I understand, Tony, with what you've been through. But for now, I'll be whatever you want me to be."

"I . . . I don't know what to say, Terri."

"Don't say anything. It's not necessary."

Neither one of them spoke for the next twenty minutes. The only sound was the rush of the salt-tinged air coursing over the top-down convertible.

Tony broke the silence. "I'm wiped out. My head is crowded with dark thoughts. Would you mind if we found a place where we could relax, get some sleep?"

Somewhat surprised, Terri quickly said, "Whatever you want."

She knew the Pacific Inn just ahead in Laguna Beach. No doubt as a result of the fears and uncertainties generated by the Thursday explosion, there were few cars in the parking lot.

Tony stayed in the car while Terri went inside. The young woman at the front desk gave her the full selection of rooms. She chose 418, which the clerk said was one of the front rooms with a charming balcony. They'd be able to see the Pacific. Terri retrieved Tony and their scant luggage, raised the Mustang roof, and locked the car. Together they took the elevator up to 418.

After they dropped their bags, Tony went to the bathroom and washed away the rivulets of tears still dampening his face.

"Are you feeling okay?" Tony asked.

"Tired, but happy we can be together."

"Terri, I need a drink. I'm too hot-wired to sleep."

"I could use one, too."

They walked down to the Beach House restaurant, where they could watch the gentle waves lap in over the sand. "I feel like I could spend the rest of my life in a beach house," Tony observed.

Terri ordered a margarita; Tony, his standard Chivas. They drank as if they were alone, separately contemplating their own experiences since the last meeting with Nasir and their own futures. How fortuitous it had all been. Would the future be equally perplexing?

It seemed as if all of the other diners were locals, and they had what Terri knew was that signature Laguna look that involved so many contradictions: dressed casually enough to be teenagers but well into their thirties, forties, and fifties; clearly concerned with fitness and appearance, yet leathery and wrinkled from so much time in the sun. It was as if they were trying to preserve their younger selves, trying to bring back the past—perhaps to understand it. It made Tony think about his own teenage years in Hialeah.

"Maybe it's my own life playing out," he said to Terri, "but it is true your view is affected by where you are, where you have been."

She slid closer, nuzzled against Tony's chest, and in a tequila-tinged whisper said, "Do you think we could end up in the same place?"

"I hope so; I really do." The waiter came by and Tony signaled for a third round. "But as our lives have already shown, luck, fate will play a big part."

By the time they got back to their room, Terri was barely awake. Tony laid her on the bed, removed her shoes, and pulled a light blanket over her shoulders.

He showered, then stretched out on the king-size bed and tried to keep himself still so as not to disturb her. Staring at the ceiling, he felt alternating waves of guilt, remorse, and bewilderment. He twisted to another position, pulling the pillow tightly to his head. He had imagined the woman sleeping next to him every night into the future would be Carol. Was it survivor guilt that kept him from completely embracing this moment, this woman? Whatever path his life might take, Carol would always be with him. Maybe the distance between them was too great for that path to have led to marriage; the image of her parents' expressions the first time they met hung in his consciousness.

What about Laura? She was one of the most enticing women he had ever encountered. Where might that adventure have gone? Laura was also the most self-centered woman he had ever known, and he had almost been the victim of that egotism. While the full circumstances of her last moments were buried in the ocean, her courage and resourcefulness were a direct reflection of John's and Mildred's genes and nurturing.

Terri could be the one, though. Maybe their similar upbringings, her hardscrabble life as an immigrant child with the determination to become a star in her profession, were the ingredients that would hold them together. He owed it to her and himself to give it a chance. But it was all too much to sort out right now.

At 4:30 a.m. Tony gently swung his legs over the side of the bed, tested his feet firmly on the deep carpeting, dressed in the same clothes he had the day before, and stepped out onto the balcony, his laptop under his arm.

The moon was still hovering above the ocean, but the early-morning light from the east was blotted by the heavy clouds that had reached the coastline during the night. Tony typed away for more than an hour. It came out in a steady stream, with hardly a pause, his eyes never straying long from the computer screen. By 6:00 he had read over what he had written, making very few changes.

He placed a memory card under Terri's pillow. It was enclosed in a hotel envelope along with a single sheet of stationery from the desk drawer. In his precise hand he had written:

Terri,

I've been thinking about Senator Billington and his prescience. These are a few of my thoughts on what has happened. I'm not suggesting anything more is going to happen, but let me say this straight: if something does happen to me that you think is suspicious, I want you to read what I've written and share it with Ambassador Talbott and Senator Stoner.

Both of us need time to think things through and make good decisions. I'm leaving the keys to the Mustang. I'll be flying back to Washington from here this morning.

I think I love you. I need the chance to be sure.

Tony

TWELVE WEEKS LATER . . .

JANUARY 20
Washington, D.C.

For the third straight time, the presidential inauguration commenced under gray clouds and subfreezing temperatures. As had become official policy, the National Park Service declined to estimate the crowd size. The *Washington Post* set it at 450,000, reporting:

> The almost million fewer in attendance than at the ceremony four years ago was consistent with other events held out of doors since the attacks involving weapons of mass destruction that began with the Mumbai nuclear explosion on September 19.

From the podium on the specially built platform on the west side of the Capitol, the new president's inaugural address prompted the multitude to applaud twenty-nine times during its thirty-five-minute duration. He concluded with the traditional call to the future:

"America is leaving the valley of doubt in which we have toiled for more than a decade. America is starting the climb to the mountain of hope and a new prosperity. We are unburdened of those policies and leaders who have slowed our progress. We have new companions, with a new vision of the nation's destiny and the roads we will travel to reach our goals.

"Our success depends upon our recommitment to God as our creator and protector; to the old American values of personal responsibility, family, and neighbor; to optimism earned by a history of achievement of a better future for each generation of Americans, better than any of those generations that have preceded us on this blessed land; and a shared sense that together—not as a nation divided by partisan labels or region or social class—we can, we shall, stand on the mountaintop."

The applause thundered from the crowd and lasted several minutes. Just as the new president signaled his wife to join him at the podium to accept and relish this surge of adulation and optimism, the sun broke through, as if heralding the dawn of a bright new age.

The applause grew even louder and more fervent.

The ovation had gone on for at least six or seven minutes when Special Agent Wilbur Wright Sullivan of the United States Secret Service, newly assigned chief of the presidential protection unit, stepped forward and approached the chief executive. With a technique so well practiced that it was all but invisible to the dignitaries assembled on the platform, he placed his left hand casually on the president's shoulder while his right hand made its way under the back pleat of his morning coat and locked firmly onto the waistband of his striped gray trousers. In this fashion, it appeared to both the crowd of onlookers and the millions of television viewers as if the president were leaving the platform of his own accord.

When he was safely inside the Capitol's vestibule, he noticed that the vice president had been secured in the same manner.

Their confusion increased as the two men were hustled up the stairs leading them back into the interior of the Capitol and a sharp turn to the left. A knot of Secret Service agents had surrounded them as Sullivan led the group to the Lyndon Johnson Room on the second floor of the Senate wing.

It was the most ornate of the suite of conference rooms circling the Senate chamber and had been Johnson's power center when he was the iron-willed majority leader. Already waiting for the president were several of his top appointees.

Secret Service agents secured the doors.

Helen Robinson, who had resigned as governor of New Hampshire to accept the appointment as secretary of homeland security, got immediately to the point.

"Mr. President, at 9:07 a.m. Pacific Time—approximately forty-nine minutes ago—the director of security for San Francisco International Airport reported an Emirates A380 on a nonstop flight from Dubai landed normally and taxied to its assigned gate at the International Arrivals area."

"I assume we are nearing the end of the 'normal' part of the story," the president said, his voice betraying both impatience and mounting apprehension.

"I'm afraid so," Secretary Robinson continued. "When the gate crew signaled cabin attendants to open the door, there was no response. No communication could be established with the cockpit crew. When several tries failed, a catering company scissors truck was brought up so the ground crew could see through the windows."

"And? . . ."

"There was no apparent sign of life, sir."

"What?"

"All of the passengers were slumped over in their seats."

"How many people were on the plane?"

"We don't have the flight manifest yet, but the A380 is the largest passenger plane in operation, and this particular one is configured for 517 passengers and 26 crew."

"The airport fire department and all emergency services personnel were immediately summoned, and the plane was towed to a remote hangar where airline mechanics opened the door externally."

The president squirmed, rotating his right index finger counterclockwise. Secretary Robinson accelerated her pace.

"When the door was dislodged, a toxic plume overwhelmed the maintenance personnel. Seven have died, and five are in critical condition. The pilot and copilot were discovered collapsed on the floor outside the flight deck, so it's assumed they succumbed when they opened the cockpit door. The fuselage has been resealed until it can be examined without further risk. Hazmat teams are standing by to examine the cabin and cargo holds as soon as we can rig up a safe, negative-pressure air lock."

"What else do we know?"

"Mr. President, I'm afraid that's most of it. We're trying to put the facts together and contain rumors as well as we can to avoid panic."

White House chief of staff Chip Burpee spoke up. "We are carrying on with the inaugural parade to maintain as much of a semblance of normalcy as possible under the circumstances."

The president nodded. "And we have no idea if this is an isolated incident or part of some larger? . . ."

"I think I should let Secretary Talbott address that," Burpee said.

Ambassador William Talbott, the president's surprise choice to be secretary of state, spoke up. "Of course, the FBI, CIA, FAA, and all relevant investigative groups are already on this. But as you and I discussed during the transition, I have felt our capability to react quickly to major crises like TERRORNUKE has been constrained by the Byzantine security apparatus we've constructed since 9/11.

"It was for this reason that I recommended a special, elite, top-secret unit hidden within my department's Bureau of Intelligence and Research, a group prepared to respond to what you and the leadership of the department consider to be the most immediate and threatening risks to America. For internal identification, we are referring to it as the Armageddon Response Team, or ART. We already have certain team members identified and assigned and can activate immediately with your say-so. I have asked the officer who saved our national hide in TERRORNUKE to head up the team."

Secretary Talbott turned to the handsome, dark-skinned man to his right.

"Mr. President, this is Mr. Tony Ramos."

ACKNOWLEDGMENTS

This book, five years in the writing and editing, was the result of my passion to tell a story—fact augmented by fiction—of betrayal and courage. I have chosen to do so as a novel in order to answer questions for which there are real answers, but answers which to date have been withheld. This work represents the next best thing: informed speculation.

As has been true for most of my adult life, all that I have undertaken has been with the encouragement and support of my wife and best friend, Adele. Our four daughters, Gwen, Cissy, Suzanne, and Kendall, and their spouses, have been invaluable reviewers, commentators, and subject matter experts as the writing progressed.

In addition to my family there were others who had to accommodate to and support my writing schedule, for which I am deeply grateful: Chip Burpee, my executive assistant, who had more late nights on this novel than Ambassador Talbott had in it; and Tom White, who was also an assistant in my office and counsel on all the Spanish language. He has left our office for an assignment I cannot disclose; Jonathan Rizzo might know.

Although he might not remember, Dr. Joseph Nye of Harvard University's Kennedy School of Government, formerly an assistant secretary in the Department of Defense and author of *The Power Game,* was the first person to suggest my concerns and ideas might lend themselves to fiction. Also at the Kennedy School, as she has been on previous occasions, Sharon Wilke was the superb op ed editor.

Two people who stimulated my initial novelistic impulses are creative writing professors at Florida International University and veteran practitioners of the art: James Hall and Les Standiford.

From the beginning to the end, I have been enormously assisted by another distinguished novelist, Mark Olshaker. He has read, critiqued, and encouraged me as the novel developed and took on its final shape.

I was very fortunate that Will Schwable, a New York author and book agent, suggested I associate with Ed Victor as an agent. Ed brought this work of a first-time novelist to the attention of Vanguard Press. Its publisher, Roger Cooper, agreed to take it on and his gifted and insightful editorial staff, Kevin Smith and Collin Tracy, gave it the final polish.

As a member of the CIA's external advisory board I submit all my writing within its scope of activity to the agency's publication review board. I appreciate the work of Richard Puhl and his colleagues in assuring that the material in this novel does not compromise national security.

Keys to the Kingdom is fact embellished with fiction, much of it based on my years as governor of Florida and then representing that state in the U.S. Senate. But a novel of this scope involves numerous individual subjects and many layers of expertise. To assure that the facts were as accurate as possible, many friends and those with whom I have become friends educated me and vetted the manuscript. While I assume full responsibility for what you will read, I want to acknowledge them for their contributions.

For nuclear details I have been advised by Dr. Howard Hall of the University of Tennessee and the Oak Ridge National Laboratory, and Michael Allen, staff director of the House of Representatives Intelligence Committee.

On matters involving aviation Tom Horne of Gulfstream Aviation and Bob Wallace, a Boeing 777 training instructor for Delta Airlines, were generous with their time and advice.

Farooq Mitha, a Fulbright scholar in the Middle East, has greatly assisted me in the presentation of cultural and linguistic matters related to that fascinating region of the world.

An old friend, Marc Henderson of the Miami-Dade Aviation Department, was kind to answer a long list of questions about the Miami International Airport, especially its parking garage.

The numerous law enforcement sections were informed by Steve Hurm, my son-in-law and a former agent for the Florida Department of Law Enforcement; Tom and Barbara McGraw, also with the FDLE; and Captain Chris Dellapietra of the Florida Highway Patrol.

I am extremely fortunate in having such devoted, interesting, and well-informed sons-in-law, all of whom were willing to be drafted into service. Bill McCullough, a former professional photographer, was my advisor on Laura Billington's photographic challenges.

Tom Gibson reviewed and critiqued the manuscript at various stages. He was also the consultant on Tony's wardrobe.

Yet another son-in-law Robby Elias, coached me on the finer points of tennis. He was assisted by my minister, Reverend Jeff Frantz of the Miami Lakes Congregational Church, who also advised on the protocols of funerals.

Robby's brother, Jaime Elias of Trivest, was very informative on the nuances of private equity.

Professor Paula Thomas of Middle Tennessee State University, Professor Larry Crumbley of Louisiana State University, and Andre Teixeira, chief financial officer of the Graham Companies, guided my character Carol Watson through her forensic accounting challenges. Morgan Ortagus of the U.S. Treasury Department was also helpful and a fine role model.

The intricacies of serving a federal subpoena were revealed by Tom O'Neil, president of the Saranac Group in Baltimore.

Dr. Jeffery Johnson, emergency room physician at the South Shore Hospital, South Weymouth, Massachusetts, educated me on the emergency treatment of John Billington.

David Price, president of the historic and beautiful Bok Tower and Gardens in Lake Wales, Florida, was my instructor on Middle Eastern landscape architecture.

The authenticity of Haitian dialect was enhanced by Joane Joseph of Shula's Hotel, Miami Lakes, Florida.

Another colleague of many years, Sandy George, and a new friend, Jorge Hayes, both of the California State University system, arranged for a visit to San Diego State University and a tour of the city. Teresa McKenzie and Tony Ramos lunched at the restaurant Jorge recommended.

The scenes that focused on the massive cargo container ship, *Petronius*, were improved by the review given by Donald Peltier of eModal, based at the Port of Los Angeles.

Colonel Randy Larsen, U.S. Air Force (Retired), executive director of the Weapons of Mass Destruction Policy Center, gave valuable technical and literary advice on the utilization of the bombs. I'm very glad such a knowledgeable and dedicated individual is on our side.

Coast Guard commander Ed Parkinson, based in Miami, educated me on maritime and helicopter subjects. Retired Army Colonel Jim Kelly was my advisor on military equipment.

Bryon Georgiou, a new friend from our mutual service on the Financial Crisis Inquiry Commission, was generous with his advice on all things Nevada. Ray Moss was invaluable on details of Kuala Lumpur and its airport.

Maybe saving the best for last or, at least, the best tasting, the recipe for the paella Tony prepared was provided by Chef Michelle Bernstein of the Señora Martinez restaurant in Miami.

There were many others who were willing to review all or portions of the manuscript as it went through a seemingly interminable set of revisions. These include but are not limited to: John Robert, Kay and Mary Middlemas, Jose Villalobos, and Mark Block, all true friends of many years; David McCullough Jr., who was there at the beginning; David Pearson, a friend of many years and my occasional vanquisher on the tennis court; Diane Roberts, Florida's best-known cultural essayist; Baruch Shemtov, a Kennedy School friend and one of the brightest people I have known; and Stu Willey who, as president of the Graham Companies, has continued The Lakes standard of excellence.

And to all the others who helped along the way, my sincere thanks.

—*Bob Graham*
MIAMI LAKES, FLORIDA
JANUARY 2011